For my son.
May you know the love of the Lord your God your whole life.

"To work miracles in our own lives, we must follow this plan: have only love in our hearts, and proceed with first faith, then works. In order for the door to heaven to open to us, we must trust that God is love, that love is what He intends for us, and love is what He wants from us. Then, through loving-kindness, we will make our way toward Him."

DR. ISSAM NEMEH
IN *MIRACLES EVERY DAY* BY
MAURA POSTON ZAGRANS

Acclaim for Erin Healy's previous works

The Baker's Wife

"A combination of suspense, mystery, religion, and even romance weaves this tale into a cohesive, compelling read."

—New York Journal of Books

"Healy's fascinating plot is fast-paced and difficult to put down once started."

—Romantic Times 4 ½ star TOP PICK! review

"A tightly woven, character-driven suspense story . . . should appeal to Dekker fans as well."

—Library Journal

Never Let You Go

". . . Will appeal to readers who like to be on the edge of their seats."

—Library Journal

"Heart-pounding suspense and unrelenting hope that will steal your breath."

—Ted Dekker, New York Times best-selling author

"Fans of Ted Dekker will appreciate Healy's chilling story of the dangers on the road back to hope and faith."

—Booklist

"Keeps you glued to the pages until the very last."

—Tosca Lee, author of Havah: The Story of Eve

The Promises She Keeps

" . . . A smartly written story . . . The Promises She Keeps will undoubtedly be enjoyed by established fans of Healy's writing, and those unfamiliar with her work, or even the genre, should give this captivating novel a read."

—5MinutesForBooks.com

"Complex characters, a plot steeped in imagery and eloquence . . . a beautiful tale of eternal love . . . Healy thrives when telling tales of spirituality and mystery."

—LifeIsStory.com

"An intricate book . . . Healy is highly skilled . . . The Promises She Keeps is beautifully written."

—The Gazette (Colorado Springs, CO)

HOUSE OF
MERCY

ERIN HEALY

THOMAS NELSON
Since 1798

NASHVILLE   DALLAS   MEXICO CITY   RIO DE JANEIRO

Published in Nashville, Tennessee. Thomas Nelson is a trademark of Thomas Nelson, Inc.

Published in association with Creative Trust Literary Group, 5141 Virginia Way, Suite 320, Brentwood, TN 37027.

Thomas Nelson, Inc., books may be purchased in bulk for educational, business, fund-raising, or sales promotional use. For information, please e-mail SpecialMarkets@ThomasNelson.com.

Publisher's Note: This novel is a work of fiction. Names, characters, places, and incidents are either products of the author's imagination or used fictitiously. All characters are fictional, and any similarity to people living or dead is purely coincidental.

Library of Congress Cataloging-in-Publication Data

Healy, Erin M.
    House of mercy / Erin Healy.
        p. cm.
    ISBN 978-1-4016-8551-5 (pbk.)
    1. Young women--Fiction. 2. Ranches--Colorado--Fiction. 3. Domestic fiction.
I. Title.
    PS3608.E245H68 2012
    813'.6--dc23

2012014076

Printed in the United States of America

12 13 14 15 16 17 QG 6 5 4 3 2 1

1

It wasn't every day that an old saddle could improve a horse's life. That was what Beth Borzoi was thinking as she stood in the dusty tack room that smelled like her favorite pair of leather boots. In the back corner where the splintering-wood walls met, she tugged the faded leather saddle off the bottommost rung of the heavy-duty rack, where it had sat, unused and forgotten, for years.

Her little brother, Danny, would have said she was stealing the saddle. He might have called her a kleptomaniac. That was too strong a word, but Danny was fifteen and liked to throw bold words around, cocky-like, show-off rodeo ropes aimed at snagging people. She loved that about him. It was a cute phase. Even so, she had formed a mental argument against the characterization of herself as a thief, in case she needed to use it, because Danny was too young to understand the true meaning of even stronger words like sacrifice or situational ethics.

After all, she was working in secret, in the hidden folds of a summer night, so that both she and the saddle could leave the Blazing B unnoticed. In the wrong light, it might look like a theft.

The truth was, it was not her saddle to give away. It was Jacob's saddle, though in the fifteen years Jacob had lived at the ranch, she had never seen him use it. The bigger truth was that this saddle abandoned to tarnish and sawdust could be put to better use. The fenders were plated with silver, pure metal that could be melted down and converted into money to save a horse from suffering. Decorative silver bordered the round skirt and framed the rear housing. The precious metal had been hammered to conform to the gentle rise of the cantle in the back and the swell in the front. The lovely round conchos were studded with turquoise. Hand-tooled impressions of wild mountain flowers covered the leather everywhere that silver didn't.

In its day, it must have been a fine show saddle. And if Jacob valued that at all, he wouldn't have stored it like this.

Under the naked-bulb beams of the tack room, Beth's body cast a shadow over the pretty piece as she hefted it. She blew the dirt and dander off the horn, swiped off the cracked seat with the flat of her hand, then turned away her head and sneezed. Colorado's dry climate had not been kind to the leather.

She wasn't stealing. She was saving an animal's life.

The latch on the barn door released Beth to the midnight air with a click like a stolen kiss. The saddle weighed about thirty-five pounds, which was easy to manage when snatching it off a rack and tossing it onto a horse's back. But it would feel much heavier by the time she reached her destination. She'd parked her truck a ways off where the rumbling old clunker wouldn't raise questions or family members sleeping in the nearby ranch house. She'd left her dog at the foot of Danny's bed with clear orders to stay. She hoped the animal would mind.

Energized, she crossed the horses' yard. A few of them nickered greetings at her, including Hastings, who nuzzled her empty pockets for treats. The horses never slept in the barn's stalls unless they were sick. Even in winter they stayed in the pasture, preferring the outdoor lean-to shelters.

The Blazing B, a 6,500-acre working cattle ranch, lay to the northwest of Colorado's San Luis Valley. The region was called a valley because this portion of the state was a Rocky Mountain hammock that swung between the San Juans to the west and the Sangre de Cristos to the east. But at more than seven thousand feet, it was no low-lying flatland. It was, in fact, the highest alpine valley in the world. And it was the only place in the world that Beth ever wanted to live. Having graduated from the local community college with honors and saved enough additional money for her continuing education, she planned to leave in the fall to begin her first year of veterinary school. She would be gone as long as it took to earn her license, but her long-term plan was to return as a more valuable person. Her skills would save the family thousands of dollars every year, freeing up funds for their most important task—providing a home and a hard day's work to discarded men who needed the peace the Blazing B had to offer.

On this late May night, a light breeze stirred the alfalfa growing in the pasturelands while the cattle grazed miles away. The herds always spent their summers on public lands in the mountains while their winter feed grew in the valley. They were watched over by a pool rider, a hired man who was a bit like a cow's version of a shepherd. He stayed with them through the summer and would bring them home in the fall.

With the winter calving and spring branding a distant memory, the streams and irrigation wells amply supplied by good mountain runoff, and the healthy alfalfa fields thickening with a June cutting in mind, the mood at the Blazing B was peaceful.

When Beth was a quarter mile beyond the barn, a bobbing light drew her attention to the west side of the pasture, where ancient cottonwood trees formed a barrier against seasonal winds and snows. She paused, her eyes searching the darkness beyond this path that she could walk blindfolded. The light rippled over cottonwood trunks, casting shadows that were indistinguishable from the real thing.

A man was muttering in a low voice, jabbing his light around as if it were a stick. She couldn't make out his words. Then the yellow beam stilled low to the ground, and she heard a metallic thrust, the scraping ring of a shovel's blade being jammed into the dirt.

Beth worried. It had to be Wally, but what was he doing out at this hour, and at this place? The bunkhouse was two miles away, and the men had curfews, not to mention strict rules about their access to horses and vehicles.

She left the path and approached the trees without a misstep. The moonlight was enough to guide her over the uneven terrain.

"Wally?"

The cutting of the shovel ceased. "Who wants to know?"

"It's Beth."

"Beth who?"

"Beth Borzoi. Abel's daughter. I'm the one who rides Hastings."

"Well, sure! Right, right. Beth. I'm sorry you have to keep telling me. You're awfully nice about it."

The light that Wally had set on the ground rose and pointed itself at her, as if to confirm her claims, then dropped to the saddle resting against her thighs. Wally had been at the ranch for three years, since a stroke left his body unaffected but struck his brain with a short-term memory disorder. It was called anterograde amnesia, a forgetfulness of experiences but not skills. He could work hard but couldn't hold a job because he was always forgetting where and when he was supposed to show up. Here at the ranch he didn't have to worry about those details. He had psychologists and strategies to guide him through his days, a community of brothers who reminded him of everything he really needed to know. Well, most things. He had been on more than one occasion the butt of hurtful pranks orchestrated by the men who shared the bunkhouse with him. It was both a curse and a blessing that he was able to forget such incidents so easily.

Beth was the only Beth at the Blazing B, and the only female resident besides her mother, but these facts regularly eluded Wally. He never forgot her father, though, and he knew the names of all the horses, so this was how Beth had learned to keep putting herself back into the context of his life.

"You're working hard," she said. "You know it's after eleven."

"Looking for my lockbox. I saw him take it. I followed him here just an hour ago, but now it's gone."

Sometimes it was money that had gone missing. Sometimes it was a glove or a photograph, or a piece of cake from her mother's dinner table that was already in his belly. All the schedules and organizational systems in the world were not enough to help Wally with this bizarre side effect of his disorder: whenever a piece of his mind went missing, he would search for it by digging. Dr. Roy Davis, Wally's psychiatrist, had curtailed much of Wally's compulsive need to overturn the earth by having him perform many of the Blazing B's endless irrigation tasks. Even so, the ten square miles of ranch were riddled with the chinks of Wally's efforts to find what he had lost.

"That must be really frustrating," she said. "I hate it when I lose my stuff."

"I didn't lose it. A gray wolf ran off with it. I had it safe in a secret spot, and he dug it up and carried off the box in his teeth. Hauled it all the way up here and reburied it. Now tell me, what's a wolf gonna do with my legal tender? Buy himself a turkey leg down at the supermarket?"

Wally must have kept a little cash in his box. She could understand his frustration. But this claim stirred up disquiet at the back of her mind. Dr. Roy would need to know if Wally was seeing things. First off, gray wolves were hardly ever spotted in Colorado. They'd been run out of the state before World War II by poachers and hostile ranchers, and their return in recent years was little more than a rumor. Wally might have seen a coyote. But for another thing, no wild animal dug up a man's buried treasure and relocated it. Except maybe a raccoon.

A raccoon trying to run off with a heavy lockbox might actually be entertaining.

"Tell you what, Wally. If he's buried it here we'll have a better chance of finding it in the morning. When the sun comes up, I'll help you. But they'll be missing you at the bunkhouse about now. Let me take you back so no one gets upset when they see you're gone." Jacob or Dr. Roy would do bunk checks at midnight.

"Upset? No one can be as upset as I am right now." He thrust the shovel into the soft dirt at his feet. "I saw the dog do it. I tracked him all the way here, like he thought I wouldn't see him under this full moon. Fool dog—but who'd believe me? It's like a freaky fairy tale, isn't it? Well, I'd have put that box in a local vault if I didn't have to keep so many stinkin' Web addresses and passwords and account numbers and security questions at my fingertips." He withdrew a small notebook from his hip pocket and waved the pages around. It was one of the things he used to keep track of details. "Maybe I'll have to rethink that."

Beth's hands had become sweaty and a little cramped under the saddle's weight. She used her right knee to balance the saddle and fix her grip. The soft leather suddenly felt like heavy gold bricks out of someone else's bank vault.

"Well, let's go," she said. "I've got my truck right on down the lane."

"What do you have there?" Wally returned the notebook to his pocket, hefted the shovel, and picked his way out of the underbrush, finding his way by flashlight.

"An old saddle. It's been in the tack room for years." She expected Wally to forget the saddle just as quickly as he would forget this night's adventure and her promise to help him dig in the morning.

He lifted one of the fenders and stroked the silver with his thumb. "Pretty thing. Probably worth something. Not as much as that box is worth to me, though."

"We'll find it," Beth said.

"You bet we will." Wally fell into step beside her. "Thanks for the ride back, Beth. You're a good girl. You got your daddy in you."

⌒

With Jacob's old saddle resting on a blanket in the bed of her rusty white pickup, Beth followed an access road from the horse pasture by her own home down into the heart of the Blazing B.

The property's second ranch house was located more strategically to the cattle operation, and so it was known to all as the Hub. The Hub was a practical bachelor pad. Outside, the branding pens and calving sheds and squeeze chutes and cattle trucks filled up a dusty clearing around the house. Inside, the carpets and old leather furniture, even when clean, smelled like men who believed that a hard day's work followed by a dead sleep—in any location—was far more gratifying than a hot shower. The house was steeped in the scent stains of sweat and hay, horses and manure, tanned leather and barbecue smoke. The men who slept here lived like the bachelors they were. If their daily labors weren't enough to impress a woman, the cowboys couldn't be bothered with her.

Dr. Roy Davis, known affectionately by all as Dr. Roy, was a lifelong friend of Beth's father. Years ago, after the death of Roy's wife, Abel and Roy merged their professional passions of ranching and psychiatry and expanded the Blazing B's purpose. It became an outreach to functional but wounded men like Wally who needed a home and a job. Dr. Roy brought his teenage son, Jacob, along. Now thirty-one, Jacob had never found reason to leave, except for the years he'd spent away at college earning multiple degrees in agriculture and animal management. Jacob had been the Blazing B's general operations manager for more than five years.

Jacob and his father shared the Hub with Pastor Eric, who was a divorced minister, and Emory, a therapist who was once a gang leader. These men were the Borzois' four full-time employees.

The other men who lived at the Blazing B were called "associates." They occupied the bunkhouse, some for a few weeks and some for years. At present there were six, including Wally.

When Beth stopped her truck in front of the Hub's porch, Wally slipped off the seat of her cab, closed the rusty door, and went directly around back to the bunkhouse. She pulled away and had reached the end of the drive when a rut jarred the truck and rattled the shovel he'd left in the truck bed.

In spite of her hurry to take Jacob's saddle to the people who needed it, she put the truck in park, jumped out, and jogged the tool up to the house. The porch light lit the squeaky wood steps, and she took them two at a time. Jacob would see the tool in the morning when he came out to start up his own truck and head out to whatever project was on the schedule. She'd phone him to make sure.

She was tipping the handle into the corner where the porch rail met the siding when the Hub's front door opened and Jacob leaned out.

"Past your bedtime, isn't it?" he said, but he was smiling at her. Over the years they had settled into a comfortable big-brother-little-sister relationship, though Beth had never fully outgrown her adolescent crush on him.

"Found Wally digging up by the barn," she said.

Surprise pulled his dark brows together. "Now? Where is he?"

"Back in bed, I guess. He said he followed a wolf up to our place. You might want Dr. Roy to look into that. Your dad should know if Wally's . . . seeing things."

Jacob nodded as he stepped out the door and leaned against the house. He crossed his arms. "Coyote maybe?"

"Try suggesting that to him. And when was the last time we had a coyote down here? It's been ages—not since Danny gave up his chicken coop."

"I'll mention that to Dad. It's probably nothing. What had you out at the barn at this hour? Horses okay?"

"Fine." Beth's eyes swiveled down to her truck, to Jacob's saddle, both well beyond reach of the porch light. She tried to recall all her justifications for taking the saddle, but in that moment all she could think was that she should get his permission to do it. She'd known this man more than half her life. He was kind. He was wise. He'd say yes. He'd want her to take it.

But she said, "I'm headed out to the Kandinskys' place. They've got a horse who injured his eye, and it's pretty bad. They let it go too long, you know, hoping it would correct itself, maybe wouldn't need a big vet bill."

"The Kandinskys have their own vet on the premises. Who called you out?"

"It's not one of their horses, actually. It's Phil's. Remember him?"

"Your friend from high school?"

"He's been working there a year or so. They let him keep the horse on the property. One of the perks."

"But he can't use their vet?"

Beth looked at her feet. "Phil's family can't afford their vet. You know how that goes. We couldn't afford him. His family doesn't even have pets, you know. They run a grocery store. The horse is his little sister's project. A 4H thing."

"Well, tell Phil I said he called the right gal for the job."

"I don't know, Jacob. It sounds really bad. These eye things— the horse might need surgery."

She found it unusually difficult to look at him, though she was sure he was studying her with a suspicious stare by now. But she couldn't look at the truck either. Her eyes couldn't find an object to rest on.

"All you can do is all you can do, Beth. That'll be as true after you're licensed as it is now."

"But I want to do miracles," she said.

He chuckled at that, though she hadn't been joking. "Don't we all." He uncrossed his arms and put his hand on the doorknob, preparing to go back inside. "I heard some big-shot Thoroughbred breeder is boarding some of his studs there," Jacob said. "Some friend of theirs passing through."

"I heard that too."

"Maybe that'll be Phil's miracle this time—an unexpected guest, someone with the right know-how or the right resources who will come to his horse's rescue."

"Angels unaware," Beth said.

"Something like that. Night, Beth."

Beth didn't want him to go just yet. "Night."

She lingered at the door while it closed, hoping he might intuit what she didn't have the courage to say.

When he didn't, she committed to her original plan. She descended the steps in a quiet rush, wanting to whisk the saddle away before he could object to what he didn't know. She wanted to be the one who did the good works, who made the incredible rescue. She couldn't help herself. It was her father's blood running through her heart.

On the driveway, her smooth-soled boots skimmed the dirt, whispering back to her truck.

"It's not your right to do it," Jacob said. Beth gasped and whirled at the sound of his voice, unexpected and loud and straight into her ear, as if he'd been standing on her shoulder. "It's not your gift to give."

But the ranch house door was shut tight under the cone of the porch light, and the bright window revealed nothing inside but heavy furniture and cluttered tabletops. At the back of the house, a different door closed heavily. Jacob was headed out to the bunk-house to check on Wally already.

Beth let her captured breath leave her lungs. She looked around for an explanation, because she didn't want to accept that the words might have been uttered by a guilty conscience.

At the base of the porch steps, crouching in such darkness that its black center sank into its surroundings, was the form of an unusually large dog. Erect ears, broad head, slender body. A wolf. She had passed that spot so closely seconds ago that she could have reached out and stroked its neck.

She took one step backward. Of course, her mind was dreaming this up because Wally had suggested a wolf to her. If he hadn't, she might have said the silhouette had the outline of a snowman. An inverted snowman guarding the house from her lies. In May.

Beth stared at it for several seconds, oddly unable to recall the landscape where she'd spent her entire life. She was distressed not to be able to say from this distance and angle whether that was a shrub planted there, or a fence post, or an old piece of equipment that hadn't made it back into the supply shed. When the shape of its edges seemed to shift and shudder without actually moving at all, she decided that her eyes were being tricked by the darkness.

Convincing herself of this was almost as easy as justifying her saddle theft.

She turned away from the house and hurried onward, looking back only once.

2

The Kandinskys' horse ranch lay a half hour's drive from the Blazing B. It seemed to belong in the rolling hills of Kentucky or New York, not to these simple plains. The white fences and ornamental gates were out of place in this land of wood posts and steel rails. The Rolls Royces parked in house-sized garages were entirely impractical, too good to drive down the two-lane highways. But the family members, though a bit standoffish, were nationally respected breeders of Fox Trotters and Morgans. They made good money in this valley acquiring reliable working stock for the ranchers. It seemed reasonable that Mr. Kandinsky's brother-in-law, a Thoroughbred breeder transferring some of his livelihood to a new ranch in California, would pick this place for a rest stop along the way.

Phil had given Beth directions to the horse breeder's secondary stables, a barn reserved for the workhorses rather than the studs. She parked near the sliding door that opened onto the stable alley.

Beth kept a first-aid kit for animals behind the driver's seat. She withdrew it, not sure if the ointments and disinfectants and dressings and poultices would be at all relevant. But the weight of the bag felt good in her hands, like confidence.

She entered the barn. Hay scattered across the ground silenced her footsteps. The entire facility, which boasted twelve stalls, was lined with fresh wheat straw and thick rubber mats and shining pine tongue-and-groove siding. If these quarters were for the lowly workers, the studs must have been housed in a crystal palace. Several of the stalls were occupied, but Phil leaned out of the box at the far end and motioned her to come.

She hoped that the horse's condition was not as bad as he had made it out to be over the phone.

Beth kept her voice low so as not to startle the animals. "Hey, Phil. Fiona," she said to his teenage sister who, judging by her sleeping bag, intended to spend the night with poor Marigold. Both Phil and Fiona had willowy statures and fine brown hair that fell into their eyes. Fiona sat on the ground, hugging her knees. Beth looked at the horse. "How's she doing?"

Fiona shook her head and bit her lip. She rocked herself gently.

"You tell us," Phil said. "It's her left eye." His tone was hopeful. For Fiona's sake, Beth thought.

Marigold lay on her side on a bank of straw, her eyes closed, and Beth took heart in the mare's peaceful appearance. There was no indication that the eyelid had been damaged. Her eyelashes were horizontal, as they ought to be. The contour of Marigold's head was smooth and free of swelling. Quite possibly, Phil and Fiona's inexperience had overstated the trouble.

Beth made a gentle clucking noise to alert Marigold to her presence before kneeling and stroking the mare's shoulder. The horse allowed it, approving with a deep sigh as Beth's fingers moved upward on the neck, caressing the jaw in the comforting way that Hastings liked so much.

When her hands approached the mare's eye, intending to lift the lid for a closer look, Marigold tossed her head away from Beth's probing. She nickered a warning and shot an open-eyed glare that caused Beth's hope to drop. The protective tissue over Marigold's eye, which should have been water clear, was a white cloud so dense that the pupil and iris were nearly invisible. And toward the rear corner of the eye, the surface was uneven and waxy, like the dribbles of a melting candle.

"Her cornea has an ulcer," Beth began.

"Is that bad?" Phil asked.

"Not normally." Corneal ulcers were one of the more common injuries a horse might receive in its lifetime. Hastings had suffered his share. "I'm sorry, girl," she said to the mare. "How long has she been like this?"

"The cloudiness—two weeks?" Phil said.

"Sixteen days," Fiona said. Beth groaned inwardly.

"But that oozing, it just started yesterday."

"Day before," Fiona corrected.

Beth shook her head at Phil's optimism. "Sixteen days ago we could have turned this around with topical antibiotics. She might have improved in a few days. But this—this is called a melting ulcer. They're wicked. Somewhere along the line that plain vanilla ulcer picked up some bacteria or a fungus. The infection is only going to get worse."

Her first-aid kit sat in the straw beside her, worthless.

Phil glanced at Fiona. "What do we do?"

"You get a vet on this right now. A licensed vet. Tonight. I can call someone for you."

"What's he going to tell us?"

"That you waited too long to call him. That Marigold might need surgery to reverse this, depending on how deep it's gone. Two weeks is a long time, you guys."

"She just didn't give any sign that it really bothered her," Fiona said.

Beth was sure the horse had. It was more likely that Phil and Fiona didn't recognize what they were seeing. "I don't mean to be cruel, but you need to understand how serious this is. She could lose her eye if you don't treat it aggressively."

Fiona dropped her head onto her knees. Phil paled. He didn't have to say what Beth knew was running through his mind. The cost of an equine surgery on a grocer's salary would hurt. Even if surgery wasn't part of the equation, the antibiotics, the anti-inflammatories, the medications to control the enzymes that were destroying the eye tissues would all add up.

Beth placed a hand on Phil's arm. "Come with me for a second. I brought something that might help."

Over the next several minutes, Beth focused on restoring hope to the siblings. She took them out to her truck and showed them the saddle's silver.

"You can remove it from the leather," she explained. "Sell it for cash. I'm sure there's enough here to cover whatever Marigold needs." It took some effort, but she eventually coaxed them into accepting the gift for Marigold's sake. Then Beth called the Blazing B's own vet and asked his phone service to rouse him from his sleep. While the threesome waited for Dr. O'Connor's return call, she sang his praises. By the time he agreed to come out in spite of the hour, Phil and Fiona had regained some of their optimism.

"We thought of the perfect way to thank you," Fiona said as Beth closed her cell phone. There was excitement in the light touch she placed on Beth's arm. "Wait here. It'll just take a few minutes."

"You don't need to do anything. Really."

"We do, we do. Give us five."

Five minutes was nothing to ask. The vet wouldn't arrive for forty-five at least.

Beth opened the tailgate and sat under the bright moon while she waited. Phil had carried the silver-clad saddle back through the stables to his own truck on the other side, and already she was having second thoughts about whether offering that up had been the right thing to do. She was disappointed in herself for not bringing it up to Jacob. And she could think of a dozen things that silver might have paid for at her very own ranch. Why hadn't she considered any of them in the hour between Phil's concerned phone call and her brilliant idea to foot Marigold's bill?

Because her idea had been inspired. Two hours ago she had no doubt that it was exactly what she ought to do. Beth sent her memory in search of that certainty so that she could hold on to it more firmly this time.

"It's not your right to do it," Jacob said, loud and close, and Beth jerked out of her reverie, expecting to see him standing beside the truck. Instead she found Fiona. The girl seized Beth's wrist and yanked her right off the tailgate, then tugged her back into the bright stables.

Phil was grinning at her, standing in the alley next to the tallest, glossiest, most beautiful Thoroughbred horse Beth had ever seen. She felt her lips form an O as admiration filled her next breath.

"What d'ya think?" he said.

Beth's sigh was awed and contented at the same time. "He's amazing," she breathed.

"Beth, meet Java Java Go Joe. Joe, meet Beth."

The horse's name was appropriate, considering the sheen of his coat, an oily dark-roasted coffee bean. The stud's track record at the races and in siring winners had lived up to the moniker too.

"Your reputation precedes you, sire," Beth said. The stallion before her, the Kandinskys' guest, was more than seventeen hands high and glistening, majestic. His lean legs made up most of the size difference between him and the ranch horses. Her father's geldings, including Hastings, averaged fourteen to fifteen hands. Those sturdy beasts saved many a cowboy's head while driving cattle through the forested mountains, where low-hanging tree limbs could steal hats and dent foreheads.

Her father objected to Thoroughbreds on the ranch. "They're too tall, too fast, and they don't have good cow sense," he always said. Beth knew a couple of ranchers who didn't seem to mind these shortcomings in their own horses, but her father was immovable.

It took Beth a long time to notice that Joe was saddled and ready to ride.

"No," her mouth said, while her heart cried *yes*.

Phil gestured to the blocks at Joe's side. "A small gesture of our appreciation," he said.

Beth stroked the animal's neck, and his muscles flickered under the skin. He seemed peaceful, easygoing, as if getting dressed out at this hour were an everyday thing.

"I shouldn't. I can't."

"Sure you can," Phil said.

"He's not even Mr. Kandinsky's."

"He's still family."

Beth shook her head. "It's wrong."

"What's wrong with giving a champion like him any excuse to relive the glory days? He's retired, you know. He resents that they only love him for his stud fees anymore. He told me so. But I said you'd love him for all the right reasons."

Beth laughed and found herself standing on the blocks.

"I guessed at your stirrup length," he said.

"Then we should see how good at guesswork you are," she said, and she was astride Joe's strong back before she could decide not to be. Her adrenaline kicked in. Beth felt him shift, evaluating her size and weight. She inserted her feet in the stirrups. Phil's estimate was perfect.

"Ten minutes," Phil urged. "No harm, no foul. In the three days he's been here he's blazed a trail all his own around the center pasture. Let him show you around. I guarantee you've never been on anything like him."

"I've never been thanked for terrible news quite like this before."

"It's not for that. It's for the saddle. Duh," Fiona said kindly.

On her perch, Beth towered over the pair. Taking the horse out to the pasture at this hour was a risky and maybe even stupid idea. And yet their upturned faces held so much expectancy. It seemed wrong to deny them. And she had often dreamed of riding a horse like this.

"He's not too old to have forgotten his top speeds, is he?"

"You're a good rider," Phil said, "but you'll be better off if he's forgotten at least a little bit."

"Are you saying he's too much horse for me?"

"Did I say that? I didn't say that." He whispered to Joe, "Go easy on her, old man."

The horse snorted as if even Phil didn't have the inside track on whatever joke he planned to pull.

"Here." Phil handed her a helmet.

"I don't need one of those for a little canter."

"Yeah yeah. I know how these things start."

She snatched up the helmet and strapped it under her chin.

"I hope you don't lose your job over this," she whispered to him so Fiona wouldn't hear.

"I won't. This is you: Princess Borzoi, Her Majesty the animal whisperer. I'm not worried about a thing. Let Joe lead the way."

That would be the easiest thing she'd done all night. Her understanding of an animal's spirit was what would make her a great veterinarian some day, her father often said to her. She could sense, in the light dance of Joe's feet as she leaned forward in the saddle, that the creature was happy to go for a ride this evening. She could sense, in the patient way he waited for her to attend to the details, that he was pleased to share the adventure.

With a gentle heel, she nudged Joe toward the fresh air. He needed no other prompt. They passed through the wide doors and then navigated a few gates, and Joe told her with his confident stride that his heart would be a reliable compass on this sky-lit night.

In the Thoroughbreds, God had married strength and grace and created a magnificent breed that few people could appreciate firsthand. *Let's go for a ride.* Beth closed her eyes. There was little for her to see, and her efforts to guide the horse might lead him into dangers worse than mere shadows cast by the moon.

She did as Phil suggested, gave Joe the reins, and trusted the animal's instincts. In seconds his walk shifted to a trot and then to a canter, and then to a gallop as pleasant as a swiftly flowing creek. Joe was an eagle born to glide above water. The surface of the pastures fell away. She leaned into the horse's neck and tucked her head and couldn't remember any sensation as wild and reckless as this.

If she gave in to her urge to grin, the bugs would hit her teeth. The thought of it, the sheer joy of this rush, brought a laugh out of her throat, and then a gasp that invited some witless insect to ride the stiff air straight back down.

The shock jolted her eyes open. Phil should have given her goggles and a mask along with the helmet, she thought. But Joe took no note of her comic sputtering, and after recovering from her coughing fit, she laughed some more. His neck stretched out and so did his stride. Together they picked up speed.

I'll love you always, Hastings, she thought, *but you're an old British butler compared to this rock star.*

She wondered how much faster than this Joe had gone in his youth, on a refined racetrack, with the jockey he trusted most. Next on her list of dreams would be to find someone who might make that experience a reality. Maybe she could arrange some kind of reality-TV career swap with a jockey for a week, or however that worked.

She envisioned a short jockey in all his pink and yellow silks, up to his armpit in the backside of a cow, testing by hand as was traditionally done to see if the bovine was pregnant or open. The image buoyed her good mood.

The horse had reached a pace that Beth understood was beyond her ability to contain. Joe was in charge of her fate now. A flicker of fear passed over her but then flew away from her mind like a rooftop in a high wind. She surrendered to Joe's confidence, and to the thrill of being out of control.

But Joe's mood shifted.

Beth noticed it first in a sudden deviation from his course, a quick and not-so-graceful dig into the earth that thrust his weight off center. The angle of his ears changed as he moved off the perimeter of the fence; they stood erect now and resisted the rushing air. And though Beth hadn't thought it possible on this unrefined terrain, the Thoroughbred accelerated, fueled by an energy that came off his back like fear.

The muscles on the inside of her thighs began to burn as she held her weight off the saddle. She took back the reins, but Joe did not respond to them. Her fingers, entwined in the leather, found the saddle horn. Her eyes, squinting and dry and unexpectedly disoriented, looked for the light of the stables. She thought they might be behind her.

Joe changed course again, zigging to the previous zag. Beth slipped an inch before she recovered her center.

"Whoa," she instructed. She didn't share his fear yet. He might respond to her steady calm. "Settle down, boy."

She attuned her own ears to the surroundings, trying to get a clue for what had upset Joe. Excitement no longer energized the horse. It was replaced by panic, frantic and panting. Beth couldn't imagine what, on this secure and sheltered land, would be so terrifying. She uttered the soothing tongue clicks and hums that Hastings liked. The sounds were trampled by the pummeling of hooves tearing up the ground, thumping like helicopter blades. Wind whistling over her ears.

A ghost-gray form floated into the periphery of Beth's vision. She glanced twice, and then a third time. The hulking spirit hovered just above the ground, gliding with a swift and otherworldly intention toward Joe's flank.

That rooftop of fear crashed back down on Beth's mind, knocking the breath out of her. She felt Joe's terror as if it were her own. His foaming sweat flew off his neck and spattered her arms, and into the vacancy of her imagination rushed Wally's wolf.

It can't be a wolf, she told herself.

Whatever it was dashed behind Joe, there and gone like the memory of a dream.

She tried to twist in the saddle, wanting to see what it really was and where it was going, but the power of the horse's speed forced her to stay forward, low above the Thoroughbred's back. All she could do was hold on, with weakening thighs and floppy ankles and fingers soft as cooked spaghetti.

Joe's desperate footwork jerked Beth awry again. Clods of dirt were flying up from behind his hooves, smacking her in the back.

Then the ghost she had lost sight of snarled, and the noise pierced all the other sounds bouncing around her ears. This sound, this primal shriek, declared that this wild dog was neither a phantom nor a fiction dreamed up by a Blazing B associate. It was physical, and it was robust, and it had performed the astonishing feat of predicting how the horse would move to evade the hunt.

The wolf had overtaken them and now came from the front, head-on. It was lunging for Joe's neck, taking an impossible leap.

The wolf's weight struck her in the face. One second Joe was solid under Beth and the next she was plunging, gasping, choking on a mouthful of fur. The leather rein caught hold of her wrist and snapped taut, shocked by the weight of her falling body as she left Joe's back. She felt the joints in her arm and wrist popping as her insignificant mass yanked against Joe's, which was a bullet train moving in the opposite direction.

She stayed connected to him by that stubborn strap. And the wild animal stayed connected to her, its claws curled into her collarbone.

Beth and beast hit the ground and bounced. She heard rocks connecting with the helmet Phil had insisted she wear. Her body flipped over onto the dog as they rolled, her distended arm still tangled in the reins, and then the animal emerged on top, teeth snapping so close to her face.

Joe might have dragged her to her death if the sudden impact hadn't jerked his neck sideways and led his hooves into a terrible misstep.

His mountainous body toppled inches from hers, but by now she was deafened by firecrackers in her skull, and she didn't hear Joe's collapse. Instead she felt the vibrations of his fall, and his heaving body pulsed atop her forearm, the one roped and pinned under Joe's shoulder like a calf tossed by a cowboy.

Beth's mind piled up sandbags against the rising flood of pain. She couldn't move.

She expected the wolf to tear into her, to finish her off. And it was a wolf. The weight, the coat, the claws—it could be nothing else. It stood on her chest, its padded feet the size of her own hands, but the animal didn't rip into her jugular or try to dig out her heart, if that was normal wolf behavior. Beth had no point of reference. If she'd been asked before this moment, she would have said no wolf could unseat a rider from a fully extended horse.

His concentrated weight bore down on her ribs so that she couldn't take a full breath. Beth prayed. *God have mercy.*

The beasty breath, full of heat and moisture and the scent of blood, caressed her chin and floated over her lips and rose through her nose into the panic centers of her mind.

She heard a voice within her ringing head say, *I will show you mercy.*

She decided the voice belonged to God.

She thought it would be a mercy to die.

3

The party for the doctor was Garner Remke's idea. As a seventy-three-year-old who'd been slowed down by liver cancer, he hadn't thrown a party for years. He wasn't sure he ever had. Pulling this one off made him feel like a kid again.

The partygoers gathered at the Burnt Rock Harbor Sweet Assembly. The building stood at the base of a spectacular cliff high in the Rocky Mountains, high above Burnt Rock itself, where the air was as pure as the spring snowmelt. Built in the fifties by a wealthy family with ties to the old mining town, the Sweet Assembly was a historic landmark. It was a museum. And it was a church of sorts, which Garner occasionally attended.

But tonight it was simply the best location in town to celebrate the work of Catherine Ransom, MD, who seemed modestly flattered by all the attention.

Nearly all of Burnt Rock's 457 residents had accepted his invitation, as happy as he was to have something partyish to do during the summer months that didn't involve entertaining tourists. For the last two hours they'd been mingling outside under the lattice-covered patios, sipping real lemonade spiked with sprigs of mint that Garner had grown in his very own basement greenhouse. Everyone who had a grill had hauled it up to the mountain overlooking their homes, fired up the charcoal, and loosened up with a local microbrew bottled near the headwaters of the Rio Grande. They ate their fill of buffalo burgers, which had been shipped up within a day of slaughter from a free-range bison ranch down in the valley. They sawed away at venison steaks and nibbled at skewered rattlesnake and ate smoky green hatch chilies whole, right out of the tumbling fire roaster.

They entertained each other with dumb-tourist stories—the Texas oil man who didn't believe the Rio Grande started in Colorado, the college thesis writer who asked if Burnt Rock had a Starbucks—and chatted up all the valley gossip and economic indicators of their tourist season, which was about six weeks underway. Would it be a boom or a bust? On a night such as this, with full bellies and warm hearts and boisterous company, everyone agreed: a boom.

Garner was as close to heaven as he figured he would ever get.

When he decided to call everyone inside, he enlisted the help of Hank and Karen Smith, who ran the hardware store. They had been sharing a table with Nova Yarrow, the bookstore owner, and Dotti Sanders, who was eighty going on eighteen and ran her own rental shack for river rafters. She winked at Garner when he leaned over Hank's shoulder, then saluted him with her rattlesnake skewer.

"When are you going to attend that herb-garden seminar in Salida with me?" Dotti asked him. "You already missed the first two of the season."

"Sign me up for the next one," Garner said, taking pleasure in the surprise that crossed her face. Dotti had been after his companionship for two years, and tonight he finally felt accommodating.

"Well it's about time," she muttered.

"And we'll have a coffee afterward. Now let's start a trend toward the indoors," he said. "Don't sneak off now, or you'll miss the desserts." Mazy had outdone herself tonight, claiming she'd been wanting to try out some new concoctions for her popular café. But before they indulged, they would all give Dr. Ransom—Cat, Garner liked to call her—a proper welcome as a true member of the community.

Cat was laughing among a small crowd of business owners: a stable manager, a quilter, a handyman, a mechanic, and a geologist who did his field work here six months out of the year. If the men weren't all married they might all have been besotted. The good doctor was a slight and fit woman, much shorter than the men in spite of her erect and easy thirtysomething posture. She wore her sleek black hair in a bob that swooped under her chin, and her lined eyes gave her the look of a brooding poet. In spite of these austere features she was much more approachable than anyone had expected the day she moved into the vacant offices previously occupied by a dentist. She never donned a white coat. Her soft turtlenecks and slim jeans did a far better job of instilling patients' confidence and assuaging any anxiety they associated with doctors' offices.

Hank and Karen were rounding up the guests when Garner took Cat's hand and gently pulled her away from the group.

"My turn with the guest of honor," he said. "We're heading in. Don't miss out!"

"You've outdone yourself," Cat said to Garner.

He sandwiched her hand in his and squeezed. "I can't think of anyone else I'd rather celebrate," he said.

"The food was amazing, and everyone is being so kind."

"You bet they are. No one else in this town is quite so easy to like as you. You're good for us all." The bookseller Nova was sitting alone at her table as Garner and Cat passed by. "Are you coming?" he asked her. Though Nova looked at Garner when he spoke to her, she gave no answer.

Mazy appeared at Garner's side. "That one's a bit off in the head," the restaurateur said of Nova in low tones.

"Balderdash. She's of sounder mind than I am," Garner said.

"And thoughtful too. She recycles all her glass jars and lets me pick out the ones I can use at the shop."

Mazy made a *pfft* sound with her lips. "Frankly, I'm surprised she's here."

"You shouldn't say stuff like that. She's always real sweet to me. And the most well-read person I've ever met. Don't you think so too, Cat? You probably know her better than anyone here."

Cat lifted her eyebrows but didn't reply, because of course, thought Garner, she was too professional and polite for this kind of nonsense.

The room where the residents of Burnt Rock gathered this lovely summer night was a theater in the round. Its beautiful domed roof boasted skylights that were big enough to see the stars sparkling in the cobalt blue sky. At the center of the circular space, a glowing fire pit that was never extinguished reflected Garner's everlasting good mood.

Almost four hundred people filed in quickly, chattering like morning birds though the sun had set, many still holding drinks and plates of food as they squeezed onto the long benches that encircled the dancing fire pit. The gathering place didn't exactly accommodate a crowd this size, but no one seemed to mind.

"Thank you, all!" Garner's strong voice rapidly settled the crowd. "Thank you for coming up here tonight to celebrate my fifty-ninth birthday!"

Everyone laughed at that, and Hank yelled from the back, "And my twenty-first is tomorrow! C'mon by the hardware store—we'll be serving shots of prune juice on the house!"

Garner drew Cat to stand next to him while the chuckling rippled around the room and finally settled into attentive silence. "All right, all right, so this old body can't pass for fifty-nine anymore, but I am here to tell you something even more unbelievable: today my oncologist called me himself to say that my aggressive cancer has met its match." Garner placed his arm around Cat's shoulder and squeezed her with a sideways hug. "It's true. That beast hasn't spread by a single cell in the last three months. Now, the oncologist is a man of modern medicine, and you all know I don't shun that—on the contrary, I'm grateful. But I know something else too. We all know it. And that is that we have a fine young doctor of our own among us, an attentive and smart woman who knows a thing or two about complementary therapies."

A flurry of whistles and applause rippled around the room.

Garner held up a finger. "You know the world's been turned upside down when someone from the big bad corporate hospitals has a kind word to say about a small-town physician." Garner looked at Cat. "He gives you his compliments, my dear. And all of us here give you our thanks."

"Hear, hear!" someone shouted.

"Until Dr. Ransom wandered into town one year ago today, we all limped along with our illnesses. We hunkered down here until our colds turned to infections and our flus turned to the plague and minor accidents became 'conditions.' We couldn't see a doctor without driving a hundred miles down the mountain to the nearest emergency care center, spending all our money on gas and those waiting room vending machines, only to be told by big shots who don't even know us to take two aspirin and come on back down in the morning."

A few people booed.

"And then this young lady showed up on my doorstep with her magic bag, wanting to buy my medicinal herbs for her new clinic, and we all felt the earth shift, didn't we?" The room rippled with bobbing heads and murmurs of agreement. "My dear Cat, you're blushing! You probably know from our collective blood pressure that we've all been sitting on pins and needles waiting to see if you'd survive your first winter here—and it didn't go easy on you, did it? No one before has loved us enough to also abide our desolate location and our annoying small-town habits. We are, after all, kind of like that extended family that gathers for Christmas dinner and gets snowed in together for unbearable weeks."

Cat rolled her eyes. "You are not."

"And yet she so far has not tired of our quirks, our complaints, or our ailments, real and—in your case, Hank—imagined. My friends," Garner said over the guffaws, "Dr. Catherine Ransom has decided to call herself one of the family. Her Burnt Rock private practice is, as of this week, officially permanent, and tonight we welcome her with joy and gratitude."

Garner led the group in applause that swelled around the room. And as it grew, he felt the warmth of the little fire at his back and the peace that had been growing in his heart across the past year. Emotion rose in his throat, and he raised his hands for quiet.

"Many of you know that I . . . that I lost a daughter many, many years ago." He briefly pursed his lips and removed his wire-rimmed glasses. "But tonight is not a night for sad stories. I just wanted to point out that the condition of our bodies is often an indication of the condition of our hearts, and when you came here last year, Cat, I was a dying man. But you . . . you have a gift of healing, and such a big heart, and I just want to say"—he resented these watery eyes that came with his age!—"that I think of you like my daughter come home."

The moment commanded a respectful silence. Cat tilted her head sweetly, accepting the compliments with the sophisticated smile of a fine woman, the kind of woman he'd once thought his only child might grow up to be.

"I'd be a fool to leave a place full of this much respect and appreciation," Cat said. "Some people have real families who are far less kind to each other than all of you have been to me. I hope you all know how much Burnt Rock has done to improve the quality of my life too. And so I thank you from the bottom of my heart for making it so easy to stay."

She placed her hand over her heart and dipped her head while everyone beamed at her. Everyone but Nova, whose wide eyes and frail body had always reminded Garner of a starving baby bird. She stood at the back of the room behind the crowd where she was nearly invisible, her brows drawn together.

Garner returned his glasses to his face and clapped his hands once. "Well, I know each person here tonight feels similarly about you in one way or another, and so—everyone! Many of you have already had much to say to Dr. Ransom, but all compliments bear repeating. She'll be manning the dessert table, and the price for Mazy's cherry cobbler is a word of thanks to our very fine, very own doctor!"

Nova's departure was as swift as it was stealthy. She received none of the syrupy cobbler and liquid ice cream at the outdoor dessert table, though she could have been the first in line. Garner tried not to fret over this. It seemed no one else had noticed. Except Cat, whose eyes alighted on Nova's tiny form for mere seconds as the bookseller left alone via the dirt trail that led back into town.

It was the only time Garner had ever seen Cat scowl.

4

Java Java Go Joe died the night of her undoing, as Beth came to think of it. She was unconscious or sleeping or some combination of the two until the moment that the beautiful broken stallion was put down, after he'd suffered for more than five hours.

While she was unaware of her surroundings—while Phil and Fiona searched for her in the blackness, found the unspeakable devastation, and then waited to get help almost as long as they'd waited to treat Marigold—Beth developed a vivid memory that could only have been a dream, except that there was physical evidence of its reality. In this state, she understood that the hundred-plus-pound wolf took the collar of her shirt in its teeth and dragged her around Joe's groaning, heaving body. Somehow, the rein that had held her wrist captive during the fall released it.

The wild dog dropped her close enough to Joe's shattered leg that Beth could smell the blood that seeped out of the Thoroughbred's broken skin. She rolled away, confusion gradually suffocating her mind. In her dream, the wolf's muzzle worked under her hip like a pry bar under a boulder, leveraging her toward the fallen horse. She resisted the force until the delusion ended.

It was the gunshot ending Joe's agony that brought her around, the burst so close to her head that she thought the bullet had split her own scalp in two. There was no wolf, but Mr. Kandinsky was bent over her throbbing, rigid body, his face a mixture of anxiety and fury.

Joe's owner, whom she soon came to know as Anthony Darling, was poised to insert his rage into the Borzois' life the way a climbing ivy invades every fissure in an established brick building and reduces it to dust. The retired champion jockey had an ego ten times the size of his own body and a net worth that could seduce any money-hungry attorney.

Near her head, Mr. Darling waved the gun he'd just discharged into Joe's ear, spewing curses at her. She would suffer long in the misery he was about to create for her, he promised her that.

Phil tried to put distance between Mr. Darling and the scene, perhaps trying to prevent the mercy killing from becoming an act of revenge as well. Mr. Kandinsky noticed this intervention as if he was noticing Phil for the first time since the drama had been exposed. He fired Phil on the spot.

The sun rising behind the eastern Sangre de Cristos caused long shadows to fall on them all. Beth wished the very mountains would collapse and bury her before she was forced to rise and face her parents' disbelief and try to make amends. She had faith that the mountain could move. She told it to. The mountain refused.

It took less than a week for the wealthy breeder to level his promise against Beth in the form of a lawsuit. This was the same as saying he had leveled his ire against her family and her family's livelihood, because she was a co-owner of the Blazing B, which all Borzois became at the age of eighteen.

The claim outlined damages for the lost horse, the lost progeny of the horse, the lost progeny of the progeny, and the reduced reputation of the breeder, who might have to wait untold years until he owned a stud of Java Java Go Joe's value once again. The demanded sum was staggering, including emotional damages for all of these real and projected losses, which had allegedly caused Mr. Darling's latent alcoholism to rear its head, which led to further damages and losses.

Blood ties spared the Kandinskys from similar litigation.

A separate suit was filed against Phil's family, but Beth didn't know the details of it. She heard from the vet that Marigold had lost her eye. She didn't call Phil, and Phil didn't call her. She had no idea what became of the stolen saddle.

The day after having been served with legal paperwork, Beth rose at her usual hour to dress and help her mother prepare breakfast. She had been awake most of the night formulating a plan to stand between Mr. Darling and her family's future, and she hoped they would be agreeable to it.

She scratched at the triple track of healing scabs across her collarbone where the wolf had clawed her. The doctor thought the cuts were inflicted by a shrub, and Beth hadn't contradicted him. She rubbed antibiotic ointment into the six-inch trails before pulling on her shirt.

Her dog, Herriot, seemed to sense that Beth's life had been disrupted, and was underfoot most days. Herriot was an Appenzell Mountain Dog, a European breed cut out for high-altitude and harsh-weather herding, even higher and harsher than Colorado's mountains. She was a solid, stocky girl about the same weight as the average coyote, but thicker in the chest and not as tall.

The dog's short-haired coat was the glossy color of melted chocolate. Rich white cream splashed across her chest and muzzle, cresting between her eyes. Streaks of caramel ran up all four of Herriot's legs and also framed her happy smile with the mischievous look of a sweet-toothed troublemaker. Twin caramel dots on the inside of her brows made her seem extra intelligent to Beth, and perhaps slightly fierce from a cow's point of view.

With the exception of Beth's father, the dog was the only living creature at the ranch who didn't seem to be judging Beth's fool actions. She pressed into Beth's legs as they went downstairs to the kitchen, bumping her haunches along the wall.

Rose Borzoi was already at the stove. Beth's mother was a striking woman made even more beautiful than she was in youth by a quarter century of admiration poured over her by her husband. No one took more pride in Rose's physical and intellectual strength than Abel Borzoi. His wife was nearly six feet tall barefoot, and she always went barefoot in the house, summer and winter. Her one vanity was her feet.

Her coarse brown hair was still as long and as thick as it appeared in her wedding picture, though it had started to gray. Rose bound it daily in a braid, then threw it back over the wide shoulders of her husband's work shirts, which were too big for her at the shoulders and yet also seemed to fit like a good trademark, rolled up to the elbows and billowing out over hips widened by childbirth and horse riding.

Beth's father was at the table, drinking his coffee.

"Hi, baby girl." He beckoned her into a snug embrace while he stayed seated. Abel Borzoi was an overweight, grizzly bear man with a wide jaw and clean-shaven face and an open spirit that smiled on sinners and saints alike.

"Sorry I'm late," she said, though the truth was her parents had risen early.

Rose acknowledged Beth by saying, "Dog goes out."

Beth put Herriot out every morning. Her mother didn't need to make a point of ordering it. Nevertheless, Beth sent Herriot out the back door without comment. The Blazing B had four dogs, and though Herriot was the only one who slept with the humans, she was not allowed to dine with them. Her food would have been already set out with the horses' near the barn.

Beth washed her hands at the sink and then fetched the pot, the water, and the steel-cut oats she'd need to make the oatmeal. There were fresh berries in a strainer in the sink, and her mother tossed slabs of ham onto a hot griddle. Her brothers, Levi and Danny, would come in at six to eat. Rose and a hired cook made the big hot midday meal for everyone down at the Hub. When it came to supper, usually cold sandwiches and leftovers, it was every man for himself.

Whatever her parents had been speaking about, they weren't going to continue in front of her.

"I'm going to fix this," Beth announced. "I have a plan. Today I'm going to go speak to Mr. Darling's attorney."

"You shouldn't do anything without speaking to ours first," her father advised.

"Hear me out—maybe we won't need him. Maybe we won't need to go to court. I'm to blame here. I did a stupid thing, and I can own up to that. I'll pay Mr. Darling what he wants. I'll pay him back for as long as it takes."

"And just where are you going to get the money for that small country it seems he wants to buy?" Rose asked.

"I'll start with my tuition."

Abel set his coffee cup on the table. "You will not. You're going to vet school in September, Beth. There's no reason for this incident to derail that plan."

Rose scoffed. "Incident. Hear her out, Abel. She has a part to play in whatever solution we've got to come up with."

Beth measured salt into her hand and tossed it into the pot of water. "My tuition will be like a down payment. And then I'll get a job. Two jobs. We'll negotiate a payment plan. Ten years, twenty years, whatever it takes. I might have to put vet school off for a few years, but I can save up for it again."

Her father shook his head. "I don't support the idea."

"If we don't come up with some money we won't be able to

support anything," Rose said. "Not this ranch, not those men, not our own flesh and blood." She stabbed at the pork with a spatula. "I can't believe you put us in this position, Beth."

"Rose, honey. You're too hard on her. We did fool things when we were her age."

"Nothing like this," her mother said. "Nothing that jeopardized the lives of a dozen other people."

Beth's insides were bound up in knots of shame. She wouldn't be eating breakfast today.

"If I make a proposal like this now, he might agree to a lesser amount of money, don't you think?" she said. "He'll avoid all the legal hassles, the attorney's fees—"

"It doesn't usually work that way," Abel observed. "Men like Darling tend to enjoy those things. And they're impatient."

"They're hiring for summer down at the feed-and-tack," Beth said. "Might turn into a full-time job. And I can work at King Soopers on the off shifts."

"And while you're working twenty-four-seven elsewhere, who's going to pick up your slack around here?" her mom said.

Beth's older brother, Levi, strode into the kitchen and snatched up a slice of ham with his bare fingers right off the griddle. "Won't be me," he said. At twenty-six, Levi had his father's broad-faced features but none of his body mass. "I'm not gonna lie in this bed Beth made."

"Yes you will," Rose said, grabbing the meat out of his hand and throwing it back down to cook longer. "We're a family. Breakfast will be ready in five."

"It's ready now," Levi said.

"Clock says it's not. Where's Danny?"

"How should I know?"

Beth said, "We already made plans to redistribute the chores when I go to school in the fall. So we make the switch a month ahead of schedule. And I won't be at school. That's all."

No one seemed to be listening to her.

Levi said, "You couldn't *sell* this land for what Darling wants out of it. He wants us to bleed."

The salty scent of ham came off the stove. Beth's water seemed unwilling to boil. She couldn't argue with the likely truth of Levi's mean-spirited point. Rose tended to the strawberries that needed slicing by slamming the colander onto the cutting block. Levi poured himself a cup of coffee.

Fifteen-year-old Danny entered the silence with a whistle and went straight to the sink to wash up.

"Taciturn and sullen, all of you," Danny said. "Who are you and what have you done with my family?"

"Beth killed them off," Levi said.

"All but you, you mean." Danny dried his hands at the sink. "You're the same as ever."

"You're early," Rose said.

"It's the ham's fault. Who can resist redolence like that?"

"Shut up, Danny," Levi ordered. "If you've got time to be *assimilating* the dictionary, you've got time to do more work around here. Beth's about to shirk all her responsibilities."

"No, I'm going to work harder than ever before," she said. She tried to remind herself that Levi's sharp edge had been honed for years prior to this moment and had little to do with her. It was the ranch that he hated—the charity of it, to be precise. His vision for how the Blazing B might reach its full potential diverged from their father's view in significant ways.

Of course, both men would perceive this suit as a terrible setback. Perhaps an insurmountable one.

"Everyone in this family works hard," Abel said. He leaned back in his chair and smoothed his shirt over his ample belly with one hand. "And no one works harder on our behalf than the Lord himself, and I expect you all to remember that. Bethesda, no mistake is beyond God's ability to repair it. Your heart is in the right place, and I know that. We'll come through it."

"Bethesda," Levi mocked. "You know you're in a bad spot when you've got the full name coming at you."

Her father dropped his fist on the table and then lifted his finger toward Levi. "Let's have some respect, son."

"She hasn't earned mine yet."

"But *I* demand it. We've got a tough row to hoe here, and if we don't do it together this is going to end as badly for you alone as it will for the Blazing B. Your mother and I named her Bethesda on purpose, and I say it as a blessing, not a punishment. You know what it means."

"House of mercy," Danny offered. He couldn't help it. And he couldn't know how his ability to irritate Levi was a salve on Beth's heartache. Rose shoveled ham slices onto four plates and left the fifth one bare. Beth stirred the pot of oats without looking at anyone.

"House of mercy." Abel's confirmation also had lighthearted warning in it for his youngest child. *Hold your tongue for a minute, would you?* "That's what we're about, isn't it? This ranch is all about showing mercy to people who need it, people who maybe haven't ever had any in their lifetimes. We are the Blazing Bethesda."

"Your great-grandpa named this place the Blazing B long before any of us were born," Levi challenged.

Beth felt his eyes on her back, resenting her status as her father's only daughter, the princess with the privileges.

Levi continued. "He named it for the Borzois, and for those Wasatch maples that turn to fire every fall."

"That's the greatness of a great name," Abel said. "It grows into itself. After five generations, we now blaze year-round with the work of the Holy Spirit. This ranch belongs to God, not to us. He'll see us through."

Levi shook his head and took his feet off the table. Danny took his seat next to his older brother. As Beth poured the oatmeal into bowls, she planned a time to call Mr. Darling's attorney.

Rose placed the oatmeal and plate of strawberries in front of her husband.

"Where's my ham?" He grabbed his wife around the waist before she could get away.

"Just what you need is another heart attack right now," she said.

He kissed her hand. "I'm three years plaque-free, Rose. I'm healthy as a horse."

"An old horse. And you're not plaque-free."

Abel winked at Beth as she sat down beside him. "She runs a tight ship, your mother. Don't take it personal. She's part of the reason why we're all going to make it. Let's pray."

5

Beth's proposal to compensate Mr. Darling in monthly install-
ments out of her steady income for as many years as it might
take was mocked and rejected. And then it bit her on the backside. Mr. Darling's counsel used her proposal as an admission of guilt.
The Borzois' attorney was almost as furious at her as her mother was.

Nonetheless, it was agreed that Beth ought to be making as
much money as possible until the final judgment was issued, and
within the following week she was able to get two jobs down the
road in Alamosa. They became a shelter for her, an escape. As
May slipped into June and then July, the ranch fell into an anxious
rhythm of silent work while everyone waited for the legal mishap,
the inspired idea, or the lottery card that would save them from the
inevitable. If the judge did not offer her grace, there would be no
way for the family to keep the Blazing B.

The associates eyed her warily, as if sensing that she might be
a weak calf about to get picked off by a coyote. On the Blazing B,
the least hardy animals were allowed to die off for the benefit of
the herd. Assistance went to the strongest stock in an effort to keep
them that way. Only Wally tipped his hat every time he crossed her
path, because he kept forgetting her offense.

The ranch hands were gracious. Dr. Roy and Jacob were practically family, very understanding family. Their unconditional love could bring Beth to tears. How could she have put their livelihood at risk? They'd poured fifteen years into this endeavor—what would they do if she destroyed it? Pastor Eric regularly offered prayers, and Emory made a habit of stopping by to see how she was holding up.

In time Beth learned to avoid them all.

One morning when she was driving off the ranch to get to her shift at the feed-and-tack, halfway between the Hub and the highway she came across a girl walking up the drive with a backpack on her shoulder. She looked barely sixteen and wore canvas sneakers with holes in the toes. Beth rolled down her window and brought her truck to a stop.

"Help you with something?" she asked.

"Is this the Blazing B?"

"It is."

"I heard—they told me I might find a job here?"

"Well I don't know who said that, but I'm sorry. We don't have a thing. We're not hiring right now."

Tears sprang to the girl's eyes, but she succeeded in holding them back. "You sure? It was the folks down at the Methodist church. They were real certain y'all might have something for me to do." She looked down at her feet. "Maybe a place to stay."

Beth weighed this. Several of their associates had been referred to them by that church, but never anyone so young. The program they ran here wasn't for minors. Or even women. But the teen's timid demeanor reached all the soft spots of Beth's heart.

"Did someone from the church give you a ride up here?"

"No, uh . . . John Adkins brought me over. My foster dad. Was. My foster dad."

"You want me to give him a call for you? Have him pick you up again?"

"Uh, no. No." She looked back in the direction from which she'd come, as if trying to decide what to do. "He won't . . . I mean, I won't be going back there."

"Why not?" Beth immediately worried that the girl was a victim of some unspeakable evil—as if whatever circumstances had put her in the system in the first place weren't awful enough.

"Turned eighteen yesterday."

Beth blinked at her.

"Aged out of the system," she clarified.

"And he just threw you out?"

"He's not a bad man. He and his wife are decent people. It just happens."

"No it doesn't. Any 'decent' person wouldn't put you on the street before you had a job or a bed to sleep in. What's your name?"

"Lorena. He said the Blazing B was a sure thing."

"You got that right. Lorena, I'm Beth." She slapped the vinyl bench seat next to her. "Get in."

Lorena ran around the hood of the truck and did as she was told. Beth started a three-point turn on the lane before the girl had closed the door, and headed back toward the Hub. She couldn't predict exactly how this might go, but already she was formulating a proposal in her mind, and she had at least three truths already at work in her favor:

Her father would never turn away someone in need.

Her mother could use some help around the house.

The lawsuit hanging over their heads wouldn't have anything to do with it.

Beth had hoped to speak to her father alone, but when she arrived at the Hub, the entire workforce was gathered at the equipment and supply sheds loading up trucks for a marathon day of fence repairs. While the cows are away, the cowboys can't afford to play, her father often said. On a ranch the size of the Blazing B, the fence repairs went on all summer, whenever the weather and other duties allowed, and the men respected this job. Each one of them had experienced the unhappy task of making emergency repairs during January blizzards. Consequently, their summer efforts were of the highest quality.

The men from the bunkhouse were already divided into teams, one led by the father-son pair of Dr. Roy and Jacob, the other by Pastor Eric and Emory. Generally, Abel teamed up with their most challenging associates, two marines who suffered from post-traumatic stress disorder. Jacob always found an excuse to pull Danny onto his team, and Levi preferred to work alone, though he rarely got what he wished. Together the men would knock out several hundred yards of dry rotted posts and rusty tangled wires before the sun set.

Beth had no choice but to barge into the group. There would be no private moment with her parents this morning, and she couldn't just leave Lorena here. She parked and indicated that the girl should follow her over to a shining black beast of a truck, an unaffordable thing that Levi had purchased for himself against his parents' advice. Her father, her brothers, and Jacob—dear Jacob, whom she had robbed—were discussing the fence lines on a large map.

"Don't let the testosterone worry you," Beth said as they approached. "They're all sweeties. All except for Levi, but you can ignore him."

Lorena carried her backpack in front of her like a shield.

"Dad," Beth called. "I've got someone here who could use a place to stay for a bit."

Abel looked up from the map. "Do you now? Hi, young lady. I'm Abel." He reached out to shake Lorena's hand, and she was forced to lower her defense. "These are my sons, Levi and Danny, and my good man Jacob."

"Look what the Blazing Bethesda dragged in," Levi said.

"I'm Lorena," the girl whispered to Abel.

"What'd you have in mind, Beth?" her father asked.

"Mom will have no trouble putting her to work."

"You know we can't take minors, honey."

"She's eighteen. Right? Can you prove it?"

"I think . . . I think . . ." Lorena fumbled with the zipper on her backpack and withdrew a brown envelope. "They gave me these documents. That's all I have. I didn't even ask what was in it."

"Let's have a look," Abel instructed. Lorena gave the packet to him.

"Her birthday kinda wrecked the arrangements she had with her foster family," Beth said.

"Well that's just wrong," Jacob said.

Beth thanked him as best she was able with her eyes. "That's what I think."

"Felonious," Danny said. He tipped his hat up at Lorena and flashed a smile. Jacob smacked down the brim and shoved him off toward the shed to fetch a toolbox.

Levi said, "We've got processes in place for this kind of thing. And women just don't fit into it."

"Your mother and sister do just fine," Abel said as he flipped through the paperwork. "You ever worked on a ranch before, Lorena?"

She shook her head.

"You graduate high school?"

No again. "But not because I can't learn," she said. "And I'm the hardest worker you'll ever meet."

"No." Levi had folded the fence map and now let it slap against the hood of the John Deere. "This isn't some charity we run here."

"Sure it is," Abel said. "What would you call it, Jacob?"

"The best church in town," Jacob said.

"We've got fifteen people to feed, near five hundred cows to bring in, and more than six thousand thirsty acres to keep well oiled. We got a pool rider to pay and grazing permits to renew. We got alfalfa to harvest and winter feed supplements to stock up on. And we got a dragon breathing fire at our back door, thanks to my little sister. Who the heck is going to pay for one more expense?"

"Well, your little sister just took two jobs. That's worth something."

"That's worth squat."

"In a few months, maybe you'll be right. But today, we have what we need to help a girl out. Why wouldn't I do that?" Abel stuffed the papers back into the envelope and handed them back to Lorena.

"This is a do-or-die kind of bad season we're in, Dad. We can't take in everyone who knocks on the door."

"We don't."

"I swear we could be operating in the black if we just used a better model than this."

At Levi's raised voice, several of the other men turned to look. Rose arrived with a truck full of brimming water containers that would be sent out with each team. Abel waved her over as Jacob left them to distribute the water.

"Rose, honey, I think our Beth has brought you someone who will be of great help around the house."

"That would be something, wouldn't it?" She wiped her brow with her long cotton sleeve and introduced herself to Lorena.

"Would that work for you?" Abel asked his wife.

"We could give it a go. I'd be grateful. Can you cook?"

At this, Lorena brightened. "Love to."

"You're not even going to run a background on her?" Levi protested.

"There's plenty of time for all that," Abel said.

"We've all gone nuts."

Beth saw Jacob smirk at a distance. He slid two five-gallon jugs off the tailgate and carried one in each hand to the other vehicles.

"How long'll this be for?" Rose asked.

"Long as it's working, I guess," her husband answered. "Until you can land a real job," he said to Lorena. "But we got rules, and you have to follow them."

"I'll do anything. Thank you. Thank you so much."

"Rule number one: you may not apply for a real job until after you have secured your GED. Ergo, you have any free time—and trust me, Rose is a good woman, but she's stingy with stuff like that—you'll be working on getting that diploma. Understood?"

"Yes, sir."

"Rule number two: no drinking, no drugs. You can dance all you want, but that's as loose as it gets around here."

"That's just fine."

Levi stalked off at this point.

"Rule number three: church on Sundays, ten sharp. If we miss church, church comes to us." Abel pointed at Pastor Eric, who took his hand off a post-hole digger to wave.

Wally was passing by the group with a bale of razor wire in his gloved hands. He saw Lorena and nodded. "Howdy. I'm sure we've met before, so I hope you'll forgive me for not remembering the name that goes with your lovely face."

"It's Lorena," Beth provided.

Wally hesitated. "And you're the one who rides Hastings?"

"Yes! That was great. Name's Beth."

He beamed at her. "Beth, that's right. The good girl. You're going to help me find my lockbox," he said.

"It's still missing?"

"Sad to say. That wolf, he's crafty like a fox."

The mention of the wolf was like cold fingers on Beth's neck. She collected herself by whispering to the teenager as he moved on past them: "Wally's harmless, just forgetful. He loves fence-repair days. He gets to dig."

"Which leads me to rule number four," Rose said. She shielded her eyes from the mounting sun. "Don't go anywhere away from the house by yourself. We are a ranch for men, after all, and your being here will be something new for all of us. C'mon now, and I'll show you the house." She glanced at the backpack. "Is that all you've got? Good, then. I'll have to think up a place for you to sleep."

"She can stay with me," Beth said.

Rose shrugged. "That'd be fine."

"If you don't mind sharing a bed," Beth said to the girl.

"I don't. Of course I don't. It sure beats the floor. And I sleep small."

Abel chuckled. "I don't know what that means, but I can guarantee you'll be sleeping hard. This is no resort we're running, much as Levi would prefer that approach."

Lorena grabbed his outstretched hand in both of hers and pumped it up and down. "I can't thank you enough." Then she jogged away. Rose was already climbing back into her vehicle.

"Your shoes," Beth called out. "You won't last a day in those. See if you can find something in my closet."

Her mother waved acknowledgment. She'd have Lorena all set up and sweeping the floors before the hour was out.

"Well that was easy enough," Abel said. "Let's get on with it, men. Where'd my map go?"

Beth watched Rose and Lorena drive back toward the Borzoi house and wondered why she felt a gnawing regret in the back of her stomach. Usually she felt joy—excitement, hope, peace, a dozen other positive emotions—whenever a new associate came onto the ranch. But in this moment she felt strangely like she'd been cast off.

The truck crested the slight rise and then descended the back side of the hill, out of sight.

"It's not going to happen," Jacob said, beside her startlingly close. Water droplets had spotted his leather work boots. His hair tended to curl up around his ears underneath the rim of his dusty hat, which sat low on his brow and accentuated how wide set his clear-blue eyes were. His laugh lines and crows' feet were prematurely deep but made him look kinder rather than older. His close-cut mustache and beard was his only flaw, Beth thought. It covered a dimple to the left of his mouth and made him look more country singer than cowboy.

Whenever Jacob sang, the cows bellowed their protest.

"What's not going to happen?" she asked.

"You, getting replaced."

"Everyone's dispensable. But that's not what I was thinking about." She didn't in fact remember exactly what she'd been thinking about. At the moment, her mind was consumed with a terrible guilt about his silver-plated saddle, and the knowledge that she would never, ever have the character to confess her crime before it came to light.

"No one's dispensable," he said. "But I don't think anyone's as generous as you."

"My father—far more."

"He's never shared his bed with an associate."

Beth laughed. "No, his calling's a little higher than mine."

"No calling's higher or lower than anyone else's. We all do what we can with what we've got."

She turned to him, intending to say that she'd been overly generous with things that were not hers to give, and the cost of her generosity might be more than anyone here could afford. This was why she was losing her place at the Blazing B. This was why she had to leave the ranch to work two jobs, and why her mother could so easily take another young woman into the house. Already Beth had been moved out into the margins of the family's life.

"Well, my bed's all I've got these days. And Lorena doesn't have one. Anyone would share it."

He shook his head. "If you say so," he conceded. "See you around."

His praise sat in her stomach like too many helpings of rich dessert.

6

On the afternoon that the black clouds rolled over the mountain ridge and poured down into Burnt Rock like an avalanche in summer, Garner Remke was balanced precariously on a ladder in his basement, because he was replacing a high-output fluorescent light tube in one of his heat lamps. It was to his credit that he'd unplugged the fixture before beginning work on it, because at the moment that the tube connected with the contact plate, the thunderstorm passed over his house.

This high in the Rocky Mountains there was little difference between an electrical storm that passed over one's house and one that shot directly through it. The light he had been using to illuminate his work sizzled and then sputtered out.

Burnt Rock was an inhospitable location to be sure, a high-altitude mining town that no longer had an operating mine and was more capable of sustaining tourists than trees. Gardens were out of the question. And yet Garner had converted the basement of his home into a climate-controlled environment capable of growing a host of healing herbs. Many people relied on Garner's Garden, Inc.: the residents of Burnt Rock, the tourists who discovered him on a summer's day, and the enthusiasts who shopped his quality blends on the Web. They could be assured that his nettle leaf or spearmint or lavender or fennel or chamomile or any one of dozens of other helpful, healthful plants was of the highest quality. Though not all of them were entirely legal.

Garner first invested in this pastime for his own physical comfort after the cancer diagnosis. Then he did it for the challenge of bringing plants to life in a pit, and then because it allowed him to stay connected to people, and to be admired for doing something important. Few things were as rewarding as harvesting rosemary and mint for a roasted-lamb supper with friends while a blizzard raged. He certainly didn't do it for the money. He had plenty of that to last him the rest of his life.

Before his family abandoned him, Garner had been a wealthy man, and a man of faith. Not a priest or pastor or any such thing, but a successful businessman who had simple beliefs about God's goodness and love. Today he was wealthy and skeptical. The thing that had caused Garner to turn away from the more childlike notions wasn't the classic problem of why God allowed bad things to happen. There were plenty of viable answers for that type of question.

Instead, Garner's crisis of faith came when first his wife and then his daughter rejected his love. He had offered it unconditionally, expecting nothing but love in return, and they treated his gift as if it was unworthy of their standards. He slaved for them, worked long hours for them, provided them with an expensive house on the most stunning piece of real estate in the San Luis Valley, and showered them with all the fringe benefits of financial security.

"You think you're being loving, but you're not," his wife had yelled at him the day she walked out. *"I don't care about your intentions. Your results are pathetic."*

His daughter left on a similar note a few years later, when he objected to her choice of husband. When Rose announced her engagement to Abel Borzoi, an established cattle rancher, Garner couldn't help but be concerned for his daughter's well-being. The Blazing B was not a ranch concerned about expanding its profitability. The Borzoi clan could promise nothing but a life of toil. Besides that, Abel was far too old for her. What kind of father would approve of such a future?

Garner and Rose had not spoken in the twenty-seven years since she stormed out of his house, slamming the door so hard that she cracked all nine of its tiny panes of glass.

This is what made no sense to him: not that the human race had the capacity to do wrong, but that it had equal capacity to reject kindness and decency and all manner of goodness, even—and perhaps especially—within the bonds of family ties.

And if love was so worthless, then perhaps the God of love was even less valuable. His defining essence was being squandered on people who didn't want it. There was no hope for such a race, nor for such a God.

But in the dustiest corners of Garner's heart, hope lingered. At age seventy-three he didn't have the heart to sweep it out, because he had nothing more appealing to put in its place. So he poured what love he had to offer into the lives of people who would accept it, such as Cat Ransom. And he waited for a sign that, at the right time, his daughter might return to him. He told no one about his wealth. For some reason love went further when it wasn't connected to money.

On the late-July afternoon when the thunderstorm passed over, into, and through his house, the walls complained, and a faint smell of something burnt seeped into the blackened basement. Electrical wiring, Garner guessed, or old wood siding cooked by lightning. At an altitude of nine thousand feet, even sturdy structures cowered when thunderheads rumbled.

In the darkness, Garner felt his way around tables stacked with live plants. He reached the stairs and climbed to the main level of the house, where the hall light had survived the zapping. The red gardening clogs on his feet thumped heavily on the unfinished pine steps.

The thunder was great and his house was small, and the atmospheric vibrations always caused his windows and his inventory to rattle. In the front room, which had been converted into a small store, his glass jars of homemade herbal teas and prized recipes of tinctures and salves were displayed on neat shelves and secured behind wood rails. He checked these first, though to date no storm had ever damaged them.

Even so, a small buzzing noise in his left ear suggested that this routine summer disturbance was anything but routine. His mind filled with the idea that something was about to break—something strong that couldn't stand up against the will of God. An oak tree, perhaps, bowed under the Lord's thumb.

Garner entered his kitchen, searching for the electric stench. There was a window at the sink that looked out over a hillside jagged with black volcanic rocks and sparse plant life. It was a stunning panoramic view. If God had not selected this house for a target, it was possible that Garner might witness someone else's devastation.

After making sure his house was not on fire, Garner decided to eat a snack. He wouldn't replace those basement bulbs until after this storm ended.

He went into his pantry for a jar of peanut butter and some round crackers. They sat on the shelf above a case of empty apothecary jars and a selection of essential oils, which he needed to restock—an activity for after eating, if the electricity was still down. He tucked his meal into the crook of his elbow, fetched a plate and a knife, and took everything to the table for assembly.

A flash of light and the exploding stink of scorched tar shingles startled him so badly that he crushed the first dry cracker he picked up. The black skies became an apocalyptic floodlight that sliced through his head to the back of his solid skull. Within the very same second, even as he blinked, the lightning's booming electrical charge clapped the humid air right into his kitchen.

The window over the sink burst like a water balloon, showering glass and rainwater across the stainless basin and the old utility carpet. The force knocked Garner off his chair, which tipped backward, and he found himself on the floor, shielded by his heavy table.

The ensuing gust swept the plate up off the table and clapped it against the wall, then released it to gravity with a clatter.

The sight of the destroyed window filled Garner with a quivering anticipation. Surely it was a sign. The sign. This spectacular breaking of glass, as theatrical as his daughter's smoldering exit, told him the time for reunion had come. It came now because Garner had finally in his heart let Rose go, because he'd accepted another daughter to replace her—Cat Ransom, a woman who needed her own father figure. Wasn't that always how it worked? For his years of suffering and loneliness, Garner's life would be doubly blessed, like Job's.

With no concern for the weather pouring in, or for the glass stuck in the carpet like glittering stalagmites—those could wait—Garner rose from the kitchen floor and found his rain jacket in the hall closet. The peanut-butter-covered table knife was still in his fist. He returned the utensil to the howling kitchen, then slipped into his mud boots, pulled up his hood, and went out into the driving rain toward Cat Ransom's offices.

He hoped the marriage had finally tanked. It wasn't that Garner thought Abel was a bad man. His daughter's husband was, from what Garner could tell, decent and hardworking and descended from tough Russian stock, the kind that could survive Siberian winters with only a pocketknife and a bearskin and a bottle of vodka. The problem was simply that Rose's marriage to him was beneath her. The Blazing B was a millstone on her neck. She had within her the brains, if not the will, to be a fine doctor. As a girl, that had been her dream. It wasn't too late.

He still had the means to fund her opportunities if she would accept his willingness to do it. He would give her whatever she needed to start over.

Garner walked to Dr. Ransom's offices briskly, ignoring the storm. The anticipation of his daughter reentering his life after two and a half decades filled him with optimism and fresh energy. She would need him again. Finally. The fast rain poured onto the leathery earth with too much impatience to be absorbed. On the dirt path between his house and the town's only paved road, where Dr. Ransom's building was located, Garner's boots splashed through puddles that had been mere depressions in the land that morning.

It took Garner less than five minutes to reach Dr. Ransom's offices, which had been a medical office since miners first settled Burnt Rock in the late eighteen hundreds. The flat-roofed, box-shaped building was wrapped in horizontally mounted tongue-and-groove siding and painted white. A second-floor balcony supported by turned-wood posts and decorative bracings provided a covering over the walkway.

Garner thought the place looked eternally ready to stage a fight between drunken gunslingers. But there wasn't a cowboy in sight. Electrical lights installed under the balcony swung from their chains in the gusty air and threw grim shadows around the ineffective shelter.

Cat shared her building with Nova's bookstore. It was an eclectic pairing, but the entire town was that way. Across a gravel driveway was a twin building that held Mazy's café and Hank's hardware store. On the opposite side of the road, the only paved road in all of Burnt Rock, was a drugstore that doubled as a post office, the town hall, and a gift shop that sold polished rocks and tiny bottles filled with gold leaf. Two zigzagging miles up the mountain behind the gift shop, hidden now by dense clouds, was the Burnt Rock Harbor Sweet Assembly church-slash-museum-slash-monument.

Garner pounded on the glass window to which gold letters had been applied in an arc. "Catherine Ransom, M.D. If the Doctor Isn't in, Dial:" And her cell phone number was listed beneath this. Publishing her cell phone number saved Cat the expense of having to hire an office assistant to take appointments and man the office whenever she wasn't there.

The door-pounding was only an announcement of his presence, not a request to be let in. Garner entered without waiting and brushed water off his slick jacket onto the dry floor of the doctor's waiting room.

"Cat, girl! Have I got news!"

Catherine Ransom emerged from her back office holding a cup of something steaming. She set down her drink and came around the counter quickly to take Garner's coat.

"Garner! Are you all right? Why are you out in this mess?"

He held the coat closed at his neck, intending to talk her into taking him out of Burnt Rock as soon as possible. "I need a ride."

"You should have called. I'd have come and picked you up."

Garner laughed, because the very sensible idea of calling this woman, who was more like a daughter this past year than Rose had ever been, hadn't occurred to him.

"I can't keep up with that kind of common sense, can I?"

"You're not sick, are you?"

"Oh no. It's my daughter."

A shadow flitted across Cat's face as one of the lamps outside moved through its wind-tossed arc.

"Rose is sick?" she asked.

"No, no. Rose is, well, I don't know exactly *how* she is, but it's time. I need you to take me to the ranch. I need to see her." Garner didn't own a car, though he could have afforded whatever private transportation he wanted. He preferred to walk to wherever he needed to go, and when that wasn't possible, to pay others for their wheels and their company. He never had need to make the hair-raising drive down the mountain alone when there were so many kind souls willing to do it for him. People seemed to find noble purpose in getting a cancer-riddled man to his various medical appointments down in civilization. Cat, especially, was never too busy for such a thing.

But tonight she didn't seem to understand Garner's urgency.

"Why do you need to see her right now?" she asked.

"Because something has happened!"

Cat's eyebrows rose expectantly. She seemed to want him to explain.

He said, "My window broke," and heard the inadequacy of the words. "She needs me. I don't know exactly why yet, but she needs me now. It might be that she's finally seen the limitations of her marriage, or that she's . . ." Overcome by a troubling possibility, Garner's mind shifted gears. "Heaven help me, if that man filed for a divorce—"

"If she's anything like you, I suppose she'd be the one to do it," Cat said. He saw in her light smile that she meant to calm him, though she knew he hadn't been the one to torpedo his own marriage.

"Right. True."

"In which case her situation might not be as dire as you think it is."

The lightning, the shattering, the force that knocked him off his seat were all quite dire, Garner thought. Indications of some-thing big and devastating. An oak tree uprooted from the earth.

"Oh my," Garner murmured.

"What?" Cat laid a warm hand on his arm.

"Abel must be dead. I think he died."

Cat did not offer him any calming answer to this. He thought he detected her sigh.

"Do Abel and Rose have children?" she asked.

"I don't know."

"How can you not—I'm sorry. Garner, let's call the ranch. We can find out the truth right now."

"No. No, I wouldn't know what . . ." Did he have grandchildren? It was an overwhelming thought at the moment, though he'd often wondered. It was better that he focus on the object of his own resentment, Abel. "I don't know how she'd react. All these years, Cat. I need to see her. Plain and simple. Her husband is gone. I know it in my soul."

Instead of making a grab for her coat and keys as Garner expected, she suggested they wait to drive down into the valley until the next day, after the storm blew over.

"It's a four-hour drive," she said.

"But a man is dead."

"We'll be dead if we attempt those mountain roads in this storm." She didn't meet Garner's eyes. Cat lifted the cup to her lips, and steam snaked out around her cheeks and drifted to the back of her head like the ties of a spooky carnival mask, cloaking her expression.

Of course driving now was foolishness. What was he thinking? And yet—he sensed something more than practicality at work in Cat's reticence. It came to him immediately. He strode across the waiting room and placed his hand firmly on Cat's shoulder.

"You have nothing to worry over, girl. Rose can't replace you in my life. I'm a lucky old man. I'll have two daughters now! She'll love you as much as I do."

When Cat didn't reply right away, Garner grew uncomfortable. He feared he'd exposed some vulnerable spot in the woman's soul. Or maybe he'd overstepped his bounds in asking for a favor.

"But you should finish your tea first," he said. "Is that my lemongrass blend? Yes, I can smell it. You take your time, girl, and then you'll know I'm right. Tea fixes everything. Just everything."

The doctor regarded Garner over the lip of the mug. Her blue eyes seemed unnaturally dark in the poor light of the storm, and Garner noticed that not one table lamp in the comfortable space was lit. They spoke by the shifting beams of the swinging lamps outside, and by the weak backlight that spilled out of her rear office. The effect was momentarily unsettling.

But then Cat offered him a half smile before she took another sip. She said, "Of course it does, Garner. Especially your tea. You know I'd do anything for you. But we'll go tomorrow, not now." Then she drank again, and the tight spot in the middle of Garner's stomach relaxed.

"There's no rush to leave this second," he agreed.

"It's safer that way."

"It is."

"Come have a cup with me."

"Thank you. I will."

"The dead are never in a hurry."

It wasn't the dead Garner wanted to see, but he found himself nodding in agreement anyway.

7

It had become Beth's habit, when the timing of her work shifts allowed it, to take Hastings out for a ride in the summer evenings. Rather than face her family, she would slip onto the Blazing B from a rear access road, park on the backside of the barn, and fetch Hastings' saddle before anyone knew she was home.

The first few times Beth did this, she was distracted and delayed in the tack room by the sight of the empty rack that had held the silver saddle, but she soon learned not to look at the accusing vacancy. She became efficient at saddling Hastings quickly and riding off to a creek that separated the ranch from the bordering public lands, where she'd stay until the sun set.

The day Lorena joined the family, Beth discovered Hastings waiting for her, already saddled up, gnawing on a tuft of grass that had poked its green fingers into the dusty corral. He abandoned it at the sight of her and whinnied. Descending sunlight reflected off his chestnut coat, marbling it with gold. Storm clouds gathered behind the foothills. It would be raining hard up in the San Juans.

She wondered who had noticed her habit and made this kind gesture. Even as she asked herself the question, she caught sight of a rider heading southward, away from the stables. By now he was the size of a figurine, an erect cowboy on a snowflake Appaloosa. Both the spotted mare, Gert, and the Indiana Jones hat crammed low over the man's ears belonged to Jacob Davis.

If he had ever noticed his saddle missing, he hadn't mentioned it to her.

Beth watched Jacob's form diminish. "Are you courting Gert without my consent?" she murmured to Hastings while stroking his nose.

The gelding nickered, a polite insistence that butlers did not deserve their reputation as covert agents.

"Okay, then," she said. "Let's go."

She mounted him from the corral rail and felt the stabbing ache in her shoulder where the wolf's paw had torn it. The skin had healed, but the deep wound remained. Beth didn't hint to anyone that it had been a wolf's paw, not the blow of the fall, that crushed her. There simply was no evidence that a wolf had ever set foot on the Kandinskys' land, or on the Blazing B. As everyone else saw it, with Phil's help she'd kidnapped Joe, forced him to ride blind into a lather, and turned his leg in a snake hole.

When she reached a high branch of the creek, Beth dismounted and let Hastings wander while she followed the water upstream to her favorite rock, which was squat and flat. The rocks in this area were mostly black and coarse, remnants of a catastrophic super-volcano. The La Garita Caldera, a crater twenty-two miles wide and forty-seven miles long, was not far away from this very spot as the eagle flew. Eons ago, when La Garita had erupted and devastated most of the state of Colorado, it released enough pyroclastic material to have buried California in thirty-nine feet of the stuff. The event was granted a ranking in the upper tiers of Earth's most destructive volcanic eruptions ever. And then, like a toddler wasted of energy after a tantrum, the cooling caldera had settled into a peaceful sleep.

At the base of Beth's volcanic rock, clean snowmelt continued to run through the creek even at this time of year. The runoff had come down out of the mountains, racing downhill east of the Continental Divide toward the larger streams and rivers, watering the valley. It was pure water, famed water that poured out of these Rocky Mountains, and to Beth it represented hope. God willing, she too might emerge clean from the volcanic disaster of her own making.

From her perch she was able to lie down on her stomach and scoop a palmful of water from the stream. She drank, then washed her face and neck. After her shift at the feed-and-tack, she smelled like a barn and was covered in oat dust. Her hair, sweaty from her efforts to relocate pallets of feed sacks, had dried in stiff strands at the base of her neck and the tops of her ears.

Beth sensed the wolf before she saw it. The depression behind her collarbone seemed to deepen, and the faintest remnants of the claw tracks along her neck began to itch, way under her skin where she couldn't have scratched. It came onto the scene like wind, not there when she reached out for the water, there when she lifted her face and felt the cool liquid running off her nose and chin. It stood on the opposite bank, head low, smudges of blood on its white muzzle.

The canine's eyes were clear and piercing. She didn't feel fear, not right away, though her nerves sent a low vibration along the surface of her ribs. The beast had passed up the opportunity to kill her at least once.

It was both beautiful and awful. In that instant of realizing she was not alone, before the fear set in, she felt aware that some imbalance in the world was shifting, correcting itself, that something bigger than her own trouble was about to unsettle all of her assumptions about how God worked.

Beth wiped the water off her cheek with her shoulder, eyes wide and locked on the wolf, seeing it in daylight for the first time. A male, tall and strong. It was true that the "common" *Canis lupis* had been hunted into exile by Colorado's ranchers and hunters as World War II was dawning. But this animal was no ghost or spirit of the past. The light in his golden eyes was real, and the blood on his jaw glistened like the silver water between them, and his growl warned her that there might be a real, non-ghostly cost to her if she continued to lie there on the rock.

He was much larger than Beth in her limited experience had imagined wolves to be, at least twice the size of Herriot. The wolf's legs were longer than she expected, and its wide head was almost too big for its slender body.

Beth stood slowly and whistled for Hastings, then sent up a prayer for God's protection on them both. She hoped the bloody muzzle meant the wolf was no longer hungry. As her spine straightened, the wolf blinked and his shoulders relaxed, the same way Herriot did just before a stretch and a yawn.

Beth stepped off the rock. The wolf matched her step and entered the water. She headed downstream, toward the place she'd last seen Hastings, keeping the wolf in her peripheral vision. The beast crossed swiftly and came up on her side of the bank.

Dark memories of long claws at her throat and hot breath on her eyes quickened her pace. Was this the same animal that had attacked her? The seed of fear in her mind bloomed. Could he detect this emotion, the way predators could sense which targets were easiest to catch? Her airways seemed inflamed. She began to jog, her ankles wobbling on uneven ground. His stride matched hers, an easy trot.

"God have mercy," she whispered as she ran. Last time, he had. *I will show you mercy.*

The voice that answered was not her own, wasn't audible to her ears, but to her heart, the same as before. This time, though, the words filled her with peace instead of foreboding.

Nothing, nothing about this encounter made sense. Not even

her decision to stop running, which wasn't a decision so much as a reflex. She halted and turned to face her hunter. She had no wisdom that might keep her alive for a minute longer, but she was no longer afraid.

The wolf ran up to her and then stopped and sniffed the ground at her feet, eyes upward on her face. Seconds passed loudly in Beth's ears like a roaring prairie wind that might be followed with equal chances by a sudden calm or a life-threatening tornado. He circled her, and she remained as still as the eye of a storm, taking deep, sweet breaths, watching him. Behind his shoulders, his lightweight fur coat stood on end and revealed long scars that ran the length of his back, four parallel stripes running all the way to his hindquarters, as if he'd narrowly escaped a predator of his own.

His orbit finished, he stopped sniffing but remained in a hostile posture, the fur on his back electrified, his muzzle low, his eyes high. And then the wolf bared his teeth and growled.

Beth scrabbled backward. Her heel met a stone and took her legs out from under her. She landed on her seat in the stream. Water soaked through her jeans in the two or three seconds it took her to get vertical again. The wolf didn't attack but continued to press in, the way Herriot might goad a stubborn cow.

Now the ears flattened back against his head; his nose dropped another inch and his head leveled out with his neck; the lip riding high on his teeth flickered.

They understood each other then, wolf and woman. Silently, Beth agreed to follow the canine's direction. Yielding to his push, she began a cautious backward walk in a weaving line along the bank of the creek. The sun was west of her, glaring on the ridgeline in a way that made it difficult to see. She strained her eyes to their limits, demanding they include the wolf and stumbling hazards at all times.

A scrubby stand of thinleaf alder trees had taken root near the stream. Beth reached out for one when she was close enough to touch it. The growth was sprawling and might provide a place for predator and prey to circle until she could make a plan.

She lifted her left arm behind her, into her blind spot, reaching out for leaves and branches. Her hand hit the shrub, and the foliage rustled. At the same moment, the wolf stopped. Beth froze too, and waited to see what he would do.

The air was still and the earth, dampened by the moving water, smelled like it was less than a day old.

A panting reached Beth's ears, the quick and short breaths of someone in pain. It was the sound of her ten-year-old self the time she slipped off a boulder and caught her ankle in the marmot hole beneath it. The hurt had been so bad that long minutes passed before her body remembered where to find its tears.

But this sound wasn't coming out of her memory. The sound wasn't even human, and it was rising from the backside of the alder. Beth took her eyes off the wolf and looked for the source of the heaving lungs.

She immediately realized her mistake and whipped her head back around, expecting claws and snarling teeth bared under a bloody gray muzzle.

The wolf was gone.

Beth spun, searching and backing into the protection of the tree's shelter at the same time. The slender branches of the tree-shrub snagged her hair. She had never imagined a wolf could vanish like that. The only thing worse than a wolf on the hunt, she thought, was an invisible wolf on the hunt.

Branches scratched at her cheeks and neck and hands as she circled, watchful.

At the place where the alder roots reached for the water, she stumbled over an animal lying at her feet, and the shock of the encounter pulled a yelp out of her throat. It wasn't the wolf, though.

The heaving shape of its rounded belly was smooth and short-haired, the golden color of winter grass. Its pure white underside and matching short tail looked soft as angora, and three matching stripes circled the creature's throat like the wide necklaces of an African beauty.

It was a pronghorn antelope. A bloody bite placed high and in front of the shoulder seemed positioned to rip these stripes right off the animal's neck.

Perhaps Beth's perceptions were running unnaturally high, but when she saw the wounds her hand went first to the claw scars at her own neck.

His breathing faltered when she squatted to touch the buck's flank. When it resumed, she could hear a gurgle under the effort. Her heart broke for the animal's suffering.

Beth's first thought was that the wolf should have forced her *away* from his trophy. It was possible that she didn't understand one thing at all about wolf behavior, but his pressing her this way, here, trumped all expectation.

The antelope's head was on his side in the creek. Crimson ribbons of life floated away on the current. Water teased one of the animal's eyes and fully submerged the animal's horns, which reminded Beth of something better suited for a prehistoric beetle: dark brown and with pincer-sharp points, they rose above the head and arced together as if trying to form a heart shape. Shorter prongs, pointing forward, branched off the main antlers.

At the water's edge, silky mud gave way under her shoes. The creek rushed the antelope's nostrils and then fell back. He snorted but didn't try to lift his head. Another ripple rose all the way over his jaw. The animal didn't flinch. If the beast didn't drown in his own blood, he would succumb to this pristine water.

He allowed her to place her hand on his throat and try to stop the bleeding. Or was too far gone to realize what she was doing.

But the gash was too great for her fingers to cover. She took off the long-sleeved work shirt she wore over a tank top and pressed the fabric into the wound, feeling that her efforts were futile.

If she'd come in her truck instead of on Hastings, she could have fetched the rifle in it and ended this creature's misery. The weapon would help her to hold the wolf at bay too. She tried to think of a way to end the antelope's suffering without a gun or knife.

The sun fell behind the ridge before her clothes were dry. She was shivering, but the antelope was warm.

The wolf remained in hiding. A part of Beth sensed the animal lurking, waiting—for what? Nothing prevented him from demanding this feast.

It was as if the wolf had offered it to her.

Her peaceful stroking lengthened out across the antelope's ribs and flank, heating her hands as she calmed him. She could feel the weak pulse in his veins and the gentle rise and fall of his shallow breath as she borrowed what warmth remained in him.

A breeze stirred and rattled the leaves of the alder. The animal's suffering seemed eerily prolonged.

The antelope groaned and began to tremble.

The wind pushed hard enough to bow the tree branches at Beth's back and disrupt the rippling creek. The air moved upstream, against its natural course, and Beth felt it like a cold breath sneaking up the legs of her jeans. In seconds, the chill cut all the way down to her bones.

The joints of Beth's legs and hips grew heavy with a throbbing ache. She pressed against the weak antelope and buried her face into its coat while the frigid air raced up her spine and over her tense shoulders. The atmosphere sat on her, an icy weight that bent her neck and made it impossible to move.

Really impossible. When Beth realized that the sounds of the wind would prevent her ears, sharp as they were, from hearing the wolf's stealthy approach, her mind told her body to straighten up before he tore her to shreds and got two meals for the effort of one. But when Beth tried to move her limbs and they didn't budge, images of a wolf crouching over the back of her neck brought tears to her eyes.

A song bubbled up in her memory about a soul being thirsty for God the way a deer was thirsty for a brook. She began to hum, and the fear hung back. The muscles of her arms twitched. The muscles over the antelope's rib cage also flickered.

And then the icy weight that seemed to sit on her head began to melt. It came apart the way an ice cube does in the sun, pooling at the base and spreading out. A sensation of liquid warmth ran down every strand of her hair and dribbled onto her back and spilled across her shoulders onto the antelope's coat.

Beth's mental command to her body to sit up finally connected with her muscles. She jerked up, expecting to see that the rain had started. She was entirely dry.

The animal jerked too, as if he shared Beth's surprise, and then his whole body was rolling toward her, nearly pinning her knees. He threw his weight forward toward the creek, and Beth feared he would crush her. Though she wasn't paralyzed any longer, her hips and legs felt heavy and thick, and the ache in her joints had spread out into a stabbing pain that followed the lines of her skeleton. She couldn't rise.

But the antelope's two-toed hooves missed her, and when she looked up at him again he was standing on all fours in the middle of the water. He dipped his head to take a drink.

The gash in his neck had vanished like the wolf. No dangling flaps of flesh exposing bloody muscle, no gurgling breaths. Only a pale pink inky spot stained the water where he'd been lying a moment earlier. The current erased that evidence in seconds. But her cotton shirt lay on the rocks by her knees, soaked in blood.

All sensation and function returned to her limbs, and she

jumped up, her mind making gazelle-like leaps across the plains of common sense. She didn't understand what she was seeing.

The antelope lifted his head and flicked his ears toward a movement behind Beth. She turned. Levi stood several yards behind her.

He held his rifle, which at first seemed only natural and then seemed entirely unnecessary. Unless he'd also seen the wolf. The antelope behaved as if being in the presence of an armed man was no cause for alarm.

"Where did he go?" she asked.

"Am I supposed to know what you're talking about?" There was anger in Levi's tone. For all of Beth's life, as she remembered it, Levi had stooped in a posture of resentment as if his spine were a frown. He seemed to regard his little sister's birth as a conspiracy to thrust him into the demanding role of firstborn son and assassinate his privileged life as an only child. None of this had ever made sense to her. But she checked her tone.

"The wolf," Beth said. "There was a wolf."

"You were supposed to be home an hour ago, and we've all been out all day on the fences. We could use your help with all the stuff that had to be put off for that. I don't have time to chase you down."

"Sorry."

"Your apologies aren't worth much these days." He was eyeing the pronghorn.

"That antelope was injured. I was trying to figure out . . ." She didn't know how to explain.

Levi turned away. His truck was likely parked in the narrow flat around the creek's bend. Beth took a sweeping look around once more for the wolf. For Hastings.

"Levi, there was a wolf here," she called out. "I saw it. It attacked the antelope."

"The buck looks fine to me."

"We should keep an eye out."

"You go ahead. I've got the rifle." He turned away and headed back to wherever he'd parked.

"Seriously, Levi—"

"Seriously, you might think you can redeem your sins by meditating with the wildlife, but I don't have time. C'mon now, or I'll let the wolf hunt *you*."

She took a couple of leaping steps after him, her bloody shirt wadded in her hands, trying to get off the slick bank and onto drier ground. "I'm doing everything I can to get the family off this hook," she said.

Levi spun back to her and raised both hands in the air the way their easily exasperated mother was prone to do lately. But the rifle in his hand made him look more like an inflamed insurgent than a cattle rancher.

"It's your hook!" he shouted. "You ought to be dangling there all alone!"

She stood up under his accusations and just nodded.

"When that judgment comes down, you're the one who's going to pay. I'll make sure of it."

"If I could take back everything, I would. I'm so sorry."

"You'll need a miracle."

"Maybe God will—"

"Shut up. It was a figure of speech. There are no miracles, Beth. There's only sweat and blood."

"But hear me out. I'm not lying to you." She pointed to the antelope. "I don't know what it means, but that animal was dying, and I . . . and I . . ."

On this side of the spectacular moment, the scene looked unremarkable. Her story sounded outrageous. She was trying to find a way to put it into words that Levi could hear when he lifted the rifle to his shoulder.

"No. Levi."

He leveled the sight at the antelope's shoulder. Air caught in Beth's throat.

"Don't," she said. "Don't."

Her brother took the shot even while Beth was moving toward him and lifting her hands. She recoiled at the rifle's great kick. She heard bones shatter and sensed the buck collapse before she could cover her ears. Under the ringing in her head she heard the body splash down. Her mouth was open to gasp or scream, but she didn't hear herself do either.

"No miracles. See? End of story."

She dropped to her knees, and her brother stalked off.

A rumble of thunder rolled overhead, and she felt the first raindrops on her bare arms.

As her brother's footsteps faded, the wolf returned. The canine trotted so close to Beth that its tall shoulders brushed hers when he passed, but she hardly registered the sensation. He padded directly for the fallen pronghorn.

Shaking, frightened of what Levi might do if he saw the wolf too, Beth rose and followed her brother. And she didn't look back when she heard the wolf finally help himself to his meal.

8

Garner's plans to catch a ride down the mountain as soon as the storm yielded to morning light were thwarted by the stomach flu.

He had left Cat's office near four in the morning after warm tea and pleasant conversation, feeling reassured that he would see his long-lost daughter in due time, in the most pleasant of circumstances, which included blue skies and sunlight. All that was left of the storm by then were a few sloppy puddles that didn't interfere with his brisk walk back home. The fresh air rejuvenated him, and he considered skipping sleep altogether.

Against such optimism, he woke on the floor of his bedroom late the following morning, unable to recall having gotten out of bed. Perhaps he had never climbed into it. He still wore yesterday's clothes, and the odor of sickness that oozed out from the nearby bathroom was witness to events he was glad to have forgotten.

As a soldier battling liver cancer, Garner was familiar with illness, but this affliction was different. Within an hour of waking, the aches that pooled in his joints spread to his muscles and then to his stomach. He groaned aloud.

There was a pounding on his front door that matched the

throbbing in his head. He wished it away. Whoever it was would have to come back later, because he was in no condition to sell tea. He didn't even know what to advise himself to take.

He cursed under his breath when he heard the front door open anyway. This was the problem with small-town life in which everyone was more neighborly than average; there was no need to lock doors in a place where everyone looked out for each other.

An icy draft swirled into his bedroom and poked him on the floor where he lay.

"Garner?"

The voice belonged to Cat. He had a vague recollection that she'd agreed to pick him up at eleven thirty for the long drive into the valley. Was it so late already?

"What on earth happened to your kitchen window? The carpet's soaking wet! Garner? Where are you? It's freezing in here."

It was terribly glaring too. He hadn't drawn the bedroom curtains when he came in, and the east-facing window was brilliant with laser-beam sunshine that bounced off the glossy paint on his walls.

Hadn't he told her about that window? He was sure he had.

Garner said, "Up here," but the sounds that came out of his mouth sounded like an alien language.

Long seconds like hours passed before the doctor, who had seemed so smart until now, found him lying there in the unwelcome spotlight.

"What took you so long?" he demanded when her youthful figure materialized at his feet. Her bobbed hair from this angle looked like a tortoise shell. He thought she was frowning at him. He wasn't sure. The glare made him squint. "Move any slower and I'll be dead before you cross the room."

"Oh, Garner! What happened?" Cat knelt beside him and started acting like a doctor of the most irritating variety, touching his forehead and his wrist and asking him questions with a tone and vocabulary suitable for a kindergartener. He answered her clearly, but she kept saying, *"What? What?"*

"You got wax in your ears?" Garner demanded.

Doctors, of course, were not obligated to answer their patients' questions. She rose and stepped over his body and strode to the window with such authority that her stomping boots seemed to come down right on Garner's temples. She yanked the curtains' cord, and the fabric obeyed the order to close.

The relief of a dim room took the edge off his annoyance.

"There will be no trip to the ranch for you today," she said.

"The dead aren't in a hurry," Garner murmured.

"Abel's not dead, Garner."

"Yes, he is."

"No, he's not. I'm sorry."

The apology confused Garner. People didn't apologize for someone kicking death in the teeth. But on second thought, he wasn't too pleased by the news.

Cat said, as if he hadn't computed her meaning, "Your daughter is not a widow."

"I heard ya." Garner gripped his head with both hands. He thought he might throw up again. "He's not dead, says who?"

"Says a friend of mine at the county medical examiner's office. I called this morning."

"Don't trust me, huh?"

"I'd trust you with my firstborn child. It's divine messages by thunderstorm that I don't bank on."

See there? He *had* told her about the broken window. Right?

"But you don't got *any* kids, Cat."

"What's that? You're slurring, Garner. I hope this isn't a stroke. You just rest. Let me figure out what's going on with you and how we're going to make it right."

Garner returned to the sleep that his pain demanded, seeing no point in waiting for the good doctor to get him onto the bed. He didn't have to be awake for that process, anyway.

A stroke. Honest to Pete.

9

For more than a week, that pronghorn antelope haunted Beth. Twice she thought she saw it in the parking lot behind the feed-and-tack, pinned under the front bumper of someone's truck. She caught glimpses of it bleeding in the aisles of the grocery store as she passed through with boxes of vegetables piled on wheeled carts. In each case she took a tentative step toward the vision, unable to tell her mind it wasn't real. The mirage reacted to her approach as mirages do: the antelope recovered and rose, dashed away, and then collapsed once more in a heap.

What on earth was the point? She chewed on the question for days while frustration over non-answers seeped into deeper questions about the pending outcome of the lawsuit and the future of the ranch. Was it a message from God, a preview of her imminent punishment? She half expected God to help her family escape Darling's snare only to lead them all directly into an even worse fate.

That wasn't God's nature, to be so mean. Was it?

Her job at the grocery store chafed like a wool shirt on a hot day. She endured her shifts yearning to be back outside, in the dirt, with the animals, so that she could start thinking straight again. At least at the feed-and-tack she was surrounded by the proper scents.

August arrived, the hottest month of the year. After several gut-wrenching conferences and hearings, Beth finally had been slated to receive a judgment. Mr. Darling had wanted his time in court, and he got it. The light did not shine favorably on Beth, in spite of her attorney's agile mind and tongue. The judge would settle the lawsuit on Monday. The Borzois' counsel was not optimistic. Beth looked down the barrel of the longest weekend of her life.

Saturday afternoon, she left King Soopers the second her shift was officially over. She was sweating from the heat trapped by the mountain ranges, and she figured she could grill sausages on the dashboard of her old truck. She sat in the cab with both doors open and the fan on high, her cell phone balanced on her knee while she dug through the glove box for a ponytail band and waited for the steering wheel to cool. She planned to call Jacob, because she needed the kindness of his voice and the reassurance of his words to carry her through the afternoon.

Considering how long Beth had known him, she ought to have found her place in his story as a surrogate little sister. For a long time after his arrival, Jacob was blind to nearly everything but his role as Roy's right-hand man. He was polite to Rose but rejected her attempts to mother him. He openly disliked Levi and gave Beth no more attention than he gave to the cows. He worked hard, studied responsibly, spoke little, and never played. Even his participation in rodeo events was more rigor than fun. At least as far as Beth saw it.

Only the birth of Beth's little brother exposed Jacob's capacity for affection. Rose had some bleeding complications that for a few days sat over the family like the grim reaper perched on their roof. Jacob was still sixteen then, still very close to the accidental death of his own mother. He hovered over the baby to the point of skipping chores and usurped Levi's role as big brother. If Levi cared, he gave no sign.

Later, when Beth was old enough to diagnose Jacob's aloofness as the pain of having lost his mother at a young age, she thought—in her expectant adolescent way—that all he needed to be happy was a woman who loved him, and when she was just a little older he would see her as exactly that. Her hopefulness grew until she was twelve, which was when Jacob put a stop to Levi's unmerciful big-brother pranks by dropping a scorpion into one of Levi's boots. After that, her interest in Jacob blossomed into full-blown adoration, and Levi, distracted from her, turned to Jacob as a more interesting and worthy adversary.

Beth eventually realized that Jacob had diverted Levi's attention because he disliked Levi, not because he cared in some special way about her. For six months he dated a rodeo queen, a modelesque woman with platinum hair and a voice like Carrie Underwood's. Beth teased Jacob about bringing home an older woman. In one of the most embarrassing moments of Beth's life, Jacob pointed out that the woman was two years his junior—an understandable misjudgment for a girl Beth's age.

The phone rang. Jacob Davis, the ID announced. This pleased her, even though he wouldn't be calling her for the same reasons she had wanted to call him.

Beth put the phone to her ear while the hair band was still between her lips. "Mm-hm?"

"Come have a look at Gert before you run off with Hastings tonight?" Jacob asked. Gert was the pretty snowflake Appaloosa, his horse, and she'd been at the Blazing B only a few months. Beth took the band out of her teeth and wrapped it around her hair.

"What's wrong with her?"

"She's lethargic, really hot to the touch. Tongue's hanging out of her mouth."

"Is she sweating?"

"No. She never sweats."

"All horses sweat, Jacob."

"Not this one. A lady all the way."

"What kind of work were you doing today?"

"Irrigating," he said.

"That shouldn't have strained her."

"She's a brilliant cow horse, but she hates these summer outings. Next time I'm taking Hastings. He can dig his own ditches—did you know that?"

Beth smiled. "I assume Gert got plenty to drink today, if you were irrigating?"

"Evian and bonbons."

"That's your problem right there: bonbons will slow a girl down every time."

She expected Jacob to laugh and wasn't sure what it meant when he didn't.

"What's her rectal temperature?" she said.

"You *know* the reason I'm calling you is because that's your department, Beth."

"You need to take her temperature."

"That would be a gross violation of our professional relationship."

"Yours and mine?"

Now Jacob laughed, and Beth realized he was talking about the horse. She felt stupid, always the kid who was shorter than the punch lines.

"So call the vet," she said, blushing.

"But we've got you."

"No, 'we' don't." She'd snapped at him without meaning to, the way a wounded dog would bite the person trying to be kind. An uncomfortable second passed between them.

She spoke first. "Wow, the heat's making me testy today. Maybe I should go cool off."

"Stop in to see Gert first," Jacob said. "It's no extra trip for you. We're right here by the barn."

"You're at the horse pasture?" Gert was as welcome there as any other horse, but Jacob usually kept her closer to the Hub. "What are you doing there?"

Jacob didn't answer, and she thought of Hastings, already saddled and waiting for her. She thought of that silver show saddle and wondered why he hadn't confronted her yet.

His refusal to call a real veterinarian caused her concern for Gert to grow. Jacob put too much confidence in Beth to benefit any horse in real danger.

"Where's Gert now?" she asked.

"Right here next to me."

"At least put her in the barn. Or in the shade."

"You think I'm standing in the sun?"

"I'll be there as soon as I can," she said. Then she hung up and called Dr. O'Connor's office, but the real professional was out on a call. The next closest vet was some distance away.

Beth's hands were vibrating with a mix of dread and anticipation as she went through the motions of closing up the truck, putting it in gear, and pulling out onto the highway to head home. What would she do if Gert's fate was about to mimic the antelope's?

Beth drove several miles without noticing her surroundings. She was wondering what might have become of that antelope if Levi hadn't shot it—would the wolf have taken it down a second time?—when a swallow swooped across her windshield and smacked the glass, leaving behind a small greasy smudge and a few tiny gray feathers before tumbling over the hood of her cab.

Beth stomped on the brakes, then swerved to the dusty shoulder of the road and jumped out. She knew when she did it that she was hoping for an opportunity. In her swift imagination she found the bird, fixed the bird, freed the bird, and as it took flight once more, all the answers to her questions came floating down from heaven and into her mind as a kind of reward.

Could she have healed the break in Java Java Go Joe's leg and averted the lawsuit? What if she had been given a supernatural gift that might save them all? What if she was about to become a vet who could work healing magic in animals?

All her financial worries would disappear. For that matter, none of this trouble would have started. She could have waved her blessed fingers over Marigold's melting cornea, and voilà! Eye restored. Silver saddle back in the barn.

An old cottonwood provided comforting shade that covered her vehicle and the road. She found the crumpled bird in the bed of her truck, and she saw that it wasn't a swallow as she had first thought, but a house sparrow with dark brown and gray features. She picked up its body gently and noted that its neck was broken. The bundle of crushed feathers was disordered and weightless. Its back still held the warmth of the hot summer sun.

Beth cradled the tiny carcass and stroked its feathers with her forefinger, hoping for the impossible: a quickening of its heart and lungs, a sudden fluttering of wings. She tried several heartfelt prayers. She tried several songs. She closed her eyes and buried her nose in the little body just as she had done with the antelope. She had such expectation!

She waited a long time, walking circles around that cottonwood tree.

Jacob's waiting for you. Gert's waiting, her conscience muttered as she clutched the dead bird to her pounding heart.

What can I do for Gert?

More than you can do for this little guy.

More than nothing? That doesn't promise to be much.

Beth could usually accept a creature's death. Animals lived and died on the ranch, in spite of the most experienced vets' efforts to save them. But today the fury of powerlessness overcame her. Rotten luck and the whims of God would hold her responsible for the death of Joe, of a pronghorn antelope, and now of this tiny bird. She would never have the opportunity to be a licensed vet, let alone a supernatural one.

Beth let loose a yell of frustration that came up from the bottom of her belly, and she hurled the dead bird like a baseball into the cottonwood's thick trunk. She wished the bird back the moment it left her fingers. This was not the behavior of a compassionate human being. But the airborne body was beyond her reach in an instant.

The sparrow bounced off the grooved bark, and then after a shocking, flapping, noisy tumble through the air, it flew away.

Beth watched a feather float down onto the exposed roots of the tree and didn't believe what she had seen. She must have startled another bird out of the branches overhead. That was all.

When she finally uprooted her feet from the earth, she searched for the evidence of her involuntary birdslaughter. She examined the nooks of the cottonwood's roots. She ran her hands up and down the rough trunk. She covered the ground in a widening spiral.

She couldn't even find any dead leaves on the ground.

When the path of her spiral took her to the base of another tree, Beth stopped her search. She placed her hand on the grooved bark because it was real and tangible. Above her head, a bird chirped once. She looked up and was not surprised to see a brown house sparrow.

Beth tried to read nothing into it. The common birds flocked together. They all looked the same to her. Avian species were not her specialty. Still she couldn't stop sweat from breaking out across the palms of her hands.

The bird chirped again and eyed her with a cocked head. She had no idea what this might mean.

But her heart said, *Go. Gert's waiting for you.*

She had to figure out how this worked. She left immediately.

10

The horse pasture and the house where generations of Borzois had lived since the late eighteen hundreds were on the north end of the Blazing B. Here the property tapered to a narrow boundary between the county road and the creek that poured out of foothills littered with black volcanic rock. Several horse shelters protected the animals from the stiff weather of the wider landscape. A horseshoe-shaped line of ninety-foot cottonwood trees offered further protection and privacy.

Beth hurried to the barn, her head full of flying sparrows and elegant antelope and expectations for Jacob's horse. God would make everything clear. He would do it before the family lost everything, in the nick of time. Miracles always came in the nick of time.

Throughout the summer, the female trees dropped their fluffy seeds like fairies in wedding dresses onto the horses' backs. Gert was lying on her side next to the barn, covered in a veil of cottonwood white that mimicked the snowflake pattern of her lovely mottled coat. The horse's lungs worked as if she'd just run a race, but she didn't have a drop of sweat on her.

"When did she go down?" Beth asked.

Jacob was sitting in the dust by Gert's head. "Right after you hung up."

"Sorry to make you wait. Dr. O'Connor is out on a call."

"I know."

She knew then that he'd called the vet first, before her, and she felt mildly embarrassed that she'd assumed otherwise. But she couldn't figure why he wouldn't just come out and say it.

"Who else did you call?" she asked.

"Stanton, from up in Villa Grove, but it'll be another hour before he gets over."

Beth ran her hands over Gert's throat, which was quite hot and dry to the touch. She placed a forefinger under the left side of the horse's jawbone and easily found the pulsating artery there.

"Count fifteen seconds for me," she said. Jacob glanced at his wristwatch and gave her a go-ahead.

"Time," he said.

Beth multiplied her count by four. "Heart rate's fifty-six," she said.

"That's what I got too."

"You might have mentioned that."

"I answered all your questions."

"Okay, then. Is this a game? One point for you, Jacob."

"No game," he said.

"Did you take her temp by yourself too?"

"All my answers were truthful," Jacob said, tipping his hat back on his head. The band inside left a reddish impression above his eyebrows. "I respect my horse's dignity."

"But you know how to do it if you had to."

"What kind of a cowboy would I be if I didn't know how? She's pushing 103."

Beth raised her eyebrows.

"Mercury in my fingertips," he said, showing her his hands.

"You can't tell just by touching her," Beth scolded.

"You're the expert."

Separated from Jacob only by his horse, Beth could easily smell his earthy scents: sweat mixed with the dust of the day and the wet leather of his boots, which were damp and mud-crusty from his irrigation work. He smelled like all the comforts of home, the way it had been in summers before this one, which she'd ruined before it even started.

She wanted to lean into him and close her eyes and rest her head in that safe spot between his collar and his arm. The strength he'd collected from the outdoors would give her courage that fluorescent lights and air-conditioning and a windowless grocery store could not.

She wanted to shave off that facial hair and run her hand over his cheek.

Instead, she fetched a thermometer from the barn, tied a string to the end, and went through the routine motions of determining just how hot Gert was. The girl was typically compliant, but today it wasn't even necessary for Jacob to hold her head when Beth inserted the device.

An accurate reading would take three minutes. Gert closed her eyes but seemed no less relaxed. Jacob rose and leaned against the barn. Beth waited for God to use her, wondering what it would feel like this time, what it would look like. Would this event bring her any closer to figuring out his methods, or hers?

Beth lifted her eyes to the pasture to see if any other horses were affected by similar symptoms.

"You're a born vet," Jacob said.

She looked at him, wondering what had prompted the remark. "That's nice of you to say."

"Not being nice. It's just the truth."

"Well, I'm not a legal one."

"It'll happen."

"It'll take a miracle."

"Miracles happen."

They do! she thought. She nearly said it—she nearly told Jacob everything about the antelope, the wolf, and the bird. Something stopped her, though: the sight of Gert lying there in the same condition as when Beth had arrived, the truth that she didn't have a formula to explain God's work, a flicker of wavering faith. Doubt.

"Do you think so?" she said instead.

With his head tipped back against the barn siding, Jacob crossed his arms and his ankles and regarded her carefully. His eyes were the same color blue as hers and should have been unremarkable in their familiarity. Instead, the direct and thoughtful attention, as if he possessed a clear answer but didn't think she could handle it, caused her to speak over any reply he might have offered.

She continued, "Or do we just call anything we don't really understand a miracle?"

"Nope. Miracles happen," he said again.

She wanted his certainty.

"If I get Gert off the ground in the next fifteen minutes, will that be miraculous?"

Jacob frowned now, and a deep line crouched between his brows.

Beth cleared her throat. She hadn't meant to be flippant. "What I meant is, what do you call a miracle?"

"Do you believe God loves you?" he asked.

"Sure. He loves everyone."

Jacob shrugged. "For starters, then, I guess I think it's a miracle that he loves someone like me."

"What do you mean, someone like you? You're a straight-up guy, you work hard, everyone likes you, you're good to people." She sighed. "You've never stolen a horse and killed it."

He didn't reply to that, and she might have apologized for her self-pity if he hadn't cracked that smile at her—the kind of unfunny, condescending smile older people gave when they were thinking, *I'm wiser than you are, young'un, but I'll hold my tongue.*

The smile goaded her to be just a little sassy. She was really bungling this whole conversation. She said, "If I get off light in this lawsuit, will that be a miracle? I'm sure Darling would say it's an injustice."

"Encouragement is hard to come by," Jacob said. "Maybe you should just take it at face value when it shows up."

He was right, of course.

He said, "Maybe it's a miracle you weren't hurt worse than you were when Joe threw you."

"Okay, okay—forget I brought that up." She turned back to Gert. "I'm thinking she's got heat stress."

Jacob glanced back at the reclined horse. "I know it's hot, but none of the other animals show signs. And she's not sweating. Isn't that how horses cool off?"

"Generally speaking. Animals with fur pant; animals with hair sweat."

She removed Gert's thermometer. "One-oh-two point nine," she read. "Might as well be 103. You score again."

"Wish I'd been wrong about that number."

"It is a bit high. Did you really just guess?" He nodded, and she said, "I'm impressed. I mean it."

"What do you recommend?"

The question brought to mind a story she'd read in one of James Herriot's books. In this particular tale, the vet had been summoned to treat a collapsed bull. The owner, befuddled over the bull's condition, put a lot of stock in cutting-edge medicine and expected Herriot to wow him with a complex diagnosis and high-tech treatment. When Herriot told him the bull had heat stroke and would recover with shade and a cold spray from the hose, the owner was downright disappointed to see his valuable animal come back to life so quickly.

"Sometimes things are never anything more than what they seem," she muttered.

"Then it should be okay to call a miracle a miracle," he said.

She laughed and felt forgiven. "You are worse than a dog on a rabbit," she said. "I was talking about Gert. Let's try to cool her off." There was a hose wound like a rattlesnake at the side of the barn. She unwound it and attached it to a spigot, then turned on the water and directed a gentle spray at Gert's legs. In a few short minutes, the horse's terrible breathing began to slow.

"I hereby diagnose her with heat stroke," Beth said.

Jacob was too nice to ask her again about the lack of sweat, but she knew he was thinking it. That was one mystery that her diagnosis didn't solve.

"How long have you had her again?" Beth asked.

"Since last October. She went with me when we went up to fetch the cows."

"Okay. I remember that. So she hasn't been with us through a summer before—or an August. Did her previous owner mention any trouble with her?"

"None."

"Where's she from?"

"Montana."

"Right."

An odd idea was emerging from the back of her mind, a factoid she'd tucked away long ago for a time such as this, when she'd have to apply it to a practical situation. "I've heard that some horses don't sweat."

"No kidding? How does that work?"

"Not too well. I read about it once—it's a condition called . . . what's it called? Hydro-something. Too little sweating. Antihydro . . . adiapho . . . oh—anhidrosis. A tendency to overheat."

"That so, Dr. Borzoi?"

"Don't take my word for it. We'll have to ask Dr. O'Connor what he thinks."

"Your word's good enough for me."

"You ought to reserve judgment."

"Gert's smiling. That's all I need."

"She is not!"

"Your future as a large-animal doctor is secure. I'll take that game-winning point now."

He tipped his hat at her, and she flicked the spray of the hose lightly in his direction. A spatter bloomed on his blue shirt. "You're kinder than I deserve, Jacob."

"Anyone who's ever lost a dream needs a kind person in his life," he said.

"I promise," Beth said. "If I ever get my second chance, I won't blow it."

"That's not what I—" Jacob sniffed and shook his head, resigned. His eyes followed the water slipping off of Gert and pooling in the dry grass under her flank. "Well. Never mind. What can I say, you've got a healer's touch. Miracle worker."

She couldn't tell if he was teasing or genuine. She was afraid to ask, because her need for clarity would only make her feel like a little girl again. He crossed his arms and turned his face to the sun as Beth directed the water over Gert's ribs and back.

Awhile later she asked, "You ever lose a dream? In college maybe? I didn't expect you to come back here afterward. You could've gone anywhere. Why didn't you? Why don't you? It's been eight years— nine already."

He didn't open his eyes at first. "Are you saying I've worn out my welcome?"

"C'mon now, be serious."

Gert snorted once and lifted her nose into the direct spray of water. She seemed to be enjoying it.

"All my dreams are right here," he said. "Simple as that."

"I'll probably keep coming back to the valley too. If they don't throw me out."

"Good place."

"I don't really want another life."

In fact, Beth had never been attracted to the busier world beyond the valley, the world that beckoned with glossy careers in entertainment or politics or big industry. Days of physical exertion spent mostly outdoors, alongside family, capped by a night's untroubled sleep, was the most rewarding life she could imagine. Depending on the judgment that would come down on them Monday, though, this simple life that she loved so much might change dramatically, or even vanish completely.

Anxiety crept back up on her once more. The magnitude of how this consequence would affect Jacob was suddenly heavy on her heart. She wondered why he didn't seem worried about it, or embittered in the same way that Levi was. It was Jacob's home and livelihood at stake as much as any Borzoi's.

Maybe Jacob really was just being kind to her, hiding his true feelings. Would he be so supportive if he knew about that saddle?

She stole a look at him. He'd lifted his head and was regarding her with a kind of sideways grin that didn't seem to be pretending anything other than friendly amusement. His dimple showed through his beard.

"What?" she said.

"I've just been wondering. What was it like to ride that Thoroughbred? I want to know everything."

She couldn't tell him everything, of course, but she told him what she thought he really wanted to know—about the thrill, the adventure, the speed. Someday, she thought, she might also be able to tell him about the rest. Until then, she took his advice and accepted the encouragement of their conversation at face value. It was a gift between two friends who might or might not be in the middle of a miracle.

And when Gert stood up twenty minutes later, looking every inch her old self, Beth counted the dusky evening as one of the most pleasant of her life.

11

Cat Ransom's life began to fall apart, again, on Monday morning.

In truth, the crumbling had begun the night lightning struck Garner Remke's window and rekindled the man's hope for a family reunion. Since then, Garner had fully recovered from his illness. It was no stroke or flu that had afflicted him, but a very carefully measured brew of elderberry-bark tea, disguised as something less toxic. Just enough to give him pause while she got to the bottom of the facts. Of course, she had no medical examiner "friend" in the valley. But she had loads of common sense. All that was required to confirm Abel's non-death was a phone call to the Blazing B, a claim to be a supplier returning a call to Mr. Abel Borzoi, and a hasty hang-up when the calm person on the other end of the line said, "Let me fetch him for you."

That was how Cat ended rumors of falling skies.

She hadn't expected when she moved here to find a quaint kind of mysticism at work in the day-to-day thinking of its residents, the kind that let Garner read signs from God in broken glass and lured miracle-seeking tourists by the busloads to the Burnt Rock Harbor Sweet Assembly church, which was not a church in any traditional or reasonable sense. If not for Garner's surprising devotion to her in spite of all this, she might have left before the first winter was over.

Devotion was all Cat had ever wanted from anyone, and until Monday morning she had thought Burnt Rock's devotion to her was secure.

Her first indication that it was not came in the form of a phone call from Garner. They had plans to drive south of town and collect yarrow together while it was still at its peak.

"Cat, girl, you don't mind if I take a rain check on our plans to head down the mountain today, do you?"

"But it's not raining. It's a gorgeous day!"

"A scorcher already."

"You've never minded the heat," she said.

"It's not the heat, Cat. It's . . . I don't know what it is exactly, but I still don't feel a hundred percent."

She sank onto her sofa, feeling disappointed. "I understand. You should listen to your body, or all that progress we've made on your cancer will lose momentum. Hang the Closed sign on your shop and go straight to bed. I can bring you something to eat in a bit if you like."

"Ah, Cat. You are so good to me. But it's not like that. My body feels fine. It's the old sentimental heart that's blue today. I thought I'd attend Hank's service at the Sweet Assembly and see if that might cheer me up a bit."

Hank the handyman officiated short, meaningless services daily for the busloads who visited the site. For the entire summer he recycled the same twenty-minute inspirational message about creating one's own miracles through the power of belief. She sat through it once. It was a load of tripe designed to bring in donations to keep the facility in attractive shape.

"You know I support anything that makes you feel better, Garner. But it stretches my imagination to think an old speech from Hank will do you more good than a fresh-air outing with me."

"It probably won't, and you'll prove yourself right again. But this is where I need to be today. I hope you'll understand."

"Of course I do," she said, though she didn't at all. She looked ruefully at the collection kit and the picnic she had already prepared and placed by her door. Garner had never broken a commitment to her, for any reason. "If you don't mind I'll go out solo anyway. I'll bring you a good share of whatever I find."

"You're the best, Cat. You really are."

Those words soothed the hurt a little. Just a little. After they ended the call, Cat gathered up the bags and carried them down the rear stairs of the apartment. These stairs led down to a public hall and an exit from the building. At the left end of the hall was a private entrance to her doctor's office, which was the one she used most of the time. Her patients entered from Main Street into the front waiting room. At the other end was a similar private entrance for Nova Yarrow's bookstore, and a similar stairway that led up to the bookseller's residence. A small atrium separated the businesses and the apartments.

Cat had the misfortune of timing her exit to match Nova's emergence from her home. She thought Nova pretended not to see her as she locked the door.

The woman's dislike of the doctor was as confounding to Cat as anyone's faith in that silly little church up the hill. She had never, to her knowledge, done anything to offend Nova. Perhaps because she was feeling the sting of Garner's decision to ditch her, Cat tried one more time to make a connection with her neighbor. She caught Nova's eye and put as much goodwill as she possessed into her voice.

"Was it a good weekend for you? Looks like the tour buses are still coming up full."

"It was fine." Nova's descent was as unhurried as her words. She seemed sluggish, and her olive skin was pale. Cat paused with the bags in her hands.

"I was just thinking of you this morning. I'm going out to collect some yarrow—how's your supply? Want me to bring any back for you?"

"No, thank you." Nova arrived at the bottom step and sighed. "I can get what I need from Garner."

"But I can bring it to you fresh, and for free," Cat said lightly. She smiled until her eyes crinkled. Nova didn't even register amusement.

"I don't need any."

"Honest? I find myself recommending the stuff almost every day. I need enough to get everyone through the winter. They stop flowering in September, you know. There's nothing you can't use it for—stomachaches, hemorrhoids, toothaches, first aid. It even lightens up the menstrual cycle if that's a concern. But I'm sure you know all this, since you share the name."

Nova put her key into the door of her bookshop. Cat noticed the tiny tendrils of sleek but sweaty hair that had fallen out of their knot and lay on Nova's collar. Her neck had a rosy sheen to it.

"Are you okay, Nova?"

"Yes."

"You look a little—"

"Tired. Nauseated. It's nothing. I'm fine, really. I'm—"

"Pregnant," Cat said, seeing it all in a flash. "You're expecting! Of course you don't want to be taking medicinal herbs right now. Though I should mention that you could still rub the yarrow on your skin as an insect repellent. Congratulations! What great news."

The woman was short and bird thin. If she reached full term, she might not tip the scales at much over a hundred, Cat thought.

Nova pulled her door open now and held it ajar with one hand as she turned halfway back to Cat. Her eyes held poorly veiled annoyance, but her voice was level.

"There is no news yet, Dr. Ransom. I'm sure you understand."

"Of course I do. Don't be silly. When it comes to doctor-patient privilege I am more discreet than a Victorian grandmother. You should come in so we can get your prenatal care underway. Are you already on vitamins? I have samples—let me fetch some for you." She set her bags down and turned in the direction of her offices. "You should feel free to use my rear entrance for as long as you want to keep your news private."

She couldn't fathom who the father might be. If Nova was seeing anyone from the area, she was a queen of stealth.

"I am in need of nothing," Nova said before she reached the door. This time, her tone held a warning.

Cat's keys dangled from her fingertips. "Okay. But I can get you on the appointment books. It's no trouble at all."

"I don't intend to make an appointment," Nova said.

"What? Of course you will. What are you talking about? This is a small town, but we're civilized here."

"If that was a reference to my Ute heritage, I will overlook it. But even if it is not, let's understand each other: this baby I carry is a gift from the heavens. He is blessed. He is specially protected by the sign of his conception, and the sign of his delivery. It's a fortuitous pairing. And the two of us, I'm glad to say, won't be needing your services."

Cat's lips parted, but nothing came out. This nutcase was putting the health of her fetus in the hands of a *horoscope*? Was this what Nova's hatred was all about—astrology versus medical science?

Nova's door floated shut behind her before Cat summoned the boldness to ask.

⌒

All Cat had ever wanted to do was help people stay alive. She aimed her 4-wheel drive up and out of Burnt Rock's basin, rose to meet the paved highway, and then dropped by twisty mountain miles into lower elevations, where the vegetation was more lush and varied. She wondered what kind of a world it was where such a noble desire to serve people could ever be called criminal, while people like Nova could turn up their noses at common sense and simply be called eccentric.

Cat felt deeply wounded by this, and the beauty surrounding her didn't ease the hurt, as it usually did. Probably because she was alone.

She had been left alone by Garner. She had been rejected by Nova.

Innumerable shades of green fluttered along the steep hillside, seeming to race her downhill. Densely growing spruce trees began to yield ground to the long-needled ponderosa pines and silvery quaking aspens.

On sunny days like this one, when the thermometer pushed into the high eighties even on the mountaintops, it was hard for Catherine to imagine that within six months this same region would be subjected to winter-weather blockbusters, the kind that featured avalanches and road closures and small snowbound towns at the heart of cannibalistic tales. Burnt Rock had no such morbid history, though it was occasionally cut off from the outside world, and this was one reason why Cat Ransom had chosen it for her home. She had ruled out the tourist trap fifty miles south because of its tacky museum commemorating a historic flesh-eater born there two hundred years ago.

"There's no point in trying to leave one's mark where the competition is so long established," she had said to Dotti Sanders of that town and its clinic a few days after setting up office in Burnt Rock. The spunky octogenarian who still went river rafting had made an appointment for a stubborn infection in her foot. Dotti was reclined in a dentist's chair, which had been left behind by the previous physician.

Dotti raised an eyebrow while Cat gently peeled away the old dressing and then said, rather fearlessly Cat thought, "You don't plan to eat my toes, do you?" And Cat had laughed, because she hadn't realized that the remark might have been interpreted that way. It wasn't what she meant at all.

"You have nothing to fear," she'd replied. "I'm all about keeping people alive."

Today the brightness of the sky cut through Cat's windshield as she followed the downward turns in the highway. The descending lane hugged the mountainside and set her back twelve feet from the precipitous cliffs. Few guard rails protected the ascending side. What protected careless drivers also made hard work for snowplows. Except in particularly dangerous spots, the state had opted to go without the rails so that heavy snows could be pushed away without obstacle. Leaving Burnt Rock never generated the same anxiety in Cat's nerves that returning to it did. Besides the risk of accidentally tumbling off the road, there was always the chance that her secrets had been discovered in her absence.

Not so long ago, Cat was known in a western state as Katrina White. Dr. White had been unfairly stripped of her license to practice medicine and likely would have spent some time in prison had she not thrown herself at the mercy of the plaintiff and the court, convinced both that she posed no flight risk, and then fled the state with cash and a new identity.

Catherine Ransom wiped Katrina White off the map.

Cat pulled her car into a scenic turnout that featured a pleasant waterfall when the snow melted off. At the other end of the lot, Garner and she had marked their own private trailhead, which was cloaked by shrubs and untrod grasses, and defined by a familiar boulder here and an aging spruce there. The all but invisible path led to a meadow rich with wild herbs, especially the cheerful yellow arnica and the more dour stinging nettle.

Cat retrieved from her trunk the backpack she used for herb gathering. It contained gloves, paper lunch bags, a small trowel and gardener's pruning shears, rubber bands for binding cut stems, cheese-cloth for wrapping more fragile cuttings, and a pocketknife. She set off, expecting the short hike to take less than two hours one way.

Since leaving the West Coast, she'd devoted her primary efforts to a greener form of healing. Her newfound focus on herbal remedies had resulted in an advantageous bond with Garner, whose impressive basement provided Cat with much of what she needed that didn't grow in the Rocky Mountain wilds, and at a much better price than she could have it online. And as it turned out, her singular attentiveness to his personal well-being had actually been good for his health.

She'd invested more money in her new identity than she'd initially planned. But the extra expense gained her the licenses and numbers she needed to conservatively write prescriptions under her new name. In this way she could present herself to the world as an open-minded, even-keeled physician who treated patients' symptoms with every resource available to her.

With only a few, unimportant exceptions that Cat was able to pass off to more traditional doctors down in the valley, the Burnt Rock residents were happy to have such a doctor among them: one who respected the natural order of the world, who prescribed artificially concocted remedies only when nature needed assistance, and who had escaped the evil clutches of those politicking pharmaceutical giants by choosing this humble, small-town life of modest means. It seemed the whole aching world was rushing her door for healing compresses dipped in her arnica liniment, made from the fresh blooms steeped in rubbing alcohol. From the dried flowers, she could make salves to last through the colder months. She picked up a few extra stalks when she gathered the yarrow.

As Dr. Cat Ransom became more and more adored, Dr. Katrina

White receded into the shadows of Cat's imagination. Nevertheless, the two women shared one unfading quality: selfless devotion to the well-being of others. No court would ever strip her of that.

As she worked, however, Cat's hatred of the Sweet Assembly's magnetism grew, as did her distaste for the commercial promises of astrologers and so-called psychics. No wonder she and Nova would never get along. She hoped Garner wouldn't also lose his head.

After a productive hour of gathering as much as she could reasonably store and use in the coming winter, she felt better. Renewed. Cat began the walk out of the field and was startled to take note of a sprawling growth of stalks about two feet tall. This relative of the lily bore clusters of small creamy white flowers, like a spear, that were beginning to drop. The leaves, slender and floppy, rose like tall blades of grass around the stalk.

Uprooted, the bulbs resembled green onions, with small edible bulbs. Well, the blue-flowered stalks, the common blue camas, were edible. These with the white flowers were so toxic from top to root that it was said they were deadlier than strychnine. They were called the death camas, and though they had killed more livestock than humans, no doctor or outdoorsman was cavalier about them. When the flowers weren't in bloom, the blue and white camas were nearly impossible to tell apart. And yet they weren't even in the same plant genus.

In Colorado, one generally assumed that no camas was edible. Blues tended to be rare in this part of the Rockies, whereas the white death camas came in two varieties: the fatal mountain death camas, and the seven times deadlier meadow camas.

Nonetheless, Garner once told her that all mountain residents should be educated in the life-and-death consequences of their local botany. He taught her a trick to help distinguish between the two, a bit of lore that had never failed him yet, though he hadn't seen it documented by a qualified scientist anywhere.

He had cut off a death camas stalk about two inches above ground. At the cross section, the leaves around the stalk folded into each other to form the general shape of a triangle. Then he pulled the bulb out of the soil and sliced it in two horizontally. The core of the fatal onion twin also resembled a triangle. Similar cross-sections of the blue camas bore tidy little circles rather than three-sided designs.

"I think we ought to name these Bermuda onions," she had said. "As a mnemonic device."

"I don't get it."

"You know—the triangle?"

"Oh. Well, death camas is far more poetic, don't you think?" he said. "And I think the real Bermuda onion growers would object."

At this time of year, identification by slicing was unnecessary. The alluring white flowers and the egg-shaped bulbs that didn't smell like onions were all the clues she needed.

Cat had no practical use for these plants, but she thought she should collect some. Play with it a little. It was wise to be prepared for all possible events, in and out of season, and *Zigadenus venenosus* wasn't exactly available online.

Wearing her gloves, she stripped a slender aspen branch of its leaves and used it to help pry the death camas out of the earth undamaged. She hardly needed the tool; summer rains had softened the earth, and nearly all of them uprooted with ease.

Cat filled a large brown sack with a couple dozen. Surely more than she needed, but she found the gesture cathartic after such a difficult morning. Just one of these bulbs could kill a child and two could kill a man, and she was no murderer. But such a large bag did make her feel a little bit powerful.

She would need to take great care with how she labeled it, to prevent an innocent soul, even herself, in a split second of distraction from accidentally applying the meadow death camas to a tragic use. Because she was all about keeping people alive.

12

The day of the judgment was blazing hot with the heat of a classic Western. The sun was molten and broiled the earth, weighing down breezes and evaporating much of the water spray that arced over the hayfields. The air rippled above blacktop roads, and the vibration of the elements seemed audible, a low and ominous hum.

Inside the air-conditioned courthouse, the oxygen was almost too thick to breathe. Beth and her father sat next to each other, elbows touching, the only souls on a wood bench worn shiny by use. Only her father had joined her today. Her mother refused to spare the ranch anyone else for "Beth's drama."

It was easy for Beth to forgive her mother, who was more frightened about the outcome than anyone.

A very small audience, mostly friends whose pity had carried the Kandinskys through this trying time, heard the judge award Mr. Anthony Darling all the damages he sought. It was a devastating number, much larger than Beth could comprehend in that second when it was uttered, even greater than the number their attorney had called a "worst case." The decision was read and received dispassionately by those in attendance, but the murmur of agreement continued to swirl around Beth's head after the judge rose and left his seat.

There was no mercy, only judgment. No nick-of-time miracle, only the expected reality. The girl with nothing was forced to give all to the man who had everything, because she had made a grave error.

Darling passed by without looking at the Borzois. Their attorney said how disappointed he was in the outcome, gave them instructions to contact his assistant for an appointment in the coming weeks, then left abruptly, as if he'd already overspent his time with this family that had no more money to give him. The courtroom emptied.

Beth had eighteen months to pay Darling. If she didn't, or couldn't, the court would proceed by issuing liens against the Blazing B, forcing subdivisions and sales of land and property if necessary. It would be necessary. The two jobs she'd taken wouldn't even skim the fat off the top of this stew.

Abel picked up the cowboy hat that sat on the seat next to him. A new frown line over his nose that matched the cleft of his chin was the only indication that he'd heard the judge's words.

Abel was older than the fathers of Beth's peers, nearly old enough to be her grandfather, having married Rose late in his life. The sun-sunk lines of his wide round face were deep, and his hair, which was once the same gold-red as Beth's, was entirely gray now, including his mustache and eyebrows.

It was his ready smile and peaceful approach to the world that made him seem young—his smile and his eyes, which were still as blue as a stellar jay's tail feathers. But when he took Beth's hand and pulled her out of her shocked state, drawing her gently off the bench, he looked old to her, and tired.

"Can we appeal it?" she asked. Hope was an invisible gas that she couldn't grab hold of. The last atoms of it floated away on her father's shuddering sigh.

"We'll figure this out, honey," he said. He wiped a beaded line of sweat off his brow, then reseated his hat. More moisture clung to the tiny hairs at his temples. "God can do anything."

"I'll think of something."

Her father shook his head as they walked down the long, empty hall. "Sometimes there's nothing to think up but belief. Faith that God can do something incredible."

God, Beth feared, would ask the family to let everything go. Equipment, vehicles, livestock, land. Staff. Livelihood. Dreams. More dreams. Maybe even love—her parents' love, her brothers' love. Even all that might not be enough.

Abel said, "Sometimes God brings us to the end of our options so that when he does his will, no one else can take the credit for it."

"I wish I had your faith that he'll save the ranch," she whispered.

"I said God *can* do something incredible, not that he will. Maybe the ranch has served its purpose. My faith isn't in good outcomes, Beth, only in the goodness of God."

Father and daughter exited the courtroom, and then the air-conditioned building. Outside, the sun bounced off the walls of the white courthouse and the reflective concrete lot, cutting through sunglasses. Abel held on to her hand as if knowing she'd need his help to wade through the dense heat. It slowed her movements and her thinking. It seemed to pry at their sweat-slicked palms. Her life was heavy as water, and she wished to be ripped away on a drowning current, but her dad's hold was lifesaving. Somehow his silence reassured.

Inside his melting, sticky-vinyl Ford, Beth developed the beginnings of an idea. Her father turned on the A/C and pulled out onto the highway.

"Cut me off," she said. "I'll sell my share of the ranch to Levi. I'll leave the valley. If I'm not connected to the Blazing B, they can't come after it."

Abel shook his head. "We'd had to have done that long before this trouble, if that's what we wanted. Which I don't, by the way."

"Do it anyway. To protect yourselves."

"That's no protection, honey. I don't know the law, but I'd guess your mother and I'd become accessories in breaking it."

He took a long breath and placed one hand over his heart.

"It's not fair that you have to pay for my mistakes. Not like this."

"This is what it means to be a family."

She feared that Levi and her mother would harbor a different sentiment.

"You wouldn't say that if we were talking about the herd," she muttered.

"What? A family is not a herd, young lady."

"All my life you've said it's healthiest for the weak ones to be culled. If a coyote takes a calf, you let it go. And you won't ever waste anyone's time tracking down that coyote."

"Coyotes do what coyotes do. We don't waste resources trying to stop that."

"My point is, the predators sense the weakest calves. And the weak ones weaken the entire herd. I'm the weak one, Dad. You've got to let me go."

The rare frown between Abel's eyes deepened, and Beth thought she might be making some inroads.

But then he said, "You thought I was talking about the calf? You're twenty-two, and you've grown up thinking we should let *predators* cull the herd?"

"What else could you have meant?"

"Those calves were killed by the natural order of the world, honey. But the culling was never about the calf, it was about the parent—the cow who failed to protect her baby. If all the other cows can keep their little ones safe from the hunter, what's wrong with the one who can't? We don't want to keep breeding those. We single out the mamas who fail. *We* cull the herd—your mother and me, Jacob. That's not the coyotes' job."

Beth's argument leaked out of her. "And those mamas who fail go into the group you sell each year."

"What did you think was happening to them?"

"I knew they were sold, but I thought it was for other things. There's a dozen reasons why certain cows go."

"If you think you're weak, maybe it's because your mom and I have let you down," Abel said.

"You know that's not what I was trying to say. I'm an adult. You're not responsible for my poor judgments, Dad."

"Most parents I know feel like they are, on some level. Doesn't matter how universally imperfect kids are—or how good. You're one of the good ones, honey."

"You feel responsible because my mistakes have affected the whole family, the whole ranch."

Her father smiled at her, his unforced, unconditional smile that brought some light back to his tired eyes.

"So my cull-the-calf metaphor breaks down," she said, "but I still think there's got to be a way to spare the family from my mess."

The truck glided by bright green circular fields watered by central-pivot irrigation systems. In some fields, hay that was cut but not yet baled lay fading under the sun in wide swaths. Fresh rectangular bales the color of peas sat waiting collection. Older bales, cut and dried earlier in the summertime, stood in tall yellow stacks under shelters.

"Hot one today," Abel observed. He sounded more exhausted than she felt.

Small herds of cows not sent to the public lands to graze nibbled on fields that were rotated with the crops for this purpose. Everything in this valley was dependent on something else for survival. The ranchers on their cows; cows on the grass; the grass on the water; the water on the mountain snow. In this part of the country, every cow-calf pair needed roughly twenty acres of property to survive, and the ranchers needed enough cows to breed and to sell to keep their acreage financially afloat. They had to have enough water and soil to grow food to keep herds through the winter with a minimum of supplementation, and ideally with a little extra to sell. Permits to graze herds on public lands, which prevented valuable croplands from becoming overgrazed, ran tens of thousands of dollars.

There was almost never enough money to prosper, just barely enough to get by. In the valley, the balance between survival and ruin teetered on fragile scales. It was life-giving, life-taking work that families out here did for love, not for cash. A rancher's worth was hardly ever liquid, and most of it was tied up in the land, beautiful but demanding. Parting with assets was nearly the same as parting with water in a desert.

Anthony Darling and the courts expected the Blazing B to hand over every canteen it possessed.

They passed a field recently cut, and a man bent over the open engine of his baler, greasy parts spread out on the ground and glistening with black oil under the sun.

Worse than the judgment itself would be turning it loose on her family. The news they were carrying back to their home was a fanged rattlesnake, coiled and hostile.

"What am I going to tell Mom?" she murmured.

In answer the Ford lurched, and Beth's attention snapped to her father as the truck began to drift across the center line. Her left hand reached out for the wheel to pull them back before her mind had processed what was happening.

Her father was gripping his shirt, a fisted wad of court-worthy clean and pressed cotton directly over his heart. Pain deepened all the lines of his face, squinting around his eyes and yanking on the corners of his mouth.

"Dad?"

The weight of his own hand dragged the steering wheel in the direction opposite her efforts, with the net effect of keeping the truck square in the wrong lane.

Abel's body slouched toward the support of his door, away from her, away from life. On the short horizon, an oncoming car was swiftly closing the distance.

"Dad, I need you to let go of the wheel."

Her voice sounded disembodied, the confident authoritative voice of someone who knew exactly what to do, someone whose heart was not thrashing about, someone whose muscles weren't shaking uncontrollably.

"Let go, Dad."

Either he couldn't hear her or he couldn't will his fingers to obey.

His body stiffened in a spasm, and his legs tried to straighten. His foot floored the accelerator and the truck surged for an electric second, straining against the stick-shift gears. Then his shoe slipped off the pedal and the car lurched again, decelerating like a sky diver caught up by his chute, stalling the engine.

Beth's fight against her father's body weight became a futile competition against the entire heavy-duty vehicle. Even if her seat belt hadn't held her at this awkward angle, she wouldn't have been able to leverage the drifting truck.

Her prayer was an inarticulate cry as the oncoming car bore down on them and began to swerve. Beth released the wheel, and her sagging, unconscious father pulled them off the shoulder and across the dry grass. Thanks to the stalled engine, they hit the solid power line just hard enough to deploy the air bags, and then the truck bounced back. The hood was dented and steaming.

Beth had raised her arms in front of her face at the moment she let go, and the skin of her forearms took the sting of the bags' explosion. Her mind worked quickly, hyper alert, and her body sprang into focused action the moment the car came to rest. In one smooth motion that she had never practiced, she swept the nylon bag out of her way, released her belt, found her phone, activated the speaker, dialed 9-1-1, put the phone on the dash, and had her father unbuckled by the time the operator answered. She was able to say exactly where the accident occurred—which highway they were on, which cross street they had just passed.

"My father had a heart attack while driving. He's unconscious. He's breathing. This is his second attack." Thanks to the first one, Beth knew the latest CPR recommendations. Everything the operator told her to do made sense.

It should have been difficult to get him onto his back, and yet she had no trouble standing over him within the confines of the truck cab. It didn't occur to her to get out, to try to open his door and drag him onto the ground. Her feet found firm braces against the armrest and the gear box. Her strong legs squatted and lifted while she gripped him under the arms, locked her fingers behind his back, and turned him across the bench seat, her sticky cheek pressed into the sweat of his hair and neck. His knees angled oddly, trapped by the steering wheel. She twisted him at the waist, making his spine as flat as possible.

"He stopped breathing," she heard herself saying. She dropped all the weight of her back and arms into rapid chest compressions, knowing that there was still enough oxygen in his blood to keep his brain and body alive, so long as she could keep it moving.

Her memory pulled up his heavy sighs, his perspiring forehead, his extreme fatigue, and interpreted all these clues much differently now.

Press-press-press-press.

Was this how God would prove his goodness?

Please, don't let him die, she prayed. If only she understood the "healing touch" that Jacob claimed she had. If only the miracle worker could control her own gift.

The operator continued to speak to her, and she continued to answer. She heard the creaking of a distant car door and remembered that there was another driver somewhere. She feared his fury. She heard a man's shout but didn't know what the words were, didn't look up until a shadow fell over the truck's cab.

Her passenger door opened, and hot but fresh air rushed in, lifted her chin. Press-press-press-press. Beth registered that a man stood there, and that a small cut under his eye was blooming and had dripped blood onto his shirt, a green polo with an embroidered design on the right shoulder. Wolf Creek, it said. A mountain-pass ski resort west of the valley. She'd skied there before but had never paid attention to its logo until now. Between two mountain peaks, the head of a wolf looked down on her with piercing triangular eyes. The man's blood dotted its nose.

Press-press-press-press.

"You're bleeding," she said.

"It's stopped," he said. "I'm an EMT. How can I help?"

13

In the round sanctuary of the Sweet Assembly, Garner waited for Hank to begin his message. Garner had heard it before and liked it about as much as canned green beans that tasted like their tin containers. Even so, he had felt unseated since the storm shattered his kitchen window. The glass had been repaired, but he couldn't fix the disquiet in his heart. It was clear to him now that the storm had stirred up a need in him like sediment on the bottom of a river, and the water would not clear. He needed his daughter, Rose. He needed her to come back to him.

He needed a miracle, which is exactly what the Sweet Assembly was known for.

Garner sat in the unyielding wooden church pew with a handful of tourists who'd recently disembarked from the ten o'clock bus. There were fewer on Mondays, especially in August, when many of Colorado's children returned to school.

In Garner's opinion, calling the Burnt Rock Harbor Sweet Assembly a church was a bit of a stretch. For one, the concept of a harbor was ridiculous in these rugged mountains of this land-locked state. He supposed it was meant to be a metaphor, but still it was absurd. For another, the nature of *assembly* was intentionally undefined, so that the hardware-store retailer-slash-minister, Hank, could offer a nondenominational, interfaith, multicultural, doctrine-free inspirational message without offending anyone who dropped in. And when desired, the facility could be used for gatherings of other types, like parties for deserving town doctors.

These were shortcomings that Garner could easily overlook. Considering his present feelings about God, he didn't believe anyone who visited the Sweet Assembly needed some hard-hitting message of deliverance from sin. That wasn't why the tourists liked to come. Over the years, enough folks had claimed to have received miracles that a few people came with expectations of their own, though most seemed merely curious, hopeful of nothing except that they might be entertained by the freakish faithful among their number. Pilgrims brought prayers on papers that they tossed into the central fire pit, which burned round the clock. Some brought relics of loved ones who couldn't make the journey. A collection of abandoned canes and walkers and pill bottles and other such symbols of healing were left behind in the circular aisles.

Then Hank and his wife, Kathy, transferred these "proofs" to an attractive display in the foyer, a showcase of the many healings that had taken place at the site of Mathilde's Miracle.

In April of 1877, before Burnt Rock was even an official town, Mathilde Werner Wulff had built the original fire in desperate haste within the same ring of granite stones. Mathilde was the young wife of a German gold miner, a talented woman admired for her leatherworking skills. On a routine trek between the Wulff home and the mine, Mathilde and the Wulffs' packhorse were attacked by a famished mountain lion, whose hunger was all but insatiable so early in the spring. It chased her some distance before one great and terrible leap struck her in the left thigh, punctured her skirts, skin, and muscles, then tore her off the horse.

The first miracle, she said afterward, was that she managed to keep hold of both her head and her husband's pistol while the animal dragged her off in its yellow teeth. She withdrew the weapon from the waistband of her skirt and took a shot that might have taken off her own leg as easily as the cougar's head. She avoided inflicting further injury to herself, but she also failed to strike the snarling cat, though she spent the entire contents of the pistol. How could she not have hit it, she later berated herself, when she could have grabbed its ears in her fists? She never had an answer for this, but the ruckus convinced the wildcat to drop her and turn its attention to less hazardous, meatier prey. The terrified horse thrashed some twenty yards off, its reins tangled in the grasping arms of a fir tree.

By the time the horse was dead, Mathilde had stumbled away.

From near death to near death she fled: the mad chase, the escape, and the bleeding leg conspired to disorient her, and as night fell she knew nothing about where she might be except far away from home, and well off any trails her husband would be able to explore before daybreak. She tore up her petticoats into bandages and then went in search of shelter, counting on her dead horse to save her now. If it was possible the wild cat might still be hungry, she had no way to separate her body from the stench of the sticky blood.

She collapsed against a pile of rocks at the base of a cliff so steep that no human of the day could have scaled it. With any luck, she surmised, neither would any wild animals be dropping on her from above. Next to her was a fallen tree, an evergreen made brittle and brown by disease, its exposed roots caked with long-dried earth. Using the dry needles, the decaying bark, and slim branches she could break off with her own hands, Mathilde assembled a tiny pyramid of materials that looked, according to her simple journal sketches, strangely like a miniature wickiup, a shelter of twigs and branches favored by the region's Ute tribes. Patiently, with weak and quavering fingers, she generated enough of a spark with her flintlock to bring the little pyre to life.

When the bleeding from her thigh finally stopped, when the glinting yellow cat eyes did not appear in the light of her campfire, and when her body overpowered her mind, Mathilde gave in to sleep.

As the story went, she woke at dawn, cold and hot and delirious, but of sound enough mind to know that death would likely find her before her husband did. The fire in her pit had gone out, but the fire in her leg was an inferno of infection, and her will wasn't enough to get her on her feet. She had no hope of gathering wood or retracing her bloody steps of the day before, and her mind filled with images of all the wild animals who might bring fate to her in their teeth: grizzly bears, mountain lions, wolves, and lynx.

She asked God to send death swiftly, and without fangs.

As she lay with her cheek on the dirt, breezy fingers stirred the dry ash of her fir trees and levitated tiny pieces. They fluttered like tiny attention-starved insects in front of her eyes, which gazed on her predicament from a despairing, sideways vantage.

It was a blessed distraction, a mesmerizing dance of nature, until some of the soot floated onto her face and stuck to the tears that wet her cheeks. When she reached up to wipe it away, the ash smudged and left a greasy gray residue on her fingertips. The stain reminded her of the purple stains left on her hands when she applied iodine to her husband's mining injuries.

Mathilde had no iodine with her, but the ash smudges brought to mind a distant idea that the ash might have similar effects. And this lent her some hope.

Even for a woman of her predicament, hope would rear its head. Garner supposed this was part of the story's allure for him.

She reached into the burned-out pile and scooped out a handful of warm ash. Spitting into the flyaway flakes, she made a muddy poultice and plastered her slashed leg with it, making several small batches in her palm until she had covered her wounds and packed the pasty goo deep in her muscles.

Historians speculated that this simple procedure probably extended Mathilde's life long enough for the surgeon who eventually treated her to do her some good. The antiseptic properties of ash had long been recognized and in her case, in spite of the unsanitary way it was prepared, managed to slow down the infection.

But Garner and others had always considered that part of the story a simple tale of good luck and quick thinking, though Mathilde's journal claimed it was God's hand that stayed the infection. *That* was not the miracle that drew people to the Burnt Rock Harbor Sweet assembly.

The real appeal was rooted in what happened next: after three days in the wilderness, without food or water or fire or the ability to walk; after the limited search-and-rescue skills of the other miners gave out; after her husband collapsed of despair, having found the awful remains of her mount, Mathilde was carried into the tiny settlement on the back of a lovely Spanish horse that no one had ever seen before—and after three more days, never saw again.

She rode in on her stomach, slung over the gray-dappled white hide like a pile of trapper's furs, unconscious and dangling but alive, her unbound hair sweeping the dirt. Fine beads made of pottery, along with three eagle feathers, were woven into the horse's fine mane.

If she hadn't been so near death during the ensuing week, she might have been more overtly mocked when she finally told her story of how the horse presented itself. Mathilde claimed that on the morning of the third day, after hours of begging God for death had morphed into disoriented dreams, the sun woke her. She watched the white beams turn blue in the morning air, and then she saw them touch the ashes of the fire that had died the first night. The sun's blue rays were like the spoon of her stew pot on the hearth at home. It stirred the remains into a dusty whirlwind that gradually produced the physical forms of the horse and a man, a Native man with coarse dark hair, clothed head to toe in winter buckskins that rattled with decorative beads. He was tall and thin, formed like a runner, with a narrow jaw and kind eyes. He was spectacularly tall, well over six and a half feet, and had slender fingers that were also noticeably long. A peace pipe was tied at his waist.

He lifted her onto the horse and spoke to her in a language she didn't understand. And though she didn't know the words, her soul heard them as the words spoken by Jesus to the paralytic at Bethesda: *Sin no more, lest a worse thing come unto thee.* Then the man slapped the animal's rump, and the horse's gentle sway rocked her back to dreams.

The horse was touched, fed, watered, and sheltered by several witnesses before it disappeared from the mining settlement, which made it difficult to dismiss Mathilde's story entirely as a fever-induced hallucination. Still, there were theories about where the horse had really come from. It was wild, some said, in spite of its decorated mane. It was the lost and wandering property of a nearby tribe. It was offered by a Ute hunter who took pity on the injured woman and sent her home, expecting neither recognition nor compensation for his good deed.

It was this last theory that seemed the most reasonable to Mathilde's husband, and it was supported by the eventual discovery of the campfire site where she'd spent her precarious days, two miles above the Burnt Rock settlement. There they found the shredded bloody petticoats she'd used for bandages, and a peace pipe made of willow.

The Ute tribes of the region were known as a peaceful people, and Mathilde's husband wanted to show his gratitude to them with a gift. With Mathilde's consent he withdrew from their stores the most valuable possession they owned: a fine leather saddle tooled with mountain flowers and overlaid with pure hand-hammered silver. The fenders, the skirt, the housing, and more were heavy with the precious metal. Mathilde had made the saddle for him as a wedding gift while they were still in Germany, in anticipation of their new life together in the Wild West.

He went with a fellow miner who knew the languages of the Utes, and the interpreter made a path for him. All of the nearby villages insisted that their horses and warriors were accounted for and knew no story of a white woman hovering between this world and the next.

One tribal elder, however, claimed to recognize the willow pipe when it was shown to him. He said that the man Wulff sought lived apart from the tribes and had come to the region with white missionaries years earlier. The elder didn't know where the man could be found, but offered to accept the saddle until his next appearance. In exchange they provided Wulff with a horse, not knowing he no longer had one, and then they loaded the mule he'd borrowed from a neighbor with heavy bear furs and tightly woven baskets filled with food.

Mathilde never engaged in any debate about the believability of her story, and she never altered her account of the man and horse rising from the ashes like the mythical phoenix. She told the story once publicly, then never again, and her experience might have been forgotten in time if her grandson hadn't taken interest in the crumbling journal written in her fading hand.

In the early 1920s, Jonathan Wulff came to Burnt Rock after a season abroad in Egypt, where he'd become caught up in the excitement surrounding Howard Carter's discovery of Tutankhamen's tomb. The young archaeology student participated in little more than the grunt work associated with the great find, but that didn't dampen his plans to pursue a career in antiquities. They were temporarily interrupted, however, when he fell from a ladder into an excavated tomb and broke his left leg, which subsequently became infected. As his condition worsened he was sent away to Paris so that grumblings about the pharaoh's curse would have no reason to spread among his colleagues.

Though Jonathan improved in France, his full recovery was expected to take months. And so he chose to recuperate among the family that had enthusiastically funded his education and career with the profits of their successful mining operations.

During his stay in Burnt Rock he was gifted with his grand-mother's journal and the peace pipe that had remained in the family. His father thought that Jonathan would appreciate the romance of Mathilde's tale, which by that time had devolved to the status of family folklore. Jonathan did like it, and found the journal entries to be good entertainment in the chilly spring evenings. They were written in German, but he had the education to translate them. While his broken femur healed by the warmth of the hearth fire, Jonathan concocted his share of jokes about the ashen Spanish horse and its dusty warrior, and regaled his nieces and nephews with ghost stories of dead men who hunted recalcitrant Wulff children.

But each night, after the family had gone to bed, he'd stay up by the light of the family's one electric lamp and part the aging hand-stitched papers, searching for a certain page, a particular paragraph that humbled his academic cynicism. At age twenty-three his grandmother Mathilde, the same age as he when the journal was given to him, had written:

It does not matter what anyone has to say of my experience, or that the preacher would rather I tell it different. Christ Jesus my Lord saved my soul when I was a girl, and He saved my body now that I am a woman. That He did it as a man breathed up of the ash the way Adam must have risen on the Sixth Day is not for me to examine.

It is no matter that I lack the preacher's schooling, or that the men fear I be guilty of cavorting with the dead, or that the wives look at me from the tops of their noses as if I am addled by sickness. Whatever the explanation for my salvation, I am no senseless creature. I credit my life only to the Lord, Who numbers our days. Today I live though tomorrow I may die. But since I live when I ought to have passed on, I am bound to Truth, which is this: it is not for me to prove what God did, nor how, but only to remind all that He did it. There is no point in a miracle except that it expose the glory of the Lord, and so I'll not try to cover it up. Look at what God has done!

Jonathan found her simple thinking to be endearing, a relic of an earlier time when faith was still hanging on to reason by the skin of its teeth. But he couldn't deny that this last line of her journal touched his heart in a deep place that was hidden from everyone who knew him. He had fond memories of his grandmother, because she had lived until he was ten, and he had heard the story of her miraculous rescue long before he was aware of a journal.

If he had known her writing first, before he knew the person, he might have expected her to be austere and dogmatic, closed-minded and stern. But his memory could only recall a woman of great softness—in the eyes, in the jowls, in the hands, in the belly—whose arms and heart were always open, and whose hugs smelled of the metal-heavy mountain water she bathed in. She would greet him by cupping his chin in her hand and approving of his good health by exclaiming, "Look what God has done!" so that he sensed his very existence was a good thing.

But something more than sentiment held his eyes on the page, night after night. It was the possibility, however slim, however ludicrous, that his grandmother knew something important about this life, in this world, that he did not. And to a man of learning who respected all people of the past, this possibility was unbearable.

So on a warm day toward the end of April in 1924, when he thought he was strong enough, Jonathan gathered his cane and a rucksack and a small shovel and a canteen full of water. Not wanting to impede his healing, but knowing he couldn't make the hike on foot, he cautiously rode his father's most gentle horse uphill to the site of Mathilde's Miracle, which until that day had been her miracle alone.

The area was not preserved as anything special, and fifty harsh winters had eliminated the ashes and altered the shape of the vegetation. But the cliff that had sheltered Mathilde was identifiable by its outcroppings, which she described in detail in the journal— she'd even drawn a picture. And some months after her recovery, before the next winter set in, Mathilde had returned and placed a small ring of broken granite rocks around the spot where God had "breathed." It was her version of a monument. An altar.

When Jonathan arrived and saw the rock ring, long anchored to the ground by snow-soaked mud and durable mountain grasses, a breeze passed over him that caused him to shudder. He would tell his family later that he thought of the apostle John's account of the angel that stirred the waters at the pool of Bethesda, though no doubt Mathilde's journal entries had given him this idea. Whether the breeze was divine, Jonathan couldn't say. Still, he was compelled to show his respect for God, regardless of what modern science had to say, by dismounting his horse, cane in hand.

He planted the tip of the cane in the firm ground next to his strong leg and leaned on it for support. The carved stick snapped in two and the bottom half toppled away, and as he overcompensated for his sudden imbalance, his full weight came to bear on his injury.

It didn't stagger under the weight of the surprise. He felt no pain. Instead the wasted muscles of his unused legs seemed to coil and hum, waiting to spring him into long-awaited action. *Look, you are well again.*

The tip of the broken cane was like a pharaoh's staff in Jonathan's fist. He raised it to the sky and tilted his face to the sun and began to laugh.

"Look at what God has done," he chuckled. "Look at what he has done."

14

If you hadn't paid good money to come on this outing," Hank said in his booming voice as he leaned against the rim of the fire pit, "I might be able to make you a promise that your very own prayers will be answered here at the sight of Mathilde's Miracle, but both God and the state of Colorado frown on that, so all I can guarantee you today is a good story."

All the boom of his voice seemed to come from the depths of his large belly. He was a jovial man, which Garner had always thought accounted for some of the assembly's popularity.

"Nevertheless," Hank said sagely, "I can say that many people who come here leave as changed people. I've seen sick people get better and sad people made happy. It's a simple thing, they tell me: they believe that anything's possible."

Hank's version of Mathilde's tale was the "simpler" and "more sensitive" one, he'd often boasted to Garner. He left out the "stop sinning" part, because who ever said such a thing anymore, especially of a person like Mathilde, who was as pure as the Rocky Mountain air? And who would know or care what such a command meant, or tolerate the threat that followed it? Wasn't being attacked by a ferocious wildcat enough terror for an innocent soul to bear?

Garner didn't mind. He knew the full story—it had been

published in a book sold at Nova's store, and it was posted in a classy museum format out in the foyer for anyone who was interested. He wasn't sure how many people had read the full text of the placards. But this slant toward sugarcoated entertainment was one of many reasons why Cat Ransom refused ever to attend services with Garner: "Even if Mathilde Wulff wasn't a complete crock," she would sniff, "the people who want to make money off the tourists sure are. It's best not to believe any of it."

Garner was more willing to give Hank the benefit of the doubt. Who would give up a half hour of his day seven days a week all summer long for a sham? There had to be something worth believing in here, however commercial it had become.

He listened attentively to Hank's version of the story. Years of repetition had refined it to a very entertaining point, and he even found himself rewarding Hank with amused laughter on cue.

But his smile fell with the long hand of the clock to the bottom of the hour. Hank was wrapping up, and Garner still had not heard the thing he had hoped to hear, even though he couldn't say exactly what that was.

"The power of belief is a great force in the universe," Hank said. "Belief has given feet to terrible evils, but also to even greater good. What do you believe about the miracle you seek? Do you deserve it?"

Yes, Garner thought. *I never forced Rose to go. I respected my daughter. She was the one who ran away. I've waited patiently for her return.*

"Will the fulfillment of your miracle bring others goodness— happiness, peace, and joy?"

Yes, Garner thought. *To the whole family.* He wasn't so sure about Abel.

"Then believe and you will receive," Hank said. "Believe and receive. This is the true beauty of a miracle, its magnificent simplicity."

Garner didn't remember if this was something Hank had

drawn from the pages of the Wulff journals or from Hank's own brilliant mind. Something about it didn't sound right. Some missing element made it insipid. Garner couldn't put his finger on it.

All Garner wanted, amid all the other wants and needs transported from the accordion doors of the tour bus into the sanctuary of the church, was for that rancher who stole his daughter to die; for his Rose to return to her father's love. And then he'd stand down by that fire pit of Mathilde's and whoop and shout, "Look what God has done!"

Cat had bet Garner one hundred dollars that the pair of them would come up with a cure for cancer before he'd ever hear those words burst spontaneously from anyone.

After a dramatic pause Hank raised both hands like a priest giving a benediction.

"Thank you all for coming today. We are so pleased to be a part of meeting your life's deepest needs. You are welcome to stay here and seek your miracle for as long as it takes, or until the bus departs from downtown at two thirty." His smile was so paternal and warm. Garner smiled back. "And because I sense the great size of the hearts here today, your great capacity to give as much as you receive, I will beg your indulgence as I draw your attention to the donation boxes positioned by each one of the doors around the building. If you have been blessed today—if you seek bigger and bigger blessings—yea, miracles—across the course of your life, then please consider what part you might play in the continuance of our work. He who gives much will receive much. And that's a promise I can make. Thank you all. Go in peace."

Garner remained in the pew while the visitors trickled out. He needed a moment to ponder Hank's closing words. *He who gives much will receive much.* It sounded like it might have been from the Bible, but it was so long since Garner had cracked the spine of his that he couldn't be sure. Still, it sounded right.

Maybe that was his problem. Garner had the means to make a generous donation, though he never had. He was a smart business-man, a wise investor. But what was his net worth doing for him these days? Nothing but sitting in a bank somewhere—far more than he needed for this simple life he'd chosen, in which he didn't need to support anything.

Maybe that's what God needed him to do after all. Give up the worldly treasure to get the spiritual one. That sounded right too.

Garner rose from his seat and made his way out into the foyer. The church was a product of mid-twentieth-century architecture, built in the fifties when Jonathan Wulff's children decided money could be made off the location, if properly packaged for the public. It was a hulking low building with a roof that was also a domed skylight, and glass bricks for windows that both allowed light to enter and closed off all view of the outside world. The red tile floors were dull but spotless.

He lingered here for a time, thinking. Mathilde's story, original pages from her journal, photographs of the family, and drawings she herself had sketched were all documented and matted and framed and hung on one side of the museum-like foyer of the little church. Few people ever lingered over them. What changes to this place might bring them closer to what they actually sought? What updates might reveal the revelations that Miracle Mattie might have to give them?

Garner shook his head. He was seventy-three years old. He'd die soon enough, with or without Cat's skills to slow it down. What else was that money going to do for him? He might as well put it to some useful good.

15

Abel lived for two days.

The EMT who stopped to help Beth carried several doses of epinephrine in his personal vehicle because his wife had severe allergies. Without him, Abel might have died on the side of the road. It took thirty-seven minutes for the ambulance to arrive.

A defibrillator resuscitated him. Oxygen revived him. An emergency surgery restored him. For two days.

For most of those fleeting forty-eight hours, Beth refused to leave her father's side. She paced the waiting room during the five-hour surgery. When her family arrived, Levi scowled at Beth and Danny hugged her, but Rose refused to acknowledge her only daughter. The women hadn't spoken and yet Rose knew, somehow had lashed together the outcome of the lawsuit and her husband's heart attack in an inseparable cause-and-effect grip.

Beth locked herself in a hospital bathroom stall and cried until her eyes swelled shut.

After the procedure she stayed close but settled silently into the shadowy corners of rooms, where Rose would not object to her. Levi and Danny came and went. Dr. Roy, Jacob's father and Abel's lifelong friend, was the only other person permitted to visit.

Her father slept a great deal and had little energy for speaking while awake. Absence cost Beth her job at the supermarket, which seemed worthless now. The manager of the feed-and-tack, who'd done business with the Borzois for years, was more understanding and told her to come back when she could.

On Tuesday night, Beth's body ached for lack of sleep and peace. In bursts of shallow rest she dreamed of tiny antelope grazing on the backs of gigantic wolves, grazing on tufts of gray fur. Their pronghorns were metallic, silvery, and shaped like a stethoscope's binaural arms and ear tips. The wolves formed a long line and scaled a ski slope with graceful, sure feet, and not one antelope fell off their backs. Then the image fell away and her mind's eye took an aerial perspective. The wolf line became distant beneath her, an indistinct line on a snowy, furry field. She soon recognized it as one of the distinctive brown rings around another antelope's neck, which soon came into view.

She could see a reflection of herself on the surface of its enormous eyes. A wolf sat beside her, and she felt unafraid.

Beth's eyes popped open. Her joints seemed locked at angles in the boxy wood-and-vinyl chair. She held this fixed position, waiting for her body to catch up with her mind before she tried to shift.

The hospital room was black save for a small night-light that cast a weak orange glow across her father's bed. The heart monitor's thin green lines created identical mountains in a long range, working silently so all could sleep. Her mother had crawled onto the bed against nurses' orders. She lay with her back to Beth and her head on its own pillow, close to Abel.

Beth's parents were murmuring in the low tones of physical weakness that didn't have anything to do with the time of night, which was so still, so quiet, that she could hear every word.

". . . time to find your old man," her father was saying.

"You know we can't," said her mother.

"The years heal wounds."

"Or deepen them."

"You've scarred over, Rosy. Maybe he has too."

Her mother's silence magnified the difficulty Abel had drawing a breath.

"I don't even know for sure where he is, or if he's alive," she said after a time.

"You haven't wanted to know. I'll bet he's still in—"

"You're right. I don't want to know. He moved on—I'm the one who stayed. He knows where to find me if he wants to."

"But now—"

"The writing is on the wall, Abel. It's time to let the ranch go. We'll sell it all, get this monkey off our backs, and still have enough to buy a quiet place where you can recover."

Abel's hair grated on the pillow as he turned his head toward his wife.

"Five generations, Rosy. That ranch is the only place in the world where I can recover."

"It's land, not life."

"It's our life. The life of . . . all those men. And Lorena now."

"And what's that worth to me if it kills you?" Rose pushed herself up onto one arm. From the shadows, Beth could see the tension in the gap between her parents, though they kept their voices low.

Her father seemed so weak. "Garner has the means—"

"Don't ignore me, Abel. What will we do with this place if you leave us? Levi has no desire to fill your shoes—surely you see that? Danny would, but he's so young. And Beth"—Rose glanced over and seemed satisfied by her stillness—"her poor judgment harms us all."

"Rosy, Rosy." He lifted his IV-injected hand an inch. "I think Garner said something similar about you once upon a time."

True or not, the claim shut down the conversation. Rose got off the bed like an agile cat, quick and light, and left the room. Beth closed her eyes and pressed down on them with her fingertips.

"Beth, honey," her dad said.

She feigned sleep.

"Find Garner Remke before your mother sells the ranch."

Remke was her mother's maiden name. Was Garner a brother? An uncle? She couldn't ignore a request like this one. "Who's he?"

"It's impossible for a father to stop loving his girl."

"He's my grandfather?"

"Do you hear me, Beth?"

Slow and stiff, she unfolded from the chair and reached out to take his hand, which seemed featherlight and withered. All wrong. Not a rancher's hand.

"What happened?" she asked. "To Mom and Garner?"

"Do you hear me?"

"Yes, I'll find him."

"It's impossible for a father to stop."

Weakness sucked him back into sleep. Beth stayed next to her father and held tight to his frail words, imagining that he spoke them about her.

She gripped his fingers until dawn, her back gradually sagging until her forehead came to rest on his pillow. Still she held on, waiting for that inexplicable cold to wash over her and pass through to him. Waiting for the antelope to rise, for the bird to fly.

The claw mark on her shoulder throbbed deep below the surface of her skin.

Whatever you did before, God, please do it again now. You did it for a sparrow—a worthless sparrow! Please do it for my father. My daddy.

Please.

Please.

God would not.

On the morning that her father died, Beth fled the hospital, disbelieving everything but that God was unmerciful and cruel, that his punishments were unfair. She would have done anything to pay any price for that mistake of stealing a saddle and a ride on Joe—any price but this one, which was wrong for anyone to demand. Including God.

She walked for miles under the searing August sun until Jacob found her, hatless and sunburned, dehydrated and mindless, on the highway that led back to the ranch. She didn't know his truck when it pulled off the road in front of her, and she didn't recognize his familiar face even after he got out of the cab and came toward her.

But his voice unlatched the gate that released the bucking bull of her spirit.

"Beth," he said. He reached out to touch her arm. "Oh, Beth. I'm so sorry."

She responded with a rage like she'd never experienced, and a surge of violence she shouldn't have had the strength to deliver. All the grief in her heart kicked its way out of her throat, burning like vomit. She resented his compassionate platitude. She ordered him to get away from her. She blamed him for all the suffering in the world and demanded he justify the very existence of God.

When it became clear that she would neither reason with him or let him take her home, he grabbed her from behind in an embrace that pinned her arms. She swore and strained and then begged, sobbing, for him to let her go. But Jacob had wrestled steers more than ten times her weight, and he held on easily, though her shoes dented his knees and bruised his shins.

Beth's fury didn't burn out. She had an infinite amount of grief for fuel. But when Danny emerged from the passenger side of Jacob's truck with red-rimmed eyes, the sight of him was like the smothering blast of a fire extinguisher. Fifteen and fatherless, he'd never looked younger to her, or more frightened by the unknown, and by her lack of self-control. He had no big words to rope her with this time.

As if Jacob could sense Beth's mind shift onto Danny's needs, he released her and she reached for her brother, whose more innocent sadness encased the three of them in pained silence while they stood, lost, at the side of the road.

16

Tea had stopped fixing Garner's restlessness. He was standing in his artificially lit greenhouse basement Thursday when he noticed this. That is, he noticed the three half-drunk cups of tea gone cold and abandoned among his plants. Never before had a brew of good-quality leaves failed to put him in a good mood—energize him if he was tired, pique his mind if he was bored, calm his heart if he was agitated.

And yet now, though his stomach sloshed with tea, he seemed to stand in a garden of sadness. He had overwatered his lemongrass so that it was turning yellow, and pinched fresh buds rather than deadheads off the blooming calendula. The plant shouldn't have had any dead blooms at all, but he'd forgotten to harvest them at the right time. He feared it might not flower again for several months, and that was disappointing, because the orange petals looked pretty in a teacup, and it seemed a lot of people cared about that these days—more than they cared about the potential health benefits.

Garner laid his clippers on the table next to a plastic planter and sighed. He didn't really have the heart to do any basement gardening today, regardless of what the plants needed. He sank onto a metal stool and felt his hip bones complain about the uncomfortable seat.

The weather had been so nice, and the tourists so numerous, that he'd opened up his house upstairs to allow an afternoon mountain breeze to clear out his rooms. The scent of sunshine drifted down into the basement but did nothing to revive his passions.

Cat Ransom sat on a matching stool and clipped peppermint sprigs from a full pot that sat between them. The fantastic bunches of arnica and yarrow she'd brought for Garner were hanging up to dry under a heat lamp. Not even these generous gifts had cheered him up.

"It's a beautiful day," she said. "Maybe you should leave this for a bit and go for a walk. Want to get a bite to eat?"

He couldn't decide if he was hungry or not.

"As your friend, Garner, I have to say that you're not doing your plants any good while you're in this brooding frame of mind. The great thing about this setup of yours is that you can work down here any time of the day or night. The work'll be here when you're feeling better. Let's get some fresh air."

He continued to sit. "I don't know, Cat. What am I doing here? I've been here in Burnt Rock . . . oh, how long now? Almost twenty years. When I first came here I thought it would just be for a year or two. I needed the isolation. I never thought it would go on this long."

"It's remote, sure. But you can't say you're isolated anymore, can you?"

He shrugged. "Depends on what you mean. From friends like you—no. 'Course not. They're good people here." He took a deep breath. "For the first few years I was really obsessed with my ex. I couldn't figure out even after we split what her real complaint with me was. She said I was either a blockhead or a world-class con. I thought that after a while she might come back and explain herself a little more clearly. I was willing to give it another go, but she wasn't into second chances."

"Some people don't know how to forgive," Cat said.

"Well, she remarried. Even that didn't totally dampen my spirits. That didn't happen until the cancer took her. After all that, we were destined for the same fate."

"That's not true."

"Maybe I could've been a help to her in the end, if she'd have let me."

Cat stroked a peppermint leaf between her thumb and forefinger.

Garner cleared his throat. "Rose is all that's left of that part of my life. She was twenty-three when she walked out. And sometimes when I consider she's been away from me for more years than she was with me, it takes all the wind out of my sails. How long does a person have to wait for what's upside down to right itself again?"

"Have you tried to contact her?"

"I wrote to her for a while in the beginning. Letters, postcards. She never replied." He picked up his shears and used the tip to scrape green chlorophyll out from under his nails. "I miss her," he said.

Cat stood and averted her face as she walked down a long aisle between two of the stainless tables. "Maybe one of the reasons you're still here is because destiny knew I would need you to be my friend. My story is a mirror of yours, you know."

"You have a daughter?" Garner was surprised. She'd never spoken of family.

"No—I had a father who wouldn't accept me for what I was."

"That's outrageous. You're gifted and lovely and successful and kind. He must have been an ungrateful man."

She glanced his way. "I had pretty serious learning disabilities as a kid. A lot of struggles and delays. I think they embarrassed him."

"That's shameful."

"Things got easier. It was hard work, but I wanted to please him so badly that I doubled my efforts in everything—therapy, school, extracurricular stuff. I graduated from medical school with top honors."

"Of course you did!"

"After my graduation ceremony I took him out to dinner at his favorite restaurant. I said, 'So what do you think, Dad?' He said, 'I'll be impressed if you can complete your residency.' A client called him away before he finished eating, and he left me with the tab."

"Give me his phone number. I'll give the man a lecture."

"He died when I was in my third year."

Garner shook his head and cursed under his breath. He had the sense that Cat meant to cheer him up with that story, but it only deepened his melancholy. If there was a worthy point, he hoped she would make it soon.

"It must have been hard to cope with that," he said.

"If I had been in a different career, I might not have survived," she said. "But everyone is so grateful and affirming. I can find all the acceptance I need in my patients."

"Regardless, you didn't deserve that kind of treatment from your father, Cat, girl. No one does."

He heard footsteps cross his threshold on the floor above.

"Garner? You down there, old badger?"

On a typical day, the sound of Dotti Sanders' voice was one that brought on a certain amount of hearing loss in Garner. Today, oddly, Dotti's sweet and heavy perfume grabbed his attention. Of course, it overpowered the fresh air and had apparently killed all sense of smell in her own nose, but Dotti's energetic personality could be highly motivational, especially when it came to selling rafting trips to visitors. Garner wasn't interested in any whitewater today, but he could use some strong motivational energy.

Her thick ankles and trendy neon walking shoes—something orange and sparkly designed for the twenty-and-under crowd—appeared on the third stair from the top. She bent at the waist and peered under the hanging lights in his direction.

"Hiya, Miss Marple." Originally, he'd not given her the nickname in kindness. She was an energetic, ubiquitous, sugary sweet busybody who didn't know a thing about plants and wanted him to educate her. He hadn't known at the time that she was fond of the fictional detective and thought he was paying her a high compliment. That revelation came later, when she suggested he participate in the Women's Auxiliary Group reading of an Agatha Christie novel.

"Got any murders for me to solve today?" she asked him, bent and clutching the rail. Her curly gray locks bobbed, and he feared she might do a somersault down the stairs. On purpose.

"I lost a rosemary plant."

"Rosemary's impossible to kill, you told me."

"And yet I did it." Garner pointed toward a sorry-looking woody shrub without a hint of green on it.

"What a man you are, able to do the impossible."

"I guess that's one way of looking at it."

"Hi, Dr. Ransom."

"Hello." The tone of Cat's voice was so flat that Garner turned to look at the doctor. She appeared stricken by Dotti's interruption.

"Or we might say it was bound to happen in a dark place like this," Dotti continued, still talking about the herb. "It's just beyond me that you can keep anything alive down here."

"And yet I run a successful business doing it."

"Yes, well, there you go, doing the impossible again. Forgive me, Garner, but it's a cave in spite of these glaring lights. I fear I'll come down straight into the jaws of a saber-toothed tiger. I've come to fetch you for lunch."

"But I just ate breakfast."

"Nonetheless, an hour with a friend will do your heart good."

"My heart is perfectly healthy. And as you see, Cat's here."

"The good doctor is welcome to join us, if she has the stomach for it. Don't be a meathead, dear."

"What's this, Marple? You never give a gentleman notice?"

"That's ridiculous. I've had two husbands, and neither of them ever needed notice if I had food to put in front of them. It might be a stretch to say they were gentlemen, but that's neither here nor there."

"But what makes lunch so urgent today?"

"The sandwich shop has come up with some new 'mountaineer' concoction, and I want to try it."

"What's on it?"

"They say it's elk, but if it is, it's got to be a freezer-bitten slab from last year's hunting season."

"An elk sandwich?"

"With grilled onions and banana peppers. And melted cheese to cover up the horror of it all."

"My heart might be worse off after lunch than before," Garner said, raising his eyebrows in Cat's direction.

She said, "I'll have to advise against it."

"They're calling it a 'seasonal special,'" Dotti said. "That means they don't need repeat business, just enough people to buy it one time. I tell you, that Mazy is cleaning out before the men start to bring back their fresh kills. Can you believe the things outsiders will fall for? For goodness' sake! It's August. Who eats any kind of melt this time of year?"

"Am I to understand that your lunch invitation is actually a dare?" Garner said. This was just the medicine his spirits had anticipated.

"If that makes you more inclined to come. I'm just doing my part to keep this town alive. A twelve-dollar sandwich will take us a ways. And it'll buy you and me some goodwill come January when all she's offering to everyone else is canned tomato soup."

Garner started chuckling as Dotti returned to the main level of the house.

"I want a few sprigs of your perfect mint if you'll cut some before you come up," she called. "You put the grocery store to shame, Garner—it's algae, what they sell. Don't make me wait. Lunch rush is upon us."

When he stood, his hips were flexibly fiftyish again. He picked up his clippers and marched to the mint. Snip-snipped quickly and headed for the stairs, light on his feet. Surprise, surprise. What tea couldn't fix, perhaps a stringy, greasy meal with a decent woman would.

"You coming?" he asked Cat when he reached the bottom step and realized she wasn't following him.

"Mm, no. It's still a bit early for me to be eating."

"Well, I can see why a young thing like you wouldn't want to hang out with old fuddy duddies like us."

"I'll watch the shop if you like," Cat offered. "No appointments until three, and the tourists have been keeping themselves out of trouble."

"No, don't bother with that. I'll just hang the sign in the window."

From upstairs, Dotti hollered, "Are you down there getting cold feet? It's *lunch*, dear! Not a wedding!"

"Right there!" Garner hollered.

"And change out of those ridiculous red clogs! They're an embarrassment."

"Only if you take the tangerines off your feet!" He started to ascend. He said to Cat, "Go do something fun for once, if you have free time."

She was still nodding when he reached the top of his stairs.

Was Garner leaving her? The question rattled Cat to the core. She wasn't asking whether he was leaving her for lunch, or leaving her for another doctor. She wanted to know if he was leaving his role as her surrogate father. What man who intended to stay in her life could be tempted away so easily by a heartburn-inducing sandwich? Had he heard anything she was trying to tell him?

The story she told was true. It was the story of Katrina White's childhood.

Cat sank onto the stool Garner had vacated and stared at the rows of plants. She didn't cry. Her lifetime allotment of tears had been spent by the time she was sixteen. But she fretted and she worried. And she felt the pressure of anxiety closing in around her lungs.

Garner was a better man than her father. That much had been made clear from the first day she met the herbalist. It was *the* reason why she had decided to stay on in Burnt Rock after the first year. In twelve months the old man had showered her with more praise and affection than her father was capable of producing in a lifetime.

Cat had hoped that Garner would also be a better man than Newell Reinhart, the father of her young patient Amelia. Cat—no, Katrina—had first fallen in love with the child, a precious thing with a weak body and a strong, strong spirit. Amelia thought Katrina ruled the stars. Amelia brought her gifts. Amelia filled her office with crayon drawings and second-grade poetry.

As for Newell, Cat fell in love with his devotion to his daughter before she'd fallen in love with the man himself.

But he too went away. As it turned out, most people in the world did not know that love was created to be reciprocal. Katrina White especially was victimized by this failure, used up by ungrateful souls who demanded she cure their every ailment and then disappeared without even a thank-you the moment they could manage their own health again.

Cat's breathing had wandered into the shallow memories of Newell and Amelia Reinhart. She had cured Amelia, and in thanks,

Newell had returned the child to her previous life—a life that did not include Katrina White.

She couldn't live with that again.

Walk with me, Garner, she said to her father figure.

No, fool girl. But I will walk with Dotti.

Dotti had a sturdy build that was more agile than it appeared, and better suited to this high-altitude environment than a body that age ought to be. The doctor often thought of her—affectionately of course—as a marmot. She was squat and thick, not fat, and Cat had come to believe that at least half the woman's body was a cavern for the largest set of lungs ever found in a human being. Dotti was never breathless, although many athletes found Burnt Rock's air too thin.

Cat had to stop Garner from leaving. She needed him to stay, to remember just how much he loved his daughter. His daughter, Catherine Ransom.

Cat found a scrap of paper on a table under the wall phone and wrote a hasty note.

Garner—Dinner at my place Saturday night, 7 sharp. Bring your friend. Affectionately, Cat

17

It might have been a thunderclap that woke Beth from her nightmare. When her eyes popped open in the darkness of her bedroom, the sound of driving rain filled her ears. It trampled the roof of the house like stampeding cattle and flailed at the window like a flock of trapped birds. The fright of her dream lingered, though the images and story line had evaporated.

She thought she'd been dreaming of Levi.

Salt tracks from dried tears cracked on the surface of her cheeks.

At the foot of Beth's bed, in the trench between Beth's and Lorena's legs, Herriot was also awake. The dog's eyes and ears were alert to the closed door until Beth rose to her elbows. Herriot gave her a glance, but when Beth didn't offer instructions, the dog resumed her watch.

Lorena was dead to the world, having exhausted herself with sobbing past midnight, as if Abel had been her best friend rather than a man she barely knew. Beth had awkwardly and ineffectively tried to comfort her.

But now a noise Beth couldn't hear over the clatter of the rain brought Herriot to all four feet. Her ears, soft triangles bowed over the sides of her face, lifted, but her tail, which usually curled like a snail's shell up onto her back, drooped.

Beth pushed the sheet off her legs and slipped out of bed. When her toes touched the floor, Herriot jumped down and waited for her. The clock on the nightstand said it was after four.

She pulled the door open onto a pitch black hall and Herriot trotted out ahead of her, toenails clicking down the flight of stairs to the left of Beth's door. Danny's room was a black cave opposite hers. To her right, at a distance, was the master bedroom. Levi slept downstairs, near the kitchen, in a room originally designed for the housekeeper.

The Blazing B hadn't had a housekeeper for twenty years.

Beth followed Herriot down the stairs without turning on any lights. The stairway turned back on itself halfway down and dropped into the great room, where the red brick hearth was cold.

This room was the family gathering place from October through spring. This was where the five Borzois would assemble during rainy days, and on Christmas morning, and on winter Sundays when Pastor Eric would bring church to them. The comfortable space was spread with handwoven rugs and cracked-leather reading chairs, tables for chess or puzzles or hot coffee, an old faded pool table with several patched holes in the felt, and cues of varying lengths that Levi and Danny never put away.

The rain sounded distant on this lower level of the house. Less threatening.

Beth needed no light to cross this area. The shadows had not changed in her lifetime. She had spent years in this room looking after Danny, rolling balls to him and building Lego trains with him and reading stories aloud for him while their parents worked.

Today it was nothing more than a bleak room that harbored ghosts. She didn't reminisce, but followed Herriot's urgent trot and passed straight through, into the home's formal entryway and then the dining room beyond. The dining room was connected to the kitchen. Off the rear of the kitchen were the housekeeper's room and a mudroom. At the side, through a sliding door, was a porch enclosed by a roof, a half wall, and screens.

From the dining room she couldn't see where Herriot had gone. All was dark except for a gold glow on the porch, an oil lamp's flame held steady by a bubbled hurricane lantern.

The brass lantern held some special meaning for Danny and their dad, though the men had never told her why. She guessed it had something to do with the one time they went camping alone together and lost all their gear in a flash flood—all their packs and food and bedding, everything except a cell phone, their horses, and an old Coleman lantern. How that might have turned into a positive memory for them was a private story between father and son.

Beth emerged into the kitchen. The sliding glass door between the kitchen and porch stood open, and the new-earth scents kicked up by the rain came into the house on a breeze.

The lamp formed a halo between Rose and the screens, reducing her to a dim, bowed version of her strong self. She sat on a wicker chair facing the sleeping morning.

Beyond her, Herriot's forelegs were propped against the low wall, nose twitching against the flimsy wire mesh, as if to detect what the humans' senses couldn't. Her tail waved calmly. Outside, the distortion of rain transformed the nearby barn's moth light into a bobbing firefly.

Beth hesitated in the kitchen, unsure if it was the right time to approach her mother, and if it was, what the proper posture would be: Comforting? Penitent? Grieved? Reassuring?

"Beth's up." Her mother was looking at Herriot, and her chilly tone rooted Beth to the floor.

Half of Levi's face came into the lamplight. The other half, like the dark side of the moon, stayed in shadow. Levi was looking at their mother with barely veiled impatience. He didn't seem to care if Beth was up, but she withdrew into the kitchen shadows.

"Don't bury him here," Levi said.

"All the Borzois who ever set foot on American soil are buried here," her mother replied.

"You'd put him in the very ground that you intend to sell?"

"Maybe I don't want to sell it after all. The insurance—"

"By the time you pay for the hospital and the funeral, you won't have enough left over to buy that fat jockey Darling a breakfast!"

"Levi. Watch your volume."

He complied but stood up and leaned over her, trading one form of intensity for another. Their mother seemed unaffected by his show.

"Don't tell me a measly life-insurance policy changed your mind."

"My mind was never made up. I only thought that selling this place would be essential to his recovery. But now—I can't help but wonder if the very suggestion was what killed him."

"Beth killed him," Levi said.

Her mother didn't defend her.

Levi's voice dropped so that it was difficult for Beth to hear. "What does it matter? He's gone now. Danny's not old enough to take on this piece of hell on earth, and I don't want it."

"No one's making you stay, Levi."

"You can't make a go of this place without me."

Yes, we can, Beth thought. *We have Jacob and Roy, Emory and Eric. We just don't have any money.*

"Now's not the time to be making such big decisions," Rose said.

"When will it be right? Eighteen months will find us without our shirts in the middle of winter, and we'll all pretend to be surprised by that. Unless we act now."

"What do you propose? You want to sell this place just so you can get your investment out of the dirt and run off to your own life? Where would you go? What would you do?"

"I'd make a *living*. What kind of life is this, breaking our backs day in and day out? I pour my sweat and blood into the filth of this land, and it's never, ever satisfied." Levi's voice was filled with disgust. "I want wealth. That's all I ask for."

"You have no idea what true wealth is," Rose said.

Levi changed his approach. He squatted next to his mother's chair and took her hand, softened his tone. "Every day we hold on to this ranch we get deeper and deeper into the money hole."

Rose shook her head. "Men rely on us. We can't pretend they're not a factor."

"How do you expect to take care of them or pay Beth's debts if we don't do something drastic?"

At the screens, Herriot went still. A low growl vibrated at the bottom of her throat. Beth watched her dog through rising tears. Levi and Rose were too wrapped up in their own dilemma to worry about Herriot's distraction.

"The market for selling might be better next spring—"

"Mom, this trouble is bigger than we are."

Rose supported her forehead with her other hand. "Who wants a ranch these days? It's too big for the romantic types who think ranching is a dreamy life; it's too small for the commercial ventures."

"We're sitting on prime real estate."

"Parts of it are—what are you suggesting? That we subdivide it? What a nightmare. I wouldn't have what it takes. It would be like dicing up your father's body and feeding it to vultures. I'd rather try to reach an agreement with a single buyer. Even Darling. Maybe he'd let the four of us stay here, work the place for him."

Levi recoiled, and Beth felt nausea shake her by the shoulders.

"This land isn't going to Darling," Levi said, and he spoke it like a vow.

His tone jarred Beth's forgotten nightmare loose from her sleepy memory. In half a second she recalled everything: She and Levi standing at the creek. A wolf with a bloody muzzle sleeping at her feet. Levi raising the rifle to his shoulder and taking aim.

At their father dressed in white, standing on the opposite bank.

The rifle shot and impact were silent and weightless. The weapon didn't recoil when it was discharged. Her father didn't reel when hit. But his blood was gushing and noisy, falling into the creek water like a sudden heavy rain.

Dream and reality tangled long enough for Beth to believe Levi had murdered their father, which was ridiculous. Her eyes darted through shadows of the kitchen and porch, looking for a rifle, for blood. Of course, there was neither in this space. There was only the notable absence of any sorrow for the man who had loved them all so much.

Beth shook off the horror of the dream but couldn't shed her rising wariness of her big brother.

"I can't leave this place," her mother said. "I can't even think of it now. Maybe if your father were with me—I thought I could, but I need . . . I need time."

"What if I told you that you wouldn't ever have to leave it?" Levi said. "That I know a way to keep you here forever, without another day of worry about how we're going to make it?"

Her mother's profile was like a child's in the lamplight, with a hopeful, lifted chin.

"I called Sam Johnson today," Levi said.

The name filled Beth with as much dread as Darling's did.

"The developer?" Rose's voice reflected Beth's shock. She stood now, nearly as tall as her firstborn. Between them, Herriot's growl rose a notch and the glistening tips of her fine fur rose off the back of her neck.

"Of course the developer."

"We can't sell the land Sam wants to buy."

"We *can* sell it, it's just that no one wants to."

"Don't act so dense. It's prime," Rose argued. "Two thousand acres of our best land—the best irrigated, the best soil. We sell that, and the cows can't survive. The ranch can't survive. If you think

I'll parcel off little plots to that man and give up the Blazing B just so I can live in this house"—she stomped her foot on the drum-like floorboards—"you don't understand my love for it at all."

"Settle down. He doesn't want those acres anymore."

"Then what on earth does he want?"

"Sam's a generous man, Mom. He only wants what's best for us."

"That's not how I would have characterized the proposal he presented to us last year."

"But this time I was the one with the proposal. And he was very interested in my thoughts."

Beth leaned in, placed her hand on the cool metal door frame of the open slider, not wanting to miss a word. If Levi was about to be her savior, she'd be stunned. Grateful, but stunned. And a little frightened of what he might demand from her in return.

"Is it too much to ask that you share those thoughts with me before you go around making business proposals with the world?" Rose asked.

Levi took a step back and pretended to look wounded. "What's wrong with you? I'm standing here with a plan to bail us out of an impossible situation, and you're treating me like I'm still a kid. We all have to grow up now, don't we? Dad's gone and I'm the only one who can see straight. It's you and me now, just the two of us to save this place."

Rose took a deep breath, silenced whatever words bubbled on her lips, and turned her palm up toward him. *Fine. Continue.*

"I asked Sam to become an investor."

"No sane man would pour his cash down a drain like this."

"Not an investor in the Blazing B, per se. But a partner of sorts."

"In *what*, Levi?"

"In the Blazing B Resort."

Beth's mind crawled with an image of fat city slickers in shiny new cowboy boots and too-tight jeans riding Hastings and Gert.

"A dude ranch?" Rose's tone was disbelieving. "You want to turn our home into a dude ranch?"

"That's such a bad label for a full-scale resort. Do you know what we can do on sixty-five hundred acres? In eighteen months we can have condos up on the river and be taking reservations for pool rides in the mountains. We can have seasonal events, offer classes, spas, cookouts—"

"No. No. I can't believe you think that's a good idea."

"It's been done before, right here in this valley. How do you think ranchers are making it? Even the ones who aren't staring down the throat of a monster lawsuit have come up with all kinds of creative ways to make ends meet."

"It can't work."

"The model works. The numbers work. In fact, they work so well that Sam will tackle Darling's money for us. Wipe it off the charts."

Rose's hands were on her hips now. "At what cost to us?"

"A very small one."

"How small, Levi?"

"It's a partnership with him or lose the land entirely. No price would be too great."

"Levi. Give me a number."

Levi looked at Herriot, who dashed along the wall to the corner of the room, ears and tail alert. "We'd get to live here, with guaranteed employment for as long as the resort was operational." Rose's hands fell to her sides. Her son would not look her in the eye. "Negotiable salaries, benefits, free housing."

"He'd take the land," Rose said. "All of it."

"We'd keep a fifteen percent stake in the profits."

The insulting number dropped a smothering silence over the room. Rose had no ready reply, no retort. She sank back into her chair.

"Sam would incorporate everything. You'd get a voting seat on the board," Levi said. "Or I would, if you don't want it."

"That's why you don't want me to bury your father here. The family cemetery—"

"It will probably have to be . . . relocated. It's in a bad place. For a resort."

"You never pretended to love your family legacy more than you loved profitable thinking," Rose whispered. "The men who count on us now—there's no room for them in a place like the one you're describing. You'd throw them out."

"It's time to save ourselves, Mom. We're the ones who need help this time. Sam's offering it."

Herriot barked once, then growled again. But whatever was out there—a fox looking for shelter under the porch, a cottonwood tree bent into villainous shapes by the rainfall—was less of a threat than what was going on in this small screened room.

Beth stepped into the reach of the oil lamp's light. "What about Garner?" she asked.

Levi flinched. Beth looked at Rose.

"Dad thinks—thought Garner could help us out." Her mother's face was unreadable.

"Who's Garner?" Levi asked.

"I think he's our grandfather," Beth said. "Grandpa Remke."

"He's dead," Levi said. He looked at Rose. "You told us he died."

"But he's alive. Isn't he, Mom?"

Rose pushed herself out of the chair. The wicker creaked and squeaked. "He's dead to me," she said.

Levi's expression might have been distorted by the shadows of the flickering flame, but Beth thought he was relieved by this proclamation, as if Garner's very existence might undermine his carefully laid plans to do business with Sam Johnson.

"Dad thought Garner could help—"

"Sam can help," Levi said.

"But maybe Garner could help us"—Beth groped for words—"less . . . commercially. More personally."

"Your father meant well," Rose said, "but he was always an optimist."

"But what if we could keep Sam's fingers out of the ranch?"

"I don't think you have too much wisdom to offer us at this point, little sister."

"Why not? Because what the rest of us might want will mess up your precious business deal? Cut you out of a nice little profit? What perks are Sam going to give you for cooking up this brilliant scheme, Levi? How's he going to line your pockets with gratitude?"

"That's enough," Rose said. "That's enough. Fortunately a deal like this takes awhile to draw up. Long enough for all of us to have time to settle down. We'll pay respects to your father, and then we'll move on. Levi, call Sam in the morning and tell him I'm ready to take the next steps, on one condition."

"We're not really in a position—"

"One condition. I will make your life so much harder if you want to argue with me. You're still my son, and this ranch is still mostly mine."

Levi crossed his arms across his chest.

"Your father will be buried in that cemetery along with his father and grandfathers, and the daughter we lost before Beth came along. And Sam will just have to deal with it, because it's not going to move, and neither am I."

"Done," Levi said.

Beth wanted to blame Levi for this terrible turn of her life, and yet she was to blame for all of it.

"I think Danny should have a say in this," Beth said, and at the same time, Herriot's posture shifted and caught the corner of Beth's eye.

Divided attention, when combined with darkness, could be a deceptive thing. Her mother looked like she might agree with Beth, but before she could say so, Herriot's growl became a disturbing snarl. As Beth turned her head, the light and shadow created illusions. She thought she saw, beyond the screen, the glassy green flicker of wild-animal eyes catching the lamp's glow.

Her brain suggested *wolf* at the same time that Herriot's hind legs launched her high onto the screen. All three people in the room turned as one to the dog. Her thick claws penetrated the lightweight mesh and shredded it like newspaper as she dropped back to the floor.

Beth shouted, lunged for the dog's collar, and missed. Teeth bared and fur electrified, the Appenzeller leaped again and this time went through the fresh hole.

A terrible tumble of snarls and snapping jaws ensued.

A crevasse of dread opened up in Beth's mind. In one motion, while Levi and Rose were still statues, Beth grabbed the cool handle of the oil lamp with one hand and ripped out a floppy panel of screen with her other so that the opening was large enough for her to follow. She leaned into the wall with her hip and swung her legs over the edge, screaming at the dog fight as if words alone could break it up.

As her weight shifted forward and she felt herself slipping off the wet sill toward the ground, she remembered she was barefoot.

A ground cover of chipped granite rocks bit into the balls of her feet and, on the right, cut deep. Her disruptive shouts became a cry of pain. She fell forward into a smacking belly flop on the damp ground.

Her elbow and the oil lamp hit the ground at the same time. Her fingers released the handle. The lamp tipped, and the glass globe protecting the flame shattered.

In the *whoosh* of flame that flared to campfire size, Beth saw the dogs unfurl from their tangled ball of mud and tails into two

distinct animals that were unevenly matched. Herriot had the dis-
advantage of a smaller size and unrestrained boldness. Rain sizzled
and raised some smoke as it hit the puddle of spilled oil, but it didn't
quell the flames.

Through the barrier of fire, Beth's eyes met the wolf's. The
wild animal shuddered, as if shaking itself off of the encounter with
Herriot, then bolted. The Appenzeller gave chase, ignoring Beth's
commands that she come back.

The porch door hit the side of the house as Levi walked out
with a blanket. He approached the mess without urgency, then
unfurled the blanket and dropped it on top of the small pool of
flaming oil. The fuel was trapped by the boundaries of the soaked
ground and would burn itself out shortly. Her brother crouched
next to her body.

"You're a drain on this family," Levi said. "Expect me to do my
best to boot you out of it."

She lowered her forehead to the mud.

18

Without returning to the house for her shoes, Beth limped to the barn as the sky's intense midnight blue took on the dusty denim hue of morning. The last scattered drops of rain cut paths through the mud on her face and clothes, and the oily smoke coated her nostrils.

She needed to find Garner. She needed to find Herriot. She needed to bandage her bleeding foot. Examining it in the weak light before she shoved her toes into a pair of muck boots, she realized she might need stitches.

Tending to her injury, then, was the first thing she needed to do. But she sensed her mother was fundamentally wrong about the time it would take Levi to close a deal with Sam. If Sam had accepted it within beats of her father's last breath, Beth would assume that the two men had been in discussion behind the family's collective back for much longer than Levi claimed. Perhaps the deal was already well underway.

Beth whistled for Hastings, slipped onto his back without a saddle, and rode out. She took him past the torn-up screen in the empty porch, past the smoky puddle of lantern oil, where the broken brass lamp was still tipped on its side. She went directly to the Hub house, to Jacob and his father, Dr. Roy.

She had loved the Hub until the day she stole that saddle. It was as honest a place as any on the ranch, and she herself was no longer honest.

By the time she arrived and slid off Hastings' smooth back, blood had collected, thick and sticky, in the toe of the muck boot. She tried to walk normally up the steps to the front door, thinking the pressure would help staunch the flow. It was nearly five o'clock, guessing by the color of the sky. Everyone should be up.

Jacob opened the door before she reached it, fully dressed and alert, but sleep and sorrow still pulled at the soft skin under his eyes. He waited for her to speak.

"Got a first-aid kit?" she asked.

Less than a minute later she was sitting on the rim of an old bathtub and rinsing her injury under warm water gushing from the spigot. Her pajama bottoms and tank top were covered in mud, which also colored the tips of her long hair. At this point, only her hands and feet were clean. A slippery bar of gray soap decorated with bloody bubbles danced at the drain under the pressure of the water.

Jacob entered with the kit she'd asked for and leaned over her to set it in the dry part of the tub. In the close quarters, the width of his shoulders shielded her from the loss of her father, the risk to her dog, the greed of her brother, the grief pouring off her mother and Danny. For a fleeting moment, Beth felt protected.

Jacob straightened up and shoved his hands into his pockets. Beth flipped the box open and grabbed the bottle of peroxide, which she poured over the gash. The resulting bubbles were fierce.

"You'll need stitches," he said.

She set the bottle on the lip of the tub, then rifled the white metal box for a butterfly bandage. "Nah. I have a healer's touch, remember?"

"Even healers need their tools."

She nodded noncommittally. "I need to find Herriot."

"I sent Emory out to have a look at her tracks."

"Should be plenty. All that rain." She feared that Emory would instead discover Herriot's mangled body. "You don't think that—"

"Herriot's the smartest dog we've got. She's fine."

"It was a wolf she went after," Beth said. "A wolf. She's an idiot."

"Probably a coyote. She's big enough to handle one of those."

"I saw them," she whispered. "It wasn't a fair match."

Mud smeared Jacob's white T-shirt sleeve where she'd gripped his shoulder for support as she hopped into the house. Except for that handprint he'd be a model for a laundry detergent commercial. Next to him, Beth felt small and filthy. She focused on applying pressure to the cut.

"Well, let's wait and see what Emory thinks," Jacob said.

A new voice said, "Emory thinks we ought to let the wolves have the run of the place." Beth twisted on her perch and saw Dr. Roy at the bathroom door. The man handed a stained cup of coffee to Jacob and set a second one on the back of the toilet tank, where she could reach it.

"Better the mythical wolves than that Sam Johnson," Jacob said to his father.

Beth shot a glance at Jacob. "How'd you know about that?"

"Sam crashed the ranchers' coffee klatch yesterday," Jacob explained.

"He didn't crash it," Roy said. His teeth were stained from coffee, but his smile was so disarming as to make a person look past the imperfect hygiene. "Levi invited him to be there."

"He did?"

"No need to worry, Beth," Dr. Roy said. "We were polite. I didn't even do anything worse than to spit once in his coffee cup. Yours there, I put a little cream and sugar."

"I love you too, Dr. Roy."

"You should have been calling me just Roy a long time now, hon."

Beth shot a glance at Jacob, looking for explanation. He'd never objected to *Dr. Roy* before. Jacob was staring at the oily swirls floating on top of his black brew. Probably, she thought, it was the man's way of offering his condolences.

Dr. Roy said, "That's some cut there."

"It'll be fine once I get it clean." She washed it with soap a second time, then splashed another shot of peroxide on it.

"Better dump those boots. They'll never be the same."

"Levi didn't tell us about his proposal until just a few minutes ago," she said, eying the cut. The bleeding just wasn't going to stop.

"Well, that explains why we didn't hear it from Rose," Jacob said to his dad.

Beth glanced up. "Nothing is beneath my big brother, is it? I don't even think his timing was an accident. Dad hasn't been gone two days. We haven't even buried him yet."

After a long silence Jacob said, "I'll be there to help dig the gravesite later this morning. Okay if I bring Wally with me?"

"I'd love that. Thanks." It would be such a relief not to be alone with Levi for that job. She noticed how tense her shoulders and neck were. "How did Emory and Pastor Eric take the news?"

The men sipped their coffee in unison. After a pause, Jacob said, "Eric stuck to his routine for the day, didn't say anything."

"He stacked the hay bales three different ways," Dr. Roy said over his coffee cup.

"I guess that's Pastor Eric's response to everything," Beth observed. "Work harder, work longer."

"Pretty much."

"And Emory?"

"Emory smoked two packs of cigarettes."

"That's not good. Thanks for not saying anything to Mom."

Dr. Roy said, "I had a strong hunch things weren't as they seemed. I think the others did too."

"It's really important the associates don't hear about this," she said.

"They haven't yet," Jacob said.

"Let's keep it that way for now. A resort here would change everything. For the worse," Beth muttered. "Except that we could probably guarantee the four of you jobs for life. The others . . ." She sighed.

Jacob said, "I think Eric and Emory were of a mind to escape that kind of living."

"What kind?"

"The kind where everything's guaranteed. Where the guarantees cost a lot."

"And you?" Beth asked.

"I don't know. Maybe it's time to find my own place."

The announcement was crushing. He was more than capable of managing his own place, but she couldn't imagine him leaving them now. And she couldn't imagine trying to stop him.

"Well, this is all my fault," she said. "I did it, I'll have to undo it. Let me handle Levi."

"You're too hard on yourself, hon," Dr. Roy said.

His gentleness was like a hug from her father, a kindness that softened her.

"I tipped over the first domino," she said.

Roy shrugged. "I'd say dominoes have been falling all across this land since long before you were ever born. Who's to say which one was first? Besides, who knows what you really set in motion, little Beth? Tiles are still clickety-clacking all over the place. Make no judgment till they come to rest. There might be some good out of it yet."

Beth couldn't imagine any good greater than the awfulness of her father's death. But she hadn't come here for argument.

"Do you know a Garner Remke?" she asked Roy.

"Sure, I remember Garner. Mean old bear in real estate down

in the valley. Made his fortune years before that, in California I think. Died awhile back, didn't he?"

"You tell me."

"How can I?"

"Because no one else will. Is he my grandfather?"

Dr. Roy's eyebrows both went up. "I didn't realize your mother felt so strongly about this as to keep that a secret from you."

"But is he?" she demanded.

"Yes. Rose's father."

"Honestly, is he alive?"

"Honestly, I don't know. Why do you need to?"

"My dad said I ought to go find him."

"Aahhh." Dr. Roy nodded and let the steam of his coffee rise into his fading gray eyes.

"I know he and Mom had a falling out, and that he's rich. Or was."

"Rich enough to try to buy her love for your dad," Dr. Roy said.

"He tried to pay her not to marry?" Jacob said.

"Tried to send her to Europe, to some top-notch medical school."

"Med school? Mom wanted to be a doctor?" How had Beth reached the age of twenty-two without knowing this? Beth had wanted to be a vet since she was ten years old. It hurt that her mother hadn't tapped this shared connection.

"Garner wanted her to be a doctor. At least, that's how Abel told it. Rose wanted to be a rancher's wife. Well, Abel's wife. She picked him over her father's money."

"I can't believe he'd try to pay her out of a marriage. That's insulting, ancient thinking."

"Oh, I think the idea appeals to every girl's father now and then. It wouldn't have been beneath Abel, but you've got a good head on your shoulders."

"No, I've just never had anyone for him to object to," she joked.

"Good girl. You keep it that way. Watch out for horse thieves like this young man here." He kicked at Jacob's knee with a stock-inged foot.

Peroxide bubbles dripped off the side of her foot into the drain.

Quite late, Beth registered Roy's innuendo that Jacob was a "horse thief" she needed to keep an eye on. What was that sup-posed to mean? Jacob was leaning against the wall and looking up at the cracked plastic in the light fixture over the sink, inscrutable.

"If you had to find out whether Garner is still alive, where would you start your search?" she asked Dr. Roy. But she was look-ing at Jacob, squeezing the skin of her foot and wishing it would stop bleeding already.

"Do a title search, maybe? Find out what properties he owned back in the day, see if he still owns them. Someone down at the courthouse can tell you how to do that, I suppose. You know any-thing about that, son?"

Jacob snapped out of whatever thoughts were preoccupying him. "I'll go fetch your shoes," he said to Beth. He turned toward the doorway.

"Please don't go," Beth said.

The men bumped into each other at the door, awkwardly responding to Beth's request without understanding it. A slop of cooling coffee splashed over Jacob's hand and onto the floor. He shook his fingers free of the dripping.

She had meant that she hoped he wouldn't leave the Blazing B now. She wanted him to stay, just as he'd stayed after he graduated from college though he could have gone anywhere. She needed him, and even Dr. Roy, to stay here. She needed these trustworthy men to guide her through the additional terrible losses that lay ahead. She imagined Jacob standing by her, holding Levi at arm's length with scorpions and whatever else was needed to protect her and Danny.

Beth felt the ten years' difference in their ages as if she were twelve all over again.

"I meant, before you get my shoes, do you have any Super Glue? It'll hold better than a bandage," she said.

"Jacob, get this girl to the hospital."

"They'll just glue it there," Beth protested. "I can do it myself in less time."

"Whatever happened to good old-fashioned stitches?" Jacob asked.

"Progress."

A cut from a rock would be so simple for God to heal. She didn't understand anything.

"Won't it get infected?"

"It'll be fine. I need to get back to the house. I need to be with Danny."

Jacob bent again over her shoulder, but this time reached out to take hold of her foot, wrapping his hand atop hers. His palm was warm and his fingers were firm as he turned her ankle to see the cut on the ball under her toes.

Beth turned her head away from the closeness of his beard. Inexplicably, tears poked the back of her eyes.

"Do you have any glue or not?"

"Emory's got some."

"Go get it then. Please."

He didn't let go right away, and she felt an unexpected impatience toward him rising up in her throat. He should just do what she wanted him to do—what she needed him to do. *Stay with me. Protect me. Love me.*

She shouldn't have to ask for everything.

He released her foot, and her skin felt instantly cold. He left the bathroom, and the chill of his departure raced over her back.

Beth, feeling Dr. Roy's eyes on her, reached up and turned off the water.

19

When the Friday morning tour bus pulled up in front of the Burnt Rock post office at precisely nine forty-five, Garner and Hank rose from the bench where they'd been waiting for it to arrive.

Garner extended an envelope to Hank. The legal document inside officially designated eighty percent of Garner Remke's net worth to the Mathilde Werner Wulff Foundation. The men clasped hands.

"I am beyond words, Garner. Never in the history of the Sweet Assembly has anyone been so . . ." He seemed to have trouble finding the right word.

"Reckless?" Garner provided. "I just want God to know how much I'm expecting to receive."

Both men laughed from their bellies.

"The distributions should all be final by end of business Monday."

"That's mighty quick," Hank said.

"No time for me to have second thoughts. Dotti Sanders talked me into the worst lunch of my life on Wednesday. She's a persuasive woman. If she gets wind of this she'll have me doubting my own name within two minutes."

"Best she don't find out then. And that Dr. Ransom too. She's a fine physician, but we all know she's not fond of us."

"What are you talking about? She likes you fine, Hank."

"I meant the Sweet Assembly."

"Yes, yes. She has strong opinions."

"Well, your gift gives us permission to dream big. I can see a paved road in our future, our own buses, international marketing. For a long time Kathy's been wanting to hire a counseling staff. Do positive-thinking seminars, that sort of thing. We can turn this place into a real destination. Maybe we'll build a hotel so people can stay as long as they actually need to find peace. There's no rushing the good Lord, you know."

The pressurized doors of the bus opened with a sound like a sigh.

"'You rush a miracle man, you get rotten miracles,'" Garner quipped. He wanted the conversation to end. Already the stone of remorse was sitting heavy in his stomach. He had never been more thankful for Trey Bateman's punctuality.

The youthful tour-bus driver was never late. When Garner had first met the college student last year, he expected the kid to wash out of his job quickly. Being a tour-bus driver required a punctuality not often respected by people too young to grasp the preciousness of time.

As it turned out, Trey was both aware of the clock and uniquely able to keep track of his sense of humor. During the summer months he made two round trips to Burnt Rock four days a week and was required, because he lived on his tips rather than his wages, to tell two sets of good canned jokes twice a day without repeating himself. Tourists didn't like to tip a comedian who was prone to forgetting what he'd already said. When Trey returned to the job this past May after completing one of his college terms, Garner was impressed. He booked a ride on Trey's bus to evaluate the young man's skill.

Being a man who was sometimes pressed to remember what day of the week it was, Garner decided the kid was as good at history and trivia as he was at jokes. Trey's job gave him permission to talk as much as he wanted to about everything that excited him. He was a top-of-his-class wildlife biologist, a regular Jeff Corwin, but more nerdy. His specialty was wildlife of the Rocky Mountains, but Trey was such a story chaser that he had a brain full of worldwide trivia.

On that May day, as Garner disembarked in Burnt Rock, he had asked Trey, "What are you doing in a tin can like this? You should be pitching your own show to the Discovery Channel."

"I'm not at that point on my ten-year plan," Trey had answered. "Lord willing, I'll get there in year eight. Right now, I need to pay for grad school."

If Trey had any flaw, it was that he was as outspoken about his personal religious beliefs as he was about everything else he liked. Garner found this simultaneously irritating and admirable. He tipped the kid fifty bucks. Trey tried to refuse it, Garner refused harder, and the pair had been on a first-name basis ever since.

Today Trey stepped off the rumbling bus with a clipboard in hand. His careless brown curls were thick and long and covered his ears, but Garner forgave him this sloppiness because the hair stayed out of his eyes, which were always contagiously happy. He wore gray slacks and a maroon-colored vest and a matching bow tie around his throat, which needed a button-down collar to go with it. Instead Trey wore a "Burnt Rock Café" T-shirt underneath the vest, its design stolen by the proprietor Mazy from a more famous café elsewhere in the world.

"This here is Pastor Hank," Trey said as Hank waved and people poured off the bus with their sun hats and tote bags and hungry children. Garner quickly counted about fifteen souls. The season was winding down. A few aimed their camera phones at the post office's weather-beaten wood sign. "Everyone in search of Miracle

Mattie will want to follow him. The rest of you might want to start your Burnt Rock visit at Hank's Hardware. While Hank's away, the wife doles out some fantastic bargains."

Hank guffawed as if this were the first time Trey had ever said such a thing.

A middle-aged woman dressed neatly in athletic shoes and a green tracksuit hugged her large purse to her tummy and attached herself to Hank right away. She was quiet, her eyes shaded by the visor of an overlarge sun hat. Garner noticed her because it appeared she traveled alone, which was unusual, and also because she fidgeted as if having trouble standing comfortably. She blinked hard and often.

Trey glanced at her several times as he explained where to find the nearest restrooms, when they should gather for the tour of the little mining museum, how to secure a limited saddle on the old mule train, and what time the visitors needed to be seated on the return bus if they wanted to avoid a ride back on one of those mules, which would take three days to reach the bottom of the mountain. The large-hat woman was the only one who didn't reward Trey with a smile. Her posture was distressed. Hank kept discreetly scooting away from her; she kept not-so-discreetly matching his step and closing the gap, like a terrified child who had been refused the comfort of holding her father's hand.

Then Trey handed the group off to Hank, and the pastor-retailer stepped out of the woman's personal space as if he'd been freed from prison.

"This way to a great tale of signs and wonders!" he said, leading the cluster of people to a smaller bus provided by Dotti Sanders' rafting company. "Sorry to seat you again so soon, but trust me—you'll prefer this to the two-mile hike uphill. This way, you won't be too tired to partake of all the blessings that await you. So if you come now with an open mind, you might leave today with a lighter heart."

In front of Garner, a kid who had to keep hiking up his over-large pants whispered to his buddy, "Did he say, 'come now with an open wallet'?"

"Yes, and you're guaranteed to leave with it lighter." The friend smirked.

Garner stood aside and Trey joined him as they waited for the tourists to determine whether to go to church or out for coffee.

"Hey, old man," Trey said, extending his hand in greeting.

"Hey, young pup." Garner accepted the strong grip. "You spending your break on this sideshow today?"

Trey nodded and tipped his head toward the blinking woman. "Think I'd better keep an eye on her. She went pretty green on the way up, and it looks like she's alone."

"She sick?"

"I don't know. She ignored me when I asked if she was feeling okay."

"Women don't like anyone to call out their weaknesses."

"I don't think that's what I was doing," Trey said. "I've been praying for her. And I feel the Spirit telling me she needs God's healing touch."

"For goodness' sake, you didn't tell her that, did you?"

"Of course not. I don't proselytize on the bus. They're a captive audience. But if someone needs help I'm not just going to leave her at the curb, because in my humble opinion, that assembly doesn't represent anything truly Christian. It's come so far from what it was to Mattie and Jonathan. Want to join me? There's room on the shuttle."

Two trips to the Sweet Assembly in one week couldn't hurt Garner's case before God. Money, attendance—whatever he wanted, he could have. Even if Trey was right about the place not being a legitimate church anymore.

Garner gestured in the direction of Cat's offices. "Why don't we take her over to Dr. Ransom's? She's right across the street."

161

"This woman might be better off at Mathilde's."

Garner was taken aback. "What do you have against Cat?"

"Nothing specific. Just a gut feeling. You could try to see if the lady will go, but she's sticking pretty close to Hank. She might have to be disappointed by him before she opens up to other options."

Hank was waiting to board the shuttle last, and it seemed the woman was determined to do the same.

"Well, let her have that then," Garner said. "God can heal anywhere—you believe that even more than I do."

"True, but I'll say it again: that place up on the hill isn't exactly a paragon of holiness." Trey locked up his bus while Garner waited.

"Does it matter? Jesus didn't do any of his healing in a church, did he?"

"Or in a doctor's office, now that I think of it."

Garner laughed and clapped Trey on the back. "Okay, okay."

The blinking woman in green held her hat down atop her head, though there was no breeze to blow it off, and studied the steps of the bus as if they were Mount Evans. Hank offered her a hand, and she accepted his assistance with effusive thanks.

During the bumpy, jarring two-mile ride up the mountain she stared at the floor, though the stark ridges and sharp blue skies captured the attention of everyone else. Garner and Trey sat together in the back, bumping shoulders as the shuttle hit ruts and rocks. Garner felt pretty confident that Trey was spending the journey in prayer.

As they disembarked at the path that passed under latticed shelters and into the Sweet Assembly foyer, Trey said, "Got a favor to ask you, Garner."

"The cannabis I have is designated for legal medicinal use only—just so we're clear."

"You have a strange sense of humor."

"It is from a different generation."

"After my shift ends Saturday, I was hoping to head out for a short expedition. Want to check in on a pride of mountain lions that live up over the ridge. I'd head out before dawn Sunday, plan to be back Tuesday night. But I want to make the most of the days— any chance I can crash at your place Saturday night and Tuesday night? I can sleep on the floor, bring my own food."

"Nonsense, I'm glad for the company. In fact, I'm having dinner with a friend Saturday night. You should join us. She said I could bring someone."

"Sounds great. Wouldn't happen to be at good old Dotti's, would it?"

Garner winked at him. "Cat Ransom," he said.

"Sweet. Tell her I'm a gluten-intolerant vegan who only eats organic macrobiotics. Maybe she'll disinvite me."

"I couldn't allow it," Garner said.

In the bright foyer of the Sweet Assembly, the solitary woman in the hat paused to regard Mathilde's portrait, a photograph of her taken around 1911, when she was well into middle age. In fact, Garner noticed, she was about the same age as the woman, who reached out to touch Mathilde's cheeks with her fingertips. She stood there, lost in her own mind for quite a long time, and Garner had the uncomfortable feeling that he was intruding on the woman's private hopes in the very same way that the tourists who came here intruded on his—even if they did buy herbs at his tea shop afterward. But Garner didn't want to be guilty of that kind of invasion. And so he turned away from her and focused on the images on the other side of the room, several photographs of a Southern Ute tribe taken in the 1920s.

These people were the reason why all the details of Mathilde's spiritual perspective weren't that important, Hank had once said to Garner. What was truly miraculous about Jonathan Wulff's encounter with his grandmother's fire pit—in Hank's opinion—was that it eventually led to an amazing archaeological discovery: Mathilde had built her fire and scooped her ashes right on top of a Southern Ute burial ground, where a man of significant rank in his tribe had been buried along with his favorite horse, according to custom. The Ute people had graciously cooperated with Burnt Rock's efforts to preserve the place, because their chief at the time had said that it was clear the spirit world hadn't barred the Wulff family from its blessings.

"You know that's how Burnt Rock got its name," Trey said at Garner's shoulder. He'd left the door to peer at the photograph of several men with their horses, the lineage of which they had acquired centuries earlier from Spanish explorers.

"What? How?"

"The Ute burial customs."

"I know they killed the man's favorite horse," Garner said. "More than one, if he was important enough."

"Imagine that in our celebrity-crazed culture. Can you imagine what a rock star's memorial service would look like?"

"Young man, that is cynical and wrong."

"I apologize. The Utes also burned down the man's home and torched his possessions. Some of the rocks in the area still bear the scorch marks. Hence, Burnt Rock."

"Is that so? I've seen those black rocks, but I didn't know what caused it. Why did they do that?"

"It was believed he'd have more use of those things in the afterlife than his family would have in this one. There were others to provide for their needs. A community."

"Still, that's an unfortunate custom for the wife and kids."

"I was thinking the horses got the worst end of the deal," Trey said.

The woman at Mathilde's portrait gave a little gasp as if she realized that she'd been left behind or had been pricked by an invisible pain. The dry climate might have resulted in an unexpected shock when she rubbed her fingers across the image, which she wasn't supposed to touch. Whatever it was, she hurried into the sanctuary, hand on hat, purse on stomach, and Garner thought he saw pain line her face. She stumbled at the threshold but recovered her balance quickly and went on.

"Maybe she's not sick at all," Trey said. "Just odd."

"No," Garner said, because he recognized something wrong with the way she had stumbled, something that told him it couldn't be blamed on a wobbly shoe or frayed carpet. "I think your first instinct was correct."

"I'm sorry to hear that," Trey said.

The pair moved quickly to follow the woman inside.

Hank's voice was flowing in the theatrical manner so familiar to Garner. He told exciting anecdotes of other visitors who had come to this site and experienced deliverance from all kinds of ailments, be they of body or soul. People of all faiths had experienced the love of God in whatever manner was most meaningful to them, and this love was available to all.

The woman in green stood in the aisle listening to his words, enraptured. She began to sway, but Garner couldn't reach her before she collapsed on the floor and finally lost hold of her hat.

When her whole body went into terrible, non-spiritual convulsions, the teenage smart-aleck with a chain through his nose wondered aloud what a tabloid might pay him for exclusive photos of this miracle, and his friend suggested a YouTube video might be more lucrative.

The mortified parents dragged them by fistfuls of T-shirts out of the sanctuary.

Trey knelt beside the woman and asked if anyone present was a doctor.

"I'll fetch Cat," Garner said, and he hurried out through a rear door where he knew he could find a phone.

20

Beth's path to Garner started in the family graveyard.

She wasn't looking for him when she went there with Danny to clear rocks from the site that would be hollowed for their father's coffin. She expected to find only Levi there, working and cursing her for not coming sooner.

Danny walked along beside her. He had spoken less than a paragraph's worth of words, big or small, since their father's death. He didn't speak to her now either, but his silence toward Beth was quite different from her mother's and Levi's, which felt more like a shunning. Though Danny had given up expressions of physical affection—hugging, kissing, even wrestling—back when he was ten or eleven, today he grabbed hold of his big sister's hand and held on to it until they reached the cemetery.

Every step on her injured foot felt like a walk across inhospitable ground, stabbing, stabbing. The glue held her cut together and showed no sign of infection, and yet the pain reminded her that she had no legitimate role in this land that couldn't abide foolishness.

Danny released Beth's fingers as they passed between two boulders, the closest thing the cemetery had to an entrance.

"It's just wrong to put someone you love in a hole," Danny

said. "I mean, I get it, the whole dust-to-dust thing, but still, it's just wrong."

The private cemetery was the only disordered spot in the expanse of the Blazing B. When it came time for them to go, family members picked their sites under the shelter of mature Wasatch maple trees, whose leaves would turn fiery red in the fall. It was for these trees that the original Borzois had named the ranch. The dead inserted themselves between or beside (and in a few cases, as far away as possible from) other long-gone family members. There were no neat rows of markers here, but a gathering of marble slabs and arched granite headstones and metal crosses as eclectic as the family personalities.

Rusty wire on stakes, and sometimes short garden fences—here a white picket, there a decorative black plastic—marked the coffin locations so that no errors would be made in digging. The siblings' grandfather was here, and their great-grandfather, and the wives and children, and some of the aunts and uncles, nieces and nephews, first and second and third cousins. That is, the ones who had chosen the ranching life over an easier one. A few beloved employees had also earned spots on these history-rich acres.

Abel Borzoi had requested a spot next to the tiny headstone of Beth's unnamed sister, where there was also room for Rose.

Beth, like her brothers, had been born at the Blazing B into the hands of their mother's midwife. According to the family stories, Rose stood when she delivered her babies, letting the strength of her legs, gravity, and women's intuition do the work.

Two years after Levi was born, Rose and Abel lost the child who would have been an older sister to Beth. Not to complications during delivery, but to a kick from a frantic cow who'd been separated from her calf. Rose had been in her second trimester. After a painful delivery, also at their home, the preterm girl had been placed in the ground, where she waited for her parents to tuck themselves around her.

When Beth and Danny reached the spot where Levi was digging, Danny stooped and started scooping rocks into a bucket they'd brought along. But Beth was alarmed to see that Levi had chipped a long rectangular shape out of the ground.

If the grave had been on any other cemetery in the nation, it would have looked entirely normal. But the proper hole for a Borzoi should have been four feet square and eleven feet deep, so that the coffin could be placed in the ground standing up. These ranchers were buried, quite literally, dead on their feet. Something that had started long ago as a wry joke had become a dying wish, and then an enduring family tradition.

"What are you doing?" she asked.

"Making some changes," he said.

"Why don't you wait for Jacob and Emory?" she said, hoping not to sound confrontational. "They're bringing the backhoe and some braces." She watched Levi thrust the spade into the ground softened by rain.

Levi didn't answer her, didn't stop. Sweat oozed from his face and neck.

Beth scanned the road in hopes that Jacob and Emory would arrive quickly. "It's wrong of you to do this," she said, gesturing to the hole.

"If it's still wrong five years from now, I'll concede to that."

"What's that supposed to mean?"

"It means I'm going to do it anyway."

Danny paused with a rock in his hand. His eyes flitted from Levi to their sister.

"You're cutting across Mom's plot," Beth said, though she was sure Levi knew this. "There's no room for her if you dig that way."

"She'll remarry and decide to lie somewhere else eventually."

Danny threw his rock back into the hole Levi had dug. He aimed right for the spot where it seemed Levi would thrust his shovel next. Instead, Levi interrupted his rhythm and pointed at the rock.

"Pick it up," Levi ordered.

Danny glared at him.

"Pick it up!" he repeated, and he jabbed his shovel at Danny's feet. Slowly, Danny stepped down into the hole. His eyes were defiant even while he went through the motions of obedience. When he bent to pick up the rock, Levi hit him with the flat of the shovel. It caught Danny between the shoulder blades and dropped him to his knees.

Beth yelled at Levi and reached for Danny, but he jabbed at her outstretched hand with the blade, and she withdrew. Danny swore at Levi and left the rock in the dirt. He climbed out of the hole, then stalked off.

"What was that about?" Beth demanded. "What do you think you're doing?"

Levi tossed a shovelful of soil, including Danny's potato-sized protest, into the growing heap beside the hole. "I'm going to change *everything*."

"Why?"

"Because Dad didn't. Couldn't. All this honor-the-land nonsense, this keep-the-herd-strong talk. Love God, serve the weak, blah blah blah. It's a nice campfire story, but that's all. Ranching is a dying way of life. Dad never wanted to admit it."

Beth looked away, feeling a sickening weakness around her heart. "You don't know what you're saying."

"Actually, I think I'm the only one in the family who wasn't brainwashed by all Dad's sweet philosophies."

"Okay. If you're so alone in the world, you can make these changes by yourself."

She turned away from her brother, unsure where Danny had gone. She had no intention of letting Levi get his way, but a man like him needed to think he was getting what he wanted, or else he'd make her life even more difficult.

Beth walked the maze of markers that was her family, looking for an alternate place for her father to rest. Which was more important, that he be buried in the location he wanted or in the posture he wanted? That would be for her mother to decide, not Levi. Beth would at least give her mother that choice. She would find an appropriate spot, then she would return with Jacob and Danny to dig it right.

It didn't take her long to determine where the site should be. Her great-great-grandfather, the founding father of the Blazing B, was buried near the center of the cemetery, under the largest maple. She surmised that its roots had long since crushed the pine box that held Romanov Borzoi. There weren't many graves nearby, because the massive, tangled system made digging too difficult.

How hard could it be, really, with modern machines? Beth decided the backhoe could be driven to this spot, and that putting her father next to his founding ancestor would be fitting.

In the event Jacob found some practical fault with this plan, she decided to keep looking around until he arrived. She ventured out a little farther. There were other options, but none as poetic as the one she'd picked.

At the back of the cemetery, nearest the creek that cut through the property, her eye caught sight of a small white marker that was barely the size of a dinner plate. If it hadn't been perfectly round, too symmetrical for a natural rock, she might not have noticed it. Also, it was planted unexpectedly close to the water, too close for a pine box to go eleven feet down without a soppy consequence.

She went to see what it was.

It was a garden stone, the kind one could create from a kit, bleached by the sun. It was plain, bearing none of the decorative bits of glass or broken tile pieces one might put into something for their garden. The inscription, such as it was, might have been scrawled with a stick into the cement before it set. There were the initials G. R., and a date that Beth recognized as her parents' wedding day.

Because the stone was so small, and because the place was too small for a body, and because Beth believed Garner Remke was in fact alive, she dropped to her knees and pried up the marker with her fingers and began to dig.

She didn't have to work too hard. The metal box was buried so close to the surface that she didn't even have to fetch a shovel or trowel before she hit the lid. A flat oval rock was tool enough to scoop the packed dirt away from the sides and create enough space for her hands to reach in and pull it out.

It was an old safety box, the kind about the size of the family Bible with a keyhole at the forward side of the hinged lid. It wasn't locked, but rust had frozen the hinges, and Beth had to apply some muscle to pry it open.

Fine dirt rained onto the papers inside as she exposed the contents to the light. Inside was an envelope that looked like it bore a greeting card. It was addressed to Mr. and Mrs. Abel Borzoi, from G. Remke. The return address was from a post office box in Burnt Rock, one of the very small mining towns up in the mountains. It wasn't far away as the eagle flew, but the rugged terrain isolated the residents and made for a slow drive.

The envelope contained a wedding card with glittery silver bells on the front and a poem printed in silver ink. The card was more yellow than ivory now. Under the pre-printed sentiment inside was a simple signature: "Sorry I can't make it, Dad."

A slip of paper fluttered out of the card. Beth picked it up. It was a check made out to "Abel or Rose Borzoi" dated twenty-five years ago. Ten thousand dollars.

Beth considered what this might mean in light of the story that Garner had tried to pay his daughter *not* to marry Abel. It seemed odd to her that such a father would then turn around and give the newlyweds a gift like this.

Underneath the card was a doctor's stethoscope. There was also a photograph of a young man with a little girl. She had olive-colored skin and long dark hair, which was unruly like the man's, and was too tall for the dress she wore. They were standing in front of a long, low-roofed building next to a sign that had been erected in the parking lot. "Remke Real Estate, Alamosa's Property Broker."

"That Mom?"

"Oh! You scared me!" Beth twisted at her waist to look up at Danny, who was bent over her, studying the photograph.

"Did he die in the war or something? Her dad? Is that why she'd bury a picture, like, because we don't have a body?"

"I don't know their story," she said. "Mom only said he died before Levi was born." Rose had never encouraged conversation about her biological father, though she encouraged their relationship with her stepfather.

Beth handed the picture to Danny and then, while he held it up to the sunlight, she tucked the greeting card and old check between the layers of cotton shirts she wore. She replaced the stethoscope and closed the box, then quickly reburied it.

Dusting her hands off on her jeans, she stood. "You keep that picture," she said. "Maybe sometime you can ask Mom to tell you what really happened."

Danny handed it back to her. "Don't know if I care."

She refused it. "Sure you do."

"Maybe last week I would've. But now . . ." He shrugged and glanced back in Levi's direction. But he tucked the picture into his hip pocket.

Though she couldn't see Levi, she could hear the sounds of shovel striking dirt rhythmically.

"Levi's grieving in his own way," Beth said, not sure why she was trying to defend his behavior to Danny. At fifteen, she was sure he understood the truth. "But it was wrong of him to hit you."

"Levi and Mom got all the same DNA," Danny said. "You and I got Dad's. So I can see how this is going to go down."

"How what is going to go down?"

"There's no point in fighting him, I guess."

"Danny. Our family doesn't fight."

"We do now. And there's nothing you can do about it."

Beth tamped down the dirt over Garner's box with her boots, trying to think of what to say. Nothing came to her, and Danny left again. She scooted the marker over the box with her foot and hoped her mother wouldn't visit the site before the next rain masked Beth's intrusion.

The rumbling of a truck engine covered up Levi's noise. Beth hurried to the place where Jacob and Emory had parked. Next to Levi's rock-star truck, a shiny beast overequipped even for the Blazing B, Jacob's looked like it had just steered its way out of the Dust Bowl. The old beater towed a flatbed trailer that carried a backhoe.

Emory was unloading shovels from the truck bed, and Wally leaped out over the wheel well with his favorite shovel over his head.

"Hiya, Wally," Beth said when he landed right in front of her.

"Hello." His greeting lacked his usual enthusiasm. "You're the good man's daughter, aren't you?"

"That's right."

"These are sad times."

"They are." Beth swallowed and looked down at her dusty boots.

"It's too bad he had to go. That Abel Borzoi, he was a godly man."

"Yes, he was."

"Someone you can't forget."

"That's right."

"Tell me your name again?"

By the grace of God Beth was able to see some humor in that line of conversation. One corner of her mouth lifted. "It's Beth."

"Well, Beth, there's a rumor going around." Here he fished his small spiral-bound notebook out of his jeans and thumbed to a page toward the back. He read, "Levi is selling the ranch because his father is gone." Then he shook his head at this sad prospect as if it were the first time he was hearing it. "Is this true?"

"Not quite yet," Beth said. "I'm searching for a way to prevent it from becoming true."

"Are you now?" Wally said. "And how's that going for you?"

Beth gave her head a light shake. "How about I keep you posted? And would you please write down, 'Don't tell anyone about this'? It would be real upsetting to the other associates."

"I will. You bet. You're a good girl. You have your daddy in you. He was the hardest-working man I ever met, and that's coming from a real authority. I wasn't always a lazy bum, kicking away my days out here under the fine sun. What man wouldn't trade his soul to live a day in my shoes?"

Emory said from the back of the pickup, "You're the hardest worker we got, Wally."

"Uhn uhn uhn. You shoulda seen me as a young thing. I could stay a step ahead of Wall Street's moves all day long. Now *that* was a job. But not even any of those beasts worked as hard as Abel Borzoi. It's in your blood, isn't it? Everything's going to be all right."

"That's a real nice thought, Wally. Thank you."

Wally was nodding and smiling at her. "Beth, Beth, Beth. Maybe I'll have your name tattooed on my arm."

Emory leaned into the truck for a stack of one-by-six pine boards. "You'd better have her picture inked on too," he said. Wally laughed and laughed.

"Tell me where to dig, boss," he said. And Wally left Beth to her bigger troubles.

Jacob was unhitching the chains that attached the small back-hoe to the trailer he towed. Beth strode to him, refusing to show her limp.

"I need your help," she said to him. Emory leaned the wood braces against the tailgate, studying Levi. Beth saw the tendons over his jaw flex under the man's skin.

"Anything you ask," Jacob said.

"There's a spot over there"—Beth pointed away from Levi and toward the tallest maple, which was in full leaf and had low branches grazing the ground—"next to my great-grandfather."

"Romanov," Jacob said. "Wish I'd been named Romanov."

Beth raised her eyebrows, curious, but it was not the time to ask. "After Levi is done doing things his way, we're going to dig a new hole," she said. "A proper Borzoi hole."

"That works for me," Jacob said. One of the chains clattered into a pile at his foot.

Emory hefted a shovel in each fist and let one of the blades bang into Levi's pristine fender. He smiled at Beth and said, "And then we'll bury your brother in the grave he prefers."

Beth didn't respond to that.

"I don't know if my mom will go for this," she confided to Jacob as Emory stalked over to Levi.

"Still worth the effort," he said.

"It's extra work for you—I appreciate it," she said.

He unhooked the last chain and then lowered the back end of the trailer so he could drive the backhoe off of it. She stayed close to him.

"After all you've done for us, I hate to ask for anything else," she said in a low voice.

"Ask," he said without hesitating.

"I'm going to head out of here for a couple days," she said. "After Dad's funeral. I need to find my grandfather."

Jacob took off his gloves and squeezed them together in one hand. He stopped working to listen to the rest of what she had to say.

"Mom and Levi won't like that I'm gone. Especially if they find out why. And especially Levi."

His frown told her he wasn't too thrilled about it either, but he kept quiet.

"I can't let this deal with Sam Johnson go down."

"Sam does what Sam wants," Jacob said. "But do you want me to talk to him for you?"

"What would you say? No. Besides, it's not Sam I'm worried about. It's Danny."

"You're not planning to go see Sam by yourself?"

"No, I told you, I'm going to find Garner. Please watch after Danny. I'm worried he won't even watch out for himself. He's just giving up."

"How long are you going to be gone?"

"A lot can happen in a short time."

"Non-answer."

"As long as it takes to find Garner and put Levi in his place."

"Where're you going to look?" he asked.

"Best you don't know."

"For a smart woman, you sure can be dense," he said. "I wish you'd reconsider."

"You know I can't."

Jacob sighed, then climbed into the backhoe and turned the ignition. He directed the machine off the flatbed, and Beth suddenly worried that if all this went south, that if nothing in her life ever went right again, she might never have another opportunity to set things right with him.

She stepped forward and reached up into the cab, laid a hand on his arm. She had to yell to be heard over all the noise. "Jacob, I took your show saddle."

"I know," he yelled back.

How? she wanted to ask. *Why didn't you say anything?* "I'm sorry. I'll pay you back for it."

"No need. You've already paid a high enough price for that mistake."

"That's not the point."

Jacob cut the engine and looked at her. "Then what is the point, Beth? That you punish yourself for the rest of your life for a mistake you can't reverse? What will that accomplish?"

"I don't know. Nothing. Something. I'm trying to make it right."

"Some things you can't make right," Jacob said. "I should know."

"Then what am I supposed to do? Just sail through life without a care?"

Jacob laughed at her then. He *laughed* at her, and she felt a strange mixture of disbelief and relief and anger at his reaction.

"You could never do that. But it's not for you to say what you owe me for that saddle."

"Then what do I owe you?"

He shook his head and pulled the brim of his hat down lower over his eyes—a gesture to prevent her from seeing his unfathomable amusement, she thought. He said, "I'll tell you when you come back."

21

Saturday morning, Levi drove the family from the public memorial service to the private burial in a flashy Cadillac he'd somehow justified renting. His mother had the front passenger seat and Beth sat in back, between Danny and Lorena, and no one spoke. Beth thought only of her father traveling alone in the hearse ahead.

Rose wore a black sheath dress that Beth recognized as one Abel had bought her for their twenty-fifth anniversary celebration. The deep tones of her skin seemed pale against the unyielding color.

The Cadillac wasn't made for the Blazing B's well-traveled but uneven roads. They bobbed alongside the fence that contained Abel's massive horse, Temuche, a broad-shouldered sorrel named for a Ute Indian chief. Pastor Eric had turned him out to graze, saying that no one should ride the horse until the horse had time to mourn and then show interest in a new rider. The horse wandered nervously across the pastureland, aimless without a saddle on his back.

The wide stretch of land was home and yet no longer home, overcome by the aura of her father's absence. Temuche seemed to share Beth's awareness of the shift in the land, though the sky had returned to its cheerful blue self. She imagined Levi's resort crowding the earth, a terrible tumor, and felt sick. The horse's grazing was restless, and he startled at the sound of the approaching rental car. The problem of having no work to do was new to the animal, and Beth felt compassion for it.

A flock of finches rode the wind up into the cottonwoods. Herriot still had not returned. Beth had begun accepting the likely reason for it after Emory reported that the two sets of paw prints had vanished into the creek, near the spot where the antelope had fallen.

Heartache upon heartache and change upon change.

Beth worried over how her mother would react when she saw the hole Levi had dug. There had been no opportunity to tell her about Levi's violation or Beth's remedy. His presence in the front seat robbed her of courage to explain it now.

Jacob, wearing new jeans and a blazer, met them at the cemetery and leaned into the hearse's window to tell the driver where to park. Levi pulled in where he wanted, ignoring Jacob. Beth caught Jacob's eye as the car passed him. He nodded at her.

Rose saw the hole before Levi shifted the gear into park. Beth felt her mother's attention snap to the offense like a magnet. She opened the door and got out without waiting for Levi's help. Beth scrambled out over Lorena.

"Stay with Danny," she ordered the girl.

Rose crossed to the site, waving off Dr. Roy when he approached. Beth chased after her mom. The ache in her foot was a persistent throb today, though it continued to heal. She reached for her mother's fingers, which seemed wilted by disbelief at her son's insult.

"We couldn't stop him," Beth said, hoping to prevent a meltdown. Behind them, Emory and Pastor Eric engaged Danny and Lorena in a distracting conversation. "But no one helped him. Levi did this alone."

Rose closed her eyes and breathed deeply.

"I asked Emory and Jacob to dig another hole." Beth pointed.

"And Wally helped. I know it's not in the right place, but it's a good place. Next to Grandpa Romanov. And there's room beside him." She couldn't form the words *for you, later.* Incredibly, the four men of the Hub had stood watch in shifts through the night and managed to keep Levi from filling it in.

Her mother was shaking her head. She opened her eyes and briefly glanced in the direction of the distant second pit, which was hidden from view by trees. Then her eyes returned to the hole at her feet, and to the tiny headstone behind it that had been fashioned for her dead daughter.

"Levi can't take anything from you that you don't give him, Mom."

"God takes what he wants," Rose murmured. "It has nothing to do with what we're willing to give."

"Levi's not God," Beth said firmly. "We have choices. You have choices. Still. Dad made it clear what he wanted—"

"Not this. Not this family falling apart, turned against each other."

"No one's turned but Levi."

"And you, Beth." Her mother's gaze on her was sharp, but she kept her tone out of reach of the men who lingered by the cars, waiting to see what she would do. "What did you think would happen, stealing another man's horse? No Borzoi has ever done such a thing. You turned before Levi ever did. What he does, you forced him to do."

The sting of her words killed all others that rose to Beth's lips. She felt choked by her mother's accusation, so bitter that it didn't matter whether it was true.

"Now you do *this*. Your brother digs a grave but you insist on another. You divide us when we're most vulnerable."

The sun felt so hot on Beth's head.

"Bury him here," Rose said to Levi, pointing to the traditional hole he'd dug. "Our little girl needs her daddy."

Daddy.

Beth stood at the side of her father's grave, breathless and trembling as the men carried her father's casket and set it near her feet. Pastor Eric spoke with well-intentioned and loving words that brought her no comfort and would not take root in her memory. So Beth spoke a silent memorial of her own to honor her father. And to drown out her mother's opinion of her.

I'll remember the strength of your arms when I'm weak, carrying me.

Danny let her lean on him. Their mother stood opposite, head bowed, eyes closed, lost in her own memories. Levi stood at a distance, his face turned toward the pasture, with them but separate.

I'll remember the scent of your sweat when I work, the calluses on your hands when I ache.

A gentle breeze stirred the trees above and the shrubs below.

I'll remember your love for God, and for all the wounded people of the world.

Eric finished, and no one said anything. Danny pulled the upright shovel out of the ground and slid it into the loose dirt.

I'll remember the sound of your laugh when I can't breathe. I'll remember the sound of your silence when I need wisdom.

The coffin sounded hollow when the earth that poured off the shovel's blade struck it.

Danny thrust the scoop back into the pile, more forceful this time, taking a heavier load. Beth watched him, feeling his heartache like a physical pain.

I'll remember your love for my mother. I'll look for you in my brothers.

Levi shoved his hat down onto his brow and left them.

I'll believe that you told me the truth: that goodness is stronger than evil, that weakness is greater than strength, that humility is a measure of greatness. I'll remember your God.

There was a second shovel lying in the patchy wild grass where Levi had left it the day before. Beth retrieved it and began to help Danny. Her little brother's face was wet with tears, but his jaw was strong and his arms moved with the precision of a metronome. She could not keep up with him, but he didn't seem to mind.

It seemed she'd only been working a few minutes when Jacob took her shovel, and Roy took Danny's. But her brow was sweaty and her black cotton blouse was stuck to her back. She stepped into the shade of the nearest tree. The Davises worked shoulder to shoulder and undid the work that Levi had done, this time with her father's body under the rubble. Beth clung to the Bible's promise that his spirit had gone on to heaven.

Eventually Pastor Eric and Emory drifted away to the other hole and began to fill it in without needing to be asked. Wally was already there, filling the pit one scoop at a time. Beth had seen him arrive discreetly during Eric's eulogy. Then Jacob and Roy finished, and silently left Rose and Beth standing alone with the fresh mound between them.

"I don't see how we can repair this fracture," her mother said.

Beth waited for her to explain. Dreaded the explanation.

"You are either in favor of your brother's plan, or you're against it."

"How can I support—"

"You support it by admitting that what this family needs right now, more than anything, is to function as a unit."

"Levi is taking advantage of—"

"Don't you *see*, Beth? Don't you see? What is happening right now isn't about what's right or wrong. There is no right or wrong, there's only what's necessary. We need each other. We have to stick together. When a family falls apart . . ."

Beth's gaze lifted and went to the distant spot where she'd found Garner's marker.

"Give me a chance to fix this in my own way," Beth pleaded. "That's exactly what Levi's tried to do. He hasn't handled this any differently."

"No. I won't let you break us up one misstep at a time."

"Is that what you think I'm trying to do?"

"No more than anyone tries. That doesn't mean I can't prevent it."

"What are you saying?"

"I'm saying I think you need some time away from us, Beth."

Beth examined each word, one at a time, in her mind.

"Think of it as your getting to go abroad for a season. When Levi and I close the deal with Sam, if you still want us then, come on home."

"Where exactly do you want me to go?"

"You're an adult. That's for you to figure out."

"I'm an owner. I won't sell my share."

"If you ever want to set foot on this property again, you'll give me power of attorney for this purpose."

"No."

"Quit acting like a child!"

"*You're* the one who's breaking us up. I only want what Dad wanted."

"I want you gone by the end of next week. I'll have the attorney draw up papers before you go."

22

Saturday evening, Garner Remke and Trey Bateman sat at Cat's dining room table in the apartment over her doctor's office. The trio was finishing a simple meal of wild salmon, which Cat liked to have shipped in from Seattle for special occasions, a lemon and fennel salad, and homemade rye rolls that Cat had made especially for Garner that afternoon. Rye was his favorite. A fortunate coincidence.

Trey ate none of the bread. He said something about preferring to avoid gluten, and Cat thought he meant to mock her. And so she said, "Far be it from me to step between a man and his lifestyle. You are perfectly healthy, after all."

It was just as well. She hadn't been expecting this kid when she told Garner to bring a friend, and she wasn't interested in an outsider hanging around. It was Garner she was trying to keep close. She had been hoping that Dotti would come.

Garner was saying, "You really ought to patch things up with Nova, Cat. She's a sweet girl. You're the same age. I bet you have a lot in common."

"She's pregnant," Cat huffed. If Nova didn't want Cat to be her doctor, there was no doctor-patient privilege to worry about.

Garner stopped chewing his bread for a minute. "Yes, I heard something about that. I'll have to concede you don't share *that* status. But when did you decide to dislike pregnant women?"

"I don't dislike them. But Nova won't let me manage her prenatal care," Cat said. Then, realizing that she might have revealed her feelings too pointedly, she clarified, "She refuses to see *any* doctor."

"Is that so?"

Garner folded his hands in his lap. "Far be it from me to insert myself into a female argument, but I heard her tell Hank's wife she's got herself a good OB down in Salida. Though I suppose it's possible she made that up to keep people from pestering her."

Cat blinked. If this was true, Nova's rejection wasn't philosophical after all. It was worse. It was deeply personal, and Cat had done nothing to deserve that. She twisted the cloth napkin in her lap. "Good then. Good. I'll be able to sleep again after all."

She turned to Trey. "So, Garner tells me you're a conservationist," she said. Her thoughts felt oddly disconnected from her words, like she was speaking underwater.

"I've been a conservationist since I was old enough to sort the recyclables," Trey said. "But I'm studying wildlife biology as I can afford to."

"Do you plan to work at a zoo?"

Trey raised one eyebrow in Garner's direction. "If tourism isn't a zoo, I don't know what is. But my actual aim is for the outdoors. Field research. Specifically in regard to mountain lions and their habitats. Did you know cougars are one of the least researched predators in America? It's harder and more expensive to catch them, track them."

"That's a cat for you." Garner chuckled and raised his water glass in a toast to the doctor.

"Very funny," Cat said.

"Human encroachment is a significant problem," Trey said, "but it's surmountable. I believe God designed men and animals to live together."

"But not women." Cat couldn't help herself.

"Of course women. So I'm helping to document the cougars' territorial habits, population density, food supply, that sort of thing. The long-term goal is to reduce their confrontations with people. We use tracking collars and, if you can believe it, hound dogs."

"Hunting dogs?" Garner said. "That's surprising."

"I know. It's archaic, right? But very effective. And cameras— I'll be downloading data and doing a little maintenance on some cameras this weekend."

"I almost feel inspired to pull out my checkbook and make a donation," Cat said wryly.

"I recommend the Rocky Mountain Cat Conservancy," Trey said.

If he had caught wind of her sarcasm, he was using it against her. She disliked him more and more.

Cat cleared her throat. "I'll make a note of it." She pushed back from the table and fetched two plastic bags for the remaining rolls, which she gathered up from the neat basket in the middle of the table. "You had better take the rest home with you," she told Garner. "Freeze a bag if you like."

"Delighted to. I don't believe I've ever tasted such a fine bread."

"If it agrees with you, I'll give you the recipe."

"I'll leave the baking to you, Cat girl. It's easier to garden at this altitude than to bake. How do you manage it?"

"It's all in the ingredients. I suppose I do better at plant biology than animal biology," she said.

"You grow your own grains?" Trey's question was loaded with disbelief.

"Maybe that's what accounts for the unusually good taste," Garner said.

Cat smiled and set the bags next to the door. Garner's praise seeped into her like a silky lotion on dry skin. She could simply not get enough of it. Was it so wrong to want to be loved, and by someone who seemed so overflowing with kindness?

"I don't have the space to grow my own here," Cat said. "But I know where to find the good stuff. You boys go on into the living room. I'll make some tea."

Garner obliged, but Trey followed her into her tiny galley kitchen with his arms full of dirty dishes. After stacking them on the sink he leaned against the yellow-tiled counter while Cat filled her electric kettle with water and opened a cupboard. She rushed to put away the bag of rye flour left out on the counter. It was all very annoying.

This was not the first time Cat had used ergot-contaminated rye flour in her rye bread recipe. The fungus ergot—the source of that wild hallucinogen, LSD—grew on many grains but preferred rye. It wasn't necessary that the rye and ergot be baked together to sicken a person, though back in medieval times that's exactly what happened. In its most impressive feat, ergot once killed forty thousand people in southern France. All those poor souls had done to deserve their fate was eat their daily allotment of rye bread.

Even more eye-popping than this plague-like disaster was that the cause of the deaths wasn't understood for another eight hundred years. Until then everyone thought that ergot, which looked like a dark brown grain of rice, was a part of the grain.

Cat had no intention of killing Garner or anyone else who ate her bread, but she did want to remind the vibrant old man how good she was for him.

The human race eventually figured out how to keep ergot out of its grain crops. On the downside, no ergot-resistant breed of rye had ever been developed. This meant that the fungus was prone to rearing its head from time to time and could, with enough money and the right connections, be purchased for "scientific pursuits" from the proper sources. Ergot did have its medicinal uses, after all.

For a moment Cat worried. She hadn't factored in Garner's compromised liver when measuring the ergot. She hoped that wasn't a fatal oversight.

She opened the cabinet over her sink and revealed several rows of glass jars brimming with loose-leaf teas.

Trey said, "Do you make all these yourself?"

"Just a few. Most are Garner's." She pointed. "The lemongrass, ginger, anise and cardamom, spearmint and rosehips. Those are his. He's taught me a little, though I can't say my blends are as satisfying as his."

"And what have you made?"

The kid's extroversion was wearing thin on her.

"Let's see." Cat skimmed the dried concoctions with her eyes and alighted on one on the top shelf. "He gave me the green tea for that one. I added some jasmine to it."

"Nice."

Nice?

"Which kind would you like?" she asked.

"I'm a pretty simple guy. How are you for chamomile?"

Cat pulled down a golden-colored mix with hints of bright red throughout. "Mine has a bit of saffron in it," she said.

"Why does that sound like you've cast pearls before swine?" he said.

"I know. Garner says it's too much shabby and chic in one jar."

"Yeah, well, he just says that because he didn't think of it himself. Let me try some."

Maybe Trey wasn't so awful after all. Cat scooped the leaves into tea balls, then hung them inside of the cups on their metal hooks.

A draft around her ankles and voices on the landing outside her door drew Cat's attention out of her kitchen.

Nova was at the door chatting with Garner. Even if she hadn't spurned Cat's skills so tactlessly, she of all people had no business being pregnant. The woman was too old, too skinny, and lived at too high an altitude for someone with those risk factors. This thin air wouldn't come close to providing the oxygen her expanding blood volume would require. And to top it off, she had no family support. Cat tried and tried not to care, but Nova's rejection of her was so unfounded that she couldn't erase the offensiveness of it. The doctor went to the door.

"I have guests," she said, looking down on her neighbor's head.

"One of them called me over to ask a question," Nova said, indicating Garner.

Cat looked to Garner for an explanation.

"I heard Nova open the back door, and it made me recall a book I wanted to order," he said.

Cat saw right through that ruse. She turned to go back inside. "I see. I'm sorry I interrupted you."

"I was just telling Nova what a fine meal you made," Garner said. He rubbed his belly. "Salmon like that do not swim in this state."

"It does smell delicious."

Cat was forced to pause and acknowledge the compliment with eye contact. Her ire rose at Garner's bald-faced bridge building.

"Thank you," she said. "You're very kind. I'm sorry it's gone, or I'd invite you in."

A terrible idea came to Cat just then, while Nova was standing there at the threshold, suggesting that she'd gladly eat Cat's food while she turned up her nose at Cat's medical savvy. To be born to a woman so cold and aloof, so uncaring of others' feelings, could only be a tragedy. What did Nova think—that books were all a child needed to thrive?

Cat would show her what savvy was.

"Wait. I just remembered." She turned to the table where she'd placed the two bags of rolls. "Garner, you wouldn't mind if I gave her one of your bags, would you?" She smiled at him.

"Oh, Nova, these are a treat." Garner reached out for the bag Cat had picked up. "You have never tasted homemade rye like this."

"Please, take it," Cat said, "I insist."

Nova's face was stone, but slowly she reached out and took the gift.

"I dare you to eat just one," Garner said. "I ate four of them myself tonight."

"Thank you. That's very kind. I'll call you when your book comes in, Mr. Remke."

"Thanks, dear."

Nova descended, her footsteps lighter than whispering feathers. She didn't promise to eat the rolls, but Cat figured a small-town bookseller sure wasn't going to throw away free, nutritious, homemade food. And when she ate enough, she'd come running to Cat for consolation and restoration for sure.

23

Beth funneled the pain of her mother's expulsion into making a focused plan that did not include giving power of attorney to anyone. With the burial of her father behind her, she went to her room to change and then paced at her window.

She was grateful that Lorena was out.

Beth quickly ruled out the option to stay on the Blazing B and go along with her mother's plan. She was legally outmuscled, and once done, developing this land would be an irreversible choice.

If her father would send her to find Garner Remke, it meant that Garner Remke could be found. And it didn't really matter that Rose had symbolically buried the man. Her husband's wishes should count for something.

With her bedroom door locked to dissuade Lorena from entering unannounced, Beth packed a small backpack that wouldn't draw attention if anyone saw her driving off with it. A change of clothes, money, her laptop and cell phone, a map that showed the location of Burnt Rock, a Swiss army knife.

It would have been nice to have a full week to prepare for a weekend away from home that might turn into a winter away. Instead, she stuck with her original intention to leave in the dark hours of Sunday morning, as if she were going to work as usual. But she wouldn't go to the feed-and-tack. Instead she would stop in Del Norte for some food and other necessities before heading west.

It took her all of five minutes to pack. After that, the evening hours stretched ahead of her. She stayed in her room, studying the map. The San Luis Valley resembled the portrait silhouette of a wolf looking westward, as if its attention had been captured by some scurrying rabbit in Utah that wasn't worth a chase. Tomorrow she would drive into the mountains via the wolf's snout. Already she sensed its inhospitable snarl.

She missed Herriot.

She got on her laptop and Googled "Garner Remke Burnt Rock" and found a folksy, unsophisticated website devoted to medicinal herbs. Garner's Garden. It had a Burnt Rock post office box number that matched the one on her mother's wedding card, but the website was last updated two years ago. The phone number published there directed her call to a recorded message that said they were open for orders Monday through Friday. If she left a message a customer service representative would be happy to return her call.

"This is Beth Borzoi. I'm trying to reach Garner Remke. It's an urgent family matter. Please call me back as soon as you get this message." She left her number.

There was an order-fulfillment address in the Boulder area, several hours north of Burnt Rock. Based on the zip and area codes, Beth thought this might be where her voice mail message now resided. She decided to go to the mining town first, then head to Boulder if necessary.

Sleep wouldn't come to her. Fully dressed, Beth lay awake on top of her bedding through the hours worrying. She wondered where Lorena was and suddenly feared that the girl might have run away. It was after eleven when Beth finally rose, left the room, and went in search of her.

She went as far as the top of the stairs. From the great room at the bottom of the split flight she heard Rose and Lorena talking in subdued tones.

Immediately Beth returned to her room. She pulled up her e-mail and wrote a note to Danny, the only family tie binding her to this ranch:

Hey, Danny,

Sorry to head off without saying good-bye, but I had to leave sooner than I expected. I'll be back as soon as I can. In the meantime, if you need anything, you go to Jacob. I think Mom and Levi are going to be a little preoccupied for a while. For my part in their distraction, I'm sorry.

You're becoming a man in the worst circumstances. I wish I could fix everything that's wrong with the world, but I couldn't convince God to give me the job. Taking Joe for a joy ride kind of disqualified me, the kleptomaniac. I don't know why God won't fix what I can't fix for myself, even though I'd pay any price for his help. If God can do miracles, why doesn't he do them when we need them most?

Maybe someday we'll know, but right now I'm holding on to the only lifeline I have. There's room for you to grab hold too: Dad always said this ranch belongs to God, and he believed God's mercy is great. I must believe it too. I pray every day for his mercy to swallow me up. Maybe you can be my prayer buddy in that.

Just do your best. Back soon.

I love you,
Beth

Again she tried to sleep. Again she failed. At four o'clock she finally pressed Send on her message to Danny, grabbed the keys off her dresser, and decided she could come up with an excuse for leaving this early if she had to. She went out of the house to her truck. It wasn't in the front drive, where she usually parked.

She tried to think of who might have borrowed it, and why.

"Looking for something?" Levi came out the front door with his own keys jangling. He was shaking them unnecessarily, bursting with something to say. Had he been waiting for her? She waited for him to say it.

"Sold your truck last night."

At first Beth didn't believe him. He'd jab her and jab her and jab her until he grew bored. She headed down the side of the house intending to look for her truck at the back, where the kitchen entry was.

"Some kid needed it for the college commute. He came by for a look after dinner, had cash. The timing worked out well, I think. We were a little short on the funeral budget."

Beth was struck by how much his statement had sounded like her own justification for stealing Jacob's saddle. She couldn't come up with a retort that didn't condemn herself. Had they guessed that she would run? Were they trying to keep her close to home until the papers were signed? But it was a dumb idea to tell Beth to leave and then take away her transportation. Maybe the truck wasn't actually sold, only hidden somewhere.

"You got somewhere to go?" Levi asked.

"Work."

"It's Sunday morning. Feed-and-tack doesn't open until noon."

"There's plenty to be done before then," she reasoned.

"Well, I'm headed in the other direction or I'd give you a lift." He didn't sound sorry about that at all. "Guess you'll have to take the horse."

"Guess so."

"We wouldn't sell Hastings, you know. He'll come in handy."

When Levi's taillights were tiny red pricks in the gray morning light, Beth went to the barn. She whistled for Hastings and went inside to get his saddle. She also grabbed a bedroll, a blanket, a canteen, and a rain jacket, all of which could be easily strapped to his back. A large flashlight from one of the drawers in the feed room went into her backpack.

It didn't take long for her to be mounted and riding away. Behind her, the sun wasn't even yet a glimmer on the eastern rim of the Sangre de Cristos. She gave herself an hour to search for the truck, which wasn't really a fair shake on ten square miles of land. But she couldn't afford more time than that, or she might be discovered and made a prisoner in her own house.

She ruled out the Hub and the buildings closest to it. Levi wouldn't have put her truck anywhere the other ranch hands might have found it. They'd only deliver it right back to her doorstep. She went instead to the more remote areas of the property that backed up into the foothills, which also had more trees, shrubs, and grasses grown tall and ungrazed through the summertime. As the morning sky shifted from its dark gray hues to pinkish reds, Beth and Hastings picked their way from north to south underneath a ledge of volcanic rock that hid them in its shadow.

There was no sign of her truck. No tire tracks, no foliage crushed by a vehicle passing through. Beth looked for two hours instead of one, and the August sun quickly grew warm even in the shade.

She drew Hastings to the creek for some water and let him drink. As he filled his belly, she turned her face westward. It might be possible to ride her horse to Burnt Rock; there were plenty of trails through these rugged mountains, trails used for more than a century by miners and prospectors, and then by ranchers and pool riders driving their herds uphill for summer grazing. She'd have to check the trail maps, because leaving a marked path in these lands would be idiotic. The map she carried, unfortunately, didn't have these details.

It had been a long time since Beth had sat and listened to the sounds of the land. It was eerily silent this morning, with the cows miles away in the mountains and the hot morning air too still to stir the leaves or grasses. The water at Hastings' lips was also quiet, trickling now at the end of summer. The noise of his drinking and dribbling was a pleasant disruption.

She heard a dog bark. A faraway yip of excitement. Hastings lifted his head and flicked his ears in the direction of the sound.

When Beth was a little girl, Rose had once tried to explain to her that mothers of mammal species were uniquely equipped to recognize their offspring's cries. A cow could find its calf among thousands of cattle, even if separated by miles. A human mother was so attuned to her infant's cries that the sound alone could cause her milk to let down. And not only did a mother recognize her child's cries, but she could distinguish among these as well: the hungry cry from the sleepy cry from the sick cry, and so on.

Beth understood this on some level, because even though she wasn't technically a mother, she had raised her dog, Herriot, by hand when the mother rejected the runt. She believed she could recognize Herriot's bark and distinguish between the types: the get-along-dumb-cow bark, the intruder-alert bark, the boy-am-I-happy-to-see-you bark.

This distant bark belonged to Herriot, and it fell into the last category.

Beth nudged Hastings to cross the creek bed in the direction of the sound. She half expected Herriot to launch herself out of the shrubs and onto the horse's back, clinging to Beth and washing her face with her thick tongue until both of them fell out of the saddle.

The grasping branches of a willow caught the corners of her eyes as Hastings came up the other bank. The horse seemed to sense what Beth wanted, and needed no guidance in following the happy noise, which repeated itself in more or less the same manner every few minutes.

After gaining some height and a slightly better view on the rocky slope, where the trees were fewer in number than they were at the creek, Beth thought it strange that Herriot hadn't made any move toward her. Maybe the dog was captive, secured by a leash or a cage, and had merely caught Beth's scent.

Hastings didn't hesitate to go on, even when doubt crept across Beth's thoughts. The second realization to trouble her was that the volume of Herriot's bark hadn't changed in the half hour she'd been pursuing it. Surely it should be growing louder. Even if the rocks and trees and slopes, now rising more steeply with every quarter mile, had distorted or cloaked the source of the bark, it seemed to Beth that the volume should be changing.

Two hours later she wished she had turned back then, at the moment she thought something was wrong, before she realized that she was far from any familiar trail and had no map or food, before trees started filling the landscape once more and crowding her perspective. But the sound of her lost dog's happy cries had a stronger pull than her good sense. Truly, Beth had expected to find Herriot long before all the ponderosas started to look the same and the sun had come to a point so directly overhead that she lost all sense of direction. The dog had sounded so much closer.

Still the pleasant barking continued, and Hastings showed no sign of fatigue. What was there to do but continue until a smarter alternative presented itself?

When Beth saw the prints of a mountain lion in the rain-moistened soil, she decided she was the stupidest person to ever wander into these mountains.

It was impossible for her to tell how old the prints were. The cougar might have passed through a week ago or a minute ago. When the tracks veered north and her dog's barking stayed to the south, Beth felt relief.

She and Hastings went on like this for a long time, with the sun continuing its arc and the prompting of her dog always the same distance ahead of them. The birdsong had long shifted from busy morning chatter into the infrequent afternoon communication. They'd soon return to their nests, and it seemed more and more likely that Beth might be staying overnight outdoors, where cougars prowled.

This thought took up hardly any space in her head compared to the mystery of the sound they followed. Why was it always in front of her, like a carrot dangling from a stick tied to her own horse? She felt as if she'd lost Herriot all over again. She began to doubt that the noise belonged to anything real, though it sounded as real as Beth's own breathing.

And then the barking stopped. The white-trunked aspen trees in front of Beth parted onto a steep bluff. The lip of it dropped away into a narrow valley cut in half by a snaking stream. The water poured off rocks at the west end and then meandered away through a pass to the southeast.

Beth reined in Hastings. She paid little attention to the vista. Most of her mind was focused on the hope that she'd hear Herriot again.

A crackling of underbrush caught her attention. Beth turned her head and saw a golden mountain lion with a wide white muzzle and a tail as thick as her arm already airborne. It was aiming for a meal.

Beth's limbs seized up. Her only reflex was to call up an image of that wolf leaping out of darkness. Oddly, Hastings didn't seem to notice that he was a target. She didn't understand anything about those two seconds of her life: *Tick* and there was a fang-bared cougar flying at her; *tock* and the cat dropped to the ground like a fighter jet struck midair by a missile.

The mountain lion tangled with a mass of long gray fur that was no match for its own great size. In spite of this inequality, they tumbled all the way to the edge of the bluff, snarling and snapping.

Freed from her shock then, Beth kicked Hastings and reined him away from the fight.

The horse didn't respond.

Beth yelled at him, kicked harder, yanked on the reins.

Hastings snorted and stayed put.

The animal kingdom has gone mad!

It was a wolf that had intercepted the wildcat—no, not just a wolf, but *that* wolf, the one that had disrupted her life. The one with the four-clawed scar striping its back. The ferocious creatures fought at the brink like men with a score to settle, all teeth and claws.

Once she accepted the wolf's identity, she also knew that she wouldn't be able to run away. If Joe couldn't outrun this wolf, the butler Hastings was lost already. That would explain why he so senselessly hung around, waiting for the inevitable.

Resignation was one thing—but why wasn't he afraid? She was terrified. She thought of her pocketknife and wished she had thought to bring a gun.

Beth's own heart was straining inside her ribs. Tiny buggy spots were beginning to swim at the edges of her vision when she saw the wolf, with powerful hind legs, propel the cougar off his body and over the edge of the bluff. She heard the cat slide down the loose rocks and then, she thought, find its footing and run away down into the valley.

She couldn't see this happen because the wolf was sitting between her and the view, and its eyes commanded her to look at him.

It was the second time she'd seen the wolf in daylight, the first being that day when the antelope straddled life at the stream. She was struck again by its size, so much larger than a domesticated dog's, and yet it was half the mass of that mountain lion.

"Hi, Mercy," she whispered. "Hope you don't mind a girl's name, seeing that you're male. But it's time I called you something, don't you think?"

The wolf yawned. Hastings reacted as if the wolf were a butterfly. He flicked his tail once.

"Maybe it would have been better if you'd knocked me off my feet the way you did that mountain lion before I even got out of the barn," she said. The wolf walked away from the lip of the earth, passed under Hastings' nose, and then began to pick up its pace as it ambled into the shelter of the trees. Soon it was trotting away.

"Is this how it's going to be? With you constantly showing up and not explaining anything?"

As if in answer, Beth's mind was filled with a vivid image from her dream: the antelope with stethoscope horns climbed the mountain of her mind's eye, a mountain that was actually the back of a wolf.

She could hear the canine's movements through the brush. In the distant valley, a different dog barked.

Beth turned her head and looked down the slope. A large herd of cattle was moving out from under the shelter of shade trees onto the green plain. The cows were a variety of colors, black and tan, mahogany and yellow. And a significant cluster of them shared a brilliant copper-red that reflected the same tones of the sun. It was the red of Beth's hair, the same red she had shared with her late father. These were Gelbvieh cows, and she knew they would have the Blazing B's brand on their hindquarters: a capital B with a tongue of fire touching the uppermost curve.

A cowboy on a large black horse followed them, close to the river. Though Beth couldn't say for sure from this distance, the white hat made her pretty certain this was Ash Martin, the pool rider. A black-and-white dog bounded next to his horse, its head turned toward the meandering cows. Its bark reached Beth's ears.

Herriot.

Beth scanned the hills for the safest route to the valley floor and wasn't surprised to see that the wolf seemed to have taken it.

Hastings turned to follow Mercy before Beth gave the command.

24

Cat was treating Randy Mason, the Burnt Rock stable owner, for an infected cut in his knee when Garner stumbled through the front door of her offices. He was doubled over, gripping his stomach and squinting from a headache that couldn't tolerate the light. He had heartburn like never before, he said, and stomach cramps took him to the floor within minutes of his arrival.

Cat had been prepared for this event. She lived for those who needed her. In serving others and having her services accepted, Catherine Ransom had learned to finally capture happiness. She quickly assessed Garner, knowing exactly what was wrong with him. He was developing a fever. It was low-grade now but would probably rise soon enough. She slid a pillow under his head right there in the center of the waiting room floor, draped a light blanket over him, drew the blinds, and told him to hang in there until she could send Randy on his way.

This was her chance to shine.

She had already finished cleaning the stableman's wound. Now she applied antibiotic ointments and clean dressings, and gave him a prescription for oral antibiotics.

"When was your last tetanus shot?" she asked.

"No idea."

"Then let's get you one, and let me know Tuesday how this is doing."

"It's a good thing we have you, doc."

"I'm glad to have all of you too. Help me with something before you go?"

"Just tell me what to do."

"Help me lift him?" she asked. "I don't have a gurney to make this easy, I'm afraid."

"I can handle it," Randy said. In simple, controlled moves, Randy scooped Garner off the floor like a child and slung him over his shoulder. "Something I learned to do in the army," he said to Cat.

Within just a few minutes they had transported Garner onto a wheeled hospital bed in the patient room closest to Dr. Ransom's private office.

"Thanks, Randy."

"Any time. Call me if you need my muscle again. You get better, Remke."

Randy left, and Cat removed Garner's shoes. She ran her fingers over his hands and feet. Both were freezing to the touch. "Could be food poisoning," Cat said for Garner's benefit.

"The elk sandwich, you think?"

"Too long ago. Might have been my salmon."

"Not a chance."

"Have you eaten anything that tasted a little off?"

He barely shook his head, then frowned from the pain the movement caused.

"Have you thrown up?"

"No."

The vomiting would start soon enough. Cat turned down the lights. It was easier to appear calmly authoritative, and therefore trustworthy and comforting, in a dim room. And Garner would be more relaxed. More suggestible.

The age of the patient, the isolation of the town, the privacy of this office—all the factors in place today would surely make this easier than the time she'd employed similar methods with little Amelia Reinhart for the sake of winning her father's adoration. Already, everything had gone so much more easily.

Cat gave Garner instructions to try to sleep while she fetched a few items she needed.

Ergot brought down its victims simply enough with symptoms that could be blamed on any number of causes: nausea, vomiting, stomach cramping, headaches, numbness, fever. Such symptoms were consolable, eased by time, patience, love, and the understanding of a gentle doctor. In small amounts, the effects were reversed easily enough: all one had to do was stop eating the ergot-tainted food and let the monster run its course.

Depending on how Garner responded to Cat's TLC, she could keep nurturing him with those rye rolls he loved so much, or put him on an ergot-free diet. She'd take one day at a time.

Though Garner's liver cancer was an unknown variable, short-term exposure to ergot was easy to handle. If she decided to, she'd keep him down long enough to restore his adoration of her but not long enough to need to admit him to a hospital. If exposure to the ergot went on too long the toxicity would mount. Some patients would experience convulsions, hysteria, hallucinations, dementia. Skin infections would flare, accompanied by such unbearable pain that the condition had been known for centuries as St. Anthony's Fire. In others, especially in animals, blood flow to the extremities was reduced to the point that gangrene set in.

As Cat gathered various analgesics from her supply closet, she found herself particularly curious about how Nova's exposure to the fungus would turn out. Ergot had been used by midwives since the dawn of time to contract the uterus after the birth of a child; modern-day obstetricians used a derivative of ergot to jump-start an expectant mother's contractions. In the distant past, some women used ergot to abort their babies—though they tended to be successful only insofar as one considered the death of both child and mother a "success."

Cat could only guess how far her generous dose might go in the fetus of a woman as slightly built as Nova. It would be an unscientific experiment.

She returned to Garner's room carrying a box of medications that she might or might not administer: a vasodilator and an anticoagulant, in the event Garner's extremities began to turn black, though that would take days, maybe even weeks; activated charcoal, if any of the symptoms worsened; saline and a stomach tube, mainly for appearances. Gastric lavage was only sometimes recommended for this type of poisoning. The box contained several other sterile items, still in their sealed plastic and brown bottles, also for appearances.

But she would go through whatever motions were required to make people love her.

A shout came from the entrance. "Dr. Ransom! Where's Garner?"

Cat left Garner's side and leaned out into the hallway. Dotti had already crossed the waiting room in those bright orange sneakers and was coming straight at her.

"Randy told me Garner came in half dead." The woman's eyes and hair were both frenzied, as if she'd run here all the way from Salida. She was even slightly breathless.

"Shh, shh. He's in good hands, Dotti."

"A person can be in good hands and still be half dead. What's wrong with him?"

"I'm thinking it's a little food poisoning, nothing worse than that. It'll pass."

"Food poisoning! The man's got liver cancer. He might as well have Alzheimer's of the liver. It won't have any idea what to do with poison."

"Dotti." Cat laid a hand on the woman's arm. "Being upset won't help him get better."

The woman finally grabbed hold of some calm. She took a deep breath and said, "Well, just tell me what will help, Doctor, and I'll be doing it right away."

"Why don't you come see him? Quietly. He's sleeping, and he needs the rest. But I'm sure he'll be able to sense your positive energy." He might technically be unconscious, but Cat wasn't about to suggest that Dotti help her verify this.

Dotti silenced herself and followed Cat into the room. The feisty marmot woman approached Garner's bedside and placed her wrinkled, sunspotted hand over the top of his. Her shoulders, cloaked in a light summer jacket that said Whitewater Rush, drooped.

"No one should have to get sick like this," Dotti murmured. "Especially not someone who's been through all he's been through." Cat felt a small rumbling of jealousy in her chest. "I want to take him home and nurse him back to health. What do you say, Dr. Ransom? A few days off his feet? A ginger tea, do you think? Garner says it's good on an upset stomach, settles the nausea. I can slice some fresh—"

"He needs to be here for a while," Cat said. She tried not to be brusque. "I want to keep a close eye on him. There's always a chance he could turn for the worse."

The ensuing silence felt awkward to Cat, though Dotti nodded her agreement.

"You must be very busy with your rental company right now, with the end of summer on its way," Cat said. "Sometimes focusing on work helps me to keep my mind in an optimistic frame."

"I've got plenty of employees to do that work for me, honey. It's a perk of being old."

Cat sighed, not knowing what she'd have to do to get the woman to leave. "You know, Dotti, this sickness was so sudden— I wouldn't be surprised if Garner has left his shop unmanned. It would be a great deal to ask, I know, but if you wouldn't mind—"

"Yes, yes. That's just the thing, isn't it? He probably left his front door wide open and has busybodies crawling like aphids around his basement. I'll go stand guard." She patted Garner's hand. "Leave it to me, Mr. Herbalist. You just do the work of getting better."

Cat said, "He's got a friend staying there, but I don't think he knows as much as you about Garner's—"

"Trey Bateman?" Dotti was already in the hall. "He doesn't know squat about plants. Let him drive a bus and collar wildcats with his bare hands. I'll handle the gardening. You call me and keep me up to speed on this man's progress."

"I think Trey isn't getting back until Tuesday night."

Dotti waved her off. "I got it covered." She pushed open the front door, and Cat was overcome by pleasant relief.

"Thank you!" she called out as the door glided shut and Dotti's purposeful form crossed the front window.

She might have raised her voice too high, for Garner stirred and murmured. Cat approached and laid a reassuring hand on his arm. "It's okay, Garner, I'm here. You're going to be just fine."

His eyes opened and seemed to notice Cat, though it was impossible to tell. "Dotti?" Garner mumbled, then he saw he was speaking to someone else. "Where's Dot?" He was frowning, as if perturbed that Cat wasn't who he thought she was.

"Need Dotti," he insisted. Cat forced a painful smile. She considered cramming another rye roll down the ungrateful man's throat. Or dispensing with the vehicle of the roll entirely; she ought to just drop the fungus into his mouth one piece at a time, straight up. A man who rejected the help smack in front of him and grasped for something out of reach could hardly be worth her investment of time.

"Dot . . ." Garner's eyes fluttered closed.

"You're a fighter," Cat whispered. "Hang in there, my friend. When I say you'll be just fine, you can know I'm good for it." But if she had to compete for her patient's affection, she might stop saying it at all.

25

Beth woke as if an alarm had pulled her out of a deep sleep. One minute she was in a dreamless state, and the next she was aware that a man was watching her. A very tall man who was not Ash Martin, the pool rider. The jolt pulled her straight up onto the seat of her pants and set Herriot into a brief frenzy of barking.

"Where's Ash?" She asked this before she was fully upright. There was a low campfire between Beth and the stranger, who answered her question by nodding toward the stainless trailer set up behind them. Ash had courteously offered it to her the night before; she had opted to stay under the stars. Irrationally, she thought the wide-open space would be the wiser choice, because out here there was nothing to separate her from Mercy, though she hadn't seen the wolf since yesterday's cougar incident.

The sun had yet to rise above the surrounding ranges. Herriot stood on alert, ears and tail erect, beside Beth. But the dog was looking toward the nearby thicket of spindly gambel oaks and didn't seem at all bothered by their unknown company. Maybe man and dog had met while she slept.

Satisfied that the slender trees hid no threat, Herriot settled down beside her owner again.

"Sorry to startle you," the man said.

"You didn't."

He smiled at her the way her father used to do, wise to her false claim but willing to let her keep her pride. Her heart connected the men so immediately that a knot formed in her throat, but their similarity was intangible. She tried to put her finger on it. This man didn't *look* anything like her father. The stranger was slim and clean-shaven, brown-skinned, and his every limb was long. His fingers seemed almost skeletal, and his legs accounted for nearly two-thirds of his height. At odds with his lanky body, his face was almost perfectly round, as if boasting of his Native American ancestry. If he was from around here, it was the Southern Utes who populated most of this territory. His glistening black hair was pressed down close against his head, the effects of a hat plus days without a shampoo. A peace pipe hung from a leather strap around his neck.

The cows were active already in the dark, making their peaceful sounds of meandering, chewing, snorting, calling. Occasionally a calf lowed, looking for its mother, and got a swift response. When Beth was a girl, she had been in the habit of opening her bedroom window during the spring months between calving season and the drive to the mountains, just to hear these comforting noises.

The man dropped a small pine log on the fire. It sizzled with morning dew.

"I thought Ash was alone," she said.

"He needs his sleep. Name's Wally."

This Wally looked no more like her forgetful friend at the Blazing B than he looked like her father. It was tempting to read something into the coincidence, but what was so special about sharing a name with another man? She could only speculate how many women around the world were named Beth.

"I'm Beth. You come up to spell Ash now and then?"

Wally poured coffee from a pot into a tin cup, then stood and leaned over the warm flames, stretching out to hand it to her. She accepted this gesture as an affirmative answer to her question, then wondered why she had.

"I expected that to burn out," she said of the fire, testing the rim of the cup with her lips. The metal had, within seconds, become too hot to sip. She set it beside her to cool, and Herriot sniffed it.

"It did. But here we are."

"Well, thanks for jump-starting it."

"Your wolf was here."

A dozen questions rushed Beth's mind, but she asked this one first: "*My* wolf?"

"The one you call Mercy."

He was smiling at her again, that disconcerting, paternal, all-knowing, and gentle grin. Now it spooked her a little. She picked up the coffee, burning her knuckles as they came against the tin, and drank the scalding brew, though sealing her lips would have been a more effective way to conceal her surprise. The coffee transformed her tongue into sandpaper and then she dropped the cup because it was too hot to hold.

She exclaimed when the coffee splashed her left thigh, then madly blotted her soaked jeans with her shirt. That liquid would leave a burn, maybe even a blister that would make riding Hastings a misery.

"Wolves haven't been in these mountains in a long, long time," she said, focusing on her fiery skin.

"More accurately, you'd have to say wolves haven't been *seen* in these mountains that long. I suspect you could find someone who's seen them here and there, if you asked the right questions of the right people."

"Have you seen them?"

"I just told you your wolf was here, didn't I?"

"I meant before tonight."

"Depends what you mean by *seen*."

Beth's coffee-soaked jeans clung to her leg. She tried unsuccessfully to pull the fabric away.

"He's a bold one," Wally said. "Sat and watched you as closely as I was watching it. Right there." He pointed to the trailer's rear tire.

"So close? And Herriot didn't go bonkers?"

"You know your dog better than I do."

Beth began to believe that she was dreaming. That instead of antelopes climbing up wolves, her mind had started constructing angels out of men she knew.

"How did you know I call him Mercy?" she asked him.

Wally laughed, and a small flock of birds took flight from the thicket, chattering. The sounds were as pleasant as the lowing cows, all of nature calling to each other in a harmonious way that seemed both beautiful and strange.

He said, "Because that's the wolf's name. What else would you call him?"

I will show you mercy, the wolf had said to her as she lay next to Joe's broken body. And again when it led her to the dying pronghorn. As if wolves could speak.

Beth stared at Wally and couldn't stop herself from smiling too. Did he also have a bond with the animal? The possibility of being able to talk with someone, even if only in a dream, about her experience filled her with anticipation.

"So you know my next question," she said, leaning forward.

"You want to ask how I know its name."

She nodded.

"I know it the same way I know yours," he said. "Bethesda."

"I see. So the real reason you know all these things is because this conversation isn't real, and all of it's happening inside my mind."

"I know names because the One who does the naming happens to like me. He lets me in on it once in a while."

"And who would that be?"

Beth waited while he stared into the fire and sipped from his own cup. She noticed a small trowel standing upright in the dirt next to his hip and an old tin coffee can, the kind with a plastic lid. Perhaps he had used it to clear out the cold ashes when he rebuilt her fire.

"Well," she prodded. "Who named the wolf?"

"The same One who names all things, including you."

"My parents named me."

"Sometimes parents pick the right name. Other times the One has to work around their personal tastes."

The fire crackled. "That is very creepy one-with-the-mother-earth talk!"

His pleasant expression took on a shadow of disapproval. "Is it? I didn't say anything like that. Your ears are prejudicial."

"Prejudicial how?"

"You see that I have close ties to the original people of the valley, and you assume that because of my heritage I can't serve the same God you serve."

Embarrassment returned Beth's attention to her burnt leg. "Then tell me again what you said. Please."

He spoke slowly. "I said that the One who names all things named both you and the wolf who follows you."

"You are saying that I belong to God. And the wolf does too."

"Yes."

"And that my parents got my name right."

"Yes."

She found this funny. She laughed a little bit.

"Did your parents get your name right?"

"No. They called me Shrieking Eagle."

Beth bit down on her smile and said kindly, "Well, I can see that you don't really seem like the shrieking type, Wally."

She had never encountered an angel, but no other idea could explain this man. The pain in the skin of her thigh was all too real for a dream.

"People change as they grow. They grow into their true names. Not everyone has the privilege of understanding this."

"I don't know what you're trying to say."

"Consider your wolf. Most people see *wolf.* They think *cattle-killer,* or *endangered species,* or maybe *nice photograph.* But you see *Mercy.* It changes the way you think. His name was made known to you because your eyes were clear when you looked at him."

"The first time I met him," Beth said, "I thought I heard him . . . tell me something. He said, 'I will show you mercy.'"

"And did he?"

"If you mean did he restrain himself from killing me, yes."

"That wasn't what I meant, but it's a start."

Beth sighed. "What did you mean?"

"This wolf is going to show you mercy."

"But he already— You mean he's going to again? Later? When?"

"I don't know."

In her mind, Beth tried to assemble the strange pieces of her wolf encounters into a meaningful whole. "He showed me . . . ," she began, then tried to concentrate on each event. "He showed me a dying antelope," she said. "And I healed it."

"You did? *You* healed this animal?"

"It sounds crazy, but I don't know how else to explain it."

Wally stretched his hands out to the warm fire.

Beth looked at Herriot and said, "What did he show you, girl?"

Herriot dropped her head to her front paws, and her eyes blinked closed, the picture of contentment.

"Do you believe in miracles?" she asked Wally.

"Every day," he said.

"You mean miracles happen every day?"

"I mean I believe in them every day. Some days you get up and can't believe they're possible. Or you don't want to. So every day, I believe in them all over again."

"Have you ever seen a miracle?"

"Don't have to see them to believe in them."

"I agree. I think. But still—have you ever seen one?"

"What do you call a miracle?"

"You and I seem to need a dictionary."

He patted his jeans pockets. "I left mine at home."

"A miracle is . . . something you can't explain."

"Then why are you asking me?"

Beth crossed her arms. "It's something that happens outside of the laws of nature."

"You mean the laws of nature as we understand them?"

"That might be splitting hairs."

"No more than saying wolves haven't been here, when it's closer to the truth to say no one has seen them. Knowing many of the laws of nature is not the same as knowing all of the laws. Two very different things, not one hair that's been split."

"I healed a dying antelope. I made a broken bird fly again. I diagnosed this sick horse—"

"That wasn't a miracle."

"Helping the horse?"

"That was your own talent."

"I have no talent, just a dream of becoming a vet."

"No vet can close a wolf bite in a pronghorn's throat without stitches," Wally said.

"As I said, I'm not a vet. Wait a minute—"

"Neither are you the one who gets credit for these events. *You* did not heal the antelope. *You* didn't make the bird fly. And I'll reconsider my opinion: perhaps it wasn't even really you who diagnosed the horse."

"You're saying I have talent, but that really God did it," Beth said.

"You did what you had the opportunity to do. And the One who orders the world worked through you. We do what we can with the resources God gives us, Bethesda. We should try to do no more than that."

"I want *good* things for the people I love. Is that so much to ask?"

"You can want them, but you can't always provide them." Wally leveled his eyes at her from across the fire. "That saddle was not yours to give."

Beth put her face in her hands. It was frustration, not tears, that she was trying to hide.

"That horse would have lost her eye with or without that stupid saddle," she muttered.

"How do you know that?"

Beth dropped her hands. "Are you *kidding* me? Are you saying that if I hadn't stolen Jacob's saddle the horse wouldn't have lost her eye?"

"I don't know. Maybe she wouldn't have lost her eye. Maybe you could have healed it. Maybe you could have healed Joe's leg. Maybe you wouldn't have broken Joe's leg in the first place."

"Well, which one is it? Why don't you know?" she yelled.

"I'm not permitted to know."

"I want to know!"

"What is it, exactly, that you want to know, Beth?"

"I want to know why God would heal a stupid antelope and let my father *die*!"

Wally's eyes were full of compassion, and she wondered how her mind had thought him up. Oh yes—he was based on her dad. Her dead father, and the Wally of the Blazing B.

"I don't believe the antelope lived either."

"What?" she sputtered. "That's your answer? Do I have a gift of healing or not, Wally? Does God work miracles through me or not? Does he even *do* miracles, or is everything arbitrary? Are good and evil just flukes? I mean . . . my *father*. This is the most unfair punishment. For one mistake."

The rising sun behind the gambel oaks cast long shadows over her shoulders, but their dark and elegant fingers were swallowed by the light of the campfire. They couldn't touch her companion.

"What seems like punishment might be God's redemption," he said.

"I'm going to go back to sleep, Wally. You've been no help to me at all."

He smiled at her again. She lowered her head onto Herriot's back as if it were a pillow.

"Will it help if I tell you how to get to Burnt Rock from here?" he said.

"I thought Mercy would lead the way."

"No. I'll give you a map."

"Gee. Thanks."

"But once you reach Burnt Rock, you must follow the wolf."

"I've *been* following the wolf."

"Only very recently. Herriot figured out that part a long time before you did," Wally said. "The time to follow the wolf is when it seems like you don't need to anymore."

Beth was quite ready for this dream or visitation or whatever it was to end. She had simple questions and was tired of the complicated answers.

"He'll lead you to your grandfather," Wally said. "He'll protect you from the predators. There are more predators. More cougars."

The promise of mountain lions and the sound of a spade penetrating the ground jarred Beth's sleepy mind. She heard dirt like a waterfall pouring into a container. It was a hollow, wistful sound.

He said, "And I'll give you one last tip."

Beth felt this dream-like meeting slipping away beneath her heavy head. "What?"

"Take a bath before you go. Use this dirt I'm digging up for you. Mix it with the creek water. Put the mud on that burn. It'll wash right off."

"Sure. Whatever you say."

"Nothing's arbitrary," Wally said. "No matter what you think you see."

The second time Beth woke, the sun was higher and the towering shadow of Ash Martin was shading her tired eyes.

"Sleepin' hard for a gal who's drunk all the joe," he said, lifting the empty pot off the charred remains of the fire and shaking it. Beth pushed herself up. Herriot had wandered off, and Beth's neck was strained. The inside of her thigh felt scorched and raw.

"Wally drank it all," she said, not expecting him to understand. "I got one sip and a bad burn."

Ash examined the pot with renewed interest.

"You met Wally?" he asked, and Beth felt her stomach drop.

She looked around for the man she didn't believe was real. Her hand bumped something on the ground at her side. She picked it up. It was an old coffee can topped with a red plastic lid. She peeled it back. The can held about two cups of dirt.

"You know him? Where is he?"

"Dunno. I didn't know he was here."

Beth's throat was thick and dry. "I guess he just got in last night, then. Uh, how do you know him?"

"He's an old mountain man. Lived here in the San Juans his whole life."

"Does he travel with you?"

"Now and then, on his terms."

Beth's mind was whirling. "He likes his terms."

Ash chuckled. "That he does."

Beth stood and reached for her backpack with her free hand. She was trying to remember the details of their conversation, but the content was already elusive. In the top of her bag, poking out from the unzipped compartment, a hand-drawn line of red ink traversed her neatly folded map, and several protein bars wrapped in silver foil were tucked behind her change of clothes. She fingered the food, and it was no imagination. She thought of the dirt and the mud, and wondered if it would also be real.

"Back in a few," she said absentmindedly, and she carried her belongings and the coffee can toward the creek, walking stiffly to prevent the denim of her jeans from chafing her inflamed skin. Riding Hastings was top on her list of things she didn't want to do right now. But she had to get to Burnt Rock.

Ash must have noticed her limp.

"Going after some mud?" he asked.

Beth stopped and turned around. "How is it that two guys so far from civilization seem to know every little thing about me?"

"Just do whatever he told you to do," Ash said. "Don't ask me to explain it. Cuts, bug bites, sprains, bruises, heck—broken bones. All I know is it works every time."

"Magic mud? Maybe you ought to bottle it. Make some extra bucks."

"It's not the mud that works. It's Wally's digging that does the job. Can't bottle that."

26

The men were right about the mud. Hidden by a dense stand of alders, Beth carefully stripped off her jeans. The hot coffee had left a bright red imprint on her thigh that looked a little bit like a hand with long fingers. The shape brought to mind Wally's unusually lengthy digits, like a pianist's.

She tossed her jeans onto a rock, then waded into the water that gently lapped its sides. The chill to her toes was knife-like, nerve-severing. She tipped the edge of the coffee can into the clear water and took in enough to turn the dry brown dirt into pasty goo. Water bugs skittered out of her way, and she returned to the bank as she stirred the contents with her fingers.

The mud was silky smooth when she applied it to her burn, and the chilly texture gave her immediate relief, calming down the raw discomfort. It felt so nice that she opted not to wash it off right away, but stood there at the bank letting the brownish trickle of water trace the shape of her legs and drip off the bones of her ankles. She closed her eyes and turned her face up to the warming sun, the new heat of the day mingling with the cool salve and creating peace.

This was mercy, that all the emotions that scalded her soul like boiling coffee—her grief, anxiety, and fear—could be so easily masked by a handful of mud, if only for the moment. Beth stood there, not wanting the peace to go away any sooner than it had to. She stood there until she felt the mud begin to dry and tug on her skin, and she allowed herself to imagine that the warm sun on her head was the steadying, strengthening hand of God.

Beth opened her eyes and Mercy was on the rock, stretched out atop the jeans, head resting on his front paws. It was no surprise that he could be so stealthy; the shock came that Herriot, who never before had approached Beth without a greeting, seemed to have learned his tricks. She sat beside him on her haunches, panting happily with her tongue hanging out one side of her mouth.

"Come to see if Wally knows his stuff?" she asked them. The wolf yawned.

Beth waded back into the stream, finding the cold water more pleasant this time. She stooped and scooped the water in the cup of her hands, ladling it up over the mud on her leg, rinsing and rubbing and half expecting the process to hurt, half knowing that it would not.

When the mud was gone, her skin was smooth and clear.

She regarded this fact with a strange mixture of awe and acceptance, the kind of expectation she had that the sun would rise every morning, though the event was uniquely beautiful every time. Deep within, she knew that this couldn't have happened if Wally hadn't said it would.

A tiny rebel in her thought she ought to test this.

Beth climbed onto the bank and returned to the rock. She pulled at the jeans under the wolf's belly, and he neither objected nor moved to get off of them. She tugged them against his body weight until they were free, then used them like a towel to dry herself off.

"That kind of thing is just an everyday occurrence for you two, is it?" she asked the dogs. Herriot's happy tail started whapping the rock and Mercy as it flopped back and forth. When had the canines started getting along?

She changed into the fresh jeans she'd stuffed into the backpack, then rolled the cuffs up to her knees and sat down beside the dogs. She lifted her foot onto her knee so she could see the cut she'd received while going after these two at the ranch. The glue she'd used to seal the wound held well, but the injury remained tender and red.

It's not magic mud, she reminded herself. But didn't she have . . . a talent?

She scooped more mud out of the can and applied it to the bottom of her foot. Then she propped it on the rock to dry a little in the sun, as she had the coffee burn.

A small amount of mud coated her fingers. Using Herriot's demeanor to gauge Mercy's, Beth assumed that the wolf's docile behavior would continue. So she held the mud under his muzzle and let him sniff it.

"I don't suppose you would explain this to me, however it is that you talk," she said. "How does the healing work? Why can't I make sense of it, what gets fixed, or what lives or dies, or how, or when?"

She reached out and rubbed the tiny bit of mud into one of the scarred groves running down the wolf's back. His head snapped back and he nipped at her wrist as if she'd hurt him. She snatched her fingers out of his reach. The moment lasted half a second and was like a gunshot that launched her heart into a hundred-meter sprint.

The wolf got up and stalked off the rock. Herriot looked at Beth, accusing her of stupidity, then followed Mercy.

Some of Beth's confusion returned. Alone on the rock now, she stuck her mud-caked foot back into the stream and let it dangle there. Maybe it didn't matter if she didn't understand what was happening to her. Her journey to Burnt Rock was what she needed to be doing, and she couldn't wait for clarity on everything before she did it.

She took the map out of the top of her pack and opened it up.

With a red marker, Wally had marked out a trail that appeared to cut several miles off the journey. If she left within the hour, the map promised, she should arrive in the small town by nightfall. She wondered if she could trust the route not to put her in harm's way, or if Wally's lines would lead her to insurmountable cliffs and chasms that couldn't be crossed.

When Beth took her foot out of the water, her toes had no feeling in them, and the wound on the bottom of her foot was also numb. But it remained inflamed at the edges and ghostly white down the center. She sighed, not sure what she'd been expecting, or even simply hoping for. But then, Wally hadn't said anything about fixing her foot, had he? All he had promised was a route to Burnt Rock, and a leg that could endure the saddle on the way there.

She prepared to leave.

Dotti parked her 4x4 right in front of Garner's shop to make it look busy. Busyness drew more business these days. She'd do him proud while he recovered and would try not to worry in the meantime. Worry was exhausting, and a body needed stamina in order to be helpful.

She left her keys in the ignition, just as everyone left their front doors unlocked. More efficient that way for all the running around and car-swapping one did in a town this size. She bipped up the stairs, crossed the porch, and shook her head when she saw that the door was actually open, leaning into the house by three or four inches.

Dotti gripped the doorknob and burst in, the better to shock the thief who might think he could walk off with a few bottles of salve while the shopkeeper had stepped out.

Instead she was the one who clutched the throat of her jacket and gasped. The bookseller Nova was at the base of the stairs that led to the second-story bedrooms. She held on to the balled newel-post cap with both hands as if her knees had already begun to buckle. Her fine hair clung to her face as if she'd been swimming, and sweat had turned her light gray cotton shirt the color of charcoal around her throat.

"Mr. Remke?" The voice was so weak.

"Nova?" Dotti said. She reached out for the girl and helped her to kneel on a step.

"Where's Mr. Remke?"

"He's ill, honey. What can I do that would help you?"

"I was wondering if he has—a tincture? A cramp bark tincture?"

Dotti hadn't the foggiest idea what a cramp bark tincture might be. She'd never seen a woman suffer from menstrual cramps like these.

"I don't know. I don't know. Have you bought some from him before?"

Nova shook her head slightly, as if shaking it too hard might cause unspeakable nausea. "It's called *Viburnum*. Could you . . . could you look?"

Of course she could look, if she had the slightest idea how to spell the word. And being an ancient veteran of excellent customer service, Dotti would have looked it up and asked all sorts of questions and turned the house inside out to find precisely what this woman needed so that she could leave happy.

"My dear," Dotti said, "you seem to be beyond the help of a tincture of vubeer . . . vubur . . .

"*Viburnum*," Nova whispered, and her hand went to her stomach. Her cheeks were flushed, and Dotti thought she might lose her lunch right there. But she merely swayed.

"Let me call Dr. Ransom for you. I know right where she is."

"No, just a . . . tincture will do. Please." Nova took a deep breath, sharp and steep, and braced herself where she knelt. When the pain passed, she closed her eyes and panted lightly.

"I really think we should get you to a doctor."

At this Nova began to sob, and she dropped her forehead to one of the higher steps, and Dotti's alarm grew. She decided that she wouldn't try to sort this one out on her own. She would call Cat, then go sit with Garner while the good doctor got to the bottom of Nova's situation.

"I'm getting Catherine."

"No. Not her."

"Why not? She's a doctor. You're sick. Don't be a fool too. What do you have against Dr. Ransom?"

"She . . . killed . . . my baby," the woman sobbed. "That doctor."

The girl was ranting. The fever had made her delirious. Dr. Ransom was a physician, not a killer. And yet this did look like a miscarriage at least. There was a small puddle of dark blood forming on the stair around Nova's knee.

"Promise me you won't call her," Nova pleaded. "Promise me."

Whatever it took before that lake of blood became an ocean.

"Where is the baby's father?" Dotti demanded.

"Far away."

"Can I call him?"

"No. He . . . doesn't know. It doesn't matter."

"Well that's just dandy. Tell me who to call for you, because I'm not the person you need. Do you understand that, Nova? Who can I call?"

She shook her head. No one.

"You need medical help, and I won't be responsible for your refusing it. You came to the wrong person for that. So let's try to reach an agreement here. I will give you three minutes of my time to search the house for the vuh . . . vuh . . ."

"*Viburnum.*"

"Viburnum," Dotti repeated.

"V-i-b . . . u-r . . . n-u-m."

Dotti rushed to grab a scrap of paper behind Garner's cash register. "The Romans could have come up with shorter Latin, don't you think?"

"It's probably in a brown bottle."

Dotti quickly scribbled the word on the scrap. She started searching Garner's pretty shelves immediately. "Three minutes starting now. If I can't find it in three minutes, I am taking you directly to Catherine. Those are my conditions." When Garner came around, she would recommend he alphabetize his inventory.

Nova nodded. The rosy color of her feverish cheeks had intensified.

It took Dotti all of thirty seconds to confirm that Garner didn't have the tincture Nova needed on these shelves. She went through the kitchen and raced downstairs to the basement, knowing exactly where Garner kept what little stock he had. It took her less than a minute to pillage these small boxes. No *Viburnum.*

But then she recalled that Garner had shipments brought up from the post office by one of Hank's fine sons, who deposited these in Garner's ample pantry at the back of the kitchen until Garner could process them all. There might be something there, especially since there was nothing anywhere else in the house. Surely a fresh order of *Viburnum* awaited upstairs! She hauled herself back up into the kitchen and turned quickly into the pantry.

Nothing. Nothing. Nothing. Dotti slapped her hands together as if dusting flour from her fingers. "Well, I've held up my end of the bargain," she called out as she returned to the entry hall. "And I'm relieved. Even if I'd found a tincture, you still should have seen the doc—"

The staircase was empty except for the evidence of Nova's crisis. The front door was wide open. And Nova Yarrow was tearing away from Garner's house in the driver's seat of Dotti's 4x4.

27

The course that Wally set for Beth was steeper than the one she would have chosen. She rode Hastings, and Herriot trotted behind her. The wolf, again, had vanished. As the sun peaked and then began to sink, Beth came up the mountains behind Burnt Rock through a recovering burn area. Ten years ago, when Beth was an adolescent, a lovesick and irresponsible forest ranger—someone with no excuse—had burned her ex's letters in a campfire. Sparks of bitterness escaped the pit with the help of a summer wind.

Until this day, Beth had forgotten about that incident, which made headlines across the country. For ten years the earth had been gradually reawakening in bursts of greens among the black matchsticks of firs and pines. It would take a few more decades before all visible evidence of the scorching was erased, but even then the earth would be able to tell its story in the layers of rock and rings of trees.

The promise of restoration was mixed up together with the permanent proof of death. Beth supposed that a person might look at this scene and call it hopeful, while someone else might look at the same place and call it tragic. The burn wasn't planned and, according to prevailing opinion, never should have happened.

But what if the same blaze had been set off by a lightning strike or a drought? Such triggers raised flames in these mountains every year, and most of them went unnoticed. Was a fire destructive only when caused by a careless person, and beneficial only when scheduled, and neutral when considered to be an "act of God"? Was any event better or worse than the other?

Beth's mind wanted the world's causes and effects to make sense, and she was frustrated by the idea that they might mingle in such a sloppy way.

Some of the blackened tree skeletons stood, and some had fallen to create a maze for anyone passing through. Hastings wasn't impeded by any of it but carried her on sure footing exactly where Beth's compass and Wally's map instructed them to go.

The aspen here flourished, because aspen were not individual trees, but a unified organism that grew from a single taproot. This root was protected deep underground from even the largest, most devastating fires, and it was constantly sending up vibrant shoots while other plants struggled to be reborn from seeds in the charred soil. The great irony of the aspens' natural durability, Beth often thought, was that the wood itself was too soft for most construction purposes. When these trees were harvested, they were used to make matchsticks.

The group climbed out of the lower elevations that the aspen preferred. It took several hours and more frequent rests for Hastings, who felt the altitude as much as any human might, though he was fit to endure it. The long-needled ponderosas too eventually yielded ground to the spruces—the dusty-blue Colorados and the yellow-green Engelmanns, the hardiest of trees in this oxygen-deprived air. The undergrowth also thinned out, and Beth could see the timberline on the peaks behind the shorter slope she scaled. Even now, in August, remnants of last winter's snow caked the mountainsides' shady crevices.

And then they reached a ridgetop, and the ground fell away as if it had been chipped off by God's chisel. Beth found herself looking down onto the old mining village that was Burnt Rock, which she guessed to be about two miles away. A modern paved road wound up the mountainside and into Burnt Rock from the southeast. She saw fresh paint on restored facades, and colorful signs that shouted out to tourists of opportunities to pan for gold or tour a mine or ride a mule or experience a miracle.

That last one caught Beth's eye, but she couldn't make out the details that would explain the meaning.

She saw a hotel, and what she presumed was a post office, and a long string of conjoined shops lining the main drag. The street was like the center vein in a narrow brown leaf, with more slender veins branching off to the north and south, unpaved routes that led to free-standing buildings and boxy, haphazardly arranged homes and cars. A few multipassenger vans were parked in a wide lot at the far end of town. She spotted one building that might be a stable, with mules rather than horses ambling in the corral.

Directly beneath her at the base of the cliff was a squat building with a roof like a wagon wheel turned on its side, the hub a large domed skylight. It might be a church positioned to keep watch over the town.

To the left of Beth was a path that led downward by first going away from the sheer drop. Mercy took this route.

Herriot did not. Facing away from Mercy's path, she barked once at something Beth couldn't see. It was a vocalization like her intruder-alert bark, but something about it was different. She stood at attention, ears and tail erect.

"C'mere, girl," Beth said, and she clicked her tongue as she turned Hastings toward the trail.

Herriot bounded away from her.

"Herriot! Come!" This time Beth whistled. Her dog responded with three short barks and a plunge through a tight stand of spruces, and then she was silent.

"Herriot!"

On the trail, Mercy had come back into Beth's view and seemed to be waiting for her.

"Your girlfriend's run off again," she said to the wolf.

The wolf appeared uninterested in this revelation. He turned around and resumed his walk. Beth took a deep breath, sent up a prayer for Herriot's safety, and followed Mercy.

He led the descent down a very shallow Z-shaped trail. At one point she thought the trail might bypass the town entirely, but then a sharp left turn offered to put her in the right direction again. A signpost told her that if she didn't turn, her present course would take her up to a mine called the Caged Bird.

The next leg of the trail was no more steep, but much longer, and as she passed through a thick stand of Engelmann spruce, she lost sight of Mercy. The trees and the setting sun darkened her way considerably. But Hastings' good sense of direction didn't falter, and he brought her onto a single-lane dirt road, which was something of a driveway. To her right she was at eye level with the building she'd looked down upon from the cliff.

A landscaped welcome at the top of the road seemed at odds with its naturally rugged surroundings. A sculpted path of pea gravel, flower beds full of blooming annuals, and molded plastic benches bearing placards with donors' names invited her into the Burnt Rock Harbor Sweet Assembly. The drive appeared to make a loop around the building. A dusty 4x4 was parked at the side of this sign, in front of a lattice-covered walkway.

The wolf sat under the shelter as if he'd been waiting for her.

A piercing shriek came out of the building and sent Hastings backward three or four paces. Beth uttered calming sounds to him, though the sound had washed away the beauty of the place like a flash flood.

There was another cry, less piercing this time and angry, but also longer, more agonizing. Thickened by sadness, like a wail.

The wolf turned and padded toward the entrance of the building.

Beth followed him. She tied off Hastings at one of the split-rail fences bordering a high-altitude garden.

One of the double doors stood open. The thick wood panels bore carved designs, and the one that was closed bore a crouching mountain lion poised to leap onto a horse carrying a young woman. The image gave Beth shivers.

The wail poured through the open door. That kind of sadness in this "sweet harbor" made as much sense as all those fire-blistered tree skeletons upright in the blooming green earth.

The lobby of the church looked like a museum, dim and with track lighting illuminating art on the earth-toned walls. Beth passed through it without noticing any details. When the scream came this time, she was sure it belonged to a woman, and it was a scream of anger and protest and grief. It was exactly the scream she herself had put into Jacob's ear when he found her wandering along the highway after her father's death.

The round room seemed to be a sanctuary, with six sections of pews coming out from the center like the arms of a snowflake. One of the aisles led directly from the passage where Beth stood to the center of the room, where a low rail encircled a pit with a low-burning gas flame in the center. Directly in front of it, a woman with her back to Beth had collapsed onto her side. She appeared to be alone. One of the woman's hands still gripped the rail, elevating her right arm. The left was a pillow for her tilted head. Her keening filled the room.

For a fraction of a second the form appeared to be a fallen antelope rather than a woman, and then the vision vanished. But it was enough to propel Beth to her side. The carpet along the aisle had been stained with a dark drip.

Beth knelt beside her at her shoulders, which jerked with each hiccupping sob. Touching her might be a shock, so Beth refrained. Still, the woman sensed her and reacted immediately, but with no physical strength; she held her breath and turned her head toward Beth. Her eyes were swollen and red, and still filled with tears, and fine strands of silky black hair crossed her face.

"Let me help you," Beth said. "What's wrong?"

The woman's voice was a whisper. "Everything."

"What can I do?"

"Nothing."

"Are you sick?"

The woman released the rail, and her arm flopped to the ground. Beth wondered how the woman had come here alone in this condition.

"Can I get someone for you?"

The woman licked her lips and drew the back of her hand across her eyes. "Is God around?" She cleared her throat and sharpened the edge on her voice. "Because I'd like to talk to him about a few things."

Beth said, "I don't know everything about God, but I think a church is as good a place as any to find him."

"This is no church," the woman said. "No miracles for anyone but Mathilde."

"Can I pray for you?"

"If I die. Not before."

It was such a strange and terrible thing to say that Beth reached out and touched the woman, as if holding on to her shoulder could prevent her from leaving the material world. Her clothes were hot as if the skin beneath it boiled, and the woman flinched.

"Your hands are ice!" she cried out, but she didn't brush Beth's hand off or try to roll away. In just a few seconds the tension in her arms began to release, one muscle fiber at a time. Perhaps she was too spent.

"Is there a friend—"

"He left me."

It sounded like abandonment, though it could have been much less. *He left me here to fetch the doctor.*

There was no ring on the woman's left hand. But there was blood coating her terribly thin legs, which looked like toothpicks protruding from her black skirt.

The woman reached up and put her hand on top of Beth's. Her breathing leveled out.

"This helps," she said.

"What's your name?"

"Nova."

"That's pretty."

"It's a pointless name for an ugly life," Nova said, and Beth felt all of the woman's heartbreak in those words. She felt protective, maternal, even though she was the younger of the pair. She wondered if Nova's parents had picked the right name for her.

"You need a doctor," Beth said. It would be difficult to get this woman into the 4x4, if that was her car outside, but Beth could go quickly and come back. "Where can I find one?"

"I'm a doctor," said a voice at the back of the sanctuary.

Beth stood. A severe-looking woman with pale features and dark, shining hair that stroked the bottom of her chin was coming down the aisle Beth had just traversed seconds ago. Her walk was more of a stalk, a weighty pounding of feet designed to make a pouting child feel powerful. She aimed herself at Beth. She carried a large purse.

Beth immediately disliked the doctor and simultaneously thought that it was unfair of her to make the judgment. But Beth disliked her heavy footfall. And she hated the distrustful look the woman shot at her, as if Beth had broken into her house to steal jewelry and secret files.

"I don't know you." The doctor said it like an accusation.

"The door was open," Beth said, and then felt like a child. She shouldn't have to defend her presence in this public place.

"Who are you?" the woman demanded.

Beth might or might not have offered her name at that point. She was thinking of asking for the doctor's name first—an ID, credentials, all kinds of ridiculousness in a setting like this. But none of it mattered, because Nova started shrieking like the terrorized star of a horror flick, and she grabbed hold of Beth's leg with both hands and started kicking out at the doctor.

"Don't touch me! Don't touch me!"

Beth tried both to calm her and to pry Nova's fingers off of her boots. The sick woman's screams drowned out all of Beth's soothing words, and the doctor didn't have a chance of getting close. Nova's energy was fierce but brief, driven by a supply of adrenaline that had already been tapped. Beth's was just kicking into gear. Should she protect Nova from this "doctor" or hand her over?

Where was Mercy to show her what she should do?

"This is your fault, you monster!" Nova screamed. Already her legs had given out, but she'd scooched herself off a spot on the floor that was an awful, sopping crimson.

The doctor's attention had shifted from Beth to Nova, and her demeanor switched just as quickly from hostile to placating. The light in her eyes brightened and the lines of her brow smoothed out. Perhaps she was as protective of Nova as Beth felt. If Beth had walked in on a stranger with a sick friend, she might have reacted similarly. But Nova's reaction made little sense.

"Nova, Nova," the doctor cooed, ignoring Beth now. "I'm so sorry about your baby."

A baby! All the blood looked freshly terrible.

"Get away!"

"Nova, honey, let me help you."

The doctor had set her purse on a pew and withdrew a very

small syringe out of her bag. She uncapped the needle and then held it slightly behind her, so as not to frighten Nova any further.

"I don't want your help, Catherine. I'll sue you!"

"But you're bleeding," Beth pleaded. She got down on her knees next to the frantic woman.

"Let us help you," the doctor said, and in that "us" Beth understood that whatever the truth of this battle was, she and Catherine had just joined ranks, and Nova would soon come out on the losing side.

Nova grabbed Beth by the shoulders now and pulled their faces close. "You help me," she said, and the words were a burst of hot air across Beth's cheeks. "Not her."

As Nova begged, Beth sensed Mercy crouching behind her, invisible as he had been the day the antelope lay at her feet, baring his teeth just a little and pushing her forward into a great mystery. Beth placed her hands atop Nova's and closed her eyes and began to pray.

The doctor said, "Dotti sent me to find you, honey. Dotti . . . and Garner."

Beth lost the thread of her prayer right away. Garner sent this woman? How many men named Garner might live in a town of four hundred people?

"They're so worried about you." The doctor's words, falsely sweet, were like a knife slicing Beth and Nova apart. Beth felt Nova release her and spring backward, away, to her perceived escape. Nova's fear of the doctor strengthened her.

She was scrabbling, a blind crab. Catherine rushed her. Nova saw the needle this time. Her screams started all over. She pushed away.

The back of Nova's head connected with the hard seat of a wooden pew and she sagged against it instantly, her spine forming an uncomfortable curve.

Beth gasped. Catherine sighed and knelt to inject the contents of the syringe into Nova's arm.

"If people would just accept my help," the doctor muttered without looking at Beth, "their lives would be so much simpler."

She emptied the contents and looked up at Beth as she capped the syringe and returned it to her bag. "You can go now," she said, unaware of the wolf sitting directly behind her in the shadow of the pews. His eyes glinted.

"I think you should accept *my* help," Beth said.

28

Nova needed to awake from her sedation in her own apartment, which was located conveniently enough to Cat's own. It was the only way this scenario could end well, Cat thought, with Nova having enough time to accept her loss without blaming it on anyone.

Cat was glad for the redheaded woman's presence then, when she realized that she'd need help getting Nova home and into bed. Never before had she been so grateful that the woman weighed less than a large dog. Now that Nova had miscarried, her physical size was nothing to regret.

"Shouldn't you get her to a hospital?" the redhead asked. She stood away from Cat but also close, in that middle ground of indecision where she was probably trying to make sense of Nova's hysterics and Cat's intentions.

"What's your name?" Cat asked. She used her naturally gentle voice and warm gaze, fearing she might have set these aside too long in her efforts to find Nova. It had been lucky for her that the woman was a mystical kook who very predictably had sought out Miracle Mattie rather than a hospital.

"Beth."

"Beth, I'm Dr. Ransom. As awful as it is, this woman's had a miscarriage. That's all. They happen all the time, no medical intervention necessary. In her case, it wasn't even unexpected. Which is part of the reason why she was so upset." She touched Beth's hand lightly. "You're young. Hopefully you won't ever have to know this kind of sadness firsthand. She just needs to rest awhile in her own bed."

"It didn't seem like she trusted you."

Cat snatched her fingers back from Beth's skin. It felt like she'd dipped the tips in a sticky goo, a quicksand that would absorb and drown her if she didn't keep her distance. That was absurd, of course—this was a human being standing next to her, as fleshy as Cat herself. But she couldn't shake off the sensation. She fished for a reasonable reply that would facilitate Beth's help.

"You understand. I can't explain without violating her privacy. But you're right. She's had challenges. Difficulties outside of our control. Disappointment has taught her to mistrust the people who most want to help her. It's sad, really."

She thought Beth might be believing her.

"I heard you say that Garner sent you to help Nova."

That cold and sticky sensation of glue crawled up Cat's fingertips even though she was no longer touching Beth. She realized she was rubbing her hands together as if they were coated in crumbs. What interest could this girl have in Garner? She had only mentioned him because she knew Nova trusted him.

"I did," she said cautiously.

"Is that Garner Remke?"

"Yes."

When Beth smiled she looked more like an innocent girl than a woman trying to judge the truth of Cat's words. "I'm Garner's granddaughter. I've been looking for him. This is unbelievable, that you know him. I thought it would take longer. But I guess I shouldn't be surprised." She glanced around the room as if looking for something, then her attention came back to Cat. "Do you know where I can find him?"

"His granddaughter? I didn't know . . . Oh, this is unfortunate." This was worse than unfortunate. It was devastating, someone come to demand Garner's attention and perhaps take him away. Her mind filled with questions: *Where is your mother? Is your father alive? Why did you come on a horse?*

"What's unfortunate?"

Cat needed to think hard, and fast. She looked down at Nova's peaceful but bloodied form. "Please, help me get this woman to my car. And if it's not too much trouble for you, the two of us can get her home. Then we can talk about . . . your grandfather."

Beth agreed to the delay. She bent and lifted Nova's slight frame at the shoulders with the strength of someone used to physical labor and the stomach of a woman who'd seen plenty of live births.

"You live on a ranch?" Cat asked, knowing the answer. "The boots, your horse . . ."

"Yes, the Blazing B."

"I've heard of it. I think I've heard of your father."

"Abel Borzoi. Maybe Garner's mentioned him."

Cat didn't confirm or deny this. The less she said about Garner, the more flexibility she'd have in crafting a believable story for the man's grandchild.

"My dad passed away," Beth said. "Just last week. I need to talk to Garner."

She wasn't looking at Cat when she said this, or she might have seen the fear that reached up and took Cat by the throat.

"I'm very sorry," she murmured.

"Me too," said Beth.

They carried Nova out of the church into the darkness that had gathered while they were inside.

On the very short drive downhill from the church to the residence over the bookstore, Cat had time to settle down and think. She realized that she was angry, and her first order of business was to get to the root of her anger so that she could deal with it. If she didn't find her center, she'd make a mistake that she'd regret. That's exactly what had happened last time.

Last time . . . last time . . . when she had made the sick child Amelia well and then the sick child's entire family had abandoned her, though she might have found a secure place with them. All she wanted was a little gratitude. A little loyalty. A little recognition for her selfless work.

A chair at the family table.

Beth followed Cat's car on horseback, always just in view of the mirror. The doctor took the hairpin turns carefully as she tried to determine what she was most angry about:

Dotti, and not she, was tending to Garner at this very minute.

Nova had gone to Garner, not to Cat, for help.

A complete stranger had very nearly usurped Cat's role in aiding Nova. What could possibly be more insulting than that, to be thrown beneath the feet of people who didn't even live in town?

Soon individuals and then the whole of Burnt Rock would decide they didn't need Dr. Catherine Ransom. This was the bottom line, wasn't it? This was the truth that took all of the fury out of Cat's heart and replaced it with a nausea dead center in her gut. Again and again, she would be left behind, designated as unnecessary. A disappointment. Nonessential. Unloved.

On the bright side, the ergot had actually worked to deliver that fetus from a horrible, selfish mother. Cat hadn't expected that to succeed, although it might have been a nicer victory if the fungus had killed off mother and child both.

She would take good news where she could find it.

This effort to think positively put her mind back on task. What she was really, truly upset about, after all, was that the redheaded young woman with the blue eyes—the granddaughter Garner didn't know he had—had come with an agenda to catapult Garner away from Cat.

Coming into new mental clarity, Cat no longer cared exactly what Beth had come for. All that mattered now were these three things:

Getting Nova out of her hair.

Getting Beth Borzoi out of Burnt Rock.

Getting back to Garner.

Already, even Dotti tugged at Garner's affections, and that was trouble enough.

Cat parked at the rear of the building that she and Nova shared. She concentrated on filling her lungs with air, swelling to form a secure embrace around her rattling heart. Then she exhaled, and with these repeated, even breaths, she created a calm from the inside out, and then she created a plan to deal with Beth Borzoi.

She got out of the car and showed Beth where she could tie off the horse under a light. Then the women carefully carried Nova upstairs.

Nova's apartment was a small place, a mirror of Cat's, with the living room, kitchen, and dining room forming a large multipurpose area. Nova's sense of style was rustic, with mismatched pieces of furniture and blankets tossed over the arms of chairs. The freestanding bookcases on every wall were overflowing, and there were stacks of books on the floor, on the coffee table, on the miniscule dining table. Who could need so many books when she had her very own bookstore right beneath her feet?

It didn't matter. Besides the books was a clear spiritual element that would assist in the story Cat aimed to tell Beth. There were candle stubs in sticks, and dream catchers hanging from each corner of the ceiling, and incense cones that had crumbled and yet still hung on to their smoky aromas. There was a stack of tarot cards on the coffee table next to an academic essay about crop circles and a newsletter, *The Science of Dreams*. One bookshelf held not books but DVDs pertaining to ghosts and hauntings and the paranormal world. She saw Beth take all this in and felt certain it wouldn't be difficult to get her to believe in the version of Nova that Cat was about to create.

"She's a bit of an eccentric," Cat said. "She believes in everything except common sense. A little of this, a little of that. I personally think she's working on creating her own religion, Jim Jones style. Do you know who Jim Jones was?"

Beth glanced at her but didn't answer. Cat sensed her caution and worried about it.

With Nova slung between them, Cat and Beth waddled under an arch into a very short passageway and then to the bedroom. They easily arranged Nova on the blankets, and then Beth left. Cat let her go, gave her silent permission to get a second look at the outer evidence of Nova's inner life.

If Beth did, though, she didn't remark on it. Instead she returned with a damp washcloth and a small bowl full of warm water. She began to carefully clean Nova's bloody legs, and Cat watched her, both impressed and irritated. She itched to yank the cloth out of Beth's hands and do this caregiving work herself. Her dislike of Nova helped her to resist.

"You seem to be a natural," Cat said. Yet one more reason to get this girl out of Burnt Rock as soon as possible.

"Decency doesn't require any skill."

"Maybe not, but I know plenty of decent people who wouldn't get someone else's blood on their hands like this. It was great luck that you came upon Nova when you did."

"Luck," Beth echoed, as if she'd never heard the word before. "Was she very far along?"

"No. Look at that. Her color's already coming back. She's

resting well." Cat fluffed a pillow and opened a window. "When you're done, you'll come with me. I live next door, and you can rest there. There isn't anything else we can do for her until she sleeps this off."

"We shouldn't leave her alone."

"She won't be alone. My door is right across the atrium. I'll keep it open."

It was very difficult for Cat to believe that Beth's frown was sincere. Nova was a complete stranger to her. She couldn't be that emotionally invested already. But Beth said, "Can't we call someone? A friend of hers? Does she have family in town?"

Cat's impatience flared a little. "Like I said, she's an eccentric. If she wasn't so pretty she'd be fit for the villain of a Grimm Brothers' fairy tale. She doesn't like anyone except for when they're buying her books. You saw how she reacted to me—the very person in the best position to help her. Trust me, she'd rather be left alone than have the two of us hovering. I hate to say it, but your kindness is wasted on her."

Beth didn't seem to mind this and rinsed the cloth in the bowl, then continued the bathing.

"What did you give her?" Beth asked.

Why do you care? Cat thought. But she said, "A sedative and a painkiller. She won't wake before dawn."

A heavy minute passed while Cat waited to see whether Beth would come away. Cat's impulse to snatch the washcloth and throw the bloody bowl in the girl's face was getting harder to ignore.

"Beth, I'd like to talk with you about Garner. But not here."

"What's wrong with this place?"

"You'll understand soon enough. Please." Cat stretched out her hand, beckoning, and finally Beth placed the washcloth into the bowl. She carried these out to the kitchen, where she spent a tedious amount of time washing up.

Then she followed Cat out of Nova's apartment, and when Cat pulled the door closed behind her, Beth returned to prop it open.

Now Cat leaned into her lies in earnest. "If I'd known when I said Garner's name that you're his granddaughter, I would have been more sensitive."

"About what?"

Cat led Beth downstairs, down the hall that ran behind the little bookstore and Cat's offices, then upstairs to her own apartment.

"I lied to Nova, Beth. About Garner sending me. She's not that close to Dotti, you see. But Garner . . ."

"But you know him, right? He lives here in Burnt Rock?"

Cat opened the door to her apartment and let Beth go in first. "Nova is something of a spiritualist. I don't know exactly what to call her. Garner was one of the few people who actually broke through her barriers. He was a pretty open-minded man himself. He—"

"I want to see Garner now," Beth said. She seemed to detect where Cat was going with this and maybe even thought that if she could cut off the doctor's words, she could prevent the content from being true. She was firm. Strong. Much stronger than she believed she was. Cat could see that clearly now, and it caused her to second-guess her approach. Her faltering was brief. She quickly recommitted.

"Beth, I'm so sorry. This is very difficult for me."

"Where is my grandfather?"

"He's dead, Beth. He passed away two years ago. Liver cancer." She watched the blood go out of Beth's freckled cheeks. "Nova was so fond of him. She would have believed that his spirit, or ghost, or whatever you want to call it, would have summoned me to help her. Crazier things have happened at that church, if you know anything about it. It might have been a cruel thing for me to do, but I needed to calm her down."

Beth stood in the middle of the apartment looking like a ghost herself, forbidden from communicating with the living. Cat avoided touching her. She indicated that Beth should take a seat on the sofa. Everything else now should be easy.

"Sit here. I know this is a shock. Truly, I'm sorry."

Cat rushed into her small kitchen and decided that Beth didn't have the look of a drinker. She selected a glass pitcher of green tea over the bottle of white wine and poured some over a glass of ice. She added a small amount of herbal sweetener and then, from another cabinet, withdrew a small vial of benzodiazepine, which she punctured with a paring knife. Tasteless and odorless, the date-rape drug of choice was also good for her personal use, on nights when she was plagued by nightmares or insomnia. This stuff could wipe out any bad dream, and Cat had her share of them.

She hesitated over how much to put in the glass. It was important that Beth not get sick over this, because the goal was to get her out of town fast, not to have to nurse her for a few days. She, like Trey Bateman, was not a patient Cat wanted to take under wing.

She estimated Beth's weight, did some calculations in her head, and hoped the effects would wear off around three in the morning, give or take a half hour. That would be late enough to prevent Beth from poking around, and early enough for Beth to wake feeling normal. She could get a good start before the town woke up.

Beth was still in a speechless daze when Cat handed her the tea. She looked at the glass as if she'd just emerged from the desert, took it from Cat, and drank half of it in just a few gulps.

"How long since your last sip of water?" Cat asked.

Beth stared at the glass in her hand. "Hastings must be more thirsty than I am."

"Your horse?"

Beth nodded.

"I'll get him something."

"Where can I take him? He needs food."

"Let me take care of that for you. Don't worry. Don't worry."

"Okay." Beth's emotional strength had already left her, Cat thought. Her physical strength would follow in a few minutes. "He's dead?" She finished the rest of the glass, and Cat thought maybe the wine would have been a better vehicle for the drug after all. She took the glass.

"I'll get you a blanket."

"Was he married?"

"Who, Garner?" Cat laughed. "No."

"Is he buried here?" Beth asked.

Cat stopped laughing abruptly. She saw where this might go if she got sloppy. "Cremated," she said. "Scattered."

"Who handled his estate?"

"No idea. Do you want some more tea? I've got plenty."

"Was there an attorney?"

Cat didn't answer right away, and Beth didn't appear to notice the delay. Cat mentally pieced together the motive behind the line of questions. Did Garner have money? She couldn't imagine it, but these were the questions of a gold digger. More than anything, Cat wanted the woman to leave Burnt Rock and not come back. By morning, she'd forge a convincing rabbit trail for Beth to follow.

"I'll ask around for you. It's been years."

"Just two, right? You said two." Beth dropped her head into her hands. "What am I going to do?"

"Let's leave the big decisions for later, Beth. You rest now. Everything will look better in the daylight."

"You're right. I'm so tired."

"What did you need Garner for, Beth? I know he and your mother . . . had a falling out. Why did you come all this way? On Hastings?" She'd have to take the horse to the stables, of course. If the beast wasn't fed and watered, it wouldn't be able to carry Beth far enough fast enough.

Beth was asleep. Cat studied her, able to see now the line of Garner's nose in hers, and the length of his fingers in her hands.

She locked the door on her way out, plotting the hours so she could return before Beth awakened. It was troubling that the girl felt the need to investigate Garner's death. Cat wasn't sure how to circumvent that.

As much as she was committed to keeping people alive, she might have to resort to killing after all.

29

The room smelled wrong. The blanket was the wrong texture. The moonlight was not coming through the window at the right angle. In fact, it wasn't coming through the window at all. There was no window where it ought to have been.

The foreign shadows that crouched over Beth's head confused her. She felt cold, although the blanket was heavy. She took a deep, sharp breath and sat up, and the hulking forms in the room righted themselves into sensible objects. A lampshade there, and a tall TV cabinet over there. Phantom shapes in a coffin of a room. There was no light, only the night vision of her own eyes adjusting to shades of gray. A fan rotated slowly overhead, charcoal paddles turning on a slate ceiling. She remembered that Garner was dead, but she couldn't piece together how she knew this.

The doctor had told her he was dead.

"Dr. Ransom?" she said, hoping her tone was normal.

At the sound of her voice a large wet muzzle prodded her cheek, and she had the feeling the dog had been doing this for some time, trying to rouse her.

"Herriot?"

Beth reached over and turned on the tabletop lamp. Instead

of illuminating the room, the bulb blinded her for long seconds of blinking and squinting and shielding her eyes with her hands.

It wasn't Herriot, but Mercy. The door to the apartment was open, and he was already headed out and down the stairs.

Beth rose and knocked her shin on the coffee table, then found her way around it. In her sleep she had been dreaming of California, the state buried in mounds of volcanic ash with real estate signs staked at the top of each heap—For Sale. And she woke thinking that Roy Davis had said something about Garner making his fortune in California, which made her think that Garner's attorney or estate manager might also be from there, and this was something she ought to mention to Dr. Ransom. It might lead somewhere. She tried to imagine what circumstances would lead a man to die without his own daughter learning of it, two years after the fact.

Her feet and hands seemed unnaturally heavy, swollen. She saw the dining room, the kitchen. The red numbers of the digital clock over the stove told her it was 1:20. No wonder she felt so groggy. On the other side of the room was a small archway leading to a hall, exactly like the one in Nova's apartment.

Nova's apartment? Who was Nova? Beth didn't pull up the answer to that question until she was standing on the landing outside the doctor's door, and then she remembered everything. She wondered if the doctor had gone to check on her.

"Dr. Ransom?" she asked again. Her voice sounded louder out here, where an atrium separated the doctor's flight of stairs from an identical set leading up to Nova's home. The bottom of the stairs was joined by a hall, and an exit to the parking lot behind the building.

Beth looked across the atrium to Nova's door. It stood open just as Beth had propped it a few hours ago. The gaping door seemed wrong to Beth, but she couldn't pinpoint why. It had something to do with the doctor wanting the door closed, and with it still being open while Dr. Ransom was most likely inside.

Still dusty and fully dressed from the two-day ride up the mountainside, Beth went out of the apartment and down the stairs. In the hall, as she passed by the exit, she saw through the narrow sidelights that Hastings was gone as promised.

She reached Nova's flight and turned to go up, then stumbled on the bottom step and went down on one knee. This kind of clumsiness wasn't like her, but after three nights without decent sleep, it was probably to be expected.

"Hello?" she said at the door without waiting to be invited in. "Dr. Ransom? Are you here?" Her foot brushed a large brown bag standing near the door, and she was greeted by the happy clinking of sturdy glass knocking together. She hadn't noticed this bag the first time she was here. It was folded over and stapled shut, and the thick lip of the sack bore the penned words *Mr. Remke.*

Beth studied this printing with the same confusion that had tainted her upside-down view of the shadows in Dr. Ransom's dark apartment. Surely it would make sense to her if she could just see it from the right mental angle. But she couldn't find it. Her reasoning was too wobbly. She knelt and pulled the staples apart at the top of the bag. Inside were six wide-mouth glass jars with screw-top lids.

She closed the bag, stood, then abandoned it. She took a few steps deeper into the living room. The lights seemed different, but she couldn't say how. Darker, though that might have just been the time of day or her weary eyes.

On one wall, an art light topped a matted black-and-white photograph that looked like an enlarged copy of an old glass photography plate. The lines were soft rather than sharp, and the gray tones had a hint of yellow in them, and several white scratches marred the negative. An Indian man sat on a gentle spotted horse that reminded Beth of Jacob's Gert, and a white man stood near the horse's head, holding the bridle. The Indian sat erect on a saddle, which Beth noticed because she had always thought of the Native Americans as bareback riders, though that was probably a narrow-minded assumption. But the saddle itself caught Beth's eye. That butterfly skirt, that hand-stamped pattern of flame, that silver stirrup—she knew this saddle.

It was Jacob's saddle. The one she'd stolen. Or one exactly like it.

In that dim moment of recognition she couldn't comprehend the saddle's connection to Burnt Rock, just as she couldn't figure out what a dead man would do with a bag full of glass jars. Her mind stayed on the saddle while her body passed under the archway and across the hall into Nova's room.

"Dr. Ransom?"

The sloping lampshade next to the bed cast geometric light on the walls and a line of shadow on the diagonal across Nova's face. She was still sleeping, as the doctor had said she'd be, but she had been perspiring, and tossing herself between the sheets as if they were a straitjacket that she couldn't escape, as if she wanted more than anything to be awake. The woman's expression was so pained that Beth worried. Maybe the lamplight was distorting her features. But she came closer and realized that it was not.

Nova's condition should have propelled Beth out the door in a wider search for Dr. Ransom. Instead she felt overcome with the certainty that she could do more to help Nova than any physician. She sat on the edge of Nova's bed and took the woman's hand, tacky and cold, and began to pray for the woman's peace and physical recovery.

In spite of her own spiritual crises, Beth believed in God's compassion. She had faith in his ability to meet the physical needs of people even before they understood their own spiritual needs. Just as Jesus had done for the man at the pool of Bethesda.

Beth sensed the first change in Nova's fingers. The surface of her skin warmed, and then her stiff joints softened like a winter creek, thawing. Her quick and shallow breathing found a healthier pace at a deeper level. And then the wrinkled worry of her brow smoothed out like a rumpled blanket tugged taut.

These were the changes in Nova. Beth herself felt an inner shift like a realignment of her spine, or a tidying up of her organs. It was a slight adjustment—like a handful of pine needles tossed on a campfire, or a firm leather rein applied to a horse's neck, or a rain-soaked clod of earth falling away from a hillside.

Nova's eyes opened as if she were a baby doll set upright. Beth jumped off the bed.

"She's not welcome here," Nova whispered. Under the clinging tendrils of stringy hair, her face was pale, and it seemed she lacked the strength to sit up, though her eyes were wide and alert.

At first Beth thought Nova was speaking about her to an unseen visitor. But then Nova looked at Beth and repeated herself.

"She's not welcome here."

"Who's not?" Beth asked.

"Catherine Ransom."

"She's not here now," Beth said.

Nova sighed with relief, and her eyes returned to a more relaxed, less petrified shape.

"She told me you'd sleep through the night," Beth said, returning to the edge of the bed. Nova reached out for her hand and gripped it fiercely.

"She says what she wants people to believe."

"Why would she lie about your sleep?"

"Because she's sick," Nova said. "Sick in the head. That's my diagnosis."

"Dr. Ransom told me you had a miscarriage. Was that a lie too?"

"*Miscarriage* sounds so unintentional." The peaceful lines of Nova's face began to collapse. "My baby's dead, and it was no accident."

"What happened?"

Her voice cracked. "Poison. She did it."

Beth hardly knew what to say to that kind of accusation. She didn't know which woman might be less reliable. Nova didn't seem to be in a clear state of mind. Nova lifted Beth's hand in hers and looked at Beth's calloused, dirty fingers through full, wet eyes.

"Your hands are very comforting. I remember them. In the church, before Catherine arrived." Beth let her twist and turn them in the angled light of the lamp. "These are good hands. A healer's hands."

Nova ran her fingertips over Beth's palm the way a carnival fortune-teller might assess the wrinkles. She turned Beth's wrist gently, admiring the tops of her hands as well.

"I'm not a healer," Beth said. "A wannabe vet, but not a healer."

"You were talking about the man at the pool of Bethesda."

Beth didn't think she had been speaking aloud.

"I heard that story once, a long time ago," Nova said. Beth feared she might be slipping back into sleep. "I like that story."

"Nova, is there someone I can get for you? A friend, a relative?"

Nova frowned and slowly shook her head. "I have no one. Just like that man. That poor paralyzed man." She drew a deep breath. "Catherine gave me some food. She hates me, you know. She hates the real healers. You ought to be careful of her. Garner isn't careful enough."

It was a difficult choice for Beth, which topic she ought to chase with which question. What were "real" healers? Was this "food" the same poison Nova had mentioned? Did Nova also see herself as some kind of doctor? Beth didn't so much choose as she allowed one question to fight its way to the top of the pile.

She said, "Is that how Garner died? She told me it was cancer. Do you think the doctor killed him?"

Nova gasped and used her grip on Beth to haul herself up to sit. Beth could see the tears flow into her eyes, going up like a wall of glass. "Mr. Remke is dead?"

"Isn't he?" Beth asked.

"That monster! That witch! I'll kill her with my own hands."

"Nova—"

"When did it happen?"

"I don't know exactly."

Nova's face began to crack. "I don't understand how this could have happened. If she killed him because of me, I'll never forgive myself. I saw him Sunday morning—I went to him for some peppermint, for the nausea."

"Sunday?" The meaning of the glass jars by the door was clearer now.

"I asked him to go with me to Mathilde's, but he couldn't just then. He said he was under the weather. And Monday I couldn't find him. I needed him, but he wasn't there."

"Nova, wait—"

"When you found me I was waiting, you know, waiting for that miracle they say can happen to the right person in the right place. I've seen it once before. It's never happened to me, but if anyone needed it to happen, last night I did."

"Nova."

"You have to wait and wait for such things. I don't know why. I was in so much pain."

"Dr. Ransom told me he died two years ago."

Nova's well of words ran dry.

"Two years ago," Beth repeated. She was standing next to the bed now, ready to leap to somewhere, but she had no direction. "He was with you Sunday morning?"

"Yes. I see Mr. Remke most days. He lives two blocks from here."

"Where?"

"On the Old Stage Road. Parallel to Main Street. He's got a shop."

"Garner's Garden."

"That's right."

253

"It's not just an online place?"

"No. It's his home too."

"What's the number, the house number?"

"I don't remember. Twenty-six? Twenty-eight? There's a sign hanging from the porch."

"I'll go check on him."

Nova gestured to the phone underneath her table lamp. "Just call him."

"It's not even two in the morning."

Nova reached for the phone and, in hesitating and squinting gestures, dialed it, while Beth felt suddenly sick and certain that the reason Dr. Ransom wasn't here was because she was *there*, killing the man she'd already proclaimed dead.

Of course, it might be that Nova was a lunatic.

"Nova, I shouldn't wait."

The woman didn't answer. Those lines of worry on her forehead that plagued her sleep began to reappear the longer she held the handset to her ear. She finally lowered it and raised her eyes to Beth. "He says he sleeps like a bear in winter."

"Are you okay for me to leave you?"

Nova reached out and gripped Beth's fingers. She closed her eyes and bowed her chin to her chest, then rested her other hand atop her slender belly, which was still tucked into the sheets. It wasn't long that she stayed this way, with Beth's fingers in a knuckle-crushing clench, but every second stretched out into a long minute for Beth, who didn't understand what Nova was doing. She appeared to be praying, as far as anyone interested in alien abductions and haunted houses might pray. But color was returning to her pallid skin, and the strength of her grip came as a great surprise.

"Where do you get your power?" Nova whispered.

"I don't have any power."

"Yes, you do. I can feel it."

"Then it must be from God."

She looked up into Beth's face, and she smiled. The lamplight and tears made her eyes sparkle. "You can do anything. You could be rich and famous."

"I don't think that's what he had in mind."

"I guess we'll see, won't we?"

"Nova," Beth finally said, as gently as she could. "I need to find Garner."

"I know." Nova reluctantly let go, looking at Beth's hands rather than her face. "Find him. And look out for Catherine Ransom. She's no doctor, I guarantee it."

30

t the bottom of Nova's stairs, the wolf was waiting for Beth with his nose pressed to the rear door like a dog who urgently needed to be let outside. Beth turned the knob and he sauntered out, heading at an easy pace straight for the unpaved road that ran up the hill behind the doctor's offices and into the impenetrable night.

Using a flashlight Nova had loaned to her, Beth set out after Mercy. Nova had given her instructions to get to Garner's shop and home. These would have been unnecessary if the wolf had waited for her, and the black margins that pressed in around her flashlight beam whispered anxious possibilities. A cloud of fatigue crowded Beth's head. The crouching mountains and her foggy awareness conspired to make everything seem darker, thicker.

She walked one block along the unpaved road, then paused at a cross street. In the center of the intersection she turned in a circle and then back, trying to locate a signpost confirming that she'd found the Old Stage Road. There was none, and soon she realized she'd lost track of her original position. Which way was west? Without the sun or mountains in view, she had no idea. Her compass was back at Dr. Ransom's apartment, in her pack.

She was considering how far she might go in any direction when Mercy's heavy weight leaned up against her thigh, and Beth's chilly fingers found the thick ruff of Mercy's neck. The grogginess fell away from her mind. He turned to the left. She followed.

She began to shine her light across the fronts of buildings that might have been stores or might have been homes, or in Garner's case, both. He wasn't the only one who did business where he also slept, judging by the painted wooden signs swinging from chains above the porches. Her light passed over handmade furniture, with model pieces lined up on each side of someone's door. One yard was home to a flock of swans made of old splayed tires that had been painted white. A plaque for Becky's Quilts advertised "Affordable Tools of the Trade."

It seemed everyone slept well under the security of moon-beams, with no need for streetlights or porch lights or any kind of illumination that would deter an intruder like Beth. Or Mercy. Garner's Garden was the fourth house on the right, its front door overlooking the heart of town at the bottom of the hill. It was a gin-gerbread house with a tidy picket fence closed by a short gate. She could see no garden to speak of, only an attractive arrangement of white and pink granite rocks, a few evergreen shrubs that lay close to the earth, several of the white-tire swans, and a single spruce tree.

The windows were dark. In that moment, Nova's claims about Dr. Ransom seemed both horrific and absurd. Who would rush to kill an old man because his granddaughter had come to visit him? And yet Beth had no trouble imagining that she might find the front door ajar and an old man dead on the floor of the living room, or the same old man not quite yet dead coming after her with an ax raised over his head because the doctor had told him Beth was coming to steal his soul.

Beth turned off the flashlight and let her eyes adjust to the night before letting herself in through the gate. The hinges were smoothly oiled and made no sound when she pushed it open, but the panel sprang out of her perspiring hands and closed with a rattling clack before she was ready. Mercy was already mounting the wood-plank steps at the end of the short pea-stone path. Beth followed quickly.

She didn't know why she expected the wolf to go to the front door. Instead he followed the wraparound porch to the rear of the house and sat down to wait for her at what appeared to be an entrance into the kitchen. A window overlooking the porch had no curtains or coverings, and the stove light illuminated a small galley. The knob turned easily in Beth's hands, and the door swung open.

Mercy rushed in and passed silently through the room and into a dark hall.

Beth left the door open. She was undecided on whether to call out for Garner or sneak up on Dr. Ransom, so she made the most easily reversed choice to stay silent. She stayed close to the kitchen counter, hoping that Mercy might return to her quickly. She wasn't prepared to follow him into the house just yet.

She stood in an eat-in kitchen with the galley and walk-in pantry to her left, the dining table in front of her, and a refrigerator behind the open door to her right. There was an exit into a room on the other side of the fridge, opposite the way Mercy had gone. It seemed she could go to the right and pass through what was probably a living area and make a full circle back. If she went this way, she could keep a wall at her back at all times. She started past the fridge.

The utility carpet silenced her boots but not the old floorboards underneath it. On her third step the entire house seemed to squeal and then burst into a primal scream, and the force of its energy knocked her to the ground.

Someone had come at her, his head to her rib cage like a linebacker. He took her backward a few feet before his gangly legs tangled with hers and they both tumbled down. Her head nicked the refrigerator handle as she tipped, and her back hit the floor before her hands could escape the tackle and brace her fall. Her rattled brain seemed to push against her eyes, and her mouth gaped for long seconds. By the stove's hood light, she made out a long arm coming down on her face like a hammer, the head of which was a spider-like fist clutching . . . a glass jar?

Mercy caught the hammer-arm in his teeth before it reached Beth and wrenched it away, rotated the shoulder so the man had to follow or lose a limb. And though Beth couldn't see what happened, she heard the wolf's warning growl and the jar breaking against the wall. She felt the man's sock-clad feet thrash out and kick her knees, and the floor vibrated as a dining chair fell sideways.

Then the room stilled and a warm dog tongue was lapping her face, and the only thing that Beth could think was that Mercy had just killed a man. She took a shuddering breath, and her black-speckled vision slowly cleared.

"Herriot," she said.

Her dog barked a happy greeting. Somewhere else in the kitchen, Mercy remained silent.

Beth rolled over and pushed herself onto her bruised knees. Just a few feet away, pinned between the wall and a cheap table by a wolf standing over him, the man who'd attacked her was facing her direction, eyes closed. Glittery glass sparkled on the floor, but no blood.

His voice startled her. "Haven't seen one of these guys around here in a while," he said to her in a calm, low voice.

Herriot's happiness was uncontainable. She approached Mercy and nuzzled him under his jaw, then sat beside him. Her tail thumped the carpet hard enough to make a glass shard bounce.

"Where's Garner?" Beth asked.

"I was wondering the same thing."

"You're talking like a ventriloquist."

"I have a wolf on my chest." The man opened one eye. "Call him off?"

"He's not mine," Beth said.

"Coulda fooled me."

"Mercy does what he wants."

"If you named him, he's yours."

Beth didn't feel the need to explain anything to this man. His mass of loosely curly hair seemed to need a drum set or bass guitar to go with it. Mercy stepped off of his chest, but the man stayed pressed into the joint where wall and floor met.

"You don't seem afraid of him," she observed.

He opened both eyes but kept them on Beth. "I'm terrified. If you're not, you're a fool. But if you show it, you're dead."

She smiled at that.

"Tell me when he stops staring at me," he instructed.

"Okay."

"So . . . are you afraid of him?" he asked her.

"Yes."

"Good. I wouldn't want to have to explain to Garner how a wolf got into his kitchen and killed you."

"He's already passed up plenty of opportunities."

"Even better. He done staring at me?"

Beth checked. "Seems that way."

Even so, he avoided eye contact with the dog. He moved slowly, folding his body into a sitting position that matched Beth's, and Mercy stood aside. Beth heard the man exhale.

The wolf quickly jabbed his nose into the man's face and licked his cheek, which earned a surprised laugh.

"He says I can stay in your pack," the man said.

"This dog's in my pack too." Beth reached down and scratched Herriot between the ears. "Herriot's mine."

"That's too bad. I was thinking of keeping her."

"I wasn't thinking of giving her away."

"But she followed me home."

"Are you a friend of Garner's?" she asked.

"Trey Bateman, houseguest and generally pesky acquaintance. And you?"

"Beth Borzoi. I'm his granddaughter."

"Borzoi," Trey said. "A Russian wolfhound."

"We're cattle ranchers, actually. Fifth generation."

"Cattle ranchers, wolfhounds—they all feel the same way about wolves. Hunt them down, keep them off the land. It's not a stretch to say your forefathers did their part to drive these guys out of the state."

"You shouldn't assume. My dad, my grandfathers—they tried not to interfere too much with the natural order of things."

"Huh. Well, maybe that's why this guy attached himself to you. Animals have a sixth sense about people, you know. Maybe he sensed you're a champion for the underdog."

Trey had no idea. Levi and his developer friend Sam Johnson weren't exactly planning to develop a wildlife refuge on the Blazing B.

"I need to talk to Garner," she said.

"I don't know where he is," Trey said. Now he stared at the wolf without fear. "I can't believe I'm seeing a gray wolf in Colorado. In someone's *kitchen*. This is amazing. Just amazing."

The wolf lay in the pass-through as if he were Herriot's domesticated buddy. Trey got off the floor and indicated that Beth should move away from the fridge.

"Do you live here?" she asked as he retrieved a carton of eggs and a pitcher of something that looked like tea. He poured a cup for her and set it on the table, constantly glancing at Mercy.

"No, just visiting. I was spending a few days gathering mountain-lion data and wasn't planning to be back until tomorrow. But something got my food. A black bear, I think. Did you know that black bears come in four colors?"

"Uh, no."

"Do you want some breakfast?" he asked.

"It's not even four o'clock."

"All my stomach knows is that I just woke up for the day. Gotta eat. Bighorn sheep were expatriated from these parts for a long time too, like your friend here." Trey nodded at the wolf. "But not because of the bears. The sheep were reintroduced to the area by train about twenty-five years ago. Maybe I should consider a thesis paper on the return of *Canis lupis*. What insane timing! I love it when God does that—it is so cool."

Beth's eyes widened a bit. His energy was a little overwhelming.

"Although your friend's behavior doesn't seem very wild," he continued. "It might ruin things if he's actually domesticated. Have you seen him with a pack? Or even one or two others?"

She shook her head.

Trey put a small frying pan on the stove and started cracking eggs into a bowl.

"Look," Beth said. "About Garner. Just a couple of hours ago someone told me he's been dead for two years."

An eggshell burst in Trey's fingers as he looked up at her. "Dead? Who told you he was dead?"

"The doctor. Dr. Ransom."

"Oh. Well. She's a bit strange. It isn't Christian to say so, but I actually don't even like her. What she said probably isn't true."

Probably? "Nova told me it wasn't true. That Garner *isn't* dead."

"The bookseller. Nice lady. I buy books from her all the time. She's quiet, but very intelligent. A true seeker."

"Trey: Garner, Garner, Garner."

"He wasn't dead Sunday morning. That's all I know. Why do you call your grandfather by name?"

"Because I've never met him! So Nova's telling me the truth?"

"Yes. Garner made that tea you're drinking, and I guarantee you it's not two years old. You've never met your grandfather? I'd like to hear this story."

"Not now. Why would Dr. Ransom lie to me?"

"I don't know. I wouldn't take it personally, though. She doesn't like me either. And she's protective of him."

"Why would she need to protect him from his granddaughter?"

"Why not, if he doesn't know you and you don't even call him Grandpa or Pops, and you break into his house at four in the morning and sic wolves on people you don't know?"

His mad scrambling of the eggs with a fork demanded an answer. Frustration rose in Beth at the disappointment of not finding Garner here after coming so far. She righted the chair that had tipped over and sat down on it. She set her drink on the table.

"Why'd you bring me to his house if he's not here?" Beth said to Mercy. "You have no sense of urgency. It's starting to bother me."

The wolf stretched out on his side into the stove light cast across the floor. He closed his eyes, leaning into Herriot's side. The cattle dog panted.

"He's going to take a nap," Beth said to Trey.

"I'd be tired too, if I'd been up all night showing you around town." He poured out the eggs into a hot pat of butter and the pan sizzled. Beth felt his eyes on her but didn't look. "Is that what you meant?" Trey asked. "That this wild animal showed you the way?"

Beth sighed. "You must think I'm crazier than Dr. Ransom."

"You don't know me well enough yet to know what I think."

For the next few minutes Trey cooked his eggs and Beth watched the dogs drift off to sleep, wondering if there was anything she could do to find Garner before daylight. Trey scraped his cooked breakfast onto a plate and carried it to the table, sat, then said, "Thanks, God," before scooping a bite into his mouth. At these words, Mercy lifted his head and met Trey's eyes, then blinked and returned to his rest.

After Trey swallowed, he said, "St. Francis of Assisi is the patron saint of animals. You heard of him?"

Beth nodded.

"There's this book called the *Fioretti*—'little flowers'—it's a collection of stories about his life and miracles. One of the tales is about a wolf that was killing the poor people of this little Italian village." He pointed his fork at Mercy as if he were the very beast. "He was more hungry than mean, but he slaughtered so many that the people were scared all the time. Too frightened to go about their daily business. They wouldn't leave their village without grabbing a knife or a bow or some weapon, but that didn't stop this guy from eating them up.

"So St. Francis felt sorry for these people and went out to meet the wolf, you know, have a little word with the killer. He didn't take a weapon with him, and everyone was so sure he was walking straight to his death that they followed him, so they could watch it happen. I guess they thought so long as the wolf was eating him, they'd be safe."

Mercy's ear twitched.

"Well, the wolf saw Francis and rushed him with his jaws wide open. And Francis made the sign of the cross and said, 'Brother wolf, I command you in the name of Christ not to harm me or any other person!' And the wolf turned into a lamb and lay down at Francis' feet."

"He did not."

"He did!"

"The wolf did not turn into a lamb."

"I meant his *demeanor*. Don't wreck the story."

"He just stopped the attack and rolled over so St. Francis could rub his belly."

"I don't know if it went that far, but there's a bronze monument in the village where it happened that shows the man and wolf hugging. That's probably not historically accurate, I'd say, but you're about to miss my point."

"All right."

"St. Francis read the animal the riot act for all the killing he'd done, even though he was just hungry, after all. The friar said that wolf deserved to be strung up in the village square for harming God's creation. But then Francis said that he didn't want the wolf to die. He'd come to broker a peace deal between the wolf and the villagers. The wolf would stop killing them, and the villagers would start feeding him."

"Why would they agree to that?"

"Because Francis said their sins were responsible for their suffering, but they had an opportunity to set things straight. He said, 'The flames of hell are not like the rage of the wolf that can only kill the body.' He said if they repented God would save them from both the wolf *and* eternal fire."

"And did they?"

"Yes. They promised to change their ways and to feed the wolf, and the wolf promised—"

"How? How did he promise?"

"Well, the *Fioretti* says that his tame-as-a-lamb body language was clear, but I suppose the real proof was in the fact that he never killed anyone again. Can't argue with that. He lived in the village for the rest of his life, going and coming into houses as he pleased, and they say not even the dogs barked at him."

Trey raised his eyebrows and nodded with such solemnity at Herriot lying next to Mercy that Beth laughed at him.

"You think I'm making this up!" Trey acted offended.

"No, I think you've taken it all very seriously. And trust me, I have plenty of reasons to believe that story's true. But I still don't know what your point is. I'm supposed to repent of something?"

"Is that what you got out of that? I thought I told a different story."

"What? You told a story about repentance."

Trey shook his head and swallowed another bite of egg. "I told a story about mercy. Life instead of death for all."

Goose bumps rippled down Beth's arms. She almost told him

about the Blazing B, about her father, about Levi, the antelope, the saddle, Jacob. Instead she said, "My full name is Bethesda."

Trey chuckled. "No kidding?"

"You know what that means?"

"It means you and this guy were made for each other. Mercy and the house of mercy—the spirit and the body."

"Maybe I just gave him an obvious name."

"Did you?"

Beth slowly shook her head.

"You think this wolf is"—she wasn't sure how to say it—"a guide from God?"

"Like the Holy Spirit? I have no idea. But God has been known to use lions or donkeys or whatever to accomplish his goals. Why not a wolf? Hey, did you know that the Bible doesn't actually say that the lion and lamb will get along together, as the saying goes, but that *wolves* and lambs will?"

"Should I start calling you St. Francis?"

"As much as I love animals, that would be heresy. And it doesn't seem like you actually need my help with anything."

"Please help me find Garner."

"If that wolf led you here, maybe he'll lead you to the man himself at the right time."

"But right now, Mercy's sleeping."

"Then I guess you'll have to wait."

"I'm not very good at waiting," Beth said.

"Interesting."

"Wait with me?" Beth asked.

"And your wolf friend?"

"Of course."

"Happily."

31

It would be best to kill Beth before the benzodiazepine wore off. It would be painless that way. Humane. It was good and right to be humane. Garner, if he were not so sick in this moment, would agree with her.

Cat stood in her clinic next to Garner's bed. He was still unconscious and delirious, but stable.

It had been a long time since Cat had been afraid that someone might die. In fact, she couldn't remember ever being anxious about the possibility. But tonight, death was boiling water and this entire building was an infusion, steeping in it: Garner here, Beth upstairs, Nova across the hall.

The doctor rested her hand on the safety rail that prevented Garner from falling out of his hospital bed. It felt grimy under her palm. The floor stank of age and mountain grit, though she knew it was clean. In that moment Cat Ransom wondered why she had ever come to Burnt Rock. What precise lineup of mistakes and poor judgments could have started with love for a child like Amelia, for a man like Amelia's father—

Cat held her breath. She couldn't remember the man's name. Where had it gone from her memory? How was such a thing possible? She scrambled for it—Neil, Nelson, Nieman, *Newell*. There it was, Newell. Newell Reinhart.

What an awful name. That might explain why she had forgotten it. Or perhaps she had never loved the girl's father at all. Yes, this was true: she hated that man Newell, because he had taken Amelia away from her, because *he* was the one who'd reported her to the police—

There would be no police this time, she hoped. She hadn't thought this through. What would she use to usher death into her home?

The death camas that she had collected was still drying in her office. She could use that, though it would be difficult to administer. It might provide Cat with a necessary alibi if Beth's death was discovered and investigated. *She came to me already sick. Maybe she ate them on the trail, thinking they were onions.*

Cat's breath was coming more quickly now. She felt her blood pressure rising, and for a second, as she let go of Garner's bed rail and turned toward the dim hall, she lost sight of where she needed to go. Outside? Upstairs? The entire world was dim and she was alone in it.

She soon found herself standing in front of the medicine cabinet in her office, unable to recall exactly how she had arrived there. Garner, in the adjacent room, was mumbling nonsense. Her hand shook as she passed it over the vials and blister packs and various bottles that she'd acquired from mail-order pharmacies. She tried to focus on the vials, liquids, easily injectable. But the labels were a floating blur. All she needed was a simple overdose—1000ccs of something that should have only been 100, or 100ccs when 10 would do—and Garner would never ever know that his estranged granddaughter had been demoted from ten feet above him to six feet below.

Some level of Cat's consciousness was working, and she didn't care how. Her muscles obeyed her intellect, and her fingers snatched up a handful of vials that she had read yet couldn't read. Digitalis, a heart medication powerful enough to turn the heart inside out and squeeze all the air out of the lungs. She fumbled in a drawer for a syringe and came out with one that might or might not be the right size. She didn't check, didn't have time, didn't have enough confidence that she might actually get out of this office and reach the top of her stairs and inject humane death into Beth Borzoi's body.

But she did get out, did climb the stairs, did fit her key into the knob and turn it without dropping the vials, though her entire body wobbled as if afflicted by low blood sugar.

Somehow her action had locked the doorknob. She repeated with the key and unlocked the hardware this time. Cat stubbed her toe on the threshold and nearly fell into the very dark space that was her home. The weak hall light cast her shadow into the open doorway but reached no farther. She was startled to hear quick and heavy breathing. The benzodiazepine should have suppressed Beth's lungs considerably.

Then she realized that the hyperventilation was her own.

And then she thought that the benzodiazepine and the digitalis might work against each other, and it bothered her that she couldn't remember the potential side effects of this drug interaction. She should know such things. They should come to her when summoned like the name of every person she had ever loved. Had she brought enough vials with her for the digitalis to overpower the sedative?

Cat flicked the light switch on the wall next to her. She turned the vials in her palms. There were only three, not four.

Two epinephrine. One insulin. No digitalis.

The doctor stared at these for a long time before her peripheral vision made note of the empty sofa. A gray chenille blanket poured like a waterfall off the cushions and onto the floor.

Cat spun, looking for Beth, expecting to see her emerging from the bathroom with a tissue or from the kitchen with a glass of water. How could she have awakened so soon? And where could she have gone without the horse? Anywhere in town!

Or merely down the stairs and across the building to Nova.

Of course, Beth would have gone looking for her, not running away from her.

The foolishness of her plans to erase Beth from Burnt Rock was clear now. Beth might have told a dozen people of her plans to seek out her grandfather. All of them might have come looking for her, at the very least her mother. And Nova, who probably wouldn't die of her misguided grief, would tell anyone who asked that she had seen the girl, and that Cat had seen her too.

There had to be another way.

With killing now out of the question, Cat sank into a pool of relief and found the calm center of it. Her lungs deepened into a healthy rhythm, and the trembling in her core slipped away. She crossed the room and laid the medications and the syringe—definitely the wrong size, she could see that now—on the dining room table. She picked up the blanket from the floor and folded it across the arm of the sofa. Then she left the apartment and pulled the door behind her and went to Nova's home.

Her restored sense of well-being faltered when she saw that Nova's door was closed.

And locked.

Cat rapped gently. "Beth? Are you in there? I was downstairs in my office doing paperwork—I should have left a note."

When no answer came after several seconds, Cat put more force into her knock. "Beth?"

Perhaps she'd fallen asleep again here, the effects of the drug not being completely worn off. Cat pounded.

"Beth! Wake up!"

"*You* wake up!" Nova's voice was clear and bold, magnified rather than muffled by the wood between her and the doctor, as if she were shouting into a megaphone. "She knows about Garner, you fraud."

How could Beth know Garner was in her office even now, sickened by the same fungus that had sickened Nov—

This was not what Nova meant. Beth knew Garner was alive. Cat rattled the doorknob, and when that didn't yield, she pressed both hands to the door and pressed her forehead into the wood.

"What did you tell her?" Cat demanded.

"I told her you're a killer."

"That's a lie. You're . . . you're unstable. Crazy with grief."

"I'll prove it eventually."

Panic did a cannonball dive into Cat's pool of calm. "Prove *what*?"

"You're no more a doctor than I am."

"Where's Beth?"

"You killed—"

"Where *is* she!"

"—my baby."

"You can't kill a *fetus*," Cat hissed. "I saved a baby from a miserable life with you, you pathetic creature."

It was Nova's silence that returned Cat's words to her like a verdict. Her confession was out there, impossible to retract.

"I could have helped you," Cat said, but she didn't care if Nova heard her or replied. Nova was the least of her concerns now. Cat fled down the stairs and back to her offices, to Garner, to the only person she'd ever known who'd appreciated her love and returned it.

She couldn't stay in Burnt Rock. Nor could Garner. They had to leave. Now, within the hour, before the sunlight exposed all of Cat's lies.

She went to her desk first. She closed her computer and slipped it into her case. The laptop contained all the most important components of her false life—passwords and résumés and diplomas and operational ID numbers, all of which had cost her so much money—and contact information for the people who could provide all that to her again.

The thought of beginning once more after so little time brought an ache to Cat's head. Could she do it? Could she enter another town, another set of lives, with a life of her own so perfectly groomed and presented that they couldn't help but love her? The false her? The doctor who was no longer a doctor, who gave so much and asked for so little?

She took what her fingers touched without thinking about why she was doing it. Prescription pads that she'd throw away when Catherine Ransom ceased to exist. Pens and magnets given to her by the Burnt Rock business owners. Intake forms that existed on her computer. She left her framed license hanging on the wall.

She found several large cardboard boxes that held bulk supplies. Toilet paper, paper towels, hand sanitizer. She dumped the contents out on the floor and filled the empty boxes with her entire inventory of medications and medical supplies, items that would be almost as costly to replace as her identity. She had no time to organize or file, only to take. She thought through what Garner would need, what she would have to access easily, and placed these in a separate, smaller box. One by one she carried these out to her car at the back of the building.

The perspiration of rushing, hurrying, worrying broke out at her temples.

When she finished with the boxes she went to the supply closet and pushed aside the coat she'd stashed there last winter. It was holding up a backboard she'd used only once, when Mazy had slipped on the ice behind her diner in January. Cat took this into the room where Garner rested, fretting. She should have invested in a gurney. It had taken herself and two men to get this hospital-grade bed, then empty, into the room. There would be no getting it out now that it was occupied. She unhooked the IV bag from its pole and rested it on Garner's chest. She moved around the bed, untucking the sheets from around the mattress, preparing to slide him onto the backboard, strap him in, then drag him to her car. It would be a jarring, primitive effort.

She wedged several inches of the slim board underneath the sheet at his left side and gripped the fabric. When she gave it a firm tug, her fingernails pierced the thin cotton and ripped a six-inch gash in it. Her heart fell at the sound of the threads snapping. This was a job that generally took three or four people and sturdy materials.

She tried again, this time pulling on both the sheet and a belt loop in Garner's pants. She leaned against the edge of the board and used her hips to shove it under Garner's body. His backside came up onto the board this time, but his legs and torso bent away from her. Cat went around to the opposite side of the bed as the IV bag slipped off Garner's chest and plummeted to the floor. She failed to catch it in time, and her despair began to mount, even though the bag didn't burst and the tube was long enough that it didn't yank the angiocatheter from Garner's hand.

Even if she could get him onto the board—which after more than a minute she finally managed, first his legs and then his shoulders and head—his hundred seventy pounds might as well have been two hundred seventy. She didn't have a clear vision in her head for how this plan would work. One step at a time, one problem at a time. She wrapped the sheet around him and secured him to the board with the safety straps like a baby in a papoose.

After ensuring that the bed's wheel brakes had been set, Cat pushed the board off the end of the mattress. When it began to gently teeter she went to the foot of the bed and guided the bottom edge of the board to the floor. She jiggled it once to make sure it was stabilized and then stepped away to lower Garner's head. When she moved, her shoe caught Garner's foot and she lost her balance, and before she recovered it the board was sliding on the slick floor and Garner's head was falling, and when her reflexes sent her arm out to catch him, the board with all of Garner's weight on it fell on top of her hand and pinned it to the floor.

She watched the board bounce and rattle Garner's head before it came down on her hand a second time. The pain was so quick and intense that Cat couldn't be sure right away if her bones had been crushed or fractured or merely bruised. For several seconds she couldn't even move to get the board off of her. She lay prone on the floor, her throbbing hand trapped under the unconscious form of her dear friend, and began to weep.

It was impossible, what she was trying to do—everything was impossible, from trying to create a new life to trying to take Garner with her.

For a time, she considered staying with him. But they would only be separated in the end. By the girl, by the law, by fate—no matter how tenderly she nursed Garner back to health, not only from the ergot, but from the cancer too. No one cared about any of that.

She would have to leave him here.

As the knife-sharp pain in her bones began to wane, so did her paralysis. Cat found her knees and reached out to shove Garner's board off her hand. The wooden *thunk* was a distant sound under the dull roaring of pain in her head. She couldn't stay on the cold floor a second longer.

Without looking at Garner, without pausing to assess the damage to her hand, Cat stumbled out of the room and out of the office. The night sky in the windows had lightened almost imperceptibly from black to charcoal. To Cat the change was as loud as Cinderella's midnight tolling, counting down the final seconds of an ending dream.

She stumbled upstairs to collect the valuables she would need for her next life.

32

The front room of Garner's house, the room on the other side of the kitchen wall, was a showcase for glass jars filled with herbs and dried flowers, slender brown vials topped with medicine droppers, squatty blue tubs filled with botanical salves, larger bottles variously labeled as syrups or tonics, and several elegant teapots and cups.

Beth ran her fingers along the labels, curious about her grandfather's work. Many of them bore the green Garner's Garden logo. Others appeared to be from Europe. She saw some from China, with the contents handwritten in English on a sticker and applied over the Chinese characters. A whisper of rising red sun slipped through the lightweight curtains, likely drawn to protect the jars from direct light without darkening the room. A display case that also served as a counter bearing a register and credit card machine separated the products for sale from the shop's front entry.

"He's developed all these remedies?" she asked Trey, who was fishing a laptop out of his backpack.

"Not the stuff that requires a lab. He has a contract with one company to produce a few recipes, and he has his favorite distributors, but his specialty is the fresh plants—you should see the basement."

"I thought he was in real estate."

"Up here? This botanical interest of his makes more sense to me. He has cancer, you know." Beth turned to face him, and his eyebrows shot up. "Of course you didn't. I'm sorry."

"What kind?"

"Liver."

"Is it bad?" she asked.

"Not bad enough to keep him off his feet. He doesn't talk about it very much, except to swear by this stuff." Trey indicated the remedies on the shelves. "And by the good doctor, who calls herself holistic."

Trey dropped onto a sofa under one of the windows and opened his laptop on his knees. "So Dr. Cat told you Garner's dead. And did I tell you she wrote me off as a specimen of perfect health? What kind of doctor resents a healthy person? Let's look into her."

Beth didn't see how this might help them find Garner.

"Do we really have to wait here for him to come home?"

"When the sun's up, we'll go ask around. Garner's popular here. But right now the town sleeps. And besides, I don't mind being forced to hang out for a while with a pretty cowgirl who listens to my stories." Trey didn't seem to be teasing her, but a veil of oil covered her hair, and her jeans might be able to stand up by themselves. "How did you come by Cat and Nova?" he asked.

"Nova was sick. I found her on my way into town, up at that church."

"The Burnt Rock Harbor Sweet Assembly. Silly place. But Nova has broad beliefs about her spiritual life. Is she okay?"

"She's had a miscarriage."

Trey looked up from his computer. "Garner said something about her expecting."

"Nova told me Dr. Ransom poisoned her."

Trey didn't laugh.

"I saw Nova Saturday night," Trey said. "She looked fine to me. She came by Cat's after we finished eating dinner."

"Does everyone here make a habit of eating with folks they don't like?"

Trey's fingers flew and the keyboard clacked.

"Don't we all now and then? I think Garner was trying to patch up an argument between them. Cat was pretty nice about things, now that I think of it—she invited Nova to join us, then sent some rolls home with her when she said she didn't have time. Garner thinks I ought to get friendly with Nova. I like her and all, but she's a bit too old for me, not to mention really far out there with her belief system. You come much closer to hitting the mark—outdoorsy, friendly with the wildlife, bold."

"You're not too shy yourself."

He glanced up at her for a second and grinned. "No time to be shy. Too many cool people to meet. And I get the idea that you're a Christian?"

"Yes."

"Spectacular!"

His eyes scanned his computer screen again.

"Dr. Ransom gave Nova food? Could that have been what made her so sick?"

Trey shrugged. "Dinner sat fine with me, and Garner seemed okay last time I saw him."

"Which was when?"

"Sunday morning before I went out. Look here: I've been searching for 'Catherine Ransom, MD' and can't find squat. She's listed on the state license board, but her license is barely a year old. She's only been in Burnt Rock that long."

Beth moved to the sofa and sat next to him where she could see the computer screen. "So maybe she's from another state."

"True. I can't remember where she's from. But I don't get any

277

hits at all on her name, not anywhere, and she's not on any of the physician listings."

"If she's only been practicing for a year, they might just not be up to date."

"That's weird, isn't it? She's what—fortyish? And if Nova's right about Cat poisoning her, maybe she's trying to hide a malpractice history."

"Poisoning someone is worse than malpractice," Beth said. The day was taking far too long to get underway. Beth gripped Trey's arm. "What if she poisoned Garner?"

"Yow! Your hands are Iceland!" Beth let go of him and sat on her hands. "Cat wouldn't hurt him. They're like this." Trey crossed his fingers.

"Until I know for sure," Beth said, "I'll keep the option open. The rolls that Cat gave Nova—did all of you eat some?"

"No. I seriously swear off gluten. That offended her. But when I pointed out that she wasn't eating any either, she dropped it."

"She didn't have some? What about Garner?"

"He ate a bunch—one for each of us and two for himself."

"Trey, think about this—"

"Mind's a-whirling."

"What kind were they?"

"I don't remember. Does it matter?"

"I don't know, but Nova and Garner ate some, and you and Cat didn't. It was less than three days ago. Come on. You have a head for details."

Trey closed his eyes for two seconds. "Rye. They were rye."

Beth sighed. Rye meant nothing to her. And what did she know about poison? She scoured her mental files for anything: her very limited experience with bread baking . . . high-altitude baking . . . rye. There were a few farmers in the valley who farmed rye. It was an easy dry-climate crop that was good for livestock feed. Sometimes the rye from neighboring farms took root in the wild and spread quickly onto grazing lands, where the cows noshed it with other grains and grasses.

"When I was a kid, we bought some rye to supplement our herd's winter feed. It had been a really good year—lots of rain for the crops, but also lots of good warm weather and grazing in the mountains. We didn't have the usual losses that year and had a few extra mouths to feed. So Dad bought this supply from a new farmer who was getting into the market with some great prices."

"You're not going to tell me that the farmer poisoned the rye and killed off your herd, are you?"

"Not exactly. The crop was infected with this fungus that grows on grain crops when the weather is particularly wet and warm. I can't remember what it's called. This farmer was so green that he didn't realize what he had going on. It didn't kill our cows, but it caused gangrene in a few of the older animals. They lost parts of their hooves. A few lost ears or tails. But what made me think of it is that a whole bunch of our pregnant cows miscarried."

"Like Nova?"

"It's a stretch, isn't it? That something like that would have a similar effect on a human?"

"The weirdest possibilities are the ones that usually turn out to be true," Trey said. "Did you know that the actress Hedy Lamarr patented a frequency-hopping technology in the 1940s that was used in the development of cell phones?"

"What does that have to do with rye bread?"

"Not bread, weird facts."

"How much trivia can your big brain hold up there?" Beth asked, pointing to Trey's head.

"Not much that's actually useful," he said, and then he laughed and typed away.

It took only fifteen minutes for Trey and Beth to unearth a few grim details about rye and the history of that fungus, which was called ergot. This included a popular theory that the Salem-witch-trials tragedy might be blamed on a wet spring and ergot-riddled rye, which caused hallucinations and burning sensations of the skin and other unpleasant symptoms. They also learned about the use of ergot in midwifery and ergot derivatives in modern-day obstetrics. A few experts believed that ergot might cause abortion in the early pregnancies of women who had other underlying risk factors, though this application was inconsistent and unreliable.

After long minutes of leaning into the small screen to read search-engine summaries and pages, Beth said, "This is all interesting, but it doesn't prove anything." She reached across the keyboard and hit the cursor that took them back to the search results.

"You have mud on your earrings," Trey said. Beth had leaned in so close to him to read the pages that she'd eclipsed his view of the screen. Annoyed with herself, she withdrew, but he had already reached up to rub the caked dirt off the dangling silver, and she was forced to stay put or get a painful yank on her earlobe.

She said the only thing that came to mind. "That mud's from Wally."

Trey chuckled again, always so ready with that warm laugh. "I guess you have your own stories to tell. I'd like to hear them sometime."

Beth didn't know why her thoughts went to Jacob at that moment, or why Trey's unguarded attention made her feel both flattered and guilty. She liked his easy manner and entertaining talk, and his apparent interest in her grandfather's well-being. But she wished Jacob were here to help her find Garner too.

She took the earring in her fingers and gently pulled it out of Trey's grip. His hands, unlike hers, were wide and warm, but this time he didn't comment on her frigid fingers. He freed her from discomfort by scrolling down the search results and then clicking through to the next page.

"Look at that," she said, pointing to a link halfway down the list.

It seemed Trey had seen it at the same time. "Mentally ill physician vanishes," with the keywords *ergot* and *poison* highlighted in the summary. The link took them to an article archived two years earlier in the *Daily News*, a Los Angeles–based newspaper. At the top of the article was a photograph of Catherine Ransom, who at the time wore her hair long and blond.

Trey and Beth read together silently.

Authorities are searching for Katrina White, MD, who fled her clinic in North Hollywood hours before an arrest warrant in her name was issued Wednesday afternoon. White is accused of intentionally and routinely poisoning at least two minors in her care over a six-month period.

James Delaney filed a complaint against White after his child was hospitalized for a series of "suspicious and inexplicable illnesses" according to Detective John Kane, who is overseeing the manhunt.

Forensic psychologist Dirk Swenson believes that White suffers from a form of Munchausen syndrome by proxy, a factitious disorder in which a caregiver, usually a mother, willfully causes harm to her charge, usually a child, for the purpose of gaining medical attention, recognition, and praise for her caregiving skill. Rarely the syndrome affects physicians.

Beth became stuck on "attention, recognition, and praise for her caregiving skill." She found herself reading the same line over and over. It was unfortunately easy to see herself in that yearning. The desire to help others wasn't entirely altruistic, was it? Her hopes of being a great veterinarian, and perhaps a gifted healer, were firmly rooted in a longing for attention, recognition, and praise. From Jacob, from Levi, from Danny, from her mother. From anyone who would notice her and think that such gifts must be far greater than any of her sins.

Munchausen syndrome by proxy is difficult to detect and diagnose because of the apparent trustworthiness and devotion of the caregiver.

"She was the kindest professional you'll ever meet," says Newell Reinhart, a single father who has also filed a legal suit against White. "My daughter's fears of going to the doctor vanished when we met Dr. White. It sickens me to say they've all come back now."

According to Kane, "We might never have cornered White if not for the quick thinking of Mr. Delaney," who turned over to police the drug samples White had provided for the child from her office. The pills did not match the description on their box, and White's recommended dose was toxic. The child was immediately removed from White's care, though an investigation yielded no intent to harm.

The case might have been called an unfortunate medical error if not for the suspicions of Reinhart, who described himself as a "close friend" of the doctor's until his child began to suffer from chronic bouts of skin irritation and symptoms that "looked like dementia," said Kane. Less than three months after the Delaney investigation, Reinhart's problems were eventually traced to a natural remedy touted by White. This remedy, which White claimed would mitigate environmental allergies, contained powdered ergot, a grain fungus known for causing psychological disturbances. Traces of the concoction were found in White's home, where it appears she made the remedy herself.

The article closed with a phone number that people could call if they had information pertaining to the whereabouts of Dr. White.

Trey finished reading first and was dialing his cell phone before Beth was done. He put the phone to his ear as the call went through to the predawn state of California.

"I'm not just seeing Dr. Cat's face in that photo because I'm tired, am I?" Trey asked her.

Beth shook her head, more worried than ever about her grandfather. She rose from the sofa and went over to Mercy, then got down on her knees and lifted the wolf's sleepy head in her hands. "I know God is using you, boy. I know we're not going to find Garner without you. Please show me where he is."

The wolf put his head back on his paws. The sunlight penetrating the thin draperies was shifting from blue to red. "Can't we go now? Please? I don't understand the holdup."

Mercy closed his eyes.

Behind her Trey said, "Yes, I'm calling about an old case of Detective Kane's . . ."

33

Cat needed so little from her apartment. She took a tote bag off her closet shelf and snapped it open, overcome by a sense of déjà vu that filled her with unexpected calm. When she'd fled California, she had even less time than she did now, and most of the essentials were already in her car.

She went into the kitchen to retrieve what cash she stored in the kitchen drawer, and some photographs of Newell and Amelia that would connect her to her life as Katrina White. They were a moot concern. Fingerprints all over this apartment and office would confirm her double identity, and she didn't have time to clean. But she couldn't part with the pictures.

It was fortunate that she had no images of Garner. It would make him easier to forget.

She took her one framed photograph, a snapshot of her parents on their honeymoon, but left the frame behind. Purse. IDs. A change of clothes, her favorite makeup. Books on the region's native, edible, and medicinal plants. Perhaps she'd stay in the Rocky Mountain region. She had time to collect her favorite teas and the valuable herbs that had taken so many hours to gather and prepare for storage.

Everything else could turn to dust. She left without locking the door.

She intended to move downstairs and away from her office as quickly as possible without glancing back. She took each step downward on heavy feet, marching to a parade of new names she might pick from. Carrie. Mary. Kendall. Sherry. Clarissa. Melissa. Bernadette. Terri. She didn't want any of them.

Her foot hovered over the landing. She wanted to be Catherine, Katrina—a name that could be anything she wanted it to be, anything *anyone* wanted it to be. Cat. Cathy. Katie. Kate. It helped draw people to her, this easy way of being, this flexible label. She didn't want to let go of it yet.

And yet she had to. She had never despised her life more than at this moment.

A cry from her office cut straight through the rear entry of her offices as she passed it, and the burst of terror almost turned her head. She covered her ears and ducked her head and jumped off the last step, then ran down the common hall toward the back door.

Garner raised his voice again, and this time her name penetrated the barrier of her fists.

"Catherine . . ."

It was a weak, dry, pathetic cry. A pitiful, wasted sound that shouldn't have been able to travel past his own toes. But it sought her out and found her, and she was troubled. He never called her Catherine. Only Cat. *Cat, girl, have a look at this. Cat, child, you're on the prowl. What's bugging you?*

"She's fainted!" Garner croaked.

He was hallucinating, a side effect of the ergot. It would wear off, if he didn't die first. There was nothing to do for ergot but to let it wear off.

"You're needed at the church!"

With her purse on one shoulder and tote bag over the other,

Cat lowered her clenched hands until they shielded her heart. She told herself not to turn around. She should leave the building *now*. Her office was a fishnet and Garner's voice was the lure, and the authorities were the fishermen who would haul her off to prison and filet her soul and lay it bare on a plate, and the hungry bears would say, before they ate her alive, that she was cold-blooded and calculating and deserving of such treatment.

No one would ever know the depths of her capacity to serve, to heal. To love.

Cat reached out and touched the exit. She leaned into it. She placed her forehead on the wood.

"Cat, girl." The whisper-thin words were barbed hooks in her heart. "I need you."

The door became an immovable object. *I need you.* She had no will to force it open. *I need you.* The three words she had never in her life been able to turn away from. If only Garner knew what he was saying.

She couldn't refuse to help him. Cat returned to her office. She passed through the entry without feeling the weight of the knob under her fingers. She floated across the old looped carpet, barely touching the fibers, and reached the exam room where Garner lay as he had ten minutes ago, lashed to that board with no one to help him up. His eyes were wide and unfocused, darting around in his head as if each hole in the ceiling's acoustic tiles commanded his undivided attention.

"I'm here," she said as she stood at his feet, which were still clad in the red clogs he wore around his basement garden every day.

"Ashes fall," he murmured. "They burn." And then, more frantic, "They burn!" His fingers strained against his restrained arms, contorting to reach out to an imaginary fire.

The flames of heartbreak licked the back of Cat's eyes then, as she watched him babble and twist. It would take hours, days of this wild nonsense before Garner was himself again. And by then they would be separated, he placed in the care of another physician who didn't know or care about a fraction of Garner, the father figure. And then they would teach him to hate her.

He would protect her if he could. But now he would never know that Cat had done this for the good of their relationship, for the strength of their father-daughter bond. What her own father had severed, she had restored with the skill of a precise and patient surgeon.

Cat knew then that she would never leave Garner. She'd suffered from a momentary lapse into selfishness, and now was the time to set that aside. They would never be separated the way she'd allowed her father to separate himself from her childhood, the way she'd allowed Newell Reinhart to walk away with Amelia. Never again would anyone rob Catherine Ransom of the right to care for another person. Not relatives. Not the law. Not anyone or anything lesser than human love.

"I will never leave you or forsake you," she said to her friend. "I will not leave you to die alone. I will go with you."

Garner let loose a shriek that sent a spike of nausea into Cat's belly. She let her tote and purse slide down her arms to rest on the floor. Then she stooped and began to rifle the bags for her supply of death camas.

There was plenty for them both.

Cat locked the doors.

34

Beth was pacing in front of Garner's cash register.

"You're making me nervous," Trey said.

Beth didn't feel the least bit apologetic about that.

Trey put aside his computer. "Okay. Sun's up. Let's go knock on some doors. Lately Garner's got himself a girlfriend, Dotti, so I think we should check at her place first."

"You might have mentioned that last night."

"Why? He's not with the Cat doctor, you know that much. And if he's with Dotti, he's in good hands. I'm sure that knocking on her door in the middle of the night wouldn't have created the best first impression for either of you." Trey reached for the sturdy hiking boots that he'd kicked off at the foot of the sofa before falling asleep the previous night.

The wolf and Herriot continued to sleep next to each other, and Trey's movements didn't rouse them.

"I can't go with you," Beth said.

"Why not?"

She pointed at the wolf. "He's not budging, so I shouldn't either. I'll have to wait. It's okay if you don't get it."

Trey yanked his shoelaces tight and looked up at Beth while he looped the strings.

"I get it," he said. "I think. How do you tell the difference between when he wants you to follow him and when he just needs to . . . go outside?"

"I don't know."

"Will your friend object if I go to Dotti's myself? You're not the only one who'd like to know where Garner's gone."

Mercy woofed like a dreaming dog.

"What does that mean?" Trey asked.

Beth shrugged. "I don't speak wolf."

"Is he going to attack me if I walk out the front door? Tie me down with his teeth? Please don't tell me you don't know."

"Why don't we find out?"

Trey hesitated long enough to make Beth break into an amused grin. Then he turned his back to Mercy and strode to the front door, his stride long and theatrical.

"He's ignoring you," Beth said.

"Never let them see you sweat. Works every time." Trey threw open the door.

He startled a woman on the porch who was rifling through a purse fashioned from a reusable grocery sack. She gasped, and Trey jumped back as if Mercy had magically transported himself outside. Even Beth flinched, and all of them uttered wordless sounds of surprise. Herriot pushed herself up on her front paws for a look at the door.

"Dotti!" Trey said. "Speak of the angels."

With one hand still moving in the bottom of her bag, Dotti was looking disapprovingly at Beth. If she'd noticed the dogs lying at Beth's feet, she either hadn't noticed one of them was wild, or she believed that Beth was the greater violation.

"Young man, what are you doing in Garner's house with . . . with . . . ?"

"His granddaughter. Dotti, meet Beth."

Dotti's stern expression melted into something downright

289

grandmotherly. Her eyes widened, transforming Beth with a blink of an eye from a streetwalker into royalty. Her mouth formed a surprised O before she said, "The old mystery man never told me he had a granddaughter."

"That's because he doesn't know," Beth said, and Dotti brightened further as she bustled into the house with her hand outstretched in a greeting.

"Well this is fun. I love being the first in on a good secret, don't you? And who's this big fellow?" Mercy had finally decided to stretch and stand, and he sniffed at the air coming through the door that Trey continued to hold open. Beth wasn't sure how to answer. Dotti reached down to run her hand along his spine as he passed her, heading for the door. "Look at that. His paws are as big as my feet. He looks like he's got a bit of wolf in him."

"A bit," Beth murmured. Mercy went out the door and down the porch steps two at a time. Herriot barked once but stayed put. Beth followed Mercy and stepped out onto the splintering wood-plank porch. Here she faced a rising anxiety that they had wasted precious hours in the house simply because none of the doors was open. And this thought branched quickly into a dozen others that all contained essentially the same core idea: this wolf was not at all what Beth had made it out to be. Instead, he was as unintentional as the wind, as powerless as any wild beast who couldn't open a manmade door.

How had he entered Cat's apartment, exactly?

In one effortless leap Mercy cleared the fence and began an easy trot down the dirt lane in the direction Beth and he had come the night before. In spite of her conflicting doubts, Beth hurried to catch up. What if, what if?

"We were hoping Garner might be with you," she heard Trey say to Dotti.

"I'm sorry to say he's been so sick that Cat took him in. I'm just here to water the plants, though if I'd known you'd be here I'd have asked you . . ."

Beth broke into a run at *Cat took him in* and was soon out of earshot. If Cat had Garner—where? Of course, Cat must have a clinic for her patients. Instead of exam rooms, an image of a grisly torture chamber came to mind. Where were her offices? Beth pulled up to shout the question at Trey and found herself caught on the hillside between the people she could no longer see and the bounding wolf, who would soon be out of sight if she didn't keep up.

She stayed on Mercy's trail. If he didn't take her to the doctor's office, she could ask the humans later.

By the light of day, the road seemed much shorter than it had in the dark. They passed another residential cross street, and a building covered in white pressboard siding appeared at the next corner. She could see the paved road just on the other side of it. When she saw that he had led her to the rear entrance of Nova's and Cat's apartments, she regretted her decision.

"No, Mercy. Not here. I've been here."

Cat's small SUV was still in the dirt lot, where she'd parked when they'd brought Nova back the night before. She saw Hastings' shoeprints in the dusty earth and wondered if she should follow those.

The wolf sat on his haunches and looked up at the closed door, eyeing the knob he could turn himself if only he had thumbs. Or if he were alone, perhaps.

Garner was ill and with Cat. What had she done to him? How much time did they have? Beth stalked up to Mercy and placed her body between the wolf and the door.

"Please," she whispered. It was a prayer really, not to the wolf, but to the God of the wolf, the One who understood everything that she couldn't.

Mercy's upper lip flickered, and he lowered his head. A low rumble of a growl rose from his throat.

It seemed a near reenactment of her encounter with the slashed pronghorn antelope, which she'd failed to save. This time, though, there was no bush to shelter her from the wolf.

His muzzle snapped out at her, all fluttering gums and bared teeth clacking as they came together inches from her belly one, two, three times. She gasped and twisted away. Her hip hit the doorknob, and she grabbed at it. The wolf's air biting was followed by a snarl, and the shadow of his form rising on hind legs came over her. One claw hit the wood siding near her head and dug into it. The other came down on the same skin he'd sliced across her neck and shoulder the night he'd knocked her off of Joe—the first night she'd ignored his prompts.

She felt the old injury reopen and pulled away from it, wrenched the doorknob in her sweaty hand, and slipped between the door and the sidelight, then slammed it shut behind her. Through the slender window she saw Mercy drop to the pads of his paws and blink his eyes once, slowly, like a happy dog. He panted gently. Beyond him, Trey descended the hill from Garner's street, coming at the urgent pace of a man who'd had to spend precious time fabricating reasons why Dotti shouldn't accompany him.

Beth breathed hard, her lungs loud in the silent hall shared by the bookseller and the doctor and whoever held the first-floor apartments. The scratch at her neck oozed under the collar of her cotton shirt.

Nova would know where Cat's offices were. Beth turned toward her staircase and caught sight of the door just beyond the foot of Nova's stairs. It bore a faded handwritten sign that she hadn't bothered to read before. "Welcome to the Book Nook. Please use the front entrance."

The meaning of this simple note came to Beth in an instant. The bookseller lived over her shop. Trey wasn't coming here because he'd followed Beth, but because the doctor also lived over her offices.

Beth spun in the hall and raced to the twin door underneath the twin staircase that mirrored Nova's. At the top of the stairs, the door to Dr. Ransom's apartment gaped open. Beneath it, the unmarked door looked like a stone-faced sentry. Beth gripped the knob and shook it.

"Garner!" Her pounding on the door sounded hollow. "Dr. Ransom! Are you in there?"

She didn't wait for an answer. What she expected to find behind this blockade deserved no courtesy. She kicked at the knob and placed the heel of her boot directly through the light panel of the hollow-core door. But the hole was too small even for Beth's slender fingers to maneuver, and there was a deadbolt standing in her way.

Trey came in behind her as she continued to kick.

"Locked," she grunted.

"I'll check her apartment for a key," he said, and he leaped up the stairs.

"Or a screwdriver," she yelled. With a flathead and a hammer they might be able to dismantle the hinges, which opened onto the hall.

Beth kicked until she broke out into a sweat, but she made no headway. It was one thing for no one to open the door and welcome her in. But it was worse that no one inside objected to her forced entry. The silence began to smother her hopes.

After what seemed like hours, Trey appeared at her side with a tiny hammer that had a peen rather than a claw opposite its head. There was nothing to wedge into the hinge pin.

"She didn't even have a screwdriver?"

"Women's tool kits just aren't all that," he said. "But the front door's made of glass."

If Mercy objected to Beth exiting, she'd have to come up with something else. But the wolf that was more than a wolf had already left his post at the door.

She chased Trey around to the front of the building. These riding boots she wore weren't made for running, and they hit the ground with noise that was all wrong for this quiet town on this sleepy street that wouldn't awake until the tour busses unloaded their visitors. Back home, the hands would be digging or hammering and the horses would be nickering and the cows would be lowing and the cowboys would be clucking their tongues. Wally the forgetful digger would be humming. Bacon would be frying in the kitchen and Danny would be whooping on the buck barrel, dreaming up the ruckus of the pending stock show. It wasn't right that all those sounds of life would end if her thundering boots didn't get her to Garner Remke's side fast enough.

She skidded on the corner and grabbed a post for balance, which put a splinter in her palm. Trey was already whaling on the door with the little hammer head, which bounced off of it like a rubber ball.

"Why won't it break?" She pulled the splinter out.

"Storm glass," Trey said, and he threw his arm again. "Thick stuff. It'll give eventually."

Beth looked around for a rock, a chain, a two-by-four, a crowbar. Anything that might have more punch than that excuse for a hammer. Through the glass, Beth saw a waiting room, a reception counter, and beside this, a corridor that led to a set of swinging shutters. There were two doorways off the hall. The one on the right was dark. Light spilled from the other.

On the floor, the spindly legs of a tall man protruded into the hall. His pant legs were hiked up on his calves, and a white sheet draped his form. Red clogs covered his feet. His ankles were twitching.

Beth's heart jumped.

"Trey—"

"I know."

The hammer bounced off the glass. It was ridiculous, that glass should be so hard to break.

Beth started pounding on the window and shouting.

"Garner! Can you hear me? Garner, listen! We're coming! I'm coming. Get up! Can you get up?"

A tiny chip flew out over Trey's head and landed on the street. He took a step back and caught his breath. Beth flew to the door and started kicking the wood frame around the glass, the same way she'd thrown her weight against the other entrance. But this door was made to open inward, and she felt it rattle with more promise against the latches and locks.

"Garner!" she screamed. "Listen to me!"

She kicked again. Without making her move out of the way, Trey started back in with his hammer.

Rose was calling him. She was standing outside the sliding glass door, the one with the broken latch, the perpetually failing broken latch that would lock at the slightest vibration no matter how many times he attempted to fix it. When the trash truck rumbled past on the street, when the dog barked, when Rose jumped rope on the deck—*thwap-thud, thwap-thud, thwap-thud*—the door would lock and she would cry out, *Daddy Daddy!* and if he didn't hear her right away or was at too great a distance to come in the short seconds before her panic set in, she would resort to calling as her mother did: *Garner! Garner!* and pounding on the door, pounding until the latch became stuck for sure. But he would rescue his Rose, always rescue Rose, would never fail to pull her out of the waking nightmare in which she was forgotten and starved and carried off in the talons of hungry eagles to feed their babies.

Garner! Garner! And the pounding. He would need the right

tool to pry up that latch this time. An ice pick . . . pick, pick, prick, poke. The pricking, the piercing! The agony of cold and hot raced along his every nerve, arms and legs and head aflame with a thousand red-hot stabs of the poker, the pricking, picking, relentless jaws of fire ants eating him alive.

Eating him up, gobbling him up, savoring his skin and masticating his muscles and burrowing into his bones, leaving each super-sensory nerve fiber for dessert, until he had been whittled away into a ham hock for a soup base, and his predators were bursting, and the eagle would swoop to the locked balcony like an open field and pluck his Rose and steal her away to the nest of ravenous eaglets.

He could not let it happen, not to Rose, who needed rescue in spite of her piercing, pricking thorns.

Garner! Daddy! Garner!

"I am coming!" he shouted, and he fought the fire ants, he sloughed them off his body with his bare hands, he beat them to the ground and then rolled atop them, their fragile exoskeletons cracking and crunching under the weight of his will.

He felt their pain. It was his, and he feared he would not survive it. If it had not been Rose calling, if it had been anyone but his daughter, he knew he could not have survived.

The shudder of a terrible chill passed through him, the shadow of death. *I am coming, Rose.* How he hoped she was not already dead!

In the depths of the cold shadow he opened his eyes. He had forgotten his eyes entirely, so overwhelmed was his brain by the sensations of fire and ice. But they opened and freed a flood of water, a dam of pain, released. And in the liquid blur he saw Rose on the floor within arm's reach, her back arched like that jump rope on the upswing, her lovely black hair chopped off and splayed around her pale head, her beautiful head . . .

She breathed like a fish on dry land. *Garner! Listen to me!* But the command didn't come from her lips, stretched wide like a shark's jaw to swallow all the air in the room. He reached out to touch her, and the tears washed away his vision finally, and he could see that this was not his Rose. This was his daughter who was not his daughter, whom he loved anyway.

He couldn't remember her name.

Rose would know it. Rose, crying at the glass door. It rattled and shook and cracked under her pleading fists.

Somehow, Garner stood. Somehow, he went to her.

35

The feet clad in red shoes moved. Beth saw them turn to the side, and a few moments later, white fingers gripped the edge of the door frame. The ball peen hammer in Trey's grip made a hesitant bounce on the glass as if he had seen it too.

"That's him, right?" she asked Trey.

"Those are his shoes," he said.

Soon the rest of the man appeared, limb by limb, extracting himself from the room by turning over and then pulling his knees up under him, still holding the frame. He came out the way an adult backs out of a tunnel for children, stiff from confinement and unsure of the space behind him. He pushed back into the hallway with his head close to the ground.

Beth pressed herself up to the glass as if her desire to help him would be enough to get him off the floor. She had never been so glad to see a man alive, this complete stranger, nor so afraid that he would die when she was so close to reaching him. She pounded a fist on the window, and he pushed himself up onto his hands and knees, then turned his face in her direction, but the morning light from her window glanced off his glasses and she couldn't see his eyes. She wasn't sure that she was anything more to him than a shadow beating on the glass.

"Garner!" Trey shouted.

"Where's Dr. Ransom?" Beth asked.

"Garner!" he repeated. "Can you unlock the door?"

Beth doubted the man could see straight, let alone crawl the marathon that stretched out between them.

"Call 9-1-1," Beth ordered.

"Cat Ransom *is* our 9-1-1," Trey said. "But the sheriff will bring someone."

"You called the sheriff? Of course you called the sheriff. That's exactly what a thinking person would have done."

Garner put one hand on the wall for balance and straightened up, got his opposite foot out from under him and planted it on the ground, and then froze in this position for long seconds.

"We have to break the glass," Beth said. "We have to get to him." She reached for the hammer dangling from Trey's fingers at his side.

"He's getting up."

He was. His muscles found the coordination to push off the wall and floor together. The strength of legs, hips, torso, and arms worked together for a brief and beautiful moment, as Garner slowly, slowly rose to his feet. He was nearly erect when his head came forward, as if it thought his feet were already on the move, and then his chin went to his chest, and his entire body fell into the wall and slid down the face of it. Garner landed hard on his shoulder before rolling onto his back, where he lay still.

It seemed that shock had frozen Trey. Beth grabbed the hammer out of his hands and started beating on the window rather than the door. The vibration of the strikes buzzed like electricity down the hammer's shaft and caused the bones of her fingers to hum. She wrapped the little hammer in both hands and raised it over her head, bringing it down on the window with all her weight, again and again. She closed her eyes and was overcome by the memory of Herriot leaping through that screen window when she went after Mercy. She saw her dog's black paws and thick claws cutting through the mesh like butter, and then scrambling over the wall with no command or leash or common sense to stop her. Beth went after her grandfather with the same recklessness.

Her hammer seemed to freeze in the glass, and when she opened her eyes and looked up, she saw that the head had gone through it and become trapped in a web of fine cracks.

Trey shed his flannel shirt and shoved his hands back into the sleeves, wrapping the cuffs around his knuckles like makeshift gloves. He stripped her hands off the handle and wrenched the hammer head out of the window, then went after the breach. He was taller than Beth and able to come down on the weakness more forcefully. Beth jerked her face away as chips of glass flew.

Trey got them both into Cat Ransom's office through the shattered window. There was glass under the window inside the waiting room, and Beth's cowboy boots ground it deep into the chair cushions as she climbed over them, one hand in Trey's sturdy grip. A shard bit into her shoulder as he helped her over the sill. But her eyes were on Garner, who looked like another dying man she wouldn't be able to save.

Somehow she reached him before Trey did, at the precise moment when his entire body shuddered and he vomited against the wall.

Trey turned his head away. "Whoa."

"It's good, it's good," Beth said, grabbing his shoulder to roll him away from the choking hazard and into fresh air. She got him onto his other side. "Throwing up is almost always a good sign, right? His body's getting rid of toxins. We have to find out what it is."

Trey shook his head and talked through his fingers. "The ergot was days ago. Would it keep doing this now?"

Beth didn't know.

Trey continued, "She could have given him anything. An overdose of something. Or drain cleaner."

Garner's heartbeat was slow but even, his airways were clear. Beth used her own sleeves to clean off Garner's mouth and nose. The physical elements of illness had never bothered her. She'd seen worse in animals—calves wasted by Johne's disease, cows with prolapsed uteri that had to be reinserted by hand, bulls made lame by foot rot more rank than any manure, horses trapped by barbed wire. It was the helplessness, not the earthiness, that punched her in the gut every time. The desire to help was so easily overwhelmed by ignorance of what to do.

Crouching over Garner now seemed so much like that moment in the crowded, suffocating cab of her father's truck, while Beth did what her father's heart couldn't. But Garner's heart and lungs were doing their own work, and her hands needed a task. They skimmed over his pallid face and shuddering chest without finding a place to land.

"His breathing is really shallow," Beth said to Trey. "See what you can find in that room he came out of. If we can find out what the poison is, maybe we can treat it."

Casting a worried glance at Garner, Trey stepped over him to get to the exam room.

"Oh no."

"What?"

"Cat's in here."

"Make her tell you what she's done."

"I think she's . . . it looks like she's unconscious."

"Stay with her," Beth said. "Do you know CPR?"

A drumming sound drew Beth's attention toward the window she and Trey had just broken. Five square panes stood at attention before the rising sun. At left, on the bottom, the shattered sixth pane gaped. The others were glaringly bright against the dark contrast of the interior, barely blue in the intensifying light. She squinted. There was nothing else to see from her position on the floor except the underside of the balcony and the roofline of an old building across the street.

She realized she had expected to see a person, a savior announcing that he was an EMT with epinephrine in the trunk of his car, and IVs and activated charcoal and heart monitors and anything else needed to reverse what she—no, what Cat Ransom had done. But there was no one. Only her, and death, and knowledge that she could apply to animals, not human beings in the throes of unknown poisons.

The head of the wolf rose before the pane of glass in the center of the row. His front paws struck it as he came up and repeated the thumping sound that had first caught Beth's attention.

The sight of the beast filled her with peace. She was deeply comforted by the possibility that God had sent the wolf—an endangered species unwanted in his native habitat—to her for a specific purpose.

I will heal him. Beth felt certain the voice that wrapped itself around her was from God, inaudible to Trey or Garner or the doctor. It was not the wolf speaking, like a creature from a fairy tale, though the wild animal was probably closer to God than she was. *I will heal him through you.*

How? I can't control this gift.

The answer was whispered into her heart with a voice so full of love that it could do no wounding. *My mercy doesn't exist because of who you are, but because of who I am.*

Then why do you need me to do it?

She asked sincerely, without disrespect, and the moment the words passed through her mind she realized that the question was backward. Of course God could heal this dying man without her; God didn't need her to accomplish his miracles. *She* was the one who needed him to do it through her. *She* needed his mercy, his redemption, his reversal of her sin and the consequence that had followed.

"You are about to show me mercy," she whispered.

I am.

"You didn't heal my father." She was putting the puzzle together, not questioning the truth.

Not all death is death, child. I promised him long ago that I would heal this family. The promise is also for you.

She would hold on to that promise tightly.

"What should I do?" she said. Her restless hands finally alighted on her grandfather's cold fingers. She took one of his hands in both of hers.

Believe me.

"I do."

As she sat on her knees, Beth clutched her grandfather's hand and pressed it to her cheek. His palm caught her tears while her forearms entwined his like a vine. His baby-soft skin smelled like fresh soil, like a garden about to sprout new life. Beth's prayer over him was wordless and open. Hope yielded to trust, doubt converted to belief, fear gave way to anticipation. She clung to Garner's hand and waited for God to do what he said he would do. She would not leave until he did.

She didn't notice time. She didn't notice whether she was comfortable or stiff, or hot or cold, or uttering her emotions aloud. She didn't pay attention to the room or anything else in the world. Eventually, words from a psalm memorized long ago formed in her mind: *Though I walk through the valley of the shadow of death, I will fear no evil; for You are with me . . . Surely goodness and mercy shall follow me all the days of my life; and I will dwell in the house of the Lord forever.*

Her grip on Garner's arm had become damp. It was the tears, she thought, the intensity of her prayers. The sweat of begging. But when she opened her eyes she saw that their arms were red and sticky. The cut on her shoulder had opened up. The wolf's claw and the knife of glass had cut through her trail-dusty shirt, sliced it open, and created an ooze of red that matched her grandfather's shoes. Even now it dripped down his elbow and left droplets on his shirt.

At his wrist, her fingers felt his strengthening pulse. The color in his skin was coming up from the sickly yellow of butter beans to the rosy glow of a belly laugh. His breathing deepened and became a lifesaving wind that pushed his boat of life out of dangerous waters and back toward home.

He slept like Adam in God's garden, before the world ever knew death.

Beth released her grasp of his arm and laid his hand over his heart. He would wake up when he was ready. Perhaps God had a few things to say to him too. The wolf had vanished from the window frame.

She remembered Dr. Ransom, and Trey, and turned to find them.

Trey was standing in the hall behind her, staring. "You're about to tell me you're related to Mathilde, aren't you?"

"What?" She got to her feet.

"It's actually a who—Miracle Mattie? Never mind. That. Was. Amazing. You should have watched that transformation! I could see him change, like one of those time-lapse films! Is he okay? He looks better. What happened? What did you do?"

She couldn't think of any answer that would satisfy Trey's curiosity right now. "Is Dr. Ransom—"

"On the brink of hell."

"Did you do CPR?"

"She's breathing. Her heart's beating. I don't know what else to do for her. I'm not even sure I'd want to if I knew how. Just being truthful."

Beth took a step toward the room. Trey stepped in front of her and swept a flyaway curl behind his ear. "It's ugly, Beth." He held up an empty gallon-size bag labeled *Zigadenus venenosus* and pointed to the words. "That translates to English as 'eat me and you die.' Meadow death camas. It looks to me like she boiled up some kind of decoction for Garner, then pumped it into his IV bag."

He pointed to the floor, and Beth noticed a trail of plastic tubing still connected to Garner's hand, the one she hadn't been clutching. It trailed along the hall and around the door frame to a floor littered with more plastic tubing, and needles, and a nearly empty bag of some cloudy liquid. Beth stepped over a backboard as she entered the room. On the counter, an electric kettle was tipped over, and a mess of translucent pulp that looked like mashed onions soaked in water.

"Get that out of him."

"Already did." Trey held up the detached tube. "So the reduction of death was for Garner. But it looks like our doctor consumed hers raw."

Beth glanced around for Dr. Ransom but didn't see her.

"Which is worse?"

"I wouldn't know. Survival classes just teach you to stay away from the stuff. They don't tell you how to prepare it for a murder-suicide."

The bulbs in the hot pot wouldn't have filled a sandwich bag, let alone the empty gallon-size storage bag hanging from Trey's fingers.

The room contained medical equipment and monitors that gave it the appearance of a hospital room. Opposite the counter, a hospital bed stood at an odd angle away from the wall. Trey nodded at it, and Beth moved around the foot.

Dr. Ransom lay on her side as if she'd fallen off the bed. She was pressed tightly into the joint where the wall met the floor, her legs unnaturally rigid and jammed at right angles between her hips and the bed. Her shoulders were rolled inward, collapsing her chest, and Beth couldn't see any movements of breathing. The doctor's neck was strained upward, tendons pushing against skin, as if her head were trying to escape her body, and her eyes were open, blind but terrified. White bubbles of saliva coated her lips and tongue and left streaks on her cheeks. Beth could see where the doctor's convulsing had spattered the wall and floor with the terrible poison.

The long, dried stems of the poisonous plant protruded from Dr. Ransom's frozen fist.

"Stay with Garner," Beth told Trey as she pushed the hospital bed aside so she had room to kneel and search for a pulse.

"Is she dead?" he asked.

"Not yet."

"You're not going to do what you did for—"

"It's not for me to say," Beth said.

"Well, I think some people deserve what they get."

Beth pushed damp strands of black hair out of the woman's terrified eyes. "Mercy's all about what we don't deserve."

"What?"

"Stay with Garner. Just stay with Garner."

36

As Cat lay on the floor choking on her last worldly hopes, she watched Garner rise from the dead and walk out of the room. He saw her, and then he left her. The pathetic turn of events brought a soundless laugh to her silenced throat, and she sputtered more frothy drool.

She surrendered to the pain of the poison. It was less than the pain of her lifeless life. She could feel the death camas seeping into her gums, floating like mist through her throat and belly, seeking out the nerve endings that would transport its toxins to the command centers of her brain. *Slow down*, the invader would command her lungs and heart. *Slow down, shut down.* Her stomach resisted the hostile takeover, but Cat was on death's side. Let her central nervous system lose its grip; she would hold on to the contents of her stomach more tightly than this unfriendly mountain held its precious metals.

It was her last intentional action before she was overtaken, like dry brush in an inferno, like a person drowning in the ocean. And then the water quenched the fire, and the moisture evaporated in the heat, and the world became black and silent.

There was no pain. She could not move. Her ears strained and couldn't even hear the sound of her own breath. Her eyes were wide and sightless and full of dry heat that radiated from the ground. What was first a comforting warmth quickly deepened and sucked up all her tears, vacuumed all moisture out of her mouth, parched her throat. It grew in intensity and seemed to melt her clothes to her skin, and she could smell the synthetic fibers burning, and she could feel the metal buttons and rivets of her jeans, the buckle of her belt, the wires and hooks of her bra, the jewelry on her fingers and in her ears—all of it become molten and begin to drip from her body, *through* her body, which was as pliable as wax.

Still, no pain. And complete silence. And unbearable heat that would melt away the very memory of her soul. She was fading away, she was already gone.

The first stab of agony was a sound, a voice rising from the saturated blackness like an invisible fanged snake. The voice of a child, tender and happy. Amelia's voice.

Dr. Ransom! Dr. Ransom!

Her heart was still beating after all; Cat discovered this when the twin cry clamped down on it and held it tight in its jaws. And then the heartache serpent began to thrash. It raised her up and slammed her down and rattled the sight back into her eyes, and she could see, high in the infinite blackness above her, a pinprick of light that was little Amelia, coming down.

I am lost, Cat thought. *Come quickly, child.*

The light grew. The point sprouted wings and became like a white butterfly, like an angel descending from heaven to the bottom of the black pot where Cat melted. Amelia's love fluttered. It rippled with hope on outstretched arms. The closer it came—though still it was so, so far away—the more violently the serpent flailed with her disintegrating body in its jaws. The harder the knocks to the back of her head. The deeper the piercing fangs.

This was the true pain of death: the memory of lost love.

It was no memory, though, not in this layer of existence where the human senses went haywire and reality was bent by hyper-real perceptions. It was a new experience, not from the past but from the future. A reality she had not known until this moment.

Amelia was coming for her. Love, finally, was coming for her.

The floating gauze of the girl's sleeves were angel wings, the tips pointing upward, out of this despair. The shape of Amelia descended, coming closer to Cat's upturned face, her whiplashed head. But as she approached, all but her pure white wings changed shape. Her hands and feet vanished. Her skirt turned gray and merged with the darkness. She bowed her faceless head, and the hair of her crown turned black and shiny. And under the wings, a terrible chasm began to open up. The blackness peeled back and exposed a bloody red mouth more terrifying than the consuming heat, and glowing white fangs stronger and longer than the ones gripping her heart.

She was not looking into the body of an angel, but the muzzle of a fierce gray wolf. He dropped his snout toward her, the white wings of snowy fur splayed out under his eyes, golden irises like new sunlight. She couldn't hold the gaze. She couldn't look away.

He snarled, and the reptile slamming her heart into the ground released her but left his venom behind. Her dead heart would never beat again on its own.

Dr. Ransom. Amelia's tender voice was so very far away.

The wolf sniffed her, and his hot breath was like a cool breeze in hell. And then it opened its mouth wide, and Cat watched as its jaws became unhinged, gaping over her battered head. It closed the final gap between them, and she felt its razor teeth on her jaw, on her temples, as he took her entire head inside of his mouth.

And then it swallowed her whole.

Beth was unprepared for the mystery of what had happened to Garner and Dr. Ransom. She had not anticipated the intensity of God's healing work, the exhaustion and the exhilaration that ran circles around her mind. She knew she would never be able to adequately explain what had happened to her or to the others in those moments after she placed her hands on them and before she opened her eyes again.

But she was even less prepared for the aftermath.

On the cold floor of the exam room, Dr. Ransom's body began to quiver. Beth was sitting at her head, hands gently cradling her skull while she prayed for God's will to be done in this broken life. The convulsing began in Dr. Ransom's foot, in a spastic ankle that jerked the toe of her shoe against the floor, and then it moved upward through every joint and along every muscle long enough to contort until it reached her head, which she began to knock against the floor so violently that Beth expected the force to break one of her fingers. She entwined them in the doctor's hair to prevent the woman from cracking her skull.

Then there was the retching, overwhelming and foul and necessary, as purging of any kind always was. Beth was unaffected by the stench, relieved that it had finally happened. And when it was finished, Dr. Ransom opened her eyes, and Beth smiled at her, overcome by the generosity of God.

Cat Ransom looked up into Beth's upside-down gaze and began to shriek. She took into her lungs all the air that had been denied to her and expelled every last bit of it in endless streams of piercing noise. With unexpected strength, she yanked her head out of Beth's protective grasp. She fought Beth's hands and pushed them off her head as if fighting a helmet. Then she created quick distance between them, a gap too far for Beth to bridge with a calming hand or soothing words. The doctor's noise settled down into a stream of fierce curses.

"You're not Amelia," Beth made out between gasps and shouts. "Where's Amelia, you devil, you dog?"

At first Beth was too stunned to answer, and then she opted not to say anything until Dr. Ransom's panic subsided on its own. Instead, the disruption mounted. It seemed the doctor's outburst had roused Garner from his peace in the hallway. There was a confrontation of words between Garner and Trey that Beth couldn't make out in her corner of the office, where Dr. Ransom's yells ricocheted around Beth's head.

When the doctor saw Garner enter the room, her screaming stopped like a car crash, and for a few brief and wonderful seconds, the only sounds were of breathless lungs trying to catch up with the moment. Beth drew in a breath and looked to her grandfather, who was on his feet in the doorway, blocking Trey from entering. The stern gaze he was leveling at her looked so much like her mother's.

"Garner," Dr. Ransom said.

Garner didn't respond to her.

"Who are you?" he said to Beth, and then without giving her a chance to reply, he said: "Where is my daughter?"

37

Cat was a mess, a screaming, hysterical, delusional mess, and Garner's heart broke with paternal love for her. As he pieced together the emerging stories told by Trey, Dotti, and Nova, who floated onto the scene and took Garner's hand like a pale ghost, he found the logic to understand what Cat had done.

The sheriff arrived. An ambulance arrived. And the entire town of Burnt Rock came out to see what the trouble was all about.

Garner refused to press charges against Catherine. He simply couldn't.

He was examined and found to be in apparently fine health. He knew no one would be able to prove, even if he cooperated, that Cat had given him a fatal dose of death camas. That was an experience he'd hold privately, in his memory. And he was willing to bet no doctor would find any cancer in his liver anymore. His entire body shuddered with wellness that he hadn't known since he was forty-six years old.

He resented that health with all his heart.

The girl who claimed to be his grandchild was mostly silent and watchful. Her hands were buried in the full ruff of a pretty cattle dog at her side, but Garner could see her fingers trembling.

Nova did most of the talking. She did not share Garner's opinion that Cat could be forgiven. Even if she had, Cat's future had been set for her by her past.

So when the EMTs finally sedated the doctor, and the sheriff cuffed her to the gurney, and the convoy of flashing lights finally pulled out of town, Garner came to see his miraculous recovery as another undeserved punishment from the hand of God. Another daughter taken from him. Another twenty-seven terrible years loomed ahead. He wished he had died before he understood any of it.

Garner didn't want Beth Borzoi, daughter of the aloof and unforgiving Rose Borzoi, in his basement the next morning. He didn't want her in his house, in his town. Ever. He wouldn't have allowed her within ten miles except that Dotti was manning the shop, "protecting" Garner's privacy, when Beth barged in. Dotti welcomed her and, effervescent with positive thinking, ushered the cowgirl downstairs.

Beth, not Rose, stood in the dim corner of his basement while he worked. He snipped ferociously at his plants as if they were responsible for his daughter's failure to appear in his darkest hour. He couldn't fathom how he'd mistaken this fair redhead for his own flesh and blood, but she had produced an aging wedding card and a brittle check, both written out to her mother in his hand. Garner decided Beth was the feminine derivative of her father, that porcelain Russian, so unlike Garner's dark-skinned Rose that only a DNA test would convince him the girl wasn't the love child of some other woman. Not all the hallucinogenic toxins in the world could lead him into such an embarrassing error again.

Such errors littered his past. He had always been a poor judge of character, hadn't he? In particular of women. Of wives and daughters who abandoned their families, of doctors who tried to kill their patients, of healers who wanted . . . He wasn't sure what this girl wanted yet, but he was confident that he wouldn't like it.

He lived in a sick and twisted world. What good were flimsy herbs in such a place? He pruned blindly.

Garner glanced up to see if Dotti had left him alone with the girl, but Dotti stood at the bottom of the stairs like a muted moth, large and soft. She offered him a daring smile that likely meant *Go on now. Take the lead with this granddaughter of yours.*

He would not. And while he was not taking the lead, he decided he also would not open his doors or his heart to Dotti anymore either. Who knew what she might do to him?

"This greenhouse is impressive," Beth said, reaching out to touch a blooming spear of foxglove.

"Don't touch anything." He pointed the hook of his clippers at her, and she snatched her hand back. "Plants'll kill you if you don't know what you're dealing with," he said. "And I'll just use your body for fertilizer."

In the silence, he almost felt terrible for saying such a thing. But what could one expect of an old man who'd been cast off, used, and dragged to the brink of death by God and by people at least three times by his reckoning?

Beth was looking at him with a gaze that seemed like pity, which only angered him further. He picked up a pot and turned around, looking for some other place to set it so he wouldn't have to watch her.

"I'm very sorry for what Dr. Ransom did to you," she offered.

"She couldn't do anything to me that wasn't already happening. I was a dying man. *You*, on the other hand—I'm not at all sure yet what kind of witch you are."

"Garner," Dotti scolded.

"Miracle worker, then, if labels matter," he said.

"They don't," said Beth. "I have a gift that I can't explain, a gift that's not even mine to control."

"And I have a healthy liver, and nothing to credit for it. For all I know it was those wicked plants Cat gave to me. A few alkaloids, a little zygadenine—"

"Don't be mean, Garner. The girl healed you."

"Mean?" Garner snapped, twisting to point his clippers at Dotti now. "Do you know how cancer is treated? By pumping a body full of poison, Dotti. Who's to say Cat didn't do the trick? How can a person even know the difference between what's good or bad anymore?"

"Oh, you're full of hooey, old man. You went up there to Mathilde's church looking for your miracle, and now you've got it. Why are you whining?"

"You think *this* was what I wanted?"

"If you didn't want your health, what did you want?"

"A relationship with my *daughter*! I don't have anything else that matters."

"Well, you won't be able to convince me that you wanted to *die*," Dotti said. With a huff she sat down on the bottom step of his stairway, effectively blocking his escape, should he plan to make one. "I know you better than that."

Garner pouted and slammed his pot down on a table.

"Trey told me you and Dr. Ransom were very close," Beth said.

"Closer than I was to my own daughter."

"I can understand why you're so angry."

"You can, can you? How old are you?"

"Twenty-two."

"And do you have kids, a child who trampled your love for her? No? Then don't tell me you understand. Why did Rose send you?"

Beth cleared her throat. "She didn't. She doesn't know I'm here, or she would have stopped me from coming. I came to ask you for help."

"All the help I have to offer is available online. You have a head-ache, a stomachache, a toothache? Take the little self-quiz and my website will direct you to all the products you need."

"Not that kind of help," Beth murmured.

"Oh—yes, I forgot. You have magic fingers. You don't need my help."

"I—my mother—needs money," Beth said.

"You have money?" Dotti's voice was full of surprise.

Garner turned around now to stare at Beth. The weight of the clippers seemed to make his shoulders stoop. "What for? School lunches? Daddy can't afford to feed you?"

He regretted his attitude and reveled in it at the same time. This was what happened, he thought, when pain could no longer be soothed, when all the medicinal therapies in the world fell short and all that was left were questions. Even when he was at death's door, it wasn't Rose who came to him, but a granddaughter he'd never met and didn't care about. Was his daughter so proud after all these years? Was his life worth so little to her?

Beth ran her fingers down the stalk of a bushy, woody plant so that the fine green needles broke off and released a pungent aroma.

"Don't touch it if you don't—"

"Rosemary," Beth said, crushing it between her fingers and holding it up to her nose. "My father died a week ago. It was my fault that he died."

Garner wiped his fingers on his apron. How long ago was it that he had hoped for this announcement? The wish belonged to another man, in another life. Now he could summon only a fatigued kind of grief, and the curious question of whether Rose was suffer-ing the way he himself had suffered when his wife ran away.

Yes or no, Rose didn't seek his consolation.

"Your fault, your problem," Garner said. "You've got the magic. You figure it out."

Beth brushed the broken herb off her hands and turned away from her grandfather. An emptiness welled in him at the sight of her back—a gaping hole that had once been filled with the fear of a terminal illness, with the hope of a family reunion before his death. Now, both fear and hope were gone. It was not the end he'd envisioned.

This must have been the way Mathilde Werner Wulff felt in the hours that she lay bleeding to death, slashed open by the claws of a mountain lion, thinking about her unreachable husband and the children they'd never have. The only difference was that Garner knew he'd never be rescued.

"I have two brothers," Beth said. "Levi is named after you—his middle name is Garner. He hates the ranch too. You have that in common."

A namesake. The first tangible evidence that the Rose who'd lived in his mind for a quarter of a century was not the same Rose who actually walked the earth. What did it mean?

"Danny is fifteen, gentle as a calf. Smart as a stock horse. He could memorize the Latin names and all the properties of all these plants within a day. Keep you talking about what you love for weeks."

This idea stirred the ashes of Garner's heart like the breath of God on embers. No one but Cat had ever taken such interest in his work—no, not even she, now that he saw through the lenses of hindsight. Dotti more than Cat, in fact. A smart boy. The son of Rose couldn't be otherwise.

Beth had come around the table and now stood beside him without touching him, standing in the gap between their hearts without forcing him to look at her.

"Families go on, don't they?" she said. "You pass along the good and the bad even if you don't mean to. But mostly good, I think. You grow all these plants because you want to help people feel better, don't you? You learn their secrets, you use that knowledge for good. I was going to be a vet, an animal healer. Maybe I got that from you."

"You were going to be?"

"My father had that in him too—not the veterinary skills, but the goodness. I think you would have liked him if you hadn't misjudged him so badly. All he ever wanted to do was help people get through life with their heads up. He gave them everything he had—kindness, trust, and this beautiful place to live, good food, the chance to do hard work so they can sleep on their satisfaction at night. I don't really understand why you objected to it. Isn't it the same thing that you're trying to do with all this?" She indicated all the healthy greens and colorful blooms.

"It isn't safe or smart to surround a woman and her children with maniacs." The argument lacked his usual passion.

"These 'maniacs' have never caused a fraction of the trouble you and I have caused to the people we love most."

"I'm not to blame for anything!" Garner objected.

Beth's momentary silence caused him to feel childish and stupid.

"You offer a type of mercy to people who need it," Beth said. "That's all my parents and I ever wanted to do. And Danny too. Levi . . . well, I don't know. Maybe he needs someone like you to help him figure that out. But now *we're* the ones who need mercy, I need it. And I don't have the resources. God gave me this . . . *gift*, but it can't pay the bills. Would you please do it for my mom, if not for me? For the sake of everything that is good about that ranch— I'll agree to anything. Name your terms."

"I can't," he said, and he saw Beth's confidence falter.

"Levi has already made plans to sell the property to a developer. These men who need the ranch most will lose their home, their livelihood. What I'm asking for isn't entirely for us, do you see? It's for them too."

Garner cleared the knot out of his throat. "They won't be the first to face that kind of hardship."

"Mom will lose everything."

"I'm sorry." His heart filled with sincerity and his eyes brimmed with disappointment. *Any ending but this one, God. It would have been better if you'd let me die.*

"I'm begging you. Please."

"I can't."

"You can, but you won't! You stubborn bull!"

"Careful, girl, I don't owe you anything."

"And God didn't owe you a second life either! But he gave it to you—what are you going to do with it?"

Garner slammed his pruning shears down on the table and took off his gloves. "Is that how this works? You go around giving people gifts they don't want and then expect something in return? No, I won't be used that way. But even if I would, it doesn't matter. There is no money, Beth! Get it? I don't have squat, and I don't know who told you I did!"

"You're lying!"

"I'm telling you the truth like it has never been told in this family. I gave it away! There *is—no—money!*"

Grandfather and granddaughter faced each other underneath the harsh fluorescent lights. Back when he'd allowed his imagination to dream up grandchildren, he had never envisioned a woman who seemed so worn out, her eyes sinking into black bowls of skin, her lips thin and dragged downward by the weight of the world. She was too young to be so old. Her need and his inability to meet it sucked all the fight out of him.

"Okay," she whispered.

"Do you believe me?"

"Yes."

"I'm sorry, Beth." And he truly was.

"I'm going to go . . . walk," Beth said. She was small enough to slide by Dotti's bulk, and her feet were weightless on the stairs, as if she was already vanishing from his life. Here, gone. Garner listened to her boots clack lightly across the floor over his head, heard the squeal of the wood-and-screen door swing open and then slap shut as she left the house.

"So, how much money do you really have?" Dotti asked.

He turned to her. "A fraction of what Hank has."

"Hank? You gave your money to *Hank*?"

"To Mathilde. Got myself a brass plate and a bench for it."

"Was it enough to save a ranch?"

Garner sighed. "It was enough to buy ten ranches."

Dotti fell silent, and Garner found it impossible to look at her. But then she started laughing. "I can't believe you gave it to Hank! I could have given you class-six whitewater rides *for life*! Much more exciting."

Garner didn't find that the least bit funny.

"It's just as well," she said, and she pushed herself off the steps and dusted off her backside with the palm of her hand. "People who have money believe it's the answer to everything. Which, of course, it's not."

38

Beth stood with Garner's yard gate closed firmly behind her and started to cry. *You said you were going to show me mercy. I don't know what you meant.*

She would have to go back to the Blazing B empty-handed. After all that.

Before she left, however, she had a question to ask Nova. A question that might actually have an answer. Beth walked the unpaved roads between her grandfather's shop and the doctor's abandoned offices. She passed in front of the broken window that still had not been boarded up. And then she walked into Nova's bookstore, drying her tears as she entered.

The aisles were narrow and the shelves were short enough to allow a person to see the entire room. Beth saw Nova at the back, rearranging some books. When she saw Beth enter, she raised her hand in a hesitant wave, and Beth thought how nice it would have been to know her older sister, the one now tucked in beside her father in the grave.

Nova spoke first. "I thought you'd have gone home by now."

Beth shook her head. "I had some things to take care of first. I'll probably go back today." It was already late morning, though, and the thought of another night in the mountains—more cougars, more detours—took everything out of her. "Or maybe tomorrow. How are you feeling?"

Nova tipped her head to one side and aligned the spines of several books on the shelf. "It's a sad time."

"It is."

They were quiet for a minute. Beth picked up some of the books Nova was shelving.

"I wanted to ask you about a photograph I saw in your apartment," Beth asked.

"Which one?"

"The men with the horse—a white man and a Native American."

"The white man is Jonathan Wulff."

"Wulff?"

"The grandson of Mathilde Werner Wulff."

"I don't know who she is."

"She is the one behind the Sweet Assembly. The church where you found me Monday night."

"Miracle Mattie?" Beth asked, recalling something Trey Bateman had said.

Nova nodded.

"I guess I'm not up to speed on the story."

While Nova arranged her books, she told Beth the tale of Mathilde's journey, of the cougar attack, of the mysterious Indian man who rose from the cold fire pit and took her home. In the rich vision of the story world that Nova built, Beth momentarily forgot her troubles.

"Come over here," Nova eventually said, and Beth followed her to the front of the store to a shelf labeled *Regional*.

"Mathilde's original journal is still with the Wulff family," Nova said as she ran her fingers along the titles, searching for one in particular. "There are excerpts on display at the Sweet Assembly. But about twenty years ago one of her descendants published it." She found the slim paperback volume and pulled it out for Beth. *The Personal Account of Miracle Mattie.*

"Jonathan Wulff wrote the foreword," Nova pointed out.

"The man in your picture," Beth confirmed.

"Yes, the one whose leg was healed at the same place. Please take the book. It's a small thing, but I'd like you to have it. For comfort in your own sad time."

"Who is the other man in the photograph? The one riding the horse."

"My great-great-grandfather. He was an elder among the Southern Ute in the 1930s. Jonathan married his daughter."

"And I'm guessing that the saddle on the horse is the one Mathilde made for her husband—the one they gave to the tribe as a gift of thanks?"

"That's right."

"What happened to it?"

"I really don't know. By the time it came into my grandfather's hands, alcohol had damaged his authority as an elder. It is rumored that he traded the saddle for a case of whiskey."

Was that like trading the saddle to save a horse's eye? No— what Beth had done was worse. At least Nova's grandfather had the right to trade it.

Beth looked at the plain book cover in the light of the large window. She fell into wondering how the saddle had traveled across the decades from a whiskey trader to Jacob, the taciturn son of a psychiatrist, without being dismantled. Knowing the history of this old piece now, she could barely believe that she had suggested Phil and Fiona strip it of its silver.

But she was pulled back to the conversation when a mental puzzle piece fell into place.

"Wait—that means you're related to Mathilde?"

"Yes," Nova said reluctantly. "I am her great-great-*great*-granddaughter."

"That's something."

"I find it best around here not to draw attention to it."

"Why?"

"Because people ask questions I can't answer. There's no rhyme or reason to why some people get what they need and others don't, though men like Hank try to explain it. Good people say their prayers, give their money. They beg and plead and leave crying. What kind of God could turn his back on such people? Grandfather Wulff thought the Sweet Assembly would be for everybody. But it's only for the lucky few. I take no pride in it."

"But that's where you went when you had nowhere else to turn," Beth observed.

Nova turned her eyes back to the book spines as if she was looking for something, and she clasped her fingers behind her back. "Yes. Well. Maybe I'm a fool."

"Or maybe you're just hopeful," Beth said. The morning sun coming in through the storefront was a comforting blanket around her shoulders.

Nova turned around and reached out to touch Beth's arm. "I would not find it hard to put my faith in a person like you, after what you did for me. And for Mr. Remke. People are talking. They don't believe, but it's easy for me." She pulled Beth down onto a narrow wooden bench in front of the bookcases as if she would prevent her from ever leaving. "You have power."

Her words and her touch alarmed Beth, who tried to pull away. "No," Beth said. "I told you I don't. Only God has real power."

"Then tell me how you get it. Tell me how you make your God do what you want him to do. How did you heal me? How did you raise Mr. Remke from the dead?"

324

The childlike desire in Nova's question melted away Beth's panic. It was the question she herself had been trying to figure out from the moment her life began to fall apart. Her search for a formula that she could apply to God was no different from what Nova wanted.

She took Nova's hand. "It doesn't work that way," Beth said. "I came here hoping for my own miracle, Nova. And I didn't find it. I couldn't make it happen. Other things happened—other miraculous things that I couldn't have dreamed up. But they weren't what I asked for."

Nova frowned. "And what would be the purpose of that?"

"I don't know yet. Maybe I won't ever know."

"Maybe *you're* the fool."

Beth smiled at that. "Do you think I am?"

Nova appeared to be caught in the awkward space of not wanting to call her healer a fool. She said, "Why do you follow such a God?"

The answer came to Beth's mouth swiftly. "Because I believe he is *good*. Not because he gives me what I want, but just because he is. He doesn't owe me any other explanation." And in that moment she recalled her father's faith, his close-to-dying words, which she was so far from understanding at the time: *"My faith isn't in good outcomes, Beth, only in the goodness of God."*

It was enough to bring her to her feet. She wanted to go home. She wanted to be with the people she loved, regardless of the outcome.

Nova was shaking her head and staring at her hands. "He has not been so good to me."

There was more pain than defiance in her words, a resignation to life's difficulties that broke Beth's heart. She reached out and took both of Nova's hands. "Maybe you just don't know what you're looking at, Nova. God is present even when life is so hard. Ask him to show his goodness to you. He'll do it. I promise you."

A new voice entered the conversation. "Mind if I eavesdrop?"

Beth turned. Trey Bateman was leaning against a display behind the women. His hands were crammed into dress pants, and he wore a T-shirt under a maroon-colored vest, and a matching maroon bow tie.

"Is that your work uniform?" Beth giggled at him while also wiping moisture from her eyes. Nova stood up too and withdrew her hands from Beth's.

"I'm a trendsetter, what can I say?"

Beth nodded. "Did you just pull in?" She glanced out the window and saw his bus in front of the post office.

"I did. Saw you come in, but it takes a little while to pull away from the visitors."

"That's okay."

"I've got an hour before I have to guide a group through the mining museum." He jerked his thumb over his shoulder toward the door. "Do you have time to get a coffee or something? I thought we could talk."

Nova slapped Beth lightly on the arm and busied herself with her books again. Beth looked at him and found his question too difficult to answer.

"About your wolf," he said.

"What?"

"We could talk about your wolf. Or about whatever you want. I'm just a curious guy. About you. And wolves. And all the ways you've weirded me out in the last thirty-six hours."

She laughed at this.

"But maybe now's not a good time," he said.

"It's not a bad time. But I think I need to go home."

"I can walk you back up to Garner's."

"I mean to the ranch. To my family. Garner isn't very happy with me right now."

Trey sighed. "So when are you going to leave? Wait—are you going to ride back? On your horse?"

"Well I don't have a car."

He shook his head. "Let me drive you. It's a big bus. No room for the horse—"

"That's really nice of you, but—"

"It's too late to start out on horseback."

"Maybe I won't go until tomorrow."

"Even so. Where did you sleep last night?"

"At Dotti's."

"She'll let you stay with her again."

Nova touched Beth's elbow. "Actually, I was hoping to talk you into staying with me tonight. I have more questions."

Trey started bobbing his head. "There, see? Now you can't go until tomorrow. It would be rude to leave sooner." He reached out and took Beth's hand and pulled her toward the door. "But I have first dibs on talking with our new pal," he said to Nova. "You'll have to wait. I'll have her back in an hour."

Nova waved them out of her store. And Beth accepted Trey's and Nova's friendship. It was a good gift from a good God.

39

Garner lay awake on his bed. His curtains were parted and he stared at the gibbous moon, which cast white light across his floor. He tried to sleep by first emptying his mind, but his efforts were futile. The face of his granddaughter kept popping in, followed by imagined faces of the brothers she had described. And even Rose showed up, reaching out to him.

He was cold. On this August night he was so strangely cold that he had donned socks and pulled the blanket at the foot of his bed up and over his chest, but all that hadn't properly warmed him.

He turned his attention to filling his mind instead of emptying it. He fetched about for something worth pondering. He thought up a new tea recipe, but then Cat butted in to tell him what she thought of it. He thought up a vacation, but no matter what destination he wanted, he kept ending up at the Blazing B. He thought up a date with Dotti at Mazy's, but when they arrived, all the tables were taken by members of the Borzoi family.

Garner finally sat up in bed and placed his stocking feet on the floor, square in the beam of moonlight. He braced his hands on the sides of the mattress and locked his elbows as he leaned forward, desperate to lose himself to the blackness of sleep. Tea did not sound good to him.

An earth-shattering crash from downstairs catapulted him off the bed. It sounded like another one of his windows had been broken. That kitchen window had been no small expense to replace, though it was one of his smallest panes.

Since giving his money to Hank, Garner thought about expenses.

He stood erect in the heaven's spotlight, and his mind raced with possibilities. A burglar? A vandal? He welcomed the threat. It was just the distraction he needed. His blood was flowing. His brain had fired up the emergency adrenaline production line. He grabbed a heavy walking stick fashioned from a gnarled piece of western juniper and carried it out of his bedroom, hefting it like a spear, and crossed the hall like a hunter. The house at the base of his stairs was dark. With his free hand Garner balanced himself as he carefully took each stair down. His knees were less nimble than they used to be.

At the bottom, the same moonlight that spread across his bedroom floor penetrated the curtains and became a night-light on the living room. The picture windows were all in one piece.

"Hello?" he said.

Not even the summer-night insects responded. But a breeze caused the wide legs of his house pants to flutter. It seemed to be coming from the kitchen.

Walking stick still raised over his head, Garner trod softly past his showcase of natural wellness, past his cash register, and past the staircase to the basement, which glowed with the fluorescent warmth of artificial sunlight.

In the kitchen he flipped on the overhead bulb, lowered the walking stick to his side, and swore. The kitchen window—the barely three-month-old, double-paned, energy-efficient window— had been reduced all over again to a pile of glitter on the floor.

"How did this happen?" he asked aloud.

He searched for a rock, a brick, any projectile that might explain it. But there was nothing but glass to be seen. If kids had done this he would have heard the thunder of their escaping feet on the floorboards of the porch. His mind went to Beth. He had assumed she left town, but he hadn't bothered to verify it. Could she be mad enough to cause this kind of damage? Could she be lingering, watching?

In his basement, a clay pot fell and was dashed on the concrete floor. Garner knew the sound, having accidentally smashed his share of plant containers over the years. His whole body turned toward the noise.

There was someone in his basement garden.

He repositioned his grip on the walking stick and turned to face the staircase. He paused at the head and said, "Who's there?" in his most intimidating voice. Another pot fell over. Judging by the sound of the impact, this one was plastic, and it merely cracked.

There was a terrible rattling of his steel tables, and several foreign sounds he couldn't pinpoint: a wet sort of clacking, a smacking of lips, a tearing of grass and leaves.

The unfinished staircase creaked slightly under his weight, but this signal didn't give any sort of pause to the basement ruckus.

When the truth of the matter came into view, Garner thought perhaps he had fallen asleep after all and was now dreaming. Or experiencing a night terror.

A great gray wolf that easily surpassed a hundred pounds stood atop one of his stainless tables and was eating the herbs and plants. In the two to three minutes it had taken Garner to come down from his room, the wolf had already devoured a fifth of Garner's inventory.

The creature raised its eyes to Garner and masticated a gallon of thyme as if he were a cow. Man and beast stared, gazes locked on each other. Only one of them breathed—the same one who also ate.

All steadiness went out of Garner's legs. He sank to sit on the step he had reached, which was about halfway down the flight.

There was no way he could climb these stairs again right now even if the wolf jumped off that table straight for Garner's jugular. He lacked strength to move, yes, but he was also riveted by the scene. There was a wolf in his basement. Not just any wild creature, which would have been amazing enough, but a wolf, an endangered wolf who had, apparently, jumped right through a glass window and was eating his *plants*.

"Aren't you supposed to be a carnivore?" he said. Each one of the dog's feet seemed nearly as large as Garner's face.

The wolf ripped into a patch of blooming purple comfrey and tore the fine stems off the roots. He was eating at an astonishing rate, moving within seconds from comfrey to bloodroot to the spectacular bryony vine on the wall. He leaped to the floor to uproot the vine from its six-foot-long planter box, and the table tipped over. The crash rattled through Garner's ears. The wolf's muzzle was coated with a lumpy clumping of soil.

Garner watched this with growing wonder. The vine, like many of the plants in this room, was toxic in large quantities. The wolf seemed to swallow without chewing, and he stripped the trellis itself from the wall as he devoured. The unnatural sight went on for long minutes. Would he choke on a tendril that caught in his throat? Would a woody stem puncture his stomach? Would the poisons finally accumulate and do their deadly work?

It wasn't until the wolf turned his eye onto the goldenseal, which had taken four years of nurturing to reach its present maturity, that Garner's practical side kicked in.

The canine snapped at the five-leafed stem.

"Hey!" Garner rose off his step. "That's valuable!" All of it was valuable. This was his livelihood now, not just some hobby. "Stop that!"

He brandished his walking stick but stayed where he was on the steps. He was no physical match for this wild animal, whose strength might be as abnormally great as his appetite. Surely the wolf would swallow Garner as easily as he could put down a mandrake.

The wolf polished off each one of the precious goldenseal roots and turned toward the cannabis. Garner wasn't growing it legally, though he had been using it legally for medicinal purposes. Cat had prescribed it for him. They had developed a wonderful marijuana-candy recipe.

"I *need* that!" he shouted, and at this outburst the wolf turned his head lazily in Garner's direction.

This is not what you need, Garner thought. But the thought seemed to belong to someone else. It was true enough, though. He knew in his knower that he didn't need that particular medicine any more, except that the candy was a lucrative asset.

As the wolf devoured every last ounce of his fan-leafed pain-killer, Garner wondered about the granddaughter who had dissolved his cancer. With a skill like that, who needed to ask for money?

How had she healed him? And why? More than any other question in the world, why?

Garner couldn't bear to watch the rest of the garden's destruction. He turned away feeling quite old again, and chilled in every extremity. He used the juniper stick to fortify his defeated walk back up the stairs. The loss of Cat, the loss of his family dream, the loss of his savings, of his income—it all bore down on him at once, so that he didn't even care about the mystical wolf.

But Cat would have liked him, Garner thought. *And Nova will be amazed.*

As he stepped up onto the main level of his home, Garner felt the cool air coming through the shattered kitchen window. It caused him to shiver. He turned down the hall toward the other flight of stairs and climbed them, heart-mind-and-bone weary.

The short walk to his bedroom stretched out like an unbearable hike. Somehow he returned to his bed and lay down on it. The moon had risen an inch in the sky. The moonbeams on his floor had shifted by degrees. He stared at them and was able to watch them creep. He wondered how long it would take for the wolf to eat everything and finally leave.

Would he turn on the jars of tea next? Would he cast them off their shelves and lap up the broken glass with his tongue?

When Garner heard the weight of those tremendous padded feet loping up the stairs to the bedrooms, he knew the wolf did not plan to leave. Garner closed his eyes and waited. He was calm. He was ready to face his fate.

The graceful dog leaped up onto Garner's bed, depressing the mattress and pinning the floppy legs of Garner's house pants beneath his paws. The animal sniffed around the bedspread, and then his hot breath poured over Garner's face, taking in the old man's scent. His tail swept the surface of the bed, brushing across Garner's knees. The man lay still, preparing for death.

The canine opened his mouth and panted, and Garner could smell the aromas of all his finest herbs and medicines on the wolf's tongue. They were worth nothing now. He braced himself for violence.

Instead, the wolf stretched out his long body next to Garner and released a sigh. Then he laid his huge head across Garner's chest, so that the man's drumming heart seemed to leap into the wolf's throat rather than his own. In a very short time, his heart began to settle down. The dread slipped away. Their breathing found a synchronized rhythm.

Peace overcame Garner. He finally felt warm.

He slept.

He dreamed of waking in his daughter's home, where she had made him breakfast. Breakfast with a capital B, topped by a tongue of flame. Bacon and eggs and hash browns. And not an herb or a vegetable in sight.

40

Beth had said her good-byes to Trey at Mazy's after they shared a dish featuring meat of a questionable texture. He lived at the bottom of the mountain in Salida, which was an easy drive from the Blazing B. She suggested that he ought to visit the ranch before it changed into something unrecognizable, and he promised to. She promised to start keeping records for him of Mercy's appearances.

Nova had shown Beth to the laundry where she could wash her stiff clothes, and then she fed Beth dinner. Afterward she pressed Beth's blouse and told stories about Burnt Rock and the people who populated it, including Mr. Remke, who was one of Nova's favorite people. Beth was touched by this chance to see Grandpa Remke in a different light, and she felt sad rather than angry about her lost opportunity to know him.

So the following morning when she left Nova's home in fresh clothes, with a backpack full of food over her shoulder and Herriot at her heels, she wasn't expecting to see Garner standing in the middle of the dirt parking lot with a light-blue hard-sided suitcase at his feet.

He looked down at it when she emerged, as if it might contain what he wanted to say.

"Hi," she said. Herriot ran up to Garner and sniffed his shoes, then his suitcase.

"Dotti said I could find you here." His eyes moved around her, landing everywhere but on her face.

"Everyone has been really hospitable," she said.

"Almost everyone. Every small town has to have its crank."

She smiled and tipped her head to one side. "I know I was a shock."

"The last several days have been a shock," he said.

She adjusted her backpack on her shoulder and silently agreed.

"You headed out?" he asked.

"I am. I was aiming for the stables just now. My horse is there. Where are you going?"

"I am going . . . I was thinking . . . It's really true that I don't have any money."

"I know."

"I feel bad about that. If you knew how short a time ago I lost it—"

"Garner, I'm the last person you need to explain yourself to."

He wrinkled up his nose. "I'm a stubborn old man, Beth."

"You'll fit right in, then."

Now Garner looked her in the eye. "Right in where?"

"At the ranch. That's where you want to go, isn't it?"

He nodded. "I really miss . . . Do you think your mother will be glad to see me?"

"I really don't know."

"It's been a lot of years, a lot of bitterness. I'd rather be going down there with money lining my pockets."

"We do what we can with what we have," Beth said. "Even if it's nothing. I'm starting to believe God can work with that."

"You sure came a long way for nothing," he said.

"Not if you come back with me."

He grinned at her then.

"So," she said. "I have a horse and a dog. They're not going to get the two of us very far."

"Dotti said we could use her car," Garner said. He bent down to pick up his case. "Either that or she'd shoot us downriver in one of her death traps."

"I don't know what that means, but a car sounds safer."

"So long as you're driving, it will be."

"I really like the idea of getting back home in just a few hours."

"Then that decides it," Garner announced. "This way to Dotti's." He tipped his head in the direction of Main Street and began to lead.

"We'll have to stop by the stables on my way out so I can make arrangements to send up a trailer for Hastings later."

"Easy peasy."

They turned the corner of the abandoned doctor's office.

"So what changed your mind?" Beth asked.

"Beth, girl, you wouldn't believe me if I told you."

Several hours later, when Beth turned off the highway, Garner began to second-guess his decision to come to the ranch. They passed under the wrought-iron entry that framed a plank announcing the location. *Blazing B* had been formed of block letters with a large wood-burning tool, and decorative flames that had rusted to an appropriate vermillion danced along the top rail against a summer sky.

Beth was silent too. Herriot sat up in the backseat as if aware they were close to home now.

"I guess we both have reason to be a bundle of nerves," Garner observed.

"We'll go to the Hub first," Beth said. "I can introduce you to whichever men happen to be there. Then we'll go to the main house. It'll be a smoother entrance that way. I think."

Garner glanced at her but had no opinion on how to go about this.

The spectacle of the ranch took him off guard. He was familiar with this valley, and with the properties here, but he'd been away long enough for their loveliness to fade in his mind. Now the golden grassland stretched ahead of him like a new day that took the edge off his anxiety. The San Juans in the west were protective, towering shades of purple and gray.

The dirt road took more or less a straight line west, and soon a house, several outbuildings, and various fenced corrals came into view. Beyond these were harvested fields that smelled of winter feed, and protective shelters that housed hay bales stacked to the roof.

Herriot woofed, and Garner pointed to the south. Three riders on horseback were approaching the house that Beth had called the Hub.

"That's Jacob in the front, on the Appaloosa," Beth said. She seemed to relax at the sight of this man. Even the tone of her voice became less taut. The trio was looking in her direction and probably wondering who this 4x4 belonged to. She'd be close enough for them to recognize her soon. "And that's Danny, behind him."

"Your younger brother," Garner said.

"Yes." Beth glanced at Garner. "Your youngest grandson."

But Garner's eyes had already moved to the rider at the rear, a tall woman in an overlarge plaid work shirt, her thick hair pulled back into a long braid down the center of her back. He could see from here the strands of gray striping her hair. Had it been so long? She was such a kid when she left.

"There's my Rose," he said.

Beth rolled down her window and reached out to wave as they rumbled along the drive. The one called Jacob tipped up the visor of his hat, studied her for a moment, then waved back and turned to say something to the others. At this Rose kicked her horse into a trot and quickly passed the men.

Garner turned his head to look out his window in the opposite direction.

Rose got to Dotti's car before they reached the ranch house. She pulled the horse alongside Beth's open window and spoke down into the car from her mount.

"I've worried myself sick, Beth," she said. And Garner thought she sounded like the saddest soul he knew.

"I know, Mom. I'm sorry. I had to go. I had to try—"

"I should never have told you to leave. That day it wasn't possible for me to think straight. I said all kinds of things—they were just confused. They were all wrong. I hope you'll forgive me. I'm so glad you're back. If I had lost your father *and* you . . ." It seemed she couldn't finish that thought.

Even though they hadn't reached the looping driveway in front of the house, Beth stopped the car.

"Of course I forgive you. I should have called."

"Danny said you left a note."

"I did. But still."

Beth opened the door and slid off the seat while her mother dismounted her roan mare. Herriot jumped over the seat and escaped, making a beeline for Jacob and Danny.

"Where did you go? Where's Hastings?" Rose encircled her daughter in a tight embrace that Garner watched from the corner of his eye. He had no idea what to do. "Whose car is this?"

Rose, now at eye level with the car, seemed to notice for the first time that Beth had come with a passenger. She placed a hand on the retracted window of the driver's side door and stooped to have a look.

Garner waited. His ears rang with the deafening buzz of uncertainty. Rose put her hand over her mouth and took long seconds to form a reaction. He couldn't tell if she was going to faint or start screaming at him. He couldn't stand not knowing.

He grabbed the handle of his door and pushed it open at the same time that Beth took a step away from her mom. Rose didn't let her get far. She grabbed hold of her daughter's hand and pulled Beth along behind her around the front of the car, reaching out to her father with her other hand and touching him in just a few long strides. Her arm went around his shoulders and she pulled her to him hard.

She breathed into his shoulder quietly, and as she clung to her father, she tugged Beth into the circle of his embrace. He wrapped his arms around his girls. It was so easy to hold them both.

"I don't have anything to bring you," Garner said. "I can't do anything to save this place."

"I don't care," Rose whispered. "It doesn't matter. You have to stay. Whatever happens, I hope you will stay. Everything will be all right then."

"If you insist."

"I *dreamed* of this day. I knew you would come."

When the time was right, he would give credit to Beth for that. If not for her, father and daughter would have each dreamed the same dream until they met at the gates of heaven.

He heard Danny say to Jacob, "Is that my grandpa Remke?"

Garner replied, "It is, son. Back from the grave." He added so that Beth would hear, "In more ways than one."

Danny was beaming. "Prodigious," he said.

Garner laughed, still holding Rose and Beth close to him. "Now that sounds like something I would have said when I was your age."

"You two already have something in common," Jacob said. Garner saw the man cast a smile at his granddaughter, though he was talking to Danny. His first thought was that this cowboy was far too old for Beth—and then he turned his back on the thought.

He had no desire to travel that judgmental road again. He despised the destination.

Rose tilted Beth's forehead toward her and planted a firm kiss on it. "I can't believe you did this," she whispered.

"Why don't you take your dad back up to the house?" Jacob said to Rose. "Danny and I can keep looking for Wally."

Beth stepped out of Garner's embrace. "What's happened to Wally?"

"He ran off during the night," Rose said. "Sometime after bed check."

"He was upset yesterday," Jacob told Beth. "That lockbox of his is gone again. He accused one of the other men of stealing it. You know how they tease him sometimes."

"We try to keep that sort of thing to a minimum," Rose said to her father. "Most of the time the men are really decent."

"He took a couple of shovels and went off last night, then didn't show for breakfast. The three of us have been all over the southern property line, but so far, nothing."

"It's easy to dig down there by the creek," Beth said. "And there's lots of places to hide something."

"Those were our thoughts," Jacob said.

"I looked there for my truck when—did Levi really sell it?" she asked.

"No! Why would he tell you that?" asked Rose. "And when?"

"It doesn't matter now. Who else is searching?"

"Everyone," Rose said. "Eric and Emory are searching the west side, Roy's on the north, and Lorena's keeping a lookout at the ranch house." She looked at Garner and squeezed his hand.

"Everyone except Levi," Danny said. "He's got higher priorities."

"Respect your brother, Danny," Rose said.

"I know, Mom. But c'mon. We all know that Levi's the reason why Wally's so agitated," Danny said. "Jacob's just too respectful to say so."

"What do you mean?" Beth asked, looking at Jacob.

Rose said, "Sam Johnson has been on the property a lot this past week—he and Levi are already drawing up plans."

"I haven't surrendered my share yet," Beth said.

"No one has. But they're moving ahead. In any case, Wally was up at the cemetery while Sam and Levi were surveying those acres, and—you tell it, Jacob. I guess everything I know I heard from you."

"Wally said he heard them talking about relocating the family plots."

Beth looked at her mother. "Levi promised not to."

"I know, hon."

"That sounds bad," Garner said.

"Downright iniquitous," said Danny. Garner liked this boy more and more.

Jacob continued, "Wally barged in and started objecting. He threatened to tell you all about their plans, Beth."

"Me?"

"He hasn't stopped talking about you since the day we buried your dad. He's been wanting to know where you are. Levi told him you were dead, and that's why you hadn't been around."

Beth paled.

"Spawn of the devil," Garner said. Danny belted out a laugh. Rose shot him a look of disbelief. "Oh, I didn't mean *that*," Garner said.

"Wally came back around suppertime out of his head," Jacob continued. "He said he couldn't find his lockbox and Levi had stolen it. He was desperate to get it back."

Beth's sigh was heavy. "I suppose Levi denies it all."

"Not in so many words. You know the notebook Wally carries?"

"Yeah, it's how he remembers things."

"He pulled it out and started taking notes of their conversation. Levi took the notebook, nothing else, he says. I got it back and thought that would settle Wally down. By the way, I assured him that you are *not* dead."

"Where else might a man hide something around here?" Garner asked. "It's a mighty big place." He would try to redeem his spawn-of-the-devil remark as fast as he could. And yet Rose's posture was already withdrawing from him. Not offended, but fearful, aware she had jumped toward him across a great chasm on a flimsy bridge that might not hold.

"We're racking our brains," Jacob said. "We've gone up and down the entire creek, the irrigation ditches. I'm starting to worry he might have gone off the property."

"We're giving ourselves until sundown," Rose said to Beth. "Then we'll call the sheriff."

"Did he say anything about a wolf?" Beth asked. She was facing north, twisting a piece of hair around her finger.

"Nope," Jacob said. "What makes you ask that?"

Beth fell silent. Garner, curious about the wolf in her question, tried to follow her secret thinking.

"But you know what he did say that I thought was odd?" Jacob asked.

She looked up at him.

"When I told him you were alive, he was so relieved. And he said, 'That's good news, because Beth promised to help me dig.'"

Beth said, "I think I know where he is."

41

B eth drove north along the access road, her mother in the passenger seat and her grandfather in the back. The ranch looked the same but seemed so different from when she had left it.

"I can't believe you're here," Rose kept murmuring. "I can't believe you're both here."

Danny and Jacob stayed at the Hub to water the horses, and Beth promised them a phone call as soon as she knew whether her hunch turned out to be correct.

"You've done well for yourself, Rosy," Garner said from the backseat, admiring the beauty of the land.

"Appreciate it while you can," she said. Her tone was more gentle than Beth had heard in months.

"I'm sorry about Abel. I was wrong about him, you know. Very wrong. Clearly, he was a fine man."

"Thank you, Dad."

Apology accepted. Simple words carrying father and daughter toward each other. Beth imagined the real work of mending this relationship would take months. Years even. A slow and careful return. She imagined her grandfather here on the land in October, sipping tea and gazing out the screens of the enclosed porch while the cows returned to the property. It was a moment she hoped to witness.

Months ago she had found Wally digging in the cottonwood grove and used this same road to take him back to the Hub. Today she traveled toward the grove, where she had never kept her promise to help him dig. She wondered when he had remembered it. The car passed the ranch house, and Beth saw Lorena standing behind the porch screen that Herriot had jumped through. The mesh had been repaired. Beth waved at the girl. Lorena lifted a tentative hand.

The road ran alongside the horse pasture, the barn, the winter lean-to shelters—all empty now while the animals were out helping to search for Wally. Beyond the pasture at a walking distance, two hulking boulders marked the entrance to the cemetery. Beth looked in the direction of her father's grave. A flash flood of sadness entered the space in her chest that had been filled the past week with urgency and sleeplessness and frantic prayers. Had it only been a week since her father passed? It felt like a year.

Today, however, there was no frantic desperation mixed up with Beth's grief. She noted a new feeling of peace.

Later she would pay her respects. Right now it was more urgent that they find Wally. She turned her head to the cottonwood grove when the car passed it on the left. If Wally was there, he was hidden by the thick trunks and undergrowth.

A hundred yards past the grove, Beth parked Dotti's 4x4 where the road ended, under the shade of a lush Wasatch maple, in the same place where she had left her truck the night she'd stolen Jacob's saddle. Her mother and grandfather got out of the car and followed her back to the trees. The leaves rustled in a light breeze.

Dozens of small holes punctured the ground, everywhere that the roots would allow a shovel to enter.

They entered the grove and stepped over and around the

prodded earth. The trees backed up against a steep hillside, a tiny intrusion of San Juan's foothills, and it only took a few minutes for the threesome to reach the upward-sloping ground. They spread out then and turned down the narrow strip of earth. It was much longer than it was wide.

Beth found Wally's shovel first, when she stepped on the blade and caused the gray wooden handle to rise up off the ground.

"Wally?" she called out.

"Who wants to know?" he answered.

Her heart lightened at the familiar question.

"Abel's daughter," she said.

"Beth!" he answered. "Over here." She was quickly joined by Rose and Garner.

They found Wally seated on the ground with his back to them, one knee drawn up to his chest, shining a flashlight at a wide trunk that grew at an angle from the knobby hillside. She wondered why he needed the flashlight while the sun was still high. He twisted and looked up at her right away.

"You remembered my name," she said, smiling at him.

"That cowboy said you . . . went on a trip. Actually, I don't remember where he said you went. I only recall that you are not dead. Which I am so happy to see is true."

"Me too," she said.

"I've been waiting for you to get back. If you told me how long it would be, I forgot to write it down." His little spiral-bound book was lying on the ground next to him, and he pointed at it. "This is all the memory I've got some days."

Wally's pleasure at seeing her faltered when he spotted Garner, and for a second she thought Wally might be as upset as if Levi had shown up.

"Doggone it," Wally said. "Each time I think I'm getting better . . ."

Beth understood. "You haven't met him before, Wally," she said. "This is my grandfather, Garner Remke. Garner, my friend Wally."

Garner extended his hand. "I'm Rosy's dad."

"It's a pleasure, sir," Wally said. "I'm sure it will be a pleasure each time. For me anyway. Howdy, Mrs. Borzoi," he said to Rose.

"You okay, Wally?" she said. "Everyone's worried about you."

"Yes, ma'am. I'm surely sorry if I've caused any trouble. I'm just in a bit of a dilemma here, and you showed up at a fine time to bail me out of it."

He glanced back toward the tree and lifted the flashlight again. He hadn't been shining the light on the trunk as Beth first thought, but alongside of it. A tall Apache plume grew here, the shrub's downy leaves and pink-feather flowers looking like a fluffy pillow behind the cottonwood.

Wally leaned in and pressed the silvery branches aside to expose another hole, this one larger than the pockmarks in the grove, deeper, and running straight back into the hillside rather than down into the ground. The flashlight's beam disappeared into blackness.

"Did you dig that yourself?" Rose asked, bending over his shoulder.

"No, ma'am," Wally said. "Something else dug this."

A metallic glint on one side of the hole about twelve feet back caught Beth's eye.

"Is that your lockbox?" Beth asked.

"I do believe it is," he said.

Garner uttered the first question to pop into Beth's mind. "How did it get way back there? The hole's too small for a man."

The answer came just as swiftly to Beth's heart: "Mercy put it there," she said.

"Who?" asked her mother.

Beth looked at Wally. "The night it first went missing, you told me the wolf took it."

"What wolf?" Rose demanded.

"That I did," Wally said. "Says so right here." He released the shrub and picked up his notebook, then began to flip through the pages.

"The wolf's name is Mercy," Beth said without thinking, and she noted her grandfather raised his eyebrows. Though he had yet to explain the reason for his change of heart, she was beginning to suspect that Mercy might have had something to do with it. "I first saw him"—she wished she could close this can of worms—"that same night."

"Him?" Wally asked. "The wolf I saw was a girl. Any chance your memory's starting to go?"

This silenced Beth. Garner started chuckling.

"Yes, I've got it here," Wally said. "I drew a little wolf face to remind me. Put the box in her mouth and a bow over her ear. See?" He held the sketch out under Beth's nose.

"What wolf is this?" said Rose again, straightening up and crossing her arms.

"And I made a note," Wally said. "'May 23. Gray wolf. Mile 6.25 fence post, cottonwood grove.' That'd be here. Been back here a lot since then, but I just found this last night."

"So what's your dilemma?" Beth asked.

"My dilemma, right. Well, as . . . as this fine man here has already observed"—he indicated Garner—"I'm a little too big for the opening, and I'd like to get my box back. But that's a minor detail. Bigger one is I can't leave this spot, because your brother knows where to find it for himself. After all the work I've done, he'd surely find this place a lot quicker than I would."

"Levi took your notebook," Beth said, recalling Jacob's account of their argument.

"Read it back to back, no doubt," Wally accused. "No telling what that boy might do if I let this place out of my sight."

Garner was kneeling by the hole now, holding back the Apache plume and looking in.

Rose's voice took on a more gentle tone. "What's in your box that Levi would want, Wally?"

Wally's expression took on a sudden look of anxiety.

"Your 'legal tender'?" Beth prompted, recalling Wally's frustration the first night the box went missing. "You have money in the box?"

"What? Fifty bucks? Pfft. He can have it," Wally said. "I used to be a rich man, you know, back in my Wall Street days. Wish I still was—once upon a time I could have helped you all out. But the people who call themselves my family sank their teeth into that gold mine long ago. Where there's money, there's always someone who wants it. It's something I like about the Blazing B, you know. The simple life."

He was talking over his worry now, Beth thought: he couldn't remember why it was so important he guard the lockbox from Levi. There was no proper response to that, just as it wasn't right for Beth to speak the truth: the survival of this "simple life" was dependent on quite a large sum of money.

Oddly, though, that truth didn't drive a knife through her heart the way it might have a week earlier. She looked at her mother and grandfather. There was something good and right about this moment, these three family members making their way through loss by returning to each other, each of them having nothing, and repairing what was broken.

Wally licked his thumb and began to search for the answer in his book. "It was important." He seemed flummoxed that he couldn't find what he had previously written down. "It was really important."

"It's okay, Wally," Beth said. She knelt beside him and rested her palm on his shoulder. "We can stay here until it comes to you. Let's think of a way to get it out. I might be small enough to climb in."

"You will not," her mother ordered.

Garner fished through some fallen leaves for Wally's discarded flashlight, found it, and aimed it into the hole for a clearer look.

Wally sighed. In his right hand he let his notebook fall shut, and he raised his left hand to press it against Beth's cheek. His skin was dusty and cracked and as gentle as a loving father's touch.

"Do you ever see something and find that it reminds you of something else, but your mind can't make the connection?" he asked her. "That's what most of my days are like now, since the stroke. But the reason I could always remember your father is because when I laid eyes on him, my old, broken brain always made the connection. I could remember why I came to this ranch, and what a gift that man had extended to me."

Beth placed her own hand atop Wally's, holding it next to her skin.

"My family found a way to get my money, but they couldn't be bothered by the old man who has trouble remembering what he ate for breakfast. You know what kind of life awaits someone like me?"

Beth could guess. She nodded once.

"Your father gave me something that exceeded every imagination, every hope. And he never asked about the money. Never needed it. Such a man is impossible to forget."

Beth closed her eyes and called up her own unforgettable memories of the man she missed so much. She heard Wally's notebook hit the dirt, and he placed his other hand on her other cheek and pulled her bowed head toward him. He planted a soft kiss on the middle of her forehead and then let her rest her face on his narrow shoulder. He smelled like alfalfa and rainwater. She leaned into his kindness, his hands warm on her back.

Her nose picked up another scent too, in the breeze that enveloped them. It was musky and earthy, solid, rich. It was the scent of Mercy, growing more familiar to Beth with each passing day.

A flinch in Wally's wrists brought her back to the present. She lifted her head, and his eyes were shining.

"I remember," he said.

"What?"

"It's not the box that needs protecting."

Beth waited.

"It's them," Wally said, and he pointed over her shoulder.

Before she was able to turn, Beth caught sight of her mother's face. Rose was pale and looking past Wally's outstretched finger. "Don't move," she whispered, but she herself took a step backward.

At the mouth of the hole, behind the bent shrub, Garner looked up and then rose from his belly. Beth turned. As she came around, a wet muzzle swiped the side of her cheek, and Beth tipped backward on her hands. The gray wolf Mercy pressed in and ran his moist nose along Beth's jaw and into her hair, sniffing as if meeting her for the first time.

"There she is," Wally said happily.

The wolf licked Beth's nose, and Rose uttered a small scream.

"It's okay," Beth said, wiping away the damp greeting. "That means I can stay in the pack."

"There's a *pack*?" Rose croaked.

"Seven of 'em," Wally said. "Ha! What do you know? I didn't even have to look that up in my little book!"

At this announcement Beth realized that the wolf who'd greeted her wasn't Mercy after all. This one's coat was a lighter gray color, more silver than ash. The dog's frame was slightly smaller, and the gender was, just as Wally had claimed, female.

The dog left Beth and padded up to Rose, who clamped her eyes shut and murmured, "Will she hurt me?"

"She's wild," Beth said wryly.

"This one won't," Garner said. And this time it was Beth's turn to raise her eyebrows and laugh.

A pattering of paws on the undergrowth announced the arrival of five adolescent wolves, neither pups nor fully grown. They leaped over Beth's extended legs and joined their mother's investigation of Rose, rising to place their front paws against her thighs.

"Get them off." Rose pulled her hands and elbows up toward her shoulders.

"People pay money for this kind of experience," Wally said.

"I don't care!" Rose was moving backward.

"At least stand still," Wally said. "Garner! Talk some sense into your daughter."

"She's got plenty of her own," Garner said.

"But these wolves need— Hey! I remembered your name." Wally reached out to touch Garner's arm. "*And* that you're her dad. Did you notice that?" he asked Beth.

One of the young wolves tired of Rose and dashed away, ducking behind Garner and the Apache plume and into the hole where the lockbox was hidden.

Beth's lips parted in surprise. "It's a den," she said.

"For the pack," Wally said, looking at her.

"A pack of endangered species." Garner nodded knowingly. "If that doesn't put a kink in Levi's plans to develop this property, I don't know what will."

He started chuckling, and Beth's smile reached all the way up to her ears. The other wolves trotted into their home, except for the female, who sat down in front of Rose's feet like a guard dog. Rose eyed her warily, all the tension still in her shoulders.

"How can you be *happy* about something like that?" Rose demanded.

"Mom, a pack of gray wolves on our land!" Beth said.

"Yes! I'm imagining the nightmare of what that will mean when the cows come home for winter!" At this, Garner's amusement became a belly laugh.

Beth said, "Mercy won't touch them. And if we can keep Levi from harming the pack—"

"He won't be able to sell the land, yes, I see that. So tell me, if Sam Johnson won't buy it, how will we get out of our financial scrape?"

No one had an answer for that.

"These wolves aren't the same as money," her mother went on.

"Maybe they're something better," Beth said.

"Better than money? What do you—" Rose gasped and put her hand on her throat. "Stars! He's huge!"

Beth followed her mother's gaze and discovered Mercy, who had silently arrived within arm's reach of Beth. She placed her hand on his head between his ears. He twisted his neck to nuzzle her palm.

"Beth, don't touch it," Rose whispered.

Garner's laughter became an outright fit of gasping.

"Is that funny to you?" Rose said to her father, though her fearful eyes stayed on the wolf. "He'll eat us alive." Except for the movement of her lips, Rose was petrified. Mercy sauntered toward her and bumped up against the female, who looked up briefly at Rose and then followed his urging into the den.

Rose put her hand on her forehead and closed her eyes. "What is happening here?" she murmured. "Why isn't anything ever simple?"

"If we had the answer to that, we could get rich off it," Beth said. Rose frowned. Beth got off the ground and went to her mother, then hugged her stiff and frustrated form. "Mom, only God knows what's going to happen to the Blazing B in the next year and a half," Beth said. "But no matter what happens, he'll take care of us." Her eyes locked on her grandfather's. They overflowed with tears of hilarity, and he wiped them off his cheeks.

"God is good," he said.

"Yes," Beth echoed. "God is good."

"You've all gone crazy," Rose accused.

Wally said, "Bananas!"

Everyone stared at him.

He beamed at Beth. "I had bananas for breakfast."

42

Later that evening, as the last rays of summer sun were slipping behind the San Juans, Beth went to the horse pasture with an apple for her father's horse Temuche. The sorrel gelding ate the juicy fruit with a great deal of chomping and then pushed at her hands looking for more treats.

"I think Hastings was holding out on me about the wolf pack," she confided "I think that's why he didn't flinch when Mercy saved us from the cougar."

Temuche pawed the dirt once.

"Were you in on the secrecy too? What else do I need to know, old fellow?"

He pawed the earth another time, and something in the ground caught Beth's eye.

The paw prints of a wolf.

Temuche didn't seem at all troubled by the tracks cutting through their feeding ground. None of the other horses did either. Maybe the horses recognized Mercy for his true self. During her journey back to the Blazing B, Beth had decided that the appearance of that wolf was a supernatural revelation of God's glory in one of the most natural expressions on earth: a wild animal returning to the home where he had once been driven out. Without anything but hope to give her confidence, she saw a promise in the family's discovery of the wolves' den—a promise that even if the Borzois were driven off this land, someday they would be allowed to return.

She followed the tracks and quickly realized that the trail was headed for the barn. The side door was wide open, and the prints headed directly inside.

The interior lights had been left on and were spilling out into the night sky. Beth rushed in.

"Mercy?" she whispered.

She heard a rustling in the tack room and moved toward it first, and as she rounded the doorway she surprised Jacob Davis, who was standing under the bare bulb of the little tack room, looking down at the corner where his empty saddle rack protruded from the rough wood wall.

He startled when she barged in, which startled her. They both stood there for a minute, she with her hand over her heart, waiting for it to settle. Jacob ran his hand through his hair and laughed lightly.

"You snuck up on me," he said.

"Sorry. I didn't expect anyone here right now."

"Me neither."

"What are you doing?" She took a few steps into the room and noted that Mercy's paw prints crossed the dusty floor and went straight into the corner where Mathilde's saddle should have been hanging. There was just one set of prints headed in one direction. They led to the wall and seemed to disappear into the saddle rack itself. She couldn't stop staring at it and suddenly wished that she wasn't here, in this room with those prints and this man and that empty rack on the wall.

He said, "Do these mysterious wolf friends of yours walk through walls?"

"Mercy opened a door by himself once, but walls—I don't think he walks through walls."

"Huh." The response was half impressed, half skeptical. Jacob crossed his arms and joined her in staring at the corner where the prints stopped so inexplicably.

"Where do you think he went?"

"He goes wherever he wants," she says.

"Maybe you can tell me more about him."

Beth nodded but didn't know where to start.

Jacob kept his eyes on the empty rack and said, "I was going to ask if you'd mind me tagging along when you and your grandfather take the car back to Burnt Rock. I can drive the trailer for Hastings. I'd like to hear the whole story."

"It's a pretty long story," she said.

"If the drive's not long enough for it, we can find something else to do until you tell it all. However long it takes."

"Okay," she said.

He said, "It took guts to do what you did. Going after your grandfather like that."

"Nothing turned out the way I wanted it to," she said.

"In my experience it almost never does. But do you regret what happened?"

"No," Beth said. She didn't even have to think about it.

He took a deep breath. "Many times everything comes out better."

"Even when we don't get what we want?" she said, suddenly needing to know he agreed with her view.

"*Especially* when we don't get what we want. Not always, but I mean, what do we know about what we really need?"

Beth laughed. He was looking at her with a serious expression, and her laughter seemed inappropriate. She cleared her throat.

"Well, who knew I had guts, huh?"

"Oh, I've always known it."

"You have, have you?"

"Yes, ever since the night when you turned that calf around inside its mother, because the vet couldn't get here through the snow."

The memory came back to Beth like a rush of pleasure. "I forgot about that. A little something I thought I could do just because I'd read James Herriot's books. When was that?"

"The coldest February night in a decade."

"I was like, what?"

"Fourteen," he said, and she was startled by the swiftness of his memory. He finally turned away from the saddle rack and faced her. He held up his big hands and turned them over. "You were the only one with hands small enough to fit through that cow's narrowness. You didn't even wrinkle up your nose."

"You coached me, if I remember right. Mr. College Grad, Expert on the Herd."

"You didn't need much coaching."

He was regarding her with a look of admiration that made her uncomfortable. Her heart was thumping harder than it needed to for a person just standing around.

"I thought you were angry with me then," she said.

His admiration turned to surprise. "Why would I have been angry? You were a crazy success."

"I don't know. I was so happy—that calf, staggering around alive because I'd pulled it out. But you didn't have much to say about it. You kind of wandered off. I just thought I'd done something wrong but you didn't want to say so, me being your boss's daughter and all that."

Jacob smiled then. "Oh. That."

"Oh that what?"

Now his face reddened, she could see it clearly even under this wicked incandescent glare, and his embarrassment so embarrassed her that she didn't dare press him to explain. She tried to rescue him from the awkwardness she'd caused.

"Mom said she's asked you to take on some of Dad's old duties. Congratulations. You are so right for that job."

"I guess Levi didn't want it."

"That would be an understatement." She pushed her fingers into her pockets.

"What do you think he's going to do?" Jacob asked.

"Look for a way around those wolves." Beth sighed. "I feel sad for him."

"One day at a time, Beth. You never can tell how God can turn a thing around. Or a person."

"This is true." She was reminded of God's promise to heal her family. Did the promise include Levi? There were so many questions unanswered still.

"I'm sorry you won't get to attend vet school as soon as you'd planned," he said.

"Me too."

"But I'm also glad you're staying here."

She liked the sound of his voice, the meaning of his words.

"I'm glad you're glad."

That awkwardness between them was back again. It could only be that tension rooted in the wrong that she'd done. She hated that it was there, preventing them from being the friends they were. And because it seemed that the only way around it was to go directly through it, Beth said the only thing to pop into her head, which was probably not the best thing she could have picked:

"I learned a thing or two about your saddle while I was up in Burnt Rock."

Jacob cleared his throat and glanced back at the vacancy where it should have been. This simple motion filled her with a great need to leave the room, to step away from Jacob's closeness and from the discomfort of the choice that she couldn't undo, even though her sin had been redeemed. Mostly redeemed. She turned away and started to walk out. She might as well get this whole thing over with.

"You said you were going to tell me what I owe you for it," she said over her shoulder.

She heard him following her out of the tack room and out of the barn and into the fresh air, where she could breathe a little more easily. She went to the metal corral gates and propped her foot on the bottom rail. He came with her but kept enough space for a horse between them.

She refused to fill the silence this time.

After a few beats he said, "When we were here that day and you were hosing down Gert, you asked me why I came back here after I finished school," he said.

Beth tried to think of how that conversation connected to his missing saddle.

He said, "I just figured there wasn't any place I'd rather be while I waited for you to grow up."

His words were like eyeglasses that instantly sharpened a fuzzy perspective. Their history took on a new light: his lack of girlfriends since that February, his aloof but brotherly treatment of her, his outspoken confidence in her abilities. She bowed her head to the rail and began to laugh softly. It was amazement running through her now, stronger than any guilt or regret or fear. "Really?"

He wrapped his fingers around the corral rail and nodded once.

"You are a patient man, Jacob Davis."

"Yes, ma'am." His smile was cockeyed and endearing.

She lifted her head and returned his pleasant expression. "But I think we ought to start with a clean slate, a zero account."

"There is no such thing. We've known each other too long."

"You really ought to tell me what I owe you for that saddle."

"Oh, I will. But now's not the time."

"Why not?"

"Because it's not what you think."

From the corner of her eye, she could see that his lopsided grin was playful.

"How do you know what I think?"

He refused to answer, only to tease silently.

"I've been wondering what became of your saddle," she said.

"It's not something I worry about."

"Still, I think I should find out."

"That's up to you." A warm breeze came down off the San Juans and lifted the side of Beth's hair across her face. She turned her back to the rails and faced Jacob. His admiring expression caused her to laugh again.

"So why don't you tell me how that saddle came to be yours. It's got quite a history from what I can tell."

"It does."

"So what's the story?"

"It's a pretty long story," he said.

"Now you're making fun of me. Tell me, please. However long it takes."

"I will. But now it's your turn to be patient, Bethesda."

"You've never called me that before."

"Do you mind it?"

She shook her head. In fact she loved it, but couldn't find the words to say so. "If you stare at me any longer your eyes will dry out."

"Small price to pay," he said. He stepped toward her and tucked her wandering strands of hair behind her ear. The rough skin of his fingertips grazed her temples. He lowered his hand to hers, and she gave it to him.

Jacob pulled her toward him and encircled her with his strong arms as protective as the shelter of trees. He gently held her head against his chest and kissed the part in her hair. The warmth of feeling safe covered Beth all the way down to her feet. His quiet sigh was full of contentment.

"Thank you," he said.

She closed her eyes. "For what?"

"For taking that saddle."

"What?" She lifted her chin to see his face. He was looking across the dusky corral. "I don't understand."

"You will," he said.

"Explain yourself, sir."

"Patience." His voice teased again.

"Tell me."

"All in due time."

"How long do I have to wait?"

"How long are you willing?"

The lighthearted banter suddenly felt weighty. She held the question in her heart. "For as long as you'll let me stand here like this," she said. "With you."

"Forever then."

"Forever," she repeated. "I can be patient."

"It's a good thing I believe in miracles."

They laughed together.

Author Note

What miracle are you waiting for?

I wrote *House of Mercy* during a season of begging God for a particular answer to prayer. Instead of giving me the solution I wanted, God gave me complications, uncharacteristic calm, and a question: *Do you believe I'm good even when I don't give you what you think you need?*

My heart said, *Right now it doesn't seem like you're being very good to me.* And my mind said, *Hey wait—is this a trick question? If I give you the right answer will you give me what I want?*

Instead of indulging my pouting, God has taken my hand and led me on a guided tour of all the ways he has proven his goodness to me across the years. That uncharacteristic calm, for example, couldn't have come from myself. My "surprise" son is a constant source of joy and laughter. I've been welcomed into a community of God-fearing people who surround me with compassion, support, and kindness that I'm sure I don't deserve. These gifts top a very long list. And all of them are from him.

The goodness of God is not a trick question. It's a reality even more real than our troubles. As this book goes to press, I still don't have the answer to my prayer. The answer that I want, that is. The one I think I need. And yet he has been more patient with me than I have been with him—proving his goodness again. When I seek him, I find him, no matter my circumstances.

Today, it seems that everyone I know is waiting for some kind of miracle. We're in need of important things. We're desperate for particular answers to our heartfelt prayers. But we are not abandoned. We hold the hand of a good God. Whatever pain, injustice, or deferred hope you face, my new prayer is that God will give you more than a happy ending (which waits for us in the next life, if not this one). May he fill you with a lasting sense of his true goodness and of his love for you.

Erin Healy
January 2012

An Encounter
with Mercy's Kin

Acouple of years ago I had a face-to-face encounter with a few wolves. I'm happy to say it was in a controlled environment and not the wild, at the wonderful Colorado Wolf and Wildlife Center in Divide, Colorado. Arriving with a storybook prejudice of wolves as a vicious kind of large dog, I was unprepared for the wolves' astonishing size, majestic demeanor, variety, and even the playfulness of their socialized ambassadors.

Kekoa is a male gray (Timber) wolf like Mercy of this novel. Gray wolves are only beginning to return to their native Colorado habitats after being expatriated from the Rocky Mountain region in the 1930s. Today they are migrating from places like Idaho, Montana, and New Mexico, where they have been formally reintroduced.

We were not allowed to stand when meeting the wolves, but if we had, and if Kekoa had put his paws on our shoulders in greeting, he would have towered over our heads at seven feet.

Shunka is an Arctic/Timber wolf mix who weighs nearly 150 pounds. It's possible he only loved me for the meat treats I had to offer him, and for the hood of my jacket, which we had to detach and toss out of the enclosure because he was determined to make it his own. But as Trey explained to Beth, Shunka's wet kiss marked my acceptance to his pack.

As this book goes to press, Kekoa and Shunka are still important ambassadors for the CWWC. A live webcam of their enclosure, as well as virtual tours and photo galleries of the rest of the pack, can be accessed at www.wolfeducation.org. But if you have the chance to visit in person, I think you will never look at wolves the same way again.

With humble gratitude to

My wise editors, who seem to have bottomless wells
of wit and insight: Ami McConnell and L. B. Norton.

The savvy fiction crew of Thomas Nelson, who devote their
days to excellence: Allen Arnold, Ami McConnell, Amanda Bostic,
Natalie Hanemann, Becky Monds, Katie Bond, Eric Mullett, Kristen
Vasgaard, Ashley Schneider, Ruthie Dean, and Jodi Hughes.

My intrepid Creative Trust agents, who boldly navigate
the waters of industry change: Dan Raines, Meredith Smith,
Kathy Helmers, Jeanie Kaserman, and Kevin Kaiser.

My early readers, who remind me of all the reasons
I should keep writing: Mike and Lynn McMahan.

The real-life Colorado ranchers who helped me tend to details:
Joyce and Merrill Bond. (Any enduring errors are mine, all mine.)

My savior in the sea of social media: Leah Apineru.
My precious family.

My Lord, my hope, whose mercies are new every morning.

An Excerpt from *The Baker's Wife*

March

The day Audrey took a loaf of homemade rosemary-potato bread to
Cora Jean Hall was the day the fog broke and made way for spring.
Audrey threw open the curtains closest to the dying woman's bed-
side, glad for the sunshine after months of gray light.

Audrey moved quietly down the hall into the one-man kitchen,
where she sliced the bread into toast, brewed tea, then leaned out
of the cramped space to offer some to Cora Jean's husband, Harlan.
He refused her without thanks and without looking up from his
forceful tinkering with an old two-way radio. Over the past month,
his collection of CBs and receivers had overtaken the small living
room. His grieving had started long ago and was presently in the
angry stage. Clearly, he loved his wife. The retired pharmacist dis-
pensed her medications with faithful precision but didn't seem to
know what else to do. If not for the radios, Audrey believed, he
might have wandered the house helplessly and transformed from
smoldering to explosive.

As Audrey arranged the snack on a tray, one of her earrings
slipped out of her lobe and clattered onto a saucer, just missing

the hot tea. She rarely wore this pair because one or the other was always falling out, but Cora Jean liked the dangling hearts with a rose in the middle of each. The inexpensive jewelry had been a gift to the women of the church on Mother's Day last year.

She put the earring back in her ear, then carried the tray to Cora Jean's room, settled onto an old dining room chair by the bed, and steered their conversation toward happy topics.

Cora Jean was dying of pancreatic cancer, the cancer best known for being unsurvivable. Audrey sat with the woman in the late stages of her illness for many reasons: because she believed that people who suffered shouldn't be left alone; because she was a pastor's wife and embraced this privilege that came with the role; because Cora Jean reminded Audrey of her own beloved mother.

She also went to the woman's home because she couldn't *not* go. In the most physical, literal sense, Audrey was regularly guided there, directed by an unseen arm, weighty and warm, that encircled her shoulders and turned her body toward the Halls' house every week or so. A voice audible only to her own ears would whisper, *Please don't leave me alone today.* It was no pitiful sound, and Audrey never resented it, though from time to time it surprised her. In these moments she thought, though she had never dared to try it, that if she applied her foot to the gas pedal and took her hands off the wheel, her car would take her wherever God wanted her to be.

This five-years familiar experience had not always involved Cora Jean, but others like her, so Audrey had long since stopped questioning how it happened. The why of it was clear enough: Audrey was called by God to be a comforter, and she was glad for the job.

Audrey had a knack for helping people in any circumstance to look toward the brightness of life—not the silver lining of their own dark cloud, which often didn't exist—but to the Light of the

World, which could be seen by anyone willing to look for it. In Cora Jean's case this meant not dwelling too long on the details of her prognosis, but in reading aloud beautiful, hopeful, complex poetry, especially the Psalms and the Brownings and Franz Wright. It meant watering the plants (which Harlan ignored) and offering to warm a meal for him before she left. It meant giving candid answers to Cora Jean's many-layered questions about Audrey's personal faith—in particular, about sin and forgiveness and justice.

And about the problem of so much suffering in a world governed by a "good" God. Cora Jean seemed preoccupied with this particular question, and her focus seemed to be connected to the yellowed family portrait hanging on the wall opposite the bed.

There were two brunette girls in the thirty-year-old picture. Audrey judged the age by Cora Jean's bug-eyed plastic-framed glasses, Harlan's rust-colored corduroy blazer, and the children's Dorothy Hamill hairstyles. Audrey had a similarly aged childhood portrait of herself with her parents. She guessed the daughters to be nine, maybe ten, and they appeared to be twins, though one of them was considerably chubbier than the other.

A pendant on a large-link silver chain hung from the upper left corner of the cheap wood frame. The pendant was also silver, crudely hammered into a flat circle, like a washer, that framed a small translucent rock. Audrey suspected it to be an uncut diamond.

It would be rude to ask whether she was right about the stone, but on the day the fog broke and the sun brought a wispy smile to Cora Jean's pale face, Audrey decided to ask about the portrait she often stared at.

Audrey lifted her teacup to her lips and blew off the steam. "Tell me about your family," she said gently, indicating the picture with her eyes.

Cora Jean's smile crumpled, and the soft wrinkles of her skin became a riverbed for tears.

Audrey wished she hadn't said anything. Meaning to apologize for having heaped some kind of emotional ache on top of the cancer's pain, she returned her sloshing teacup to the tray, then reached out and placed her hands on top of Cora Jean's, which were clutching the sheets.

That was the second unfortunate choice Audrey made that day, with a third yet to occur before the sun set. The woman's sorrow—if it could be thought of as something chemical—entered Audrey's fingertips, burning the pads of her fingers, the joints of her knuckles, her wrists. The flaming liquid pain seeped up her arms, searing as it went: elbows, shoulders, collarbone. And then the poison found her spine, an aqueduct that delivered breathtaking hurt to every nerve in Audrey's body. She yelped involuntarily. Here was a sensation that she had never experienced.

She wished that she could save the dying woman from the terror. She also wished that she had never dipped her toe into these hellish waters.

The pain bowed her over Cora Jean's fragile body, a posture at once protective and impotent, and paralyzed Audrey. The women cried together until every last drop of the agony had let itself out of Audrey's eyes.

In time Cora Jean said, "Thank you for understanding," and fell asleep, exhausted.

Audrey, who understood not a bit of what had transpired, said nothing. She tuned the radio to Cora Jean's favorite classical station, then waited, agitated and restless, for the hospice nurse to arrive.

cb

Audrey stumbled out of the house, forgetting to give Harlan a polite good-bye. She stood on the square front stoop, stunned and spent and a little bit frightened, and leaned against the closed screen door

369

for a long minute. She fiddled absentmindedly with one of her rose-in-a-heart earrings.

She began to wonder if she wasn't as well-suited for her divine calling as she had once thought. Surely sitting with a person through suffering didn't mean sharing the pain like *that*, experiencing it firsthand. How had it happened? She wasn't sure. She wasn't sure of anything except that she would prefer to avoid that kind of intensity in the future. She would do what she was able to do, and there was no point in feeling guilty about her shortcomings, if guilt was the right name for this emotion.

Audrey sighed and finally walked off the Halls' stoop and across the lawn. Cora Jean's windows weren't the only ones opened that day. Because the fog was gone, others in the working-class neighborhood had raised sashes to lure cleansing breezes into their homes. This is what Audrey would later blame for her third poor choice of the day.

Wide oaks offered shade on both sides of the street. The separation from the sun would be a gift from God come summertime, when the air was too tired to stir even a single leaf in any of the towering eucalyptus trees.

The fleeting question of whether Cora Jean would be alive then passed through Audrey's mind. She kicked it out of her consciousness, still feeling raw and drained. She moved toward her car, wanting to go home and find answers in her sleep.

When she stepped off the curb to round her parked car and climb into the driver's seat, she felt the atmosphere move. Invisible but solid, thick air stepped in front of her like a large man who intended to hijack her car or snatch her purse. Her keys, hanging from her fingertips, jangled as if she'd struck something. She steadied herself with one hand on the hood of the car, bracing her surprise. She had never experienced this "leading," as she called it, so close to another event. The effects would either pass shortly or lead her onward.

Heat like a strong arm snaked across the back of her shoulders. Audrey stepped forward to get out from under the weight. The move was reflexive, a whole-body flinch that sent her right into the invisible obstacle again. This time she was met with pressure, square and flaming over her sternum, and a crushing pain went straight to her heart. The grip on her shoulders squeezed, keeping her upright where she couldn't escape the wounding.

The hurt was blunt and weighty, a pestle grinding in a mortar. Audrey's lips parted and flattened, stretching out like a cry, but no sound came out of her mouth. The skin around her nose and eyes bunched up until she couldn't see, but there were no tears. She folded at the waist, her body bending over the car just as she had drooped over Cora Jean. This connection was unwelcome, and Audrey resisted it.

The arm let her sag, all but dropped her, and she lowered her forehead onto the hood. The drill into her heart kept turning, creating a whining noise that grew louder in her own ears until it drowned out everything else on the street. No birds, no cars, no children playing on lawns or in driveways.

And then the violence stopped. The body of heat released her, and Audrey found herself breathing heavily and wondering if anyone had witnessed her bizarre behavior. Her head pounded, every blood vessel in it taxed as if she'd been wailing for hours. Audrey rested her cheek on the smooth shell of the hood and waited for her heart and lungs to find their rhythms again.

The sound of real sobbing reached her then.

Cora Jean? Audrey jerked away from the car, looking, her breathing still deep and quick. The earth tipped, then leveled out again. The muscles at the base of her neck were painful knots.

After three or four seconds she stepped back onto the curb and crossed the grassy easement to the sidewalk. The noise wasn't coming from the Halls' house but from somewhere down the street.

She started walking, hesitant to follow the heartache, unable to do anything else.

The terrible sound pulled her toward one of the neighborhood's nicer homes, a single-story brick house with an attached garage. The cries came from an open window at the front of the house. Audrey stepped off the sidewalk and cut directly across the lawn, getting as close to the window as the bordering juniper hedge allowed. The dirt underfoot was still soft from the rain that had escorted in winter's final batch of fog. A sheer curtain in the window blocked her view of anyone on the other side.

"Hello?" She raised her voice. "Hello? Are you okay?"

Abrupt silence answered her.

"I'm sorry to intrude, but do you need help?"

The house in front of her was as still as her own when her husband and son were out. Audrey waited.

"Are you injured?"

She understood that she might be facing a delicate situation in which her confident desire to help someone could cause more problems than allowing that someone some privacy. But in her view, it was worse to be lonely than to be embarrassed by a good Samaritan—and even worse for her to disobey God's clear direction—so she decided to persist at least until the person told her to stop.

"Maybe there's someone I can call for you?" she offered.

"I know how to use a phone." It was likely that the female speaker was the same one who had been crying. Her *N* sounds were nasal and stuffy. But the tone was far more irritated than grieved. As a pastor's wife, Audrey understood the fine line between the two emotions.

"Of course you do," Audrey said gently. "But sometimes it helps to assign tasks to other people. Take a load off your own shoulders."

At the edge of the elevated windowpane, the curtain flickered.

"You're trespassing."

Audrey's defenses went up. Her compassion had been rejected on many occasions, but never beaten back with accusations.

"That's true, I am. I'm sorry, but I . . ." She had yet to land on an easy explanation for the experiences that led her to other people. Geoff's position as a church leader required that Audrey's choice of words—and confidants—be discreet. Anyone who thought she was outside of God's will, or heretical or occult or misguided or just plain loony, would frown on her husband too. Even so, Audrey believed people deserved simple, no-frills truth. The world was so full of deceptive spin that most days she worried it might gyrate right out of orbit.

"I just sensed you could use a friend right now. My name's Audrey and I go to Grace Springs Church. My husband's the pastor there. Maybe you've heard of it? Doesn't matter, I'm not trying to recruit anyone. Anyway, do you like fresh bread? Geoff and I bake bread as a hobby, to give it away. I'd like to give you a loaf. I have some with me in my car because I was visiting one of your neighbors before I heard you crying. I'm parked right down—"

A door slammed inside the house and the curtain rose, then sank.

Audrey waited for a minute while the juniper leaves tickled the legs of her jeans. Sometimes people came back. Sometimes they wanted relief so badly that they didn't care if it was offered by a total stranger.

But not this time.

Audrey left the yard, returned to the sidewalk, and started walking back toward her car, thinking about the woman inside the house. She passed the mailbox on her left, and her thoughts were interrupted. Her feet took her backward two steps, and she took another look at the side of the black metal receptacle. The name *MANSFIELD* was applied to the box with rectangular stickers, black block letters on a gold background.

Mansfield. *As in Jack Mansfield, the church elder?* She glanced at the house number. She'd have to check the church directory. Mrs. Mansfield, Jack's wife, was a math teacher at her son's high school. Ed had her for geometry his sophomore year.

Audrey resumed walking, trying to bring up the woman's face. They'd met once, at a school event. Mrs. Mansfield refused to attend church with Jack, and Audrey had understood this reality to be a tender bruise on the elder's heart, maybe even on his ego.

Julie. Her name was Julie. And their daughter's name was Miralee, which was easier for Audrey to remember because until last week, the start of spring break, her son had dated the girl for a brief time.

If that had been Miralee crying, her refusal to come out was completely understandable. And Audrey was a fool not to have realized where she was. She still wasn't sure if the kids' breakup had been Ed's call or Miralee's. Audrey's nineteen-year-old had been so strangely tight-lipped that she assumed Miralee had broken things off. Secretly, Audrey wasn't sad to see that relationship end, though she hated that Ed was in pain. Now, after being subjected to the sounds of the broken heart in that house, she wondered if her assumptions had been wrong.

The thought passed through her mind that she should go back, knock on the front door like a respectable friend, apologize, and get to the bottom of things. Fix what Ed had broken, if necessary, though Ed wasn't prone to breaking very many things in life. He was a good boy. A careful boy. Man now.

Audrey looked back at the redbrick house.

A flash of light, a phantom sensation of liquid fire tearing through her body, prevented her from returning to the Mansfields' property. She had no desire to press Miralee for details of the heartbreak. Especially not after the girl had refused.

She had done what God asked of her. This excuse propelled

her back toward her car, the sunny air rich with the scent of rosemary-potato bread pushing against her face.

Audrey didn't second-guess this decision for three months. In June the Grace Springs Church board, spurred to fury by none other than Jack Mansfield, fired her husband and barred him from seeking another post as pastor.

The story continues in *The Baker's Wife*.

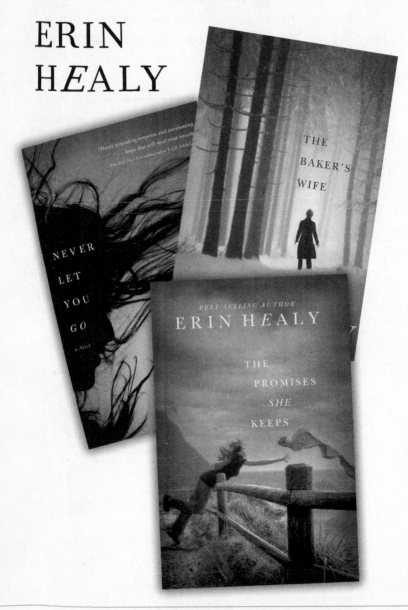